"No sex—with anyone. No scandals. Or no 'I do.'"

If no sex was important to her, how could he refuse? "Six weeks," he said hoarsely. "While we're engaged. Once we're married, all bets are off."

"We'll see. You and I don't make sense together, Hendrix, so don't pretend that we do."

She swallowed that sentence with a squeak as he hauled her out of the chair and into his arms for a lesson on exactly how wrong she was.

* * *

One Night Stand Bride
is part of the In Name Only trilogy:
"I do" should solve all their problems,
but love has other plans…

ONE NIGHT STAND BRIDE .

BY
KAT CANTRELL

First Published in Great Britain 2017
By Mills & Boon, an imprint of HarperCollins*Publishers*
1 London Bridge Street, London, SE1 9GF

© 2017 Kat Cantrell

ISBN: 978-0-263-92840-2

51-1017

Our policy is to use papers that are natural, renewable and recyclable products and made from wood grown in sustainable forests. The logging and manufacturing processes conform to the legal environmental regulations of the country of origin.

Printed and bound in Spain
by CPI, Barcelona

USA TODAY bestselling author **Kat Cantrell** read her first Mills & Boon novel in third grade and has been scribbling in notebooks since she learned to spell. She's a Harlequin So You Think You Can Write winner and a Romance Writers of America Golden Heart® Award finalist. Kat, her husband and their two boys live in north Texas.

One

The Las Vegas tourism department needed to change their slogan because what happened in Vegas did *not* stay there. In fact, what had happened in Vegas followed Hendrix Harris home to North Carolina and landed above the fold on every media outlet known to man.

He wanted his money refunded, a spell to wipe the memories of an entire city and an aspirin.

Though even he had to admit the photographer had perfectly captured the faces of Hendrix and Rosalind Carpenter. The picture was erotic without being pornographic—a trick and a half since it was abundantly clear they were both buck naked, yet somehow, all the naughty bits were strategically covered. A miracle that had allowed the picture to be print-worthy. It was a one-in-a-million shot. You could even see the steam rising from the hot tub.

And thanks to that photographer being in the right place at the wrong time, Hendrix's luck had run out.

He'd fully expected his mother to have a heart attack when she saw her son naked with the daughter of the wealthiest man in North Carolina. Especially since Hendrix's mother had warned him to keep his clothes on once she launched her gubernatorial campaign.

Joke was on Hendrix. No heart attacks. Instead, his mother was thrilled. *Thrilled* that he'd gotten chummy with Paul Carpenter's daughter. So thrilled that somehow she'd gotten Hendrix to agree that marrying Rosalind would fix everything.

Really, this whole scandal was his fault, and it was on him to make amends, or so he'd been told. The Carpenter family had old money and lots of influence, which provided a nice balance to the Harris new money.

Grumbling in his head because he loved and respected his mother too much to do it out loud, Hendrix threw himself into the task of figuring out how to contact Roz. Their naked Vegas romp had been most definitely of the one-night stand variety. Now he would have to convince her that she loved his mother's plan.

Hendrix didn't hate the idea of marriage, per se, not when it solved more than one problem. So it was now his goal to make sure a big fat yes was Roz's response to the question *Will you marry me?*

The only problem being that he hadn't actually spoken to her since that night and they'd expressly agreed they wouldn't see each other again. Minor detail. When he put his mind to something, rare was the obstacle that didn't get the hell out of his way.

Luck crept back onto his side. Roz hadn't blocked

all the web crawlers that posted her address to one of those seamy "find anyone for a price" sites. Hendrix had no qualms about throwing money at this problem.

Hendrix drove himself to the building Rosalind Carpenter lived in on Fayetteville Street instead of taking a car. Arriving with fanfare before he'd gotten this done didn't fit his idea of a good plan. After she said yes, of course there'd be lots of sanctioned pictures of the happy couple. And they'd be dressed.

His mother hadn't properly appreciated just how hard her son had worked to get his abs to look so centerfold-worthy. It was a shame that such a great shot of what had been a truly spectacular night with the hottest woman he'd ever met had done so much damage to Ms. Harris's family values campaign.

He charmed his way past the security desk because everyone liked him instantly, a fact of life he traded on frequently. Then he waited patiently until someone with the right access to Roz's floor who was also willing to listen to his tale of woe got on the elevator. Within fifteen minutes, he knocked on Ms. Carpenter's door.

To her credit, when she answered, she didn't even blink.

He did.

Holy hell. How could he have forgotten what she did to him?

Her sensuality leaped from her like a tidal wave, crashing over him until he scarcely knew which way was up, but he didn't care because surfacing was the last thing on his mind. He gasped for air in the wake of so much sensation as she tucked a lock of dark hair behind her ear. She pursed those lush lips and surveyed him with cool amusement.

"You don't follow instructions well," she fairly purred, leaning on the door, kicking one foot to the side and drawing attention to the sexy slice of leg peeking out from her long flowy skirt.

"Your memory is faulty," he returned easily, a smile sliding across his face in spite of the reason for his visit. "I recall being an instant slave to your instructions. 'Faster, harder, take me from behind.' I can't think of a single thing you told me to do that I didn't follow to the letter."

One dark brow rose. "Other than the one where I said Vegas was a onetime thing?" she reminded him with a wry twist of her lips. "That there were reasons we shouldn't hook up at home and you agreed."

Hendrix waved that off with a grin. "Well, if you're going to get into specifics. Sure. That was the only one, though."

"Then I guess the only thing left to do is ask to what do I owe the pleasure?" That's when she blinked. "Perhaps I should rephrase the question since I have the distinct impression this is not a social call."

No point in dragging it out when they were both to blame for the scandal and they both had a vested interest in fixing the problem. But he did take a moment to appreciate how savvy she was. Contrary to what the majority of women in the Raleigh-Durham-Cary area would argue, Hendrix did notice when a woman had assets outside of the obvious ones.

Roz's brain turned him on. She saw things—layers—that normal people took at face value. It was captivating. He still wasn't sure why it had taken a trip to

Vegas for them to hook up when they'd known each other peripherally for years.

"You saw the picture," he said.

"Along with half of the eastern seaboard. But it's been circulating for a week." She slid a once-over down his body, lingering along the way like she'd found something worth noting. "Not sure why that would suddenly cause you to seek me out now."

The region under her hot gaze woke up in a hurry, galvanized into action by the quick, sharp memories of this woman under his mouth as he'd kissed, licked and tasted his way over every inch of her luscious body.

"We're definitely going to have to do something about your defective memory," he growled as he returned her heat with a pointed glance of his own. "If you can look at that photograph and not want to immediately repeat the experience."

She crossed her arms over her filmy top that did little to curb his appetite. "Nothing wrong with my memory and I have no problem admitting that your reputation is well-founded. What's not going to happen is a repeat. Vegas was my last hurrah. I told you that."

Yeah, she had. Repeatedly. While they'd been naked in her bed. And maybe once in the shower. It had been an all-night romp that had nearly caused him to miss his friend Jonas's wedding the next morning. But Hendrix had left behind his delectable companion and made it to the chapel on time, assuming he'd never see her again, as instructed.

His mother, Helene Harris, presumptive future Governor of North Carolina, had reset his thinking. It had taken a week to work through the ramifications and about that long to get him on board with the idea of a

wedding as the antidote. But he was all in at this point.
And he needed Roz to be all in, too.

"Here's the thing. The picture never should have
happened. But it did. So we need to mitigate the damage. My mother's people think that's best accomplished
by the two of us getting married. Just until the election. Then her people have agreed that we can get a
quiet divorce."

Roz laughed and the silky sound tightened all the
places that she'd affected so easily by sheer virtue of
standing there looking lush and gorgeous.

"Your mom's people, Hendrix? That's so precious."

"Like your dad doesn't have people?" Carpenter
Furniture ranked as one of the top-grossing businesses
in the world. Her father had been the CEO since its in-
ception thirty years ago. He had people.

The mirth left her face in a snap. "My dad's people
aren't spewing nonsense like a *marriage* to fix a non-
existent problem. This conversation is boring me and
I have things to do, so if you'll excuse me."

"Not so fast." Hendrix stuck a foot in the door before Roz could slam it in his face. Time to change tac-
tics. "Let me buy you a drink so we can discuss this
like rational adults."

"Yeah. You and alcohol creates a rational atmo-
sphere."

Sarcasm dripped from her tone and it was so cute,
he couldn't help but grin.

"Aww. That was very nearly an admission of how
crazy I can make you."

"And I'm done with this." She nearly took off his
foot with the force of the door closing but he didn't
yank it free, despite the pinch in his arch.

"Wait, Roz." He dropped his tone into the *you can't resist me even if you try* realm. "Please give me five minutes. Then you can sever my toes all you want."

"Is the word marriage going to come out of your mouth again?"

He hesitated. Without that, there was no reason for him to be here. But he needed her more than she needed him. The trick was to make sure she never realized that.

"Is it really so much of a stretch to contemplate a merger between our families that could benefit us all? Especially in light of the photograph."

Her face didn't relax, but he could tell he had her attention. Pushing on their mutual attraction wasn't the ticket, then. Noted. So he went with logic.

"Can you honestly say you've had no fallout from our…liaison?" he asked. "Because I have or I wouldn't be standing on your doorstep. I know we agreed no contact. I know the reasons why. Things changed."

But not the reasons why. The reasons for no contact were for pure self-preservation.

He and Roz were like kindling dropped into a forest fire together. They'd gone up in flames and frankly, he'd done more dirty things in one night with Rosalind Carpenter than with the last ten women he'd dated. But by the time the sun rose, they were done. He had a strict one-time-only rule that he never broke and not just because of the pact he'd made his senior year at Duke. He'd vowed to never fall in love—because he'd been rejected enough in life and the best way to avoid all that noise was to avoid intimacy.

Sex he liked. Sex worked for him. But intimacy was off the table. He guaranteed it with no repeats.

Only at his mother's insistence would he consider making Roz his onetime exception.

"So this marriage idea. That's supposed to fix the fallout? From where I'm sitting, you're the reason for the scandal. Where's the plus for me?"

Like she hadn't been the one to come on to him on the dance floor of the Calypso Room, with her smoky eyes undressing him, the conclusion of their evening foregone the second their bodies touched.

At least she hadn't denied that the photograph had caused her some difficulty. If she had, he'd remind her that somewhere around 2:00 a.m. that night, she'd confessed that she was looking to change her reputation as the scandalous Carpenter daughter. The photograph couldn't have helped. A respectable marriage would.

That fact was still part of his strategy. "Helene's your plus. You'll be the daughter-in-law of the next governor of North Carolina. I'm confused why you're struggling with this."

"You would be." She jerked her head toward him. "I'm morbidly curious. What's in this for you?"

Legitimacy. Something hard to come by in his world. His family's chain of tobacco shops wasn't a respected industry and he was the bastard son of a man who had never claimed him.

But what he said was, "Sex."

She rolled her eyes. "You're such a liar. The last thing you need to bargain for is a woman willing to get naked with you."

"That sounded like a compliment." He waggled his brows to hide how his insides suddenly felt wobbly and precarious. How had she seen through that flippant answer?

That was what he got with a smart woman, apparently.

"It wasn't. Seduction is less of an art when you're already starting out with the deck stacked."

He had to laugh, though he wasn't quite sure if he was supposed to say thank you for the backhanded nod to his skill set. "I'm not leaving here without an answer. Marry me and the scandal goes away."

She shook her head, a sly smile spreading over her face. "Over my dead body."

And with that, she pushed his foot from the gap and shut the door with a quiet click.

Dumbfounded, Hendrix stared at the fine-grain wood. Rosalind Carpenter had just rejected his proposal. For deliberately not putting anything emotional on the line, the rejection sure stung.

Roz leaned on the shut door and closed her eyes.

Marriage. To Hendrix Harris. If she hadn't understood perfectly why he'd come up with such a ridiculous idea, she'd call the cops to come cart away the crazy man on her doorstep.

But he wasn't crazy. Just desperate to fix a problem. She was, too.

The big difference was that her father wasn't working with his "people" to help her. Instead, he was sitting up in his ivory tower continuing to be disappointed in her. Well, sometimes she screwed up. Vegas had been one of those times. Fixing it lay solely at her feet and she planned to. Just not by marrying the person who had caused the scandal in the first place.

Like marriage was the solution to anything, especially marriage to Hendrix Harris, who indeed had a reputation when it came to his exploits with the opposite sex. Hell, half of her interest back on that wild night had been insatiable curiosity about whether he could be as much trouble as everyone said.

She should have run the moment she recognized him. But no. She'd bought him a drink. She was nothing if not skilled at getting into trouble.

And what trouble she'd found.

He was of the hot, wicked and oh-so-sinful variety—the kind she had a weakness for, the kind she couldn't resist. The real question was how she'd shut the door in his face a moment ago instead of inviting him in for a repeat.

That would be a bad idea. Vegas had marked the end of an era for her.

She'd jetted off with her friend Lora to let loose in a place famed for allowing such behavior without ramifications. One last hurrah, as Roz had informed him. Make it memorable, she'd insisted. *Help me go out with a bang*, had been her exact words. Upon her return to the real world, she'd planned to make her father proud for once.

Instead, she'd found exactly the trouble she'd been looking for and then some.

It was a problem she needed to fix. She'd needed to fix it before she'd ever let Hendrix put his beautiful, talented mouth on her. And now memories of his special brand of trouble put a slow burn in her core that she couldn't shake. Even now, five minutes after telling him to shove off. Still burning. She cursed her weakness for gorgeous bad boys and went to change clothes so she could dig into her "make Dad proud" plan on her terms.

Marriage. Rosalind Carpenter. These two things did not go together under any circumstances, especially not as a way to make her father proud of her.

After watching her father cope with Roz's mother's extended bout with cancer, no thank you. That kind of pain didn't appeal to her. Till death do you part wasn't a joke, nor did she take a vow like that lightly. Best way to avoid testing it was to never make a vow like that in the first place.

Roz shed the flirty, fun outfit she'd worn to brunch with Lora and donned a severe black pencil skirt coupled with a pale blue long-sleeved blouse that screamed "serious banker." She twisted her long hair into a chignon, fought with the few escaped strands and finally left them because Hendrix had already put her behind for the day. Her afternoon was booked solid with the endless tasks associated with the new charity she'd founded.

She arrived at the small storefront her father's admin had helped her rent, evaluating the layout for the fourteenth time. There was no sign yet. That was one of the many details she needed to work through this week as she got Clown-Around off the ground. It was an endeavor of the heart. And maybe a form of therapy.

Clowns still scared her, not that she'd admit to having formed a phobia during the long hours she'd sat at her mother's hospital bedside, and honestly, she didn't have to explain herself to anyone, so she didn't. The curious only needed to know that Rosalind Carpenter had started a charity that trained clowns to work in children's hospitals. Period.

The desk she'd had delivered dwarfed her, but she'd taken a page from her father's book and procured the largest piece she could find in the Carpenter ware-house near the airport. He'd always said to buy furni-ture for the circumstances you want, not the ones you have. Buy quality so it will last until you make your dreams a reality. It was a philosophy that had served Carpenter Furniture well and she liked the sentiment. So she'd bought a desk that made her feel like the head of a successful charity.

She attacked the mountain of paperwork with gusto, cheerfully filling out forms and ordering sup-plies. There was an enormous amount of overhead that went along with running a charity and when you had zero income to use in hiring help, there was only one person to do the work—the founder.

Before she'd barely dug into the task, the lady from the first hospital Roz had called her back.

"Ms. Smith, so happy to speak with you," Roz began smoothly. "I'd like to see what your requirements are for getting Clown-Around on the approved list of or-ganizations available to work with the children at your hospital."

"I could have saved you some time, Ms. Carpenter," the liaison replied and her tone could only be described as frosty. "We already have an approved group we work with. No need for any additional ones."

That threw Roz for a loop. "Oh. Well, we'd be happy to go on the backup list. You know, in case the other group cancels unexpectedly."

"That's okay," she cut in quickly. "That almost never happens and it's not like we have scheduled times. The clowns come in on a pretty casual basis."

This was not a good conversation. Unease prickled at the back of Roz's neck and she did not like the feeling. "I'm having a hard time believing that you can't use extra cheer in the children's ward. We're talking about sick kids who don't want to be in the hospital. Surely if your current clowns come and go at will, you can add some of mine to the rotation. A clown is a clown, right?"

The long pause boded badly. Roz braced for the next part.

"To be frank, Ms. Carpenter, the hospital board would not appreciate any association with a charity you helm," Ms. Smith stated bluntly. "We are required to disclose any contact a patient has with outside parties, particularly when the patients are minors. The clowns must have accreditation and thorough vetting to ensure we're not exposing patients to…unseemly influences."

Roz went hot and then cold as the woman's meaning flashed through her. The reputation of the charity's founder preceded her apparently. "I take it I qualify as an unseemly influence. Then may I be as frank and ask why you bothered to call me back?"

"Strictly in deference to your father. One of his vice presidents is on the board, if you're not aware," she replied tightly. "If we've reached an understanding…"

"We have. Thank you for your candor." Roz stabbed the end call button and let her cell phone drop to the desk of a successful charity head. Too bad that wasn't who was sitting at it.

Wow. Her hands were shaking.

And because her day hadn't been crappy enough, the door she'd forgotten to lock behind her opened to the street and Hendrix Harris walked into her nightmare.

"What are you doing here?" she snapped, too off-kilter to find some manners when she'd already told him to step off once today. "This is private property. How did you find me?"

Not one perfect brown hair out of place, the man waltzed right in and glanced around her bare-bones operation with unabashed curiosity. "I followed you, naturally. But I didn't want to interrupt your phone call, so I waited."

"Bless your heart," she shot back and snatched up her phone to call the cops. "You have two seconds to vacate or I'm going to lodge a trespassing complaint."

Instead of hightailing it out the door—which was what he should have done—Hendrix didn't hesitate to round the desk, crowd into her space without even a cursory nod to boundaries and pluck the phone from her hand. "Now, why would you do a thing like that? We're all friends here."

Something that felt perilously close to tears pricked beneath her lashes. "We're not friends."

Tears. In front of Hendrix. It was inexcusable.

"We could be friends," he announced quietly, without an ounce of flirt. Somehow that was exactly the right tone to burn off the moisture. "Friends who help each other. You didn't give me much of a chance to tell you how earlier."

Help. That was something she needed. Not that *he* needed to know that, or how grateful she was that he'd found a way to put her back on even footing. She didn't for an instant believe he'd missed her brief flash of vulnerability and his deft handling of it made all the difference.

The attitude of the hospital lady still chilled her. But she wasn't in danger of falling apart any longer, thank God.

"Because I have a zone of crazy around me." She nodded to the floor, near his feet. "There's the perimeter and you're four feet over the line."

Problem being that she liked him where he was—one lean hip cocked against her desk and all his good stuff at eye level. Naked, the man rivaled mythical gods in the perfection department. She could stare at his bare body for hours and never get tired of finding new ways to appreciate his deliciousness.

And dang it, he must have clued in on the direction of her thoughts. He didn't move. But the temperature of the room rose a few sweat-inducing degrees. Or maybe that was just her body catching fire as he treated her to the full force of his lethal appeal.

His hot perusal did not help matters when it came to the temperature. What was it about his pale hazel eyes that dug into her so deeply? All he had to do was look at her and sharp little tugs danced through her core.

It pissed her off. Why couldn't he be ugly, with a hunchback and gnarled feet?

Which was a stupid thing to wish for because if that was the case, she wouldn't be in this position. She'd never have hooked up with him in Vegas because yes, she was that shallow and a naked romp with a man built like Hendrix had righted her world—for a night.

Now she'd pay the price for that moment of hedonism. The final cost had yet to be determined, though.

Hendrix set her phone down on the desk, correctly guessing he had her attention and the threat of expulsion had waned. For now. She could easily send him packing if the need struck. Or she could roll the chair back a few inches and move the man into a better position to negotiate something of the more carnal variety. This was a solid desk. Would be a shame not to fully test its strength.

No. She shook her head. This was the danger of putting herself in the same room with him. She forgot common sense and propriety.

"Since I'm already in the zone of crazy," he commented in his North Carolina–textured twang, "you should definitely hear me out. For real this time. I don't know what you think I'm proposing, but odds are good you didn't get that it starts and ends with a partnership."

That had *not* come across. Whatever he had in mind, she'd envisioned a lot of sex taking center stage. And that she'd have to do without because she'd turned over a new leaf.

A partnership, on the other hand, had interesting possibilities.

As coolly as she could under the circumstances, she crossed her arms. Mostly as a way to keep her hands to herself. "Talk fast. You've got my attention for about another five minutes."

Two

Hendrix had been right to follow Rosalind. This bare storefront had a story behind it and he had every intention of learning her secrets. Whatever leverage he could dig up might come in handy, especially since he'd botched the first round of this negotiation.

And the hard cross of Roz's arms told him it was indeed a negotiation, one he shouldn't expect to win easily. That had been his mistake on the first go-round. He'd thought their chemistry would be good trading currency, but she'd divested him of that notion quickly. So round two would need a completely different approach.

"What is this place?" he asked and his genuine curiosity leaked through. He had a vision in his head of Rosalind Carpenter as a party girl, one who posed for men's magazines and danced like a fantasy come to life. Instead of tracking her down during an afternoon shopping spree, he'd stumbled over her *working*.

It didn't fit his perception of her and he'd like to get the right one before charging ahead.

"I started a charity," she informed him with a slight catch in her voice that struck him strangely.

She expected him to laugh. Or say something flippant. So he didn't. "That's fantastic. And hard. Good for you."

That bobbled her composure and he wouldn't apologize for enjoying it. This marriage plan should have been a lot easier to sell and he couldn't put his finger on why he'd faltered so badly thus far. She'd been easy in Vegas—likable, open, adventurous. All things he'd assumed he'd work with today, but none of those qualities seemed to be a part of her at-home personality. Plus, he wasn't trying to get her into bed. Well, technically, he *was*. But semi-permanently, and he didn't have a lot of experience at persuading a woman to still be there in the morning.

No problem. Winging it was how he did his best work. He hadn't pushed Harris Family Tobacco Lounge so close to the half-billion mark in revenue without taking a few risks.

"What does your charity do?" he asked, envisioning an evening dress resale shop or Save the Kittens. Might as well know what kind of fundraiser he'd have to attend as her husband.

"Clowns," she said so succinctly that he did a double take to be sure he hadn't misheard her. He hadn't. And it wasn't a joke, judging by the hard set of her mouth.

"Like finding new homes for orphan clowns?" he

guessed cautiously, only half kidding. Clown charity was a new one for him.

"You're such a moron." She rolled her eyes, but they had a determined glint now that he liked a lot better than the raw vulnerability she'd let slip a few minutes ago. "My charity trains clowns to work with children at hospitals. Sick kids need to be cheered up, you know?"

"That's admirable." And he wasn't even blowing smoke. It sounded like it meant something to her and thus it meant something to him—as leverage. He glanced around, taking in the bare walls, the massive and oddly masculine dark-stained desk and the rolling leather chair under her very fine backside. Not much to her operation yet, which worked heavily in his favor. "How can I help?"

Suspicion tightened her lush mouth, which only made him want to kiss it away. They were going to have to fix this attraction or he'd spend all his time adjusting her attitude in a very physical way.

On second thought, he couldn't figure out a downside to that approach.

"I thought you were trying to talk me into marrying you," she said with a fair amount of sarcasm.

"One and the same, sweetheart." He gave it a second and the instant his meaning registered, her lips curved into a crafty smile.

"I'm starting to see the light."

Oh yes, *now* they were ready to throw down. Juices flowing, he slid a little closer to her and she didn't roll away, just coolly stared up at him without an ounce of give. What was wrong with him that he was suddenly more turned on in that instant than he had been at any point today?

"Talk to me. What can I do in exchange for your name on a marriage certificate?"

Her smile gained a lot of teeth. "Tell me why it's so important to you."

He bit back the curse. Should have seen that one coming. As a testament to her skill in maneuvering him into giving up personal information, he opted to throw her a bone. "I told you. I've had some fallout. My mother is pretty unhappy with me and I don't like her to be unhappy."

"Mama's boy?"

"Absolutely." He grinned. Who didn't see the value in a man who loved and respected his mama? "There's no shame in that. We grew up together. I'm sure you've heard the story. She was an unwed teenage mother, yadda, yadda?"

"I've heard. So this is all one hundred percent about keeping your mom happy, is it?"

Something clued him in that she wasn't buying it, which called for some serious deflection. The last thing he wanted to have a conversation about was his own reasons for pursuing Roz for the first and only Mrs. Hendrix Harris.

He liked being reminded of his own vulnerabilities even less than he liked being exposed to hers. The less intimate this thing grew, the better. "Yeah. If she wasn't in the middle of an election cycle, we wouldn't be having this conversation. But she is and I messed up. I'm willing to do whatever it takes to get this deal done. Name your price."

"Get your mom to agree to be a clown for me and I'll consider it."

That was what she wanted? His gaze narrowed as

they stared at each other. "That's easy. Too easy. You must not want me to figure out that you're really panting to get back into my bed."

Her long silky laugh lodged in his chest and spread south. She could turn that sentiment back on him with no trouble at all.

Which was precisely what she did. "Sounds like a guilty conscience talking to me. Sure you're not the one using this ploy to get me naked without being forced to let on how bad you want it?"

"I'm offended." But he let a smile contradict the statement. "I'll tell you all day long how much I want you if that floats your boat. But this is a business proposition. Strictly for nonsexual benefits."

Any that came along with this marriage could be considered a bonus.

She snorted. "Are you trying to tell me you'd give up other women while we're married? I don't think you're actually capable of that."

Now, that was just insulting. What kind of a philanderer did she take him for? He'd never slept with more than one woman at a time and never calling one again made that a hundred percent easier.

"Make no mistake, Roz. I am perfectly capable of forgoing other women as long as you're the one I'm coming home to at the end of the day."

All at once, a vision of her greeting him at the door wearing sexy lingerie slammed through his mind and his body reacted with near violent approval. Holy hell. He had no problem going off other women cold turkey if Roz was on offer instead, never mind his stupid rules about never banging the same woman twice. This situation was totally different, with its own set of rules. Or at least it would be as soon as he got his head out of her perfect cleavage and back on how to close this deal.

"Let me get this straight. You're such a dog that the only way you can stay out of another woman's bed is if I'm servicing you regularly?" She wrinkled her nose. "Stop me when I get to the part where I'm benefiting from this arrangement."

Strictly to cover the slight hitch in his lungs that her pointed comment had caused, he slid over until he was perched on the desk directly in front of her. Barely a foot of space separated them and an enormous amount of heat and electricity arced through his groin, draining more of his sense than he would have preferred. All he could think about was yanking her into his arms and reminding her how hot he could get her with nothing more than a well-placed stroke of his tongue.

He let all of that sizzle course through his body as he swept her with a heated once-over. "Sweetheart, you'll benefit, or have you forgotten how well I know your body?"

"Can you even go without sex?" she mused with a lilt, as if she already knew the answer. "Because I bet you can't."

What the hell did that have to do with anything?

"I can do whatever I put my mind to," he growled. "But to do something as insane as go without sex, I'd need a fair bit of incentive. Which I have none of."

Her gaze snapped with challenge. "Other than getting my name on a marriage license you mean?"

The recoil jerked through his shoulders before he could catch it, tipping her off that she'd just knocked him for a loop. That was uncool. Both that she'd realized it and that she'd done it. "What are you proposing, that I go celibate for a period of time in some kind of test?"

"Oh, I hadn't thought of it like that." She pursed her lips into a provocative pout that told him she was flat-out lying because she'd intended it to be exactly that. "That's a great deal. You keep it zipped and I'll show up at the appointed time to say 'I do.'"

His throat went dry. "Really? That's what it's going to take?"

"Yep. Well, that and Helene Harris for Governor in a clown suit. Can't forget the children."

Her smug tone raked at something inside him. "That's ridiculous. I mean, my mom would be happy to do the clown thing. It's great publicity for her, too. But no sex? Not even with you? There is literally no reason for you to lay down such a thing except as cruel and unusual punishment."

"Careful, Hendrix," she crooned. "It's starting to sound like you might have a problem keeping it in your pants. I mean, how long are we talking? A couple of months?"

A couple of *months*? He'd been slightly panicked at the thought of a week or two. It wasn't that he was some kind of pervert like she was making it sound. Sex was a necessary avoidance tactic in his arsenal. A shield against the intimacy that happened in the small moments, when you weren't guarded against it. He kept himself out of such situations on purpose.

If he wasn't having sex with Roz, what would they *do* with each other?

"I think the better question is whether *you* can do it," he countered smoothly. "You're the same woman who was all in for every wicked, dirty escapade I could dream up in Vegas. You're buckling yourself into that chastity belt too, honey."

"Yeah, for a reason." Her eyes glittered with conviction. "The whole point of this is to fix the problems the photograph caused. Do you really think you and I can keep ourselves out of Scandalville if we're sleeping together?" His face must have registered his opinion on that because she nodded. "Exactly. It's a failsafe. No sex—with *anyone*. No scandals. Or no 'I do.'"

The firm press of a rock and a hard place nearly stole his breath. If no sex was important to her, how could he refuse?

"Six weeks," he said hoarsely. "We'll be engaged for six weeks. Once we're married, all bets are off."

"We'll see. I might keep the no sex moratorium. You and I don't make sense together, Hendrix, so don't pretend that we do."

She swallowed that sentence with a squeak as he hauled her out of that chair and into his arms for a lesson on exactly how wrong she was. God, she fit the contours of his body like the ocean against the sand, seeping into him with a rush and shush, dragging pieces of him into her as her lips crashed against his.

Her taste exploded under his mouth as he kissed her senseless. But then it was his own senses sliding through the soles of his feet as Roz sucked him dry with her own sensual onslaught. For a woman who'd just told him they didn't work, she jumped into the kiss with enthusiasm that had him groaning.

The hot, slick slide of her tongue against his dissolved his knees. Only the firm press of that heavy desk against his backside kept him upright. The woman was a wicked kisser, not that he'd forgotten. But just

as he slid his hand south to fill his palms with her luscious rear, she wrenched away, taking his composure
with her.

"Where are you going?" he growled.

"The other side of the room." Her chest rose and fell
as if she'd run a marathon as she backed away. Frankly,
his own lungs heaved with the effort to fill with air.
"What the hell was that for?"

"You wanted that kiss as much as I did."

"So it was strictly to throw it back in my face that
I can't resist you?"

Well, now. That was a tasty admission that she
looked like she wished to take back. He surveyed her
with renewed interest. Her kiss-reddened lips beckoned
him but he didn't chase her down. He wanted to understand this new dynamic before he pressed on. "You
said we didn't work. I was simply helping you see the
error in that statement."

"I said no such thing. I said we don't make sense together. And that's why. Because we *work* far too well."

"I'm struggling to see the problem with that."
They'd definitely worked in Vegas, that was for sure.
Now that he'd gotten a second taste, he was not satis-
fied with having it cut short.

"Because I need to stay off the front page," she reminded him with that funny hitch in her voice that
shouldn't be more affecting than her heated once-overs.
"There are people walking by the window as we speak,
Hendrix. You make me forget all of that. No more kissing until the wedding. Consider it an act of good faith."

The point was painfully clear. She wanted him to
prove he could do it.

"So we're doing this. Getting married," he clarified.

"As a partnership. When it stops being beneficial, we get a divorce. No ifs, ands or buts." She caught him in her hot gaze that still screamed her desire. "Right? Do we need to spell it out legally?"

"You can trust me," he grumbled. She was the one who'd thrown down the no-sex rule. What did she think he was going to do, force her to stay married so he could keep being celibate for the rest of his life? "As long as I can trust you."

"I'm good."

He thought about shaking on it but the slightly panicked flair to her expression made him think twice. It didn't matter. The deal was done, as painful as it would ultimately end up being.

It was worth it. He had to make it up to his mom for causing her grief, and this was what she'd asked him to do. And if deep inside, he craved the idea of belonging to such an old-guard, old-money family as the Carpenters, no one would be the wiser.

All he had to do was figure out how to be engaged to Roz without trying to seduce her again and without getting too chummy. Should be a walk in the park.

Being engaged was nothing like Roz imagined. Of course she'd spent zero time daydreaming about such a thing happening to her. But her friend Lora had been engaged for about six months, which had been a whirlwind of invitations and dress fittings. Until the day she'd walked in on her fiancé and a naked barista who was foaming the jackass's latte in Lora's bed. Roz and Lora still didn't hit a coffee place within four blocks of the one where the wedding-wrecker worked.

Roz's own engagement had a lot fewer highs and

lows in the emotion department and a lot less chaos. For about three days. The morning of the fourth day, Hendrix texted her that he was coming by, and since there'd been no question in that statement, she sighed and put on clothes, wishing in vain for a do-over that included not flying to Vegas in the first place. Or maybe she should wish that she and Lora had gone to any other club besides the Calypso Room that night.

Oh, better yet, she could pretend Hendrix didn't do it for her in a hundred scandalous ways.

That was the real reason this engagement/marriage/partnership shouldn't have happened. But how could she turn down Helene Harris in a clown outfit? No hospital would bar the woman from the door and thus Clown-Around would get a much-needed lift, Roz's reputation notwithstanding. It was instant publicity for the gubernatorial candidate and the fledgling charity in one shot, which was a huge win. And she didn't have to actually ask her father to use his influence, which he probably wouldn't do anyway.

Plus, and she'd die before she'd admit this to Hendrix, there had to be something about being in the sphere of Helene Harris that Roz's father would find satisfactory. He was so disappointed about the photographs. If nothing else, marrying the man in them lent a bit of respectability to the situation, right? Now Roz just had to tell her father about the getting married part. But first she had to admit to herself that she'd actually agreed to this insanity.

Thus far it had been easy to stick her head in the sand. But when Hendrix buzzed her to gain access to the elevator, she couldn't play ostrich any longer.

"Well, if it isn't my beloved," he drawled when she opened the door.

God, could the man look like a slouch in *something*? He wore the hell out of a suit regardless of the color or cut. But today he'd opted for a pair of worn jeans that hugged his hips and a soft T-shirt that brazenly advertised the drool-worthy build underneath. He might as well be naked for all that ensemble left to the imagination.

"Your beloved doesn't sit around and wait for you to show up on a Saturday," she informed him grumpily. "What if I had plans?"

"You do have plans," he returned, his grin far too easy. "With me. All of your plans are with me for the next six weeks, because weddings do not magically throw themselves together."

She crossed her arms and leaned against the door-jamb in a blatant message—*you're not coming in and I'm not budging, so...* "They do if you hire a wedding planner. Which you should. I have absolutely no opinion about flowers or venues."

That was no lie. But she wanted to spend time with Hendrix even less than she wanted to pick out flowers. She could literally feel her will dissolving as she stood there soaking in the carnal vibe wafting from him like an invisible aphrodisiac.

"Oh, come on. It'll be fun."

The way his hazel eyes lit up as he coaxed her should be illegal. Or maybe her reaction should be. How did he put such a warm little curl in her core with nothing more than a glance? It was ridiculous. "Your idea of fun and mine are worlds apart."

A slow, lethal smile joined his vibrant gaze and it

pretty much reduced her to a quivering mess of girl parts inside. All the more reason to stay far away from him until the wedding.

"Seems like we had a pretty similar idea of fun one night not too long ago."

Memories crashed through her mind, her body, her soul. The way he'd made her feel, the wicked press of his mouth against every intimate hollow an unprecedented experience. It was too much for a Saturday morning after she'd signed up to become Mrs. Hendrix Harris.

"I asked you not to kiss me again," she reminded him primly but it probably sounded as desperate to him as it did to her.

She could *not* get sucked into his orbit. As it was, she fantasized about that kiss against her desk at odd times—while in the shower, brushing her teeth, eating breakfast, watching TV, walking, breathing. Sure it was prudent to avoid any more scandals but that was just window dressing. This was a partnership she needed to take seriously, and she had no good defenses against Hendrix Harris.

He was temporary. Like all things. She couldn't get invested, emotionally or physically, and one would surely lead to the other. The pain of losing someone she cared about was too much and she would never let that happen again—which was the sole reason she liked sex of the one-night stand variety. What she'd do when that wasn't an option, like after she said I do, she had no clue.

"Wow. Who said anything about kissing?" He waggled his brows. "We were talking about the definition of fun. That kiss must have gotten you going something fierce if you're still hung up on it."

She rolled her eyes to hide the guilt that might or might not be shuffling through her expression. "Why are you here?"

"We're engaged. Engaged people hang out, or didn't you get the memo?"

"We're not people. Nor is our engagement typical. No memos required to get us to the…insert whatever venue we're using to get hitched here. Until then, I don't really feel the need to spend time together." She accompanied that pitiful excuse of his with crooked fingers in air quotes.

"Well, I beg to differ," he drawled, the North Carolina in his voice sliding through her veins like fine brandy. "This partnership needs publicity or there's no point to it. We need to be seen together. A lot. When people think of you, they need to think of me. We're like the peanut butter and jelly of the Raleigh social scene."

"That's a nice analogy," she said with a snort so she didn't laugh or smile. That would only encourage him to keep being adorable. "Which one am I?"

"You choose," he suggested magnanimously and that's when she realized she was having fun. How dare he charm her out of her bad mood?

But it was too late, dang it. That was the problem. She genuinely liked Hendrix or she wouldn't have left the Calypso Room with him.

"I suppose you want to come in." She jerked her head toward the interior of her loft that had been two condos until she bought both and hired a crew of hard hats to meld the space into one. They should probably discuss living arrangements at some point because she was *not* giving up this condo under any circumstances.

"I want you to come out," he countered and caught her hand, tugging on it until she cleared the threshold on the wrong side of the door. "We can't be seen together in your condo and besides, there are no people walking past the window. No photographers in the bushes. I could slip a couple of buttons free on this shirt of yours and explore what I uncover with my tongue and no one would know."

He accompanied that suggestion with a slow slide of his fingertip along the ridge of buttons in question, oh so casually, as if the skin under it hadn't just exploded with goose bumps.

"But you won't," she said breathlessly, cursing her body's reaction even as she cursed him for knowing exactly how to get her hot and ready to burst with so little effort. "Because you promised."

"I did." He nodded with a wink. "And I'm a man of my word."

She'd only reminded him of his promise as a shield against her own weaknesses, but he'd taken it as an affirmation. He would keep his promise because it meant something to him. And his sense of honor was doing funny things to her insides that had nothing to do with desire. Hendrix Harris was a bad boy hedonist of the highest order. Nothing but wicked through and through. Or at least that was the box she'd put him in and she did not like the way he'd just climbed out of it.

She shook her head, but it didn't clear her sudden confusion. Definitely they should not go into her condo and shut the door. Not now or any day. But at that moment, she couldn't recall what bad things might happen as a result. She could only think of many, many very good things that could and would occur if she invited him in for a private rendezvous.

"I think we should visit a florist," he commented casually, completely oblivious to the direction of her thoughts, thank God.

"Yes. We should." That was exactly what she needed. A distraction in the form of flowers.

"Grab your handbag." The instruction made her blink for a second until he laughed. "Or is it a purse? I have no clue what to call the thing you women put your lives into."

Gah, she should have her head examined if a simple conversation with a man had her so flipped upside down. Nodding, she ducked back into the condo, snagged her Marc Jacobs bag from the counter in the kitchen and rejoined Hendrix in the hall before he got any bright ideas about testing his will behind closed doors. Hers sucked. The longer she kept that fact from him, the better.

He ushered her to a low-slung Aston Martin that shouldn't have been as sexy as it was. At best, it should have screamed *I'm trying too hard to be cool*. But when Hendrix slid behind the wheel, he owned the beast under the hood and it purred beneath his masterful hands.

She could watch him drive for hours. Which worked out well since she'd apparently just volunteered to spend the day planning flowers for her wedding with her fiancé. Bizarre. But there it was.

Even she had heard of the florist he drove to. Expensive, exclusive and very visible, Maestro of the Bloom lay in the Roundtree shopping district near downtown.

Hendrix drove around the block two times, apparently searching for a parking place, and she opened her mouth to remind him of the lot across the street when he braked at the front row to wait for a mother and daughter to get into their car. Of course he wanted the parking place directly in front of the door, where everyone could see them emerge from his noteworthy car.

It was a testament to his strategic mind that she appreciated. As was the gallant way he sped around to her side of the car to open the door, then extended his hand to help her from the bucket seat that was so low it nearly scraped the ground. But he didn't let go of her hand, instead lacing their fingers together in a way that shouldn't have felt so natural. Hands nested to his satisfaction, he led her to the door and ushered her inside.

A low hum of conversation cut off abruptly and something like a dozen pairs of eyes swung toward them with varying degrees of recognition—some of which held distaste. These were the people whose approval they both sought. The society who had deemed their Vegas tryst shocking, inappropriate, scandalous, and here the two of them were daring to tread among more decent company.

Roz's fingers tightened involuntarily and dang it, Hendrix squeezed back in a surprising show of solidarity. That shouldn't have felt as natural as it did either, like the two of them were a unit already. Peanut butter and jelly against the world.

Her knees got a little wobbly. She'd never had anything like that. Never wanted to feel like a duo with a man. Why did it mean so much as they braved the social scene together? Especially given that she'd only just realized that turning over a new leaf meant more than fixing her relationship with her father. It was about shifting the tide of public opinion too, or her charity wouldn't benefit much from Helene's participation. Roz would go back to being shunned in polite society the moment she signed the divorce papers.

Against all odds, he'd transformed Roz into a righteous convert to the idea of marriage with one small step inside the florist. What else would he succeed in convincing her of?

With that sobering thought, Roz glanced at Hendrix and murmured, "Let's do this."

Three

As practice for the bigger, splashier engagement party to come, Hendrix talked Roz into an intimate gathering at his house. Just family and close friends. It would be an opportunity to gauge how this marriage would fly. And it was a chance to spend time together as a couple with low pressure.

The scene at the florist had shaken Roz, with the murmurs and dirty looks she'd collected from the patrons. That was not okay. Academically, he knew this marriage deal was important to his mother and her campaign. In reality, he didn't personally have a lot of societal fallout from that photo. No one's gaze cut away from him on the street, but he was a guy. Roz wasn't. It was a double standard that shouldn't exist but it did.

Who would have ever thought he'd be hot to ease Roz's discomfort in social situations? It had not been on his list of considerations, but it was now. If this party helped, great. If it didn't, he'd find something else. The fragile glint in her eye while they'd worked with the florist to pick out some outrageously priced flowers had hooked something inside and he'd spent a considerable amount of time trying to unpierce his tender flesh, to no avail. So he did what he always did. Rolled with it.

The catering company had done a great job getting his house in order to host a shindig of this magnitude. While the party had been floated as casual, Hendrix had never entertained before. Unless you counted a handful of buddies sprawled around his dining room table with beer and poker chips.

Roz arrived in the car he'd sent for her and he ignored the little voice inside taunting him for hovering at the front window to watch for her. But it was a sight to see. Roz spilled from the back of the car, sky-high stilettos first, then miles of legs and finally the woman herself in a figure-hugging black cocktail dress designed to drive a man insane.

She'd even swept up her wavy dark hair into a chignon that let a few strands drip down around her face. It was the sexiest hairstyle he'd ever seen on a woman, bar none.

He opened the door before she could knock and his tongue might have gone numb because he couldn't even speak as she coolly surveyed him from under thick black eyelashes.

"Thanks for the car. Hard to drive in heels," she commented, apparently not afflicted by the stupid that was going around.

He shouldn't be, either. He cleared his throat. "You look delicious."

Amazing might have been a better term. It would make it seem more like he'd seen a beautiful woman before and it was no big thing. But she was *his* beautiful woman. For as long as they both deemed it beneficial.

That seemed like a pretty cold agreement all at once for two people who'd burned so very hot not so long ago.

She smiled with a long slow lift of her pink-stained lips. "I'll take that as a compliment, as weird as it is."

"Really? It's weird to tell my beautiful fiancée that she looks good enough to eat?" he questioned with a heated once-over that she didn't miss.

"You can't say stuff like that," she murmured and glanced away from the sizzling electricity that had just arced between them right there on his doorstep.

"The hell I can't. You said no kissing. At no point did I agree to keep my carnal thoughts to myself, nor will I ever agree to that. If I want to tell you that I'm salivating to slide that dress off your shoulders and watch it fall to the ground as it bares your naked body, I will. I might even tell you that I taste you in my sleep sometimes and I wake up with a boner that I can't get rid of until I fantasize about you in the shower." Her cheeks flushed. From embarrassment at his dirty talk or guilt because she liked it? He couldn't tell. He leaned closer and whispered, "Believe it or not, I can tell you what I want to do to you without acting on it."

A car door slammed behind her and she recoiled as if it had been a gunshot to her torso.

"Invite me in," she muttered with a glance over her shoulder. "This is a party, isn't it?"

Should have been a party for two with a strict dress code—birthday suits only. Why had he agreed to her insane stipulation that they abstain from any kind of physical contact until the wedding? It was a dumb rule that made no sense and if Jonas and his wife, Viv, weren't waltzing up the front walk at that precise moment, Hendrix would be having a completely different conversation about it with his fiancée.

He stepped back and allowed Roz to enter, slipping an arm around her waist as she tried to flounce past him into the living room. "Oh, no you don't, sweetheart. Flip around and greet the guests. We're a couple."

Her smile grew pained as he drew her close. "How could I forget?"

Jonas and Viv hit the welcome mat holding hands. Funny how things worked. Jonas and Viv had gotten married in Vegas during the same trip where Hendrix had hooked up with Roz.

"Hey, guys. This is Roz," Hendrix announced unnecessarily, as he was pretty sure both Jonas and Viv knew who she was. If not from the photo flying around the internet, strictly by virtue of the fact that she was glued to his side.

Viv, bless her, smiled at Roz and shook her hand. "I'm Viv Kim. It's nice to meet you, and not just because I love any opportunity to use my new name."

With an intrigued expression, Roz glanced at the male half of the couple. "Are you newly married?"

Jonas stuck his hand out. "Brand-new. I'm Jonas Kim. My name is still the same."

Hendrix nearly rolled his eyes but checked it in deference to one of his oldest friends. "Thanks for coming.

Roz and I are glad you're here to celebrate our engagement. Come in, please."

He guided them all to the cavernous living area that
had been designed with this type of gathering in mind.
The ten-thousand-square-foot house in Oakwood had
been a purchase born out of a desire to stake his claim.
There was a pride in ownership that this house delivered. It was a monument of a previous age, restored
lovingly by someone with an eye for detail, and he appreciated the history wafting from its bones.

The house was a legitimate home and it was his.

Curiously, Viv's gaze cut between the two of them
as she took a seat next to Jonas on the couch. "Have
you set a wedding date?"

"Not yet," Roz answered and at the same time, Hendrix said, "Five weeks."

She shot him a withering look. "We're waiting until
we pick a venue, which might dictate the date."

The doorbell rang and his mother arrived with Paul
Carpenter right on her heels. Introductions all around
went smoothly as nearly everyone knew each other. As
the CEO of Kim Electronics, Jonas had met Mr. Carpenter several times at trade shows and various retail
functions. Helene frequented Viv's cupcake shop on
Jones Street apparently and exclaimed over the baker's
wares at length. It was Paul and Helene's first meeting, however.

Hendrix raised a brow at the extra beat included in
their hand shake, but forgot about it as Roz's friend
Lora showed up with a date. Hendrix's other best
friend, Warren Garinger, was flying solo tonight,
which was lately his default. He arrived a pointed thirty
minutes late.

It wasn't until later that evening that Hendrix had a chance to corner his friend on his tardiness.

"Just the man I was looking for," he said easily as he found Warren in the study examining one of the many watercolors the decorator had insisted went with the spirit of the house.

Warren pocketed his phone, which should have melted from overuse a long time ago. He worked ninety hours a week running the energy drink company his family had founded, but Hendrix didn't think that was what had put the frown on his friend's face. "I had to take a call. Sorry."

"The CEO never gets a day off," Hendrix acknowledged with a nod. "It's cool. I was just making sure you weren't hiding out in protest."

"I'm here, aren't I?" Warren smoothed out his expression before it turned into a full-bore scowl. "You've obviously made your decision to get married despite the pact."

Hendrix bit back a sigh. They'd been over this. Looked like they were going over it again. "The pact means something to me. And to Jonas. We're still tight, no matter what."

Jonas, Warren and Hendrix had met at Duke University, forming a friendship during a group project along with a fourth student, Marcus Powell. They'd had a lot of fun, raised a lot of hell together in the quintessential college experience—until Marcus had gotten his heart tangled up over a woman who didn't deserve his devotion. She'd been a traitorous witch of a cheerleader who liked toying with a man's affections more than she'd liked Marcus. Everyone had seen she was trouble. Except their friend.

He'd grown paler and more wasted away the longer she didn't give him the time of day and eventually, his broken heart had overruled his brain and somehow suicide had become his answer. Shell-shocked and embittered, the three surviving friends had vowed to never let a woman drive them to such lows. They'd formed a pact, refusing to fall in love under any circumstances.

Hell, that had been a given for Hendrix, pact or not. Love wasn't something he even thought much about because he never got close enough to a woman to develop any kind of tender feelings, let alone anything deeper.

But the pact—that was sacred. He'd had little in his life that made him feel like he belonged and his friendship with Jonas and Warren meant everything to him. He'd die before violating the terms of their agreement.

"If the pact is so important, then I don't understand why you'd risk breaking it with marriage," Warren countered and the bitterness lacing his tone sliced at Hendrix far more severely than he'd have expected.

They both glanced up as Jonas joined them, beers in hand. "Thought I'd find you two going at it if I looked hard enough. I'm the one you want to yell at, Warren. Not this joker."

Hendrix took the longneck from his friend's hand and gave Warren a pointed look until the other man sighed, accepting his own beer. No one was confused about the significance. It was a peace offering because Jonas had already broken the pact by falling in love with Viv. Warren had not taken it well. The three of them were still figuring out how to not be bachelor pals any longer, and how to not be at odds over what Warren viewed as Jonas's betrayal.

Hendrix just wanted everything to be on an even keel again so he didn't get a panicky feeling at the back of his throat when he thought of losing the one place where he felt fully accepted no matter what—inside the circle of his friends.

"If it makes you feel better," Hendrix said after a long swallow of his brew, "the odds of me falling in love with Roz are zero. We're not even sleeping together."

Jonas choked on his own beer. "Please. Is this April Fools' Day and I missed it?"

"No, really." Hendrix scowled as both his friends started laughing. "Why is that funny?"

"You've finally met the one woman you can't seduce and you're *marrying* her?" Warren clapped Hendrix on the back, still snickering.

"Shut up," he growled. Why did that have to be the one thing that got his buddy out of his snit? "Besides, I can go without sex."

"Right." Jonas drew the word out to about fourteen syllables, every one of them laden with sarcasm. "And I can pass as Norwegian."

Since Jonas was half-Korean, his point was clear. And Hendrix didn't appreciate his friend's doubt, never mind that he'd been angling for a way to kibosh the no-sex part of his agreement with Roz. "I don't have to explain myself to you guys."

Jonas sipped his beer thoughtfully. "Well, I guess it's a fair point that this is a fake marriage, so maybe you're pretty smart to skip sex in order to avoid confusion. I of all people can understand that."

"This marriage is not fake," Hendrix corrected. "*Your* marriage was fake because you're a moron who thought it was better to live together and just pretend you're hot and heavy. I'm not a moron. Roz and I will have a real marriage, with plenty of unfake hot and heavy."

Especially the honeymoon part. He was already glancing at travel websites for ideas on places he could take his bride where they'd have no interruptions during a weeklong smorgasbord where Roz was the only thing on the menu.

Jonas raised his eyebrows. "You're trying to tell me you're waiting until marriage before you sleep together? That's highly unconventional for anyone, let alone you."

It was on the tip of his tongue to remind Jonas how late Hendrix had been to his wedding. Roz had been the reason, and these yokels were lucky he'd showed up at all. It had been sheer hell to peel himself out of Roz's bed to make it to the chapel before the nuptials were over.

But something held him back from flinging his escapades in his friends' faces. Maybe it had something to do with their assumption that he was a horndog who couldn't keep it in his pants, which had frankly been Roz's assumption, too. Was that all there was to him in everyone's mind? Always on the lookout for the next woman to nail? There was a lot more complexity to his personality than that and he was suddenly not thrilled to learn he'd overshadowed his better qualities with his well-deserved reputation.

"That's me. Unconventional," he agreed easily.

And now he had an ironclad reason to stick to his agreement…to prove to himself that he could stay out of a woman's bed.

* * *

Roz's father had smiled at her tonight more times than he had in the past five years. As much as she'd craved his approval, all this cheer made her nervous. Paul Carpenter ran a billion-dollar furniture enterprise, with manufacturing outlets and retail stores under his command as far away as the Philippines and as close as within walking distance. He rarely smiled, especially not at Roz.

"I've always liked this house," her father commented to her out of the blue as they found themselves at the small minibar at the same time.

"I think Hendrix mentioned it's on the Raleigh Historical Society's list as one of the oldest homes in Oakwood. It's really beautiful."

Small talk with her father about her fiancé's house. It was nearly surreal. They didn't chat often, though that could be because she rarely gave him a chance. After years of conversations laden with her father's heavy sighs and pointed suggestions, she preferred their communication to be on a need-only basis.

Maybe that tide had turned. Hendrix, Jonas and Warren had disappeared, likely having a private no-girls-allowed toast somewhere away from the crowd, so there was no one to interrupt this nice moment.

"You haven't mentioned it, but I'd really like it if you allowed me to walk you down the aisle," her father suggested casually.

Something bright and beautiful bloomed in her chest as she stared at his aged but still handsome face. She'd never even considered having the kind of wedding where such a thing happened, largely because it had never occurred to her that he'd be open to the idea.

They'd never been close, not even after her mother died. The experience of witnessing someone they both loved being eaten alive by cancer should have bonded them. For a long time, she let herself be angry that it hadn't. Then she'd started to wonder if he'd gotten so lost in his grief that he'd forgotten he had a daughter dealing with her own painful sense of loss.

Eventually, she sought to cauterize her grief in other ways, which had led to even further estrangement. Was it possible that she'd erased years of disappointment with the one simple act of agreeing to Hendrix's out- rageous proposal?

"Of course." She swallowed a brief and unexpected tide of emotion. "That would be lovely."

Thankfully, her fiancé was already on board with planning an honest-to-God wedding with all the trim- mings. She'd have to talk him into a longer engagement if they were going to have the type of wedding with an aisle, because she'd envisioned showing up at the jus- tice of the peace in a Betsey Johnson dress that could support a corsage. The simpler the better.

But that was out the window. She had another agenda to achieve with her wedding now, and it in- cluded walking down an aisle on her father's arm. Dare she hope this could be a new beginning to their rela- tionship?

"I wasn't sure you'd like the idea of me marrying Hendrix Harris," she said cautiously, trying to gauge how this new dynamic was supposed to work. She'd left a message to tell him about the party and its pur- pose, effectively announcing her engagement to her father via voice mail so he couldn't express yet more disappointment in her choices.

"I think it's great," he said with enthusiasm she'd rarely heard in his voice. "I'm happy that you're settling down. It will be good for you."

Keep her out of trouble, more like. It was in the undertone of his words and she chose not to let it sour the moment. She did have some questionable decisions in her rearview mirror or she wouldn't have needed to marry Hendrix in the first place. The fact that her dad liked the move was a plus she hadn't dared put on the list of pros, especially given that she was marrying a man her father and everyone else had seen in the buff.

"I think it will be good for me, too," she said, though her reasons were different than his.

"I did wonder if this wedding wasn't designed to eliminate the negative effects of that unfortunate photograph on Helene Harris's campaign." Her father sipped the scotch in a highball, deliberately creating a pregnant pause that prickled across the back of Roz's neck. "If so, that's a good move. Additionally, there are a lot of benefits to being the governor's daughter-in-law, and I like the idea of being tied to the Harris family through marriage."

That had not been a chance statement. "What, like maybe I could put in a good word for you?"

He nodded thoughtfully, oblivious to her sarcasm. "Something like that. I've had some thoughts about going into politics. This is an interesting development. Lots of opportunities unfolding as we speak."

She shouldn't be so shocked. But her stomach still managed to turn over as she absorbed the idea that her father only liked that she was marrying Hendrix because of how it benefited *him*. Did it not occur to her father that she didn't have any sort of in with He-

lene Harris yet? Geez. She'd only met the woman for the first time tonight. And Roz might only have a certain number of favor chips to cash in. The first item on her list was Ms. Harris in white face paint with big floppy shoes.

What was going to happen if she couldn't create the opportunity her father was looking for?

Everyone was expecting something from this union. Why that created such a bleak sense of disillusionment, she had no idea. It wasn't like she'd ever done anything else her father liked. It was just that for once, she'd thought they were finally forming a relationship.

Of course that wasn't the case. Fine. She was used to losing things, used to the temporary nature of everything good that had ever happened to her. It was just one more reason to keep everyone at arm's length.

But Hendrix made that vow harder to keep almost immediately, cornering her in the kitchen where she'd gone to lick her wounds.

"Studying up on my pots and pans so you can cook me a proper dinner once you're the little woman?" he asked as he sauntered into the room and skirted the wide marble-topped island that separated the sink from the 12-burner Viking range to join her on the far side.

"Unless you like your balls in your throat, I would refrain from ever referring to me as the little woman again," she informed him frostily, not budging an inch even as the big, solid wall of Hendrix's masculinity overwhelmed her. "Also, this is a private party. See yourself out."

He had some nerve, waltzing into her space without invitation. All it would take was one slight flex of her hips and they'd be touching. Hell, that might even happen if she breathed deeper.

Instead of getting huffy about her command, he just watched her, his eyes darkening. He was too close, smelled too much like a memory of sin and sex.

"What?" she asked testily as a long, sensual thread pulled at her center.

She swallowed a yelp as he snagged a lock of hair, tucking it behind her ear. But the touch was just an excuse to get even closer, of course, because once he had his hand on her, he didn't stop there. His thumb cruised down her jaw, sensitizing her entire face.

In some alternate dimension, there was a Rosalind Carpenter with the will to slap this man's hand away when he took liberties she hadn't invited. In this dimension, her stilettos had been cemented to the floor and she couldn't do anything but stand frozen as he tipped up her chin.

She braced for the crush of his lips on hers. Anticipated it. Leaned into it ever so slightly.

But then he shocked the hell out of her by tilting her head to the side and grazing her cheek as he murmured in her ear, "Wanna tell me what's got you so upset?"

Oh, no he didn't. How dare he make this about something other than sex and be dead on target about her reasons for hiding out at the same time?

"I'm not upset." Her pulse tripped all over itself, scrambling to sort his dominating presence from his uncanny ability to read her. "Maybe I like the kitchen."

And sure enough—with each breathy catch of her lungs—their bodies brushed and the contact sang through her.

"You can't snow the master of winter," he advised

her so softly that she had to lean in a little closer to hear. Or at least that was her excuse and she'd cling to it as long as she could. "So lie to your friends, your dad. Anyone other than me. We're in this together and I need you."

Her knees went a little mushy. *Mushy.* The one person she had zero intention of letting under her skin had just demonstrated a remarkable ability to blaze right past every barrier she'd ever constructed. And it didn't even seem to matter that he hadn't meant those words the way they'd sounded, like he cared about her and had her back.

No. He wanted her to stick to the deal and stop being such a big baby about the fact that her father expected favors from this union. Weren't favors the whole purpose of this marriage? For God knew what reason, the fact that Hendrix had figured out all the subtle nuances of her mood hooked something inside her.

That pissed her off. He wasn't supposed to be good at handling her. He wasn't supposed to be anything but a means to an end.

"Yes," she purred and let her hips roll forward just a touch until she hit the thick, hard length she'd been seeking. "I can feel how much you need me."

"Careful." His lips feathered against her ear, sending shafts of need deep inside *her.* "Or I might think you're trying to entice me into breaking my promise. The Roz I know wouldn't play so dirty. So I'm going to assume it's a distraction from what's really going on with you and roll with it."

Before she could blink, his arm snaked around her waist, shoving her firmly into the cradle of his body, exactly where she wanted to be.

What did it say that he knew that about her too without being told?

"Put some of that sass where it belongs," he said into her ear as their embrace got a whole lot more intimate. He pressed her back against the counter, one leg teasing her thighs like he might push between them but he'd give her a minute to think about it. "Don't let a stray comment cramp your style. Be the life of the party because no one else's opinion matters."

Her eyes burned all at once. Oh, God, he was going to make her cry. What was wrong with her that a couple of compassionate phrases from a player like Hendrix could yank loose *tears*?

Except he wasn't just a creep looking to score. They were engaged, as unbelievable as that was to reconcile, and he needed her to *pull it together*.

"You're right," she admitted. "I'm letting crap that doesn't matter get me down."

What was she doing skulking around in the kitchen when there was a party going on? More importantly, he'd given her the perfect excuse to step out of his arms as everything settled inside.

She didn't move.

"Of course I am," he told her and she could hear the smile in his voice even as she absorbed his heat through her little black dress. "Roz, this is practice for the wider swath of society that we have to wade through an exhausting number of times over the next few weeks. They're not going to be any more forgiving. But I'm here. I'm not going anywhere and I'll be holding your hand the whole time."

"PB&J for the win," she murmured and dang it, her arms fit so well around his waist that she couldn't do anything but leave them there. "Although I have to ask why we couldn't have had this conversation without you wrapping yourself around me like an octopus."

"Oh, we could have." He nuzzled her ear. "This was strictly for me. You're driving me insane in that dress and all I can think about is that I don't get to take it off at the end of the night. I deserve something for my suffering."

That shouldn't have made her laugh. Especially since the whole of his body pressed into hers felt more like the opening act than the finale.

"Also," he continued, "I didn't think you were in the mood for an audience. If anyone came through that door right now, they'd exit pretty quickly for fear of intruding on a moment between lovers."

Did the man ever miss an angle? She did not want to appreciate any of his qualities, let alone the non-sexual variety.

Neither should she be recalling with perfect clarity what he'd said to her on his front porch. He'd never been shy about using his mouth in whatever inventive way came to mind, and he had a really great imagination, especially when it came to talking dirty.

That was enough to jump-start her brain. This wasn't the start of a seduction, never mind how easily it could be. It was a Come to Jesus at the hands of her partner and she was the one who'd taken sex off the table. For a reason. The man made her forget her own name and she needed to keep her wits about her, or she'd never survive this. She had to get Clown-Around off the ground and Hendrix was nothing to her except a ticket to achieving her goals.

"The moment is over," she informed him through sheer force of will.

"I disagree." But he stepped back immediately, taking all his delicious heat with him.

Even in that, he'd read her expertly, extracting himself as soon as he sensed her consent had changed. His gaze burned hot and she had no doubt he'd sweep her back into his arms if she gave the word.

And that put the steel in her spine that had been missing. She had equal power in this partnership. He wasn't going to slip through her fingers when she wasn't looking because they weren't a couple basing their relationship on fleeting feelings. They both had goals, none of which would be accomplished when one of them moped around poking at old bruises.

Hendrix was a smart choice. Obviously. He got her in ways no one ever had and she refused to examine how much she liked that.

"We're a power couple." She held out her hand to him. "Let's go act like one."

Four

Hendrix nursed a Jack Daniel's on the rocks as he hung out near the fireplace on the east end of the house and wished like hell he could blame the whiskey for the burn in his throat. But that pain was pure Roz.

And maybe some leftover crap from the discussion with Jonas and Warren, where his so-called friends had made it known in no uncertain terms how weak they thought he was when it came to women.

He could go without sex. He could. Hadn't he walked away from Roz when she'd said walk? If that wasn't a stellar test of his iron will, he didn't know what was. And he'd passed.

So why was he still so pissed? His skin felt like a hundred ants were crawling over it as he failed yet again at keeping his eyes off his fiancée. She lit up the room as she talked to his mother. So what if anyone caught him staring? He and Roz were engaged and he was allowed to look at her. In fact, he'd say it was expected.

The unexpected part was how…fierce the whole encounter in the kitchen had made him. Someone had upset Roz and he didn't like it. Didn't like how fragile she'd felt in his arms as he did his best to beat back whatever was going on with her internally. But she'd snapped out of it like the champ she was and he'd had a hard time letting her go when what he really wanted to do was explore that lush mouth of hers. That wasn't what she'd needed. Wasn't what he needed, either.

Okay, it was what he *needed* all right. But he also needed to prove to everyone—and maybe to himself—that he had what it took to reel back his sex-soaked lifestyle. If he'd learned to do that when his mother had asked him to, Vegas wouldn't have happened and there'd be no photograph of Hendrix's bare butt plastered all over the internet.

Paul Carpenter loomed in Hendrix's peripheral vision and then the man parked near him with a lift of his glass. "Haven't had a chance to speak to you one-on-one yet."

"No, sir."

Hendrix eyed the older man whose wealth and power in the retail industry eclipsed almost everyone in the world. Certainly a smaller chain like Harris Tobacco Lounge had nothing on Carpenter Furniture, nor did people get vaguely distasteful looks on their faces when talking about the business Roz's father had founded. Tobacco wasn't in vogue any longer, not the way it had been in the late eighties when Helene had partnered with her brother to build a string of shops from the ground up. Hendrix had joined the company almost a year after Uncle Peter died and then worked ninety hours a week to pull miracle after miracle from thin air to increase revenue over the past decade as he gradually took over the reins from his mom.

But Hendrix didn't assume for a moment that a man like Paul Carpenter respected one thin dime of Harris tobacco money, regardless of how hard he and his mom had worked for their fortune.

Mr. Carpenter eyed Hendrix as he swished his own amber liquid around the ice in his highball. "I suppose soon enough you'll be my son-in-law."

"Yes, sir." Why did it feel like he'd been called to the principal's office? He'd bet every last dollar of Harris money that Carpenter didn't think Hendrix was good enough for his daughter. "Roz is pretty important to me."

Uncomfortable didn't begin to describe this conversation. Hendrix shifted his stance. Didn't help.

"She's important to me, too," Paul said with a small smile. "It's just been the two of us since she was eight, you know."

"Yes, she mentioned that her mother had passed away." It was something they had in common—a missing parent. But Carpenter hadn't thrown that tidbit in for anything close to the same reason as Roz had. At the time, they'd been playing truth or dare and doing Jell-O shots off each other's bare stomachs. "I'm sorry for your loss, sir."

The memory of Roz's hot body decked out on the bed with the little circle of raspberry gelatin covering her navel slammed through his senses with far more potency than he'd have expected given that he'd just had the woman in his arms less than fifteen minutes ago.

Problem was that she'd been dressed. And off-limits. And probably even if he'd had permission to boost her up on the counter so he could get underneath that black dress, he'd still want her with a bone-deep ache. That had happened in Vegas, too. He couldn't get enough of her skin, her abandon, the way she was always game for whatever he did next.

And that was a conviction of his crimes as much as anything else. He had few memories of Roz that didn't involve her naked. That was the way he liked it...and lent entirely too much credence to everyone's certainty that he was a walking boner, panting after the next piece of tail he could get his hands on.

God, what was wrong with him? He was having a conversation with his future father-in-law and all he could think about was casting the man's daughter in the dirtiest sex scenario imaginable.

Something that might have been a blush if he'd been a girl prickled across his cheeks. But embarrassment wasn't something he did. Ever. He had nothing to be ashamed of. Except for the handful of scandals he'd managed to fall into over the past few years—Roz had certainly not been the first. She was just the one that had been the most worth it.

He sighed as Paul nodded his thanks over Hendrix's condolences. Maybe if he thought about something else, like cars, he could pretend the hard-on he'd been carrying around since Roz walked through his front door would eventually go away.

"I'm not one to pry," Paul said in that tone people used when they meant the exact opposite of what they'd just claimed. "And it's none of my business. But I wanted you to know that if you're marrying Roz to eliminate the scandal, I approve."

"You, um…what?" Hendrix swallowed. It didn't work. Throat still burned. He gulped enough whiskey to choke a horse, coughed and then had to wipe his watering eyes.

Paul Carpenter *approved* of Hendrix's marriage to Roz. As if Hendrix was someone he might have picked out for his daughter. It was as shocking as it was unbelievable.

For the first time in his life, he'd been automatically accepted by a male of note, one he wasn't related to, whom he admired, one whose approval he would have never sought, save this specific situation. And he'd *never* expected to get it.

"It's high time that Roz take responsibility for the questionable decisions she makes, especially the one that led to so much trouble for you and your mother's campaign. I appreciate that you've been a willing party to the *fix*." Paul accompanied that word with two fingered air quotes.

The elation that had accompanied the man's initial statement fizzled. Fast.

A willing party? As if Roz had somehow seduced him into indulging a one night stand and then orchestrated the photograph? As if Hendrix had been an innocent victim of her stupidity?

Agape and unable to actually close his mouth around the sour taste coating his tongue, Hendrix let Paul's meaning filter through his brain for a good long while. At least until he felt like he could respond without punching Paul in the mouth.

"It takes two to tango. Sir." Hendrix lifted his chin. "Roz and I are partners. I'm making all my own decisions and rest assured, one of them is to treat her like the amazing, wonderful woman that she is."

He stopped short of telling Paul that he should take a lesson.

Figured the one time he'd had a few moments of approval from a man who could have been a father figure would end in the realization that Roz hadn't had a relationship with her surviving parent the way Hendrix had. Hendrix's mother loved him and while his exploits exasperated her, she never judged. Not the way this sanctimonious jerk had just judged Roz.

Roz was Paul's daughter and he should be on her side. If anything, Hendrix had been expecting a talking-to about corrupting the Carpenter daughter with his evil ways, which would have been well-deserved and easy to pretend didn't affect him. Instead, he felt like he needed to take a shower and then tuck Roz away where this man couldn't touch her.

"Well, be that as it may, I for one am quite happy with the development. Marriage will be good for Roz and with any luck, she'll stop the naked romps in hot tubs."

"Sir, I mean this with all due respect, but I sincerely hope not."

Hendrix whirled and left Paul standing by the fireplace with a bemused look on his face. Having an in with Carpenter Furniture wasn't going to pave the way to belonging in the upper echelon of North Carolina businessmen then. But what *would* make Hendrix finally feel like he was legitimate?

He found Roz talking to Lora in his study and took only half a second to gauge Roz's mood. Better. She didn't seem fragile any longer. Good. He grabbed his fiancée's hand, threw an apologetic glance at her friend and dragged Roz from the room.

"What are you doing?" she demanded once they hit the hall.

"You and I are going to go do something together. And we'll be dressed."

Then he'd have a memory of her that had nothing to do with sex. They both needed that.

"Darling, we *are* doing something together. Dressed." And Roz's sarcasm wasn't even as thick as it should be. "We're at our engagement party, remember?"

"Of course I do," he grumbled. A lie. He'd forgotten that he couldn't just leave and take Roz on an honest-to-God date.

Soon. It was an oversight that he'd beat himself up for later. He and Roz would—and *should*—go on lots of dates with each other while they weren't having sex. Spend time together. Get to know each other. Then he could stop thinking about her naked forty-seven times a minute.

But one thing he *couldn't* stop thinking about was the fact that he'd never have realized she was upset earlier if he'd been permitted to turn it into a sexual encounter. What else had he already missed because his interactions with his fiancée started and ended with how best to get into her panties? That question put a hollow feeling in his chest that stayed with him the rest of the night.

* * *

Roz took a long shower when she got home from the engagement party, hoping it would wash the evening from her brain. But nothing could dislodge the surprising things she'd learned about Hendrix in the course of a few hours. The man never did what she expected. But she'd already known *that*.

What she hadn't known was how easily he'd figure out how to bend her to his will. She'd naively assumed that as long as they weren't naked, she'd be good. Wrong. Somehow, he'd gotten her to agree to a date.

A date with Hendrix Harris. That was almost more unbelievable than the fact that she was marrying him. Yeah, their "date" was a public spectacle that he'd dreamed up as a way to push their agenda. Couldn't get society used to the idea that they were a respectable couple if they hid at home. She got that.

But for the love of God… What were they going to talk about? She didn't date. She had a lot of sex with men who knew their way around a woman's body but conversation by candlelight in an intimate booth at a swanky restaurant wasn't in her repertoire—by design. One she could handle; the other she could not. Intimacy born of conversation and dating led to feelings she had no intention of developing, so she avoided all of the above like the plague.

One surefire way to ensure a man never called you again? Sleep with him. Worked every time. Unless his name was Hendrix Harris, apparently. That guy she couldn't figure out how to shake, mentally or physically.

At least the concept of going on a date with her fiancé had pushed the unpleasantness of the encounter with her father to the background. Actually, Hendrix had almost single-handedly done that with his comfort-slash-seduction scene in the kitchen, which she'd appreciated more than she'd ever let on.

The less the man guessed how much he affected her, the better.

The next morning, she rifled through her closet for something appropriate for a date with the man who'd blown through half the female population of Raleigh. All eyes would be on her and not for the normal reasons.

Nothing. How was it possible not to have a thing to wear in an entire eight-hundred-square-foot closet? She'd have to go shopping after she got some work done.

Donning a severe suit that she secretly called her Grown-up Outfit, she twisted her hair into a sleek up-do that made her feel professional and drove to Clown-Around to push some paperwork across her desk.

Her phone rang and she almost didn't answer the call from an unfamiliar number. It was too early and she hadn't had nearly enough coffee to endure more rejection from yet another hospital.

But she was the only one here. There was no one else to do the dirty work. She answered.

"Rosalind?" the female voice said. "This is Helene Harris. How are you?"

Roz nearly dropped the phone but bobbled it just enough to keep it near her face. "Ms. Harris. I'm fine. Thank you. It was lovely to meet you last night."

"Likewise. I hope you don't mind that I asked Hendrix for your number. I'd like to take you to lunch, if you're free."

"I'm free." That had probably come out a little too eagerly. Thank you, Jesus, she'd worn an outfit that even a future mother-in-law would approve of. "And thank you. That would be lovely."

They made plans to meet at a restaurant on Glenwood Avenue, dashing Roz's notion to go shopping for a date dress, but she couldn't think about that because *holy crap*—she was having lunch with her future mother-in-law, who was also running for governor and who had presumably agreed to be a clown. Plus there was a whole mess of other things running through her head and now she was nervous.

By lunchtime, Roz truly thought she might throw up. That would put the cap on her day nicely, wouldn't it? A photo of her yakking all over a gubernatorial candidate would pair well with the one of her *in flagrante delicto* with the woman's son.

Ms. Harris had beaten her to the restaurant and was waiting for Roz near the maître d' stand, looking polished, dignified and every inch a woman who could run a state with one hand tied behind her back. In other words, not someone Roz normally hung around with.

"Am I late?" she asked Ms. Harris by way of greeting. Because that was a great thing to point out if so.

Ms. Harris laughed. "Not at all. I got here early so I didn't have to make you wait."

"Oh. Well, that was nice. Thank you." A little floored, Roz followed the older woman to a table near the window that the maître d' pointed them to.

The murmur of voices went into free fall as the two ladies passed. Heads swiveled. Eyes cut toward them.

But unlike what had happened to Roz the last time she'd braved polite society, the diner's faces didn't then screw up in distaste as they recognized her. Instead, the world kept turning and people went back to eating as if nothing had happened.

Miraculous.

Roz slid into her chair and opened her menu in case she needed something to hide behind. Ms. Harris didn't do the same. She folded her hands on the table and focused on Roz with a sunny smile that reminded her of Hendrix all at once.

"I'm so jealous that you can wear your hair up," Ms. Harris said out of the blue and flicked a hand at her shoulder-length ash-blond hair. "I can't. I look like a Muppet. But you're gorgeous either way."

"Um…thank you," Roz spit out because she had to say something, though it felt like she was repeating herself. "Ms. Harris, if I may be blunt, I need some context for this lunch. Are we here so you can tell me to lie low for the foreseeable future? Because I'm—"

"Helene, please." She held up a hand, palm out in protest, shooting Roz a pained smile. "Ms. Harris is running for governor and I hear that enough all day long. I like to leave her at the office."

"Helene, then." Roz blinked. And now she was all off-kilter. Or rather more so than she'd been since the woman had called earlier that morning. Come to think of it, she'd been upside down and inside out since the moment she'd caught Hendrix's eye at the Calypso Room. Why would lunch with his mother be any different? "I'm sorry. Call me Roz. Rosalind is an old-fashioned name that would be better suited for an eighty-year-old woman who never wears pants and gums her food."

Fortunately, Helene laughed instead of sniffing and finding something fascinating about the tablecloth the way most polished women did when confronted with Roz's offbeat sense of humor. She hadn't grown up going to cotillions and sweet-sixteen balls the way other girls in her class had, and her lack of decorum showed up at the worst times. Her father had been too busy ignoring the fact that he had a daughter to notice that she preferred sneaking out and meeting twenty-year-old boys with motorcycles to dances and finishing school.

"I think it's a beautiful name. But I get that we can't always see our own names objectively. If I had a dime for every person who called me Helen." She made a tsk noise and waved away the waiter who was hovering near her elbow. "And then try to give your own kid an unusual name that no one on the planet can mispronounce and all you get is grief."

In spite of herself, Roz couldn't help but ask. "Hendrix doesn't like his name? Why not?"

Helene shrugged and shook her head, her discreet diamond earrings catching the low light hanging over the table. "He says Hendrix was a hack who would have faded by the time he reached thirty if he hadn't overdosed. Blasphemy. The man was a legend. You'd think your fiancé would appreciate being named after a guitar hero, but no."

"He…he thinks Jimi Hendrix is a *hack*?" Roz clutched her chest, mock-heart-attack style, mostly to play along because she knew who the guitarist was of course, but she had no opinion about his status as a legend. Neither had she been born yesterday. You didn't argue musical taste with the woman who would most likely be sitting in the governor's chair after the election. "I might have to rethink this whole wedding idea."

The other woman grinned wide enough to stick a salad plate in her mouth sideways. "I knew I liked you." Helene evaluated Roz for a moment and then signaled the waiter. "As much as I'd prefer to spend the rest of the afternoon hanging out, duty calls. We should eat."

Since it sounded like a mandate, Roz nodded, trying to relax as Helene ordered a salad and water. This wasn't the Spanish Inquisition that she'd expected, not yet anyway. Maybe that was coming after lunch. She ordered a salad despite loathing them because it was easy to eat and obviously an approved dish since Helene had gotten the same.

And that was the root cause of her nervousness—she wanted Helene to like her but had no clue how to go about that when she had no practice cozying up to a motherly type. Furthermore, the woman had just said she liked her. What more did Roz need in the way of validation, a parade?

She sipped her water and yearned for a glass of wine, which would be highly inappropriate. Wouldn't it?

"Thank you," Helene murmured to her after the waiter disappeared. "For agreeing to this wedding plan that we came up with. It speaks a lot of your character that you'd be willing to do something so unconventional to help me."

"I…" *Have no idea how to respond to that.* Roz sat

back in her chair and resisted the urge to rub at her temples, which would only clue in everybody that she'd fallen completely out of the rhythm of the conversation. "I— You're welcome?"

Smiling, Helene patted Roz's hand, which was currently clenched in a fist on the tablecloth. "Another thing. You're making me nervous, dear. I can't decide if you're about to bolt or dissolve into tears. I asked you to lunch because I want to get to know you. You're the only daughter I've ever had. For as long as I've got you, let's make this a thing, shall we?"

Unexpected tears pricked at Roz's eyelids, dang it. The Harris family shared that gene apparently—Hendrix had that uncanny ability to pull stuff out of her depths, too.

"I don't have a mother," she blurted out. "So this is all new to me."

Helene nodded. "I understand that. I didn't have a good relationship with my mother. Sometimes growing up, I wondered if it would have been easier if she'd disowned me instead of spending every waking second being disappointed in me."

Roz nodded, mortified as she dashed tears away with the white napkin from her lap. This was not the conversation she'd intended to have with her new mother-in-law. She didn't believe for a second that shouting, *I still wonder that about my father!* would be the best way to foster the relationship Helene seemed to be asking for.

But Helene's story so closely mirrored the way Roz felt about her father that it was uncanny. How familiar was she allowed to be on her first one-on-one with Helene? This was uncharted—and so not what she'd expected. If anything, she'd earned an indictment for playing a role in the problems that Helene had just thanked her for helping to solve. There'd been two naked people in that hot tub, after all.

"I'm sorry about the photograph," she said earnestly and only because Helene hadn't called her on the carpet about it. That was why Roz and her father were always at such odds. He always adopted that stern tone when laying out Roz's sins that immediately put her back up.

Accepting the apology with a nod, Helene waited for the server to put their salads on the table and leaned forward. "Trust me when I tell you that we all have questionable exploits in our pasts. You just got lucky enough for yours to be immortalized forever, which frankly wouldn't have happened if you'd been with anyone other than Hendrix."

That was entirely false. Bad luck of the male variety followed her around like a stray dog, waiting to turn its canines on her the moment she tried to feed it. Roz swallowed and ate a tiny bit of salad in order not to seem ungrateful. "I have a tendency to get a little, um, enthusiastic with my exploits unfortunately."

"Which is no one's business but yours. The unfortunate part is that my son forgot that political enemies have long reaches and few scruples. You can only tell the kid so much. He does his own thing." She shrugged good-naturedly, far more so than should have been the case. It was a testament to Helene's grace, which was something Roz had no experience with.

"You're very generous," Roz said with a small frown that she couldn't quite erase. "Most parents aren't so forgiving."

At least that had never been Roz's experience. Parents were harsh, not understanding.

"I'm not most parents. Hendrix is my life and I love him more than I could possibly tell you. He saved me." Helene paused to eat some of her own salad but Roz didn't dare interrupt. "I have a bit of a wild past myself, you know."

Was this the part where Roz was supposed to nod and say, *Why yes, I have heard all the gossip about your rebellious teenage years*? Especially when Roz's own rebellious teenage years had been nothing but practice for her even more defiant twenties, when she'd really tested the limits of her father's patience.

"Getting pregnant at seventeen was a huge wake-up call," Helene recounted in the pause. "Without that baby, I might have continued in a self-destructive cycle that wouldn't have ended well. And now look at me. I created a successful business that Hendrix runs like the maestro of the boardroom that he was born to be and I'm running for governor. *Governor.* Some days, I don't know what I did to earn these blessings."

Roz's own eyes misted in commiseration as Helene dabbed at hers with her napkin. "I honestly wasn't sure what to think when you asked me to lunch. But making each other cry wasn't even on the top ten."

Helene's smile widened. One thing Roz noticed, no matter what, the woman's smile never slipped. It was a trait she'd like to learn because not for one moment did Roz believe that Helene's life was all smooth sailing. No, instead, Helene had some innate quality that allowed her to be happy regardless of the subject or circumstance. Voters must really be drawn to that happiness the same way Roz was.

Of course that apple did not fall far from the tree. Hendrix's bright personality had been a huge turn-on. Still was. He just laced it with pure carnal intentions that he did not mind making her fully aware of, and then followed through like the maestro of the *bedroom* that he was.

Roz shivered and tried like hell to reel back those thoughts because fantasizing about a woman's son while sitting with her in an upscale restaurant felt like bad form.

"I didn't plan to make you cry when I called you," Helene confessed sunnily. "Just happened. But I love that you're a companionable crier. No one wants to cry alone."

No. No one did. But that was some people's lot in life and if they didn't change the subject, there were going to be a lot more tears. The raw place inside was growing a lot bigger the longer she sat here. This wonderful woman had just said she'd be happy having a mother-daughter relationship with Roz for as long as Roz was married to Hendrix. Like that was an invitation Roz got every day and it was no big thing.

It was. And Roz wanted to cling to it, hold it and wrap her arms around it. But like everything—*everything*—in her life, Helene would be gone one day soon. Too soon. Any day was too soon because Roz had just realized that she craved whatever relationship this woman would grant her. Helene could be a...mentor of sorts. A friend. A stand-in mother.

It was overwhelming to contemplate. Overwhelmingly sad to think about having that and then giving it up.

But how could Roz refuse? She didn't *want* to refuse.

Helene was helping her blow away the scandal if nothing else and Roz owed the woman respect and allegiance for that alone.

The rest was all a huge bonus.

Five

Hendrix picked Roz up at the door of her loft for their date because he wanted to and he could. Also? What better way to prove he had all the skill necessary to resist pushing his way inside and having his way with her than not to do it?

But when he knocked on the door, she swung it wide to give him an eyeful of soft, gorgeous skin on display. Being that edible should be a crime. Her cleavage should be framed and hung on the wall of the Louvre.

"What happened to your pants?" he growled hoarsely.

Roz glanced down at the river of bare legs flowing from the hem of the blouse-like thing she had on. "What pants? This is a dress."

"The hell you say." He couldn't take her on a date in that outfit. His will would slide into the toilet in about a microsecond. Surely that would be the easiest dress in the history of time to get his hands under, even if they were someplace normally reserved for hands off, like a high-backed booth in the corner of a dimly lit restaurant.

His will made a nice whooshing sound as it flushed away and all his good intentions crumbled into dust. He might have whimpered.

Do not step over the threshold. Do not. No stepping.

"Let me make this perfectly clear to you," he ground out. "If you wear that dress—and I use that term *very* loosely—I cannot be responsible for what carnal activities may befall you in the course of this evening."

"Please." She waved that off. "You made a promise to keep your hands off me and you will, I have no doubt. What you're really saying is that you'd be embarrassed to be seen with me in this, right? So kiss off. I'm wearing it."

Oh, so it was going to be one of those nights. Not only would he have to contend with the idea that she had absolute faith in him, but she'd also assigned some kind of nefarious intent to his comments.

Her attitude needed to go and fast. "I wasn't embarrassed to be seen with you naked in a photograph. Not embarrassed now. Stop projecting your own crap all over me and get your purse. If you want to wear something that's one stiff breeze away from being illegal, be my guest."

"What's with you?" she called over her shoulder as she did exactly as he'd commanded without seeming to realize it. "You asked me on this date. If you're going to be nasty to me the whole time, then I'd be happy to slam the door in your face and order takeout."

That wasn't happening. He'd been looking forward to this date all day. "Why is it so hard to believe my objection to that dress starts and ends with how spectacular you look in it? You tell me what's with you and I'll tell you what's with me."

She smirked and flounced past him to the building's elevator. "You never had a problem with what I wore in Vegas. What's changed now? Only that we're engaged and you want me to look like a proper Harris bride."

Whatever *that* meant.

"Stop putting words in my mouth." The elevator door closed around them and they were alone in a space that got a whole lot smaller the more of her scent he breathed in. "In Vegas, I didn't care what you wore because I was taking it off you at some point. That's not the situation tonight and if you're really confused about the state of my extreme sexual frustration, the evidence is ready and available for your hands-on examination."

Her gaze flicked to his crotch, which put a little more heat into his already painful erection. Her sweet fingers on it would be legendary indeed but she didn't take him up on the invitation. Shame.

"I— You know what? Never mind." Her lush pink lips clamped together and she looked away.

Not so fast. His beleaguered senses were still working well enough to alert him that there was more here that he didn't know. "Spit it out, sweetheart. Or I'll be forced to kiss it out of you."

"What?" She slid him a sideways glance. "There's no stipulation in the rules that says you're allowed to kiss me to get information."

He shrugged. "How come you get to make all the

rules? If you're not going to be honest with me, I have to make up my own rules."

Her sigh worked its way through his gut and he was a half second away from sweeping her into his arms to show her he always put his money where his mouth was. But then she did as he suggested.

"I am projecting," she admitted.

It was as much of a shock now as it had been in the kitchen during their party—he'd figured out how to make progress with Roz. She was such a mystery, one he'd like to spend many long hours solving. Usually he would do that in bed. But that was off-limits here, so he'd been forced to be more creative. Looked like it was working. "Don't do that. Tell me what's up and then we'll go paint the town."

"Maybe you want a wife more like your mom. Smart and accomplished." She shrugged, her face blank. "That's not who I am. I have to be me, even if I don't look like I'm supposed to be here."

"What does that even mean? Of course you're supposed to be here. What, are you worried how you stack up?" The long, intense silence answered his flippant question in spades. "Are you *kidding* me? That's really something that even crossed your mind?"

Ridiculous. But apparently it wasn't to her. She rolled her shoulders back and her spine went stiff.

"Can we just forget about it?"

That wasn't happening any more than not taking Roz on this date. But first they obviously needed to get a few things straight. The elevator reached the ground floor and he waited until she reached his car.

Instead of opening the door for her, he snagged her by the waist and turned her into his arms, trapping her against the car. Instantly, everything but Roz drained from his mind as her body aligned with his so neatly that he could feel the heat of her core against his leg.

That was some dress.

"I already told you what you wanted to know, Hendrix." She glanced up at him through her lashes and the look was so sexy it put at least an inch on his already impossibly hard erection. "What are you going to do now, kiss me anyway?"

"No need." His hips fit so well into the hollow of her stomach that he swayed into her a little deeper. "This is strictly Exhibit A. B and C will have to wait."

Because he'd given his word. How had that become such a thing? Fine time for something like principles. Before Roz, he'd have said he had none when it came to women. Or rather, women said that on his behalf and he'd never corrected the notion.

"Make no mistake, though. You need kissing," he murmured, ignoring the fact that it was so backward it wasn't even funny. "In the worst way. Anytime you find yourself worried about whether you're the most gorgeous woman in the room, you think about this. Remember what my body feels like against yours and don't you dare question whether you're the woman I want to take home with me."

"I wasn't worried about that," she said and blinked her long sooty lashes coquettishly. "But I do appreciate exhibit A."

Not enough to lift the no-kissing moratorium apparently. She was crushed against his body, wearing a filmy, flirty dress that barely covered her good parts and her lips came together in the sweetest little bow that he wanted to taste so badly he feared for his sanity.

But not enough that he'd lost all decorum. Looked like his will wasn't completely broken because he found the wherewithal to step back. His chest heaved as he met her gaze. It was enigmatic and full of heat.

"Let me know when you're ready for the rest of the exhibit. I can open it up for your viewing pleasure any time."

Why were they torturing themselves like this again?

Due punishment, he reminded himself. His mom deserved to have a campaign free from other people's darts because of her son's actions. He owed it to his mother to fix it, especially after already messing up once because he couldn't resist this woman.

Plus, marrying Roz and introducing something real and legitimate into his life meant something to him, more than he'd ever admit, to her or anyone.

He tucked his fiancée into the car and slid into his own seat. She leaned on the center console instead of settling back against the leather, spilling way too much of her presence into his space.

"This seat has plenty of room for two," he murmured instead of starting the engine like a good boy.

"Don't threaten me unless you plan to follow through," she shot back and tucked her chin into her palm as if she planned to watch him the entire time he drove. "Where are you taking me? Not Randolph Room. That's where your mom took me to lunch."

"You had lunch with my mom?" That was news to him. He frowned.

Had his mother mentioned something about it last night and he'd forgotten in all the hoopla of the engagement party and the disturbing conversation with Paul Carpenter? He distinctly recalled giving Roz's number to his mom, but he'd assumed that was so they could coordinate the clown thing.

His mother usually told him her schedule and it was bothersome that she hadn't given him a heads-up about having lunch with his fiancée. He and Helene were business partners, and Hendrix sometimes offered advice on her campaign. And they were friends, which was often weird to people so he seldom talked about it.

Of course, since the photograph, she'd been a little on edge with him. It stung to find out they weren't totally back to normal.

"Yeah. She called me and asked if I was free. I wasn't going to say no."

"You shouldn't have. What did you talk about?"

"Girl stuff."

That was code for *mind your own business*. Hendrix started the car to give himself something to do that wasn't prying into the social life of his mother and fiancée. Nor did he want to obsess over the reasons why it was bothering him.

At least now he had some context for why Roz had all of a sudden joined the Helene Harris fan club and developed a complex about whether she stacked up against other women.

They drove to the restaurant where he'd made reservations and he cursed the silence that had fallen inside the car. Normally he had no problem finding something to talk about, particularly when it came to Roz, but he didn't want to spend the evening discussing all the ways he planned to have her after the wedding.

Well, he *wanted* to. There was absolutely nothing wrong with a healthy attraction to the woman you were going to marry. But he genuinely didn't think he had it in him to talk dirty to Roz and then not follow through yet again.

"Did you and my mother work out the clown stuff?" That was a safe enough subject.

"No. I mean, she mentioned it, but only to say that she's overcommitted right now and to bug her about it at lunch next week so she can fit it in. She actually said it like that. *Bug* her." Roz laughed. "As if I'd pester Helene like that. 'Mom, Mom, can you be a clown? Pleeeeease?'"

Hendrix did a double take at Roz's cute little girl voice. And the mention of additional lunches. "You're having lunch again?"

"Sure, we decided it was important to have a standing lunch date once a week from now on. Is there a problem with that?"

Yes. A huge problem. He didn't like the idea of his mom getting chummy with Roz. Why? How the hell should he know? He just…didn't. "Of course not. I was making conversation. This is a date. The whole point is to get to know each other, right?"

"That was how you posed it," she reminded him with another laugh that should have had him thinking of all the ways he could get her to do that a lot because it meant she was having fun.

Instead, his back was up and his mood had slid into a place normally reserved for tense board meetings. What was *wrong* with him? Not enough sex lately, most likely.

At the restaurant, they waited in a discreet corner as the maître d' readied their table, both of them ignoring the pointed attention from the other guests. At least Roz hadn't stiffened up like she had at the florist. He'd consider that a win.

Wedding plans. That was a good subject. Surely they could talk about that. He waited until they'd both taken their seats and he'd given the waiter their wine preference.

"So. You're going to hang out with my mom once a week now?"

She lifted a brow. "That's really bothering you, isn't it?"

Apparently. And now it was evident to them both. He bit back a curse.

When was the last time his mom had asked him to lunch? Ages ago. Not since the photograph had hit the news. She'd been really upset. But it had all blown over after he'd agreed to marry Roz—he'd thought.

And look, here he was in a restaurant with Roz. Engaged. That had been a major feat to pull off. People were noticing them together and a waiter had even taken a discreet picture with his phone that would likely make the rounds with some positive press attached. Surely Helene could appreciate all of the steps Hendrix had taken toward legitimizing his relationship with Roz so that his mom's political opponents wouldn't have any fodder to lob at her via the press.

Now would be a great time to stop sulking and get back to the reason he was torturing himself with a stunning companion whom he would not be taking to bed later. They hadn't even scored a dimly lit booth, which was good. And bad.

"This is the part where you're supposed to back me into the kitchen and stick your hands all over my body so I can have something else to focus on besides the stuff in my head," he informed her.

"I would if that would help." She eyed him nonchalantly. "But I'm pretty sure that only works on me. Instead, why don't you tell me why you're so threatened by the idea of me having lunch with your mom?"

Lazily, he sipped his wine to cover the panic that had uncurled in his stomach. The alcohol didn't help. "*Threatened* is a strong word."

And so correct. How dare she be the one to figure that out when he hadn't? The back of his neck flashed hot. That was a big wake-up call.

He'd never in a million years expected that getting married would mean he'd have to share his mother with someone. It had been the two of them for so long, and they'd become even more of a unit as he'd grown into adulthood, made even stronger after Uncle Peter had died. His reaction was pure selfishness and he didn't feel like apologizing for it all at once.

"Then you tell me what would be a better word," she said.

No quarter. If he wasn't already feeling pushed against a wall, her cool insistence would have put him there. *"Curious."*

Her small smile said she had his number and she'd be perfectly within her rights to call him on his complete lie. *Pissed off* and *tense* would be more applicable. Which was dumb. What, was he actually worried that Roz was going to steal his mother from him?

"Curious about why on earth two women who don't know each other and will soon share the same last name could possibly want to have lunch?" She watched him over the rim of her glass as she sipped her own wine.

"You're changing your name?" This evening was full of revelations.

"Yeah. Why not? That's part of the deal here, right? Marrying you is my get-out-of-jail-free card. Might as well go full throttle. Make sure everyone is clear that I'm tied to the governor's office."

"But you're already a Carpenter—" All at once, the conversation with her father slammed through his consciousness. Was he really that dense? Maybe being a Carpenter wasn't all that great for her. After being treated to a glimpse of the judgment levied in her direction, it wasn't so hard to guess why, if so. Maybe she deserved a name change.

Wow. When had he turned into such an ass?

He picked up her hand to hold it in his. Her touch bled through him, convicting him even further since she didn't pull away. "I shouldn't be jumping down your throat about having lunch with my mom. It's fine. I'm glad you're getting along."

She nodded and the mood lightened. The restaurant he'd selected featured a highly rated chef and the meal reflected that. They ate and conversed about innocuous subjects and he relaxed about halfway through dinner.

It wasn't until he escorted Roz to the valet stand that he realized the tension hadn't completely fled on her side. Her back felt stiff under his fingers. Okay, he'd royally screwed up earlier if she was still uptight over the third degree he'd given her. But why had she dropped it like everything was fine? Just like a woman to nurse a grudge and not bother to say anything about it. That wasn't going to fly.

As he pointed the car in the direction of her loft, he

glanced at her from the corner of his eye. "Silent treatment for my crimes?"

She stared out the window. "Don't be ridiculous. I don't play little-girl games with men."

He let that simmer for a few minutes as he put a tight rein on his temper before he did something like comment on big-girl games. Nothing in his experience had prepared him to do this kind of long-term thing with a woman. And they were *getting married*. For the first time, it occurred to him that maybe he wasn't marriage material, that the reason he'd shied away from relationships wasn't solely because of the pact he'd made with Warren and Jonas, but also because he sucked at navigating emotional land mines.

But like the promise he'd made to keep his hands off her, this conversation was just as much a measure of his character. It was worth it to him to figure this out, if for no other reason than to prove he could.

He pulled over into a shadowy parking lot and killed the engine, then turned to face her. "Talk to me, Roz. You're obviously still upset."

"You asked me on a date so we could get to know each other. But then when you had an opportunity to really lay it all out, you didn't. At least have the courtesy to be honest with me. You don't like me being friendly with your mom because I'm just a good-time girl you had to marry because we got caught up in a scandal. I'm not good enough to be a real wife."

He shut his eyes for a blink, as that barb arrowed through his gut nice and deep. He had no excuse for not having seen that coming. Obviously she was playing back things she'd heard from others, and he'd unwittingly stepped right in the center of the land mines.

Yep. Not marriage material. This was why he stuck to sex, which he was good at, and shied away from anything that smacked of intimacy, which he was not good at.

"Roz, look at me." She did, her eyes barely discernible in the dark as he fumbled his way through. "Don't let your father's pigheadedness color your opinion of yourself. No one here is judging you for your sins. The reason I got testy is solely because I'm a jerk who doesn't like to share. My mom has been mine alone for a long time. We're a unit. I didn't want to lose that, or have that diluted somehow if you... Wow, this sounds really bad out loud."

She smiled with the faintest stirrings of tenderness. "No, it sounds honest. Which I like."

"This is me being honest," he agreed. If that was all she was looking for, maybe he didn't have to botch this too badly. "So you have to believe me when I say earlier was a combination of you in that dress and me being territorial. And maybe a bit of foot-in-mouth disease."

Her laugh washed through him, dissolving a lot of the tension, and he had to fight the muscles in his hand so that he didn't reach for her. The reasons he wanted to were totally mixed up and he didn't fully understand this urge to connect himself with that laugh in a way that had nothing to do with sex.

"Honesty is the best policy. So I'll return the favor. I don't remember my mom from when she was healthy. I just remember her sick and in a hospital bed, dying. Today a woman I admire invited me to lunch for the first time in my adult life. The fact that she's your mother didn't even factor into why it meant so much to me. Are you starting to see why I got a little bent out of shape about you getting bent out of shape?"

Her tone walloped him, dredging through his gut with razor-sharp teeth. He'd behaved like a jackass and stabbed at Roz's wounds at the same time. This wasn't a run-of-the-mill fight, like what normal couples might go through. They were surfacing enormously difficult emotions that he shouldn't want any part of.

But he was still here.

"If I say I'm sorry, will that help?"

Her smile widened. "Maybe."

Hell, why was he fighting this insanely strong urge to touch her? He skimmed his fingertips down her jaw and feathered a thumb across her lips. "I'm sorry."

She didn't even blink, just leaned until her lips hit his, and then treated him to the longest, sweetest kiss of his experience. Everything fell away except her and he froze, letting her drive this to whatever completion she wished because this was about feeling her out, learning who she was besides the woman he'd had hot, dirty sex with in Vegas.

God, he'd needed this, needed her in ways he wouldn't have guessed. The anticipation of getting her into his arms just like this flavored it so heavily that kissing her was nearly mind-altering. And this wasn't even close to the kind of kiss he'd envisioned jumping into all night. This was something else.

She pulled back and tilted her forehead to his until they touched. "I'm sorry, too. For being difficult. But not for kissing you. You needed the reminder that *we're* a unit. Peanut butter and jelly."

Yes. *That's* what it was. A solidifying of their union. No longer was this a marriage favor he was doing for his mother. He and Roz were becoming something. What, he wasn't sure yet, but it was so much more real than what he'd envisioned.

No. That wasn't what was happening here. Something lodged in his chest and he couldn't breathe all at once. He *couldn't* care about Roz, not like they were a couple. Not like there was any possibility of something deeper than a surface connection that started and ended with sex.

She didn't think there was something bigger than a marriage of convenience happening here. Did she? Had he messed up her expectations with all the talk of dates and getting to know each other? Had he screwed up his *own* expectations?

Surely not. Maybe some things had gotten a little out of whack, strictly due to the rules she'd laid down. The solution was to marry her and get to the place where he could block all that out with lots of hot sex, obviously. The lack of it was throwing them both off, that was all. He'd been forced into this pseudo-intimacy because of the scandal and now that he'd proven he wasn't a sex addict, it was time to move on to the next level. Once things were on familiar ground, he could fix all their fights with orgasms and then no one had to apologize for anything.

"We've got to get a wedding date on the calendar and you in a dress," he muttered.

The sooner the better.

Six

Somehow, Hendrix pulled off a miracle and got the wedding planned in record time, even down to the last place-setting. Roz wasn't confused about his motivation. She'd thrown down a gauntlet that they couldn't have sex until the wedding and had unwittingly created an environment that meant they'd be tense and irritable around each other.

Frankly, she was a little tired of it, too. They didn't have anything in common other than blind lust and a desire to fix the scandal. She got that. Their one disastrous attempt at a date had ended with solid reminders that her skill set didn't extend to forming connections with people, especially not with men—because she was good at having sex with them, but nothing else. Hendrix was no exception.

After her patient attempt to work through his unexpected freak-out over what should have been a simple announcement that she'd had lunch with Helene, his response? *Let's get you in a wedding dress so I can finally get what I came for.*

Fine. They weren't a real unit. Not like Hendrix and Helene, and the reminder had been brutal. Maybe she'd started to feel a little mushy about the idea of being part of something, but it had been nothing but a mirage.

They were getting married for reasons that had nothing to do with peanut butter and jelly and she'd agreed to that. It was smart. Not romantic, and that was a good thing. Less painful in the long run.

She liked orgasms as much as the next girl, so there was really no downside. Except for the niggling feeling that she and Hendrix had been on the verge of something special in the car and then it had vanished.

Her life was spiraling out of her control faster than she could grab on to it. She combated that by sticking her fingers in her ears and pretending there was no wedding planning going on. Hendrix handled it all, finally getting the message after his fourth attempt to include her in the decisions. Except for the flowers she'd already picked out, she really didn't care.

None of it mattered. They'd be undoing it all in a matter of months. The wedding music would dwindle from everyone's memory the moment the last note faded. Who cared what the piece was called?

The morning of the wedding dawned clear and beautiful, a rare day in Raleigh when the humidity wasn't oppressive. Figured. It was a perfect scenario to wear her hair down, but the pearl-encrusted bodice of her dress required her hair to be up. She dragged herself out of bed and got started on enjoying her wedding day—likely the only one she'd ever get. If nothing else, by the end of it, she and Hendrix would be past the weirdness that had sprung up since their date.

Lora picked her up at nine to take her to the spa, where they'd planned to spend the morning pampering themselves, but Roz couldn't get into the spirit. Hell, what kind of spirit was she supposed to be in on the day of a wedding that was basically an arranged marriage? She'd moved a few things into Hendrix's mansion in Oakwood yesterday and they planned to live together for a few months, at least until the election, at which point they'd agreed to reevaluate. Everything was on track.

The spa did not relax her. The masseur had ham hands, the girl who did Roz's bikini wax burned herself—not badly, but she'd had to find someone else to finish the job—and the facial left Roz's skin feeling raw and slightly dry, so her makeup wouldn't apply correctly. Gah, she'd been putting on foundation for fifteen-plus years. Why did her face suddenly look like the Grand Canyon in miniature?

Nerves. So much was riding on this marriage. Her reputation. Clown-Around. Helene's campaign. Her father's political ambitions. And maybe deep inside, she hoped that saying *I do* would magically shift things between her and her father. It wasn't a crime to hope.

But neither was any shifting likely. So far, he'd stayed on script, expressing nonverbal disapproval in the usual ways while tossing out backhanded comments about getting chummy with Helene. It had soured her lunch dates with Hendrix's mom to the point where she had canceled the last one. It had killed her to lose that one-on-one time with Helene but Hendrix had been so weird about it that Roz figured it was better not to get too attached. Her response was mostly self-preservation at this point.

As she leaned into the mirror to work on her eyeliner, her hand started to shake.

Lora glanced over from her spot next to the bride. "You okay? You've been jumpy since this morning."

Dang it. If Lora had noticed, Hendrix would, too. Maybe she could sneak a glass of white wine from the reception before walking down the aisle. Just to settle things inside. "Brides are allowed to be jumpy."

Her friend eyed her. "But this isn't a real wedding. You've been so calm and collected this whole time. It's kind of a shock to see you having this strong of a reaction."

"It is a real wedding," she corrected, fielding a little shock of her own that Lora had classified it any other way. "And a real marriage. I'm taking his name. We'll be sleeping in the same bed. Can't get much more real than that."

That started tonight. Holy hell. That was a lot of reality, orgasms notwithstanding. She'd be an honest-to-God wife who could legally sign her name Mrs. Harris. It suddenly felt like a huge gamble with no guarantee of a payoff.

Lora shrugged and tossed her long blond hair over her shoulder, leaning into the mirror to apply her own cosmetics. "But you're not in love. It's not like he swept you off your feet with a romantic proposal that you couldn't resist. I'm kind of surprised you're going through with it, actually. You didn't plan one tiny part of the ceremony. I had to force you to pick a dress."

All of that was true. And sad all at once that such a cold recitation of facts so accurately described her wedding day. She tossed her head. "I never dreamed of my wedding or scrawled my future married name on stray pieces of paper growing up. I'm marrying a man with bedroom skills a gigolo would envy. My life will not suck. And when we get tired of each other, I get a no-fault divorce. It's a business arrangement. It's the perfect marriage for me."

She'd keep telling herself that until *she* believed it too, and ignore the huge gap in her chest that she wished was filled with something special.

Grinning, Lora waved her mascara wand in Roz's direction. "When you put it that way... Does he have a friend?"

"Sure. I'll introduce you to Warren. You'll like him." Doubtful. Lora wouldn't look twice at a man who accessorized with his cell phone 24/7. "Hendrix's other friend is married."

Jonas and Viv had come across as one of those couples who were really in love. You could just tell they both firmly believed they'd found their soul mate. Honestly, Roz thought she'd be exactly like that if she ever fell in love, which was why she hoped she never did. Her parents had been mad for each other and watching her father waste away alongside her dying mother had been a huge wake-up call. Love equaled pain. And then when it was gone, she envisioned being alone for the rest of her life, just like her father. Carpenters weren't good at serial marriage.

The one she'd get with Hendrix Harris *was* perfect for her.

Hendrix sent a limo to pick up the bride and brides-maid. Roz felt a little silly at the size of the vehicle when she spread out her white pearl-encrusted skirt on the spacious leather seat that could have held four people. But the fact of the matter was that she didn't have a lot of friends that she would have asked to be in her wedding party. She had acquaintances. They'd all been invited to the social event of the season, though she didn't fool herself for a moment that they were coming for any other reason than morbid curiosity.

All at once, the door to the chapel loomed and her feet carried her into the church's vestibule without much conscious effort on her part. Her father waited for her inside as arranged, but she couldn't quite shake the feeling of walking through a surreal dream.

"Roz," her father called as he caught sight of her. "You're looking well."

Geez. Exactly what every bride dreams of hearing on her wedding day. "Thanks, Dad."

He wasn't effusive with his praise, never had been. But was it too much to ask for a little affection on a day when she was doing something that would benefit him?

Crooking his elbow in her direction, he stood where the coordinator directed him to and then it was Roz's turn to get in line behind Lora, who was stunning in a pale pink column dress with a long skirt. It would have been more appropriate for an evening wedding, but that was one thing Roz had cared about picking out. She'd gotten the dress that looked good on Lora, not the one societal convention dictated.

She was still Rosalind Carpenter. For about thirty more minutes. Oh, God.

What if this was a huge mistake?

Music swelled from the interior of the chapel that Hendrix had insisted would lend validity to their union. That seemed be the litmus test for pretty much all of his wedding decisions—how legit the thing was. She'd never have pegged him as that much of a traditionalist but she got more than an eyeful of his idea of what a proper wedding looked like as the coordinator flung open the doors to the chapel, signaling their entrance.

Five hundred guests rose dutifully to their feet, heads craned toward Roz for their first glimpse of the bride. An explosion of color greeted her, from the bouquets at the end of each pew to the multiple stands holding baskets of blooms across the front. Hendrix had chosen pinks to complement Lora's dress, but hadn't seemed too inclined to stick with a flower theme. There were stargazer lilies she'd picked out at the florist, but also roses, baby's breath, tulips, daisies, and something that might be a larkspur, but her father started down the aisle before she could verify.

Wow, was it hot in here. Every eye in the house was trained on her. Her spine stiffened and she let her own vision blur so she didn't have to see whether they were quietly judging her or had a measure of compassion reflected on their faces. No way was it the latter. No one in attendance had a clue how difficult today was for the motherless bride.

Then her gaze drifted past all the flowers and landed on the star of the show. Hendrix. She stared into his pale hazel eyes as her father handed her off in the most traditional of exchanges. Her husband-to-be clasped her fingers and the five hundred people behind her vanished as she let Hendrix soak through her to the marrow.

"You're so beautiful it hurts inside when I look at you," he murmured.

Her knees turned to marshmallow and she tightened her grip on his hand.

That was the proper thing to say to a bride on her wedding day and she didn't even try to squelch the bloom of gratitude that had just unfurled in her chest. "I bet you say that to all your brides."

He grinned and faced the minister, guiding her through the ceremony like a pro when nerves erased her memory of the rehearsal from the night before. The space-time continuum bent double on itself and the ceremony wound to a close before she'd barely blinked once.

"You may kiss the bride," the minister intoned and that's when she realized the complete tactical error she'd made.

She had to kiss Hendrix. For real. And the moratorium on that thus far had guaranteed this would become A Moment. The carnal spike through the gut at the thought did not bode well for how the actual experience would go down.

Neither did the answering heat in his expression. He cupped her jaw on both sides, giving her plenty of time to think about it. No need. Her whole body had just incinerated with the mere suggestion of the imminent follow-through.

And then he leaned in to capture her mouth with his. It was a full-on assault to the senses as their lips connected and she couldn't do anything else but fling her arms around his waist, or she'd have ended up on the ground, a charred shell that was burned beyond recognition.

Oh God, yes. With that one hard press of his mouth, Hendrix consumed her. This kiss was but a shadow of the many, many others they'd shared, but it was enough to slide memories along her skin, through her core.

This was so very right, so perfect between them. Everything else faded—the weirdness, the nerves. This heat she understood, craved. If he was burning her alive from the inside out, she didn't have to think about all the reasons this marriage might not work.

He teased the flame in her belly into a full raging fire with little licks of his tongue against hers. Hell, that blaze hadn't ever really been extinguished from the moment he'd lit that match in Vegas. Masterfully, the man kissed her until she'd been scraped raw, panting for more, nearly weeping with want.

This was why she'd thrown down the no-kissing-no-sex rule. She could not resist him, even in a church full of people. Her body went into some kind of Hendrix-induced altered state where nothing but basic need existed. And he wasn't even in full-on seduction mode. Thank God he'd played by her rules or there was no telling what new and more horrific scandals might have cropped up prior to the wedding.

That was enough to get her brain back in gear. She broke off the kiss to the sound of flutes and strings. The recessional music. They were supposed to walk and smile now. Somehow, that's what happened and then she floated through a million photographs, a limo ride to the reception and about a million well-wishers.

All she really wanted was to dive back into Hendrix and never surface.

The crowd at the reception crushed that hope flat. No less than ten people vied for their attention at any given time and she'd lost count of the number of times Hendrix had introduced her to someone from his business world. The reverse wasn't at all true, a sobering fact that brought home the reasons she was wearing a wedding band.

She'd spent the past few years having what she'd staunchly defend as a "good time" but in reality was a panacea for the pain of losing first her mother to cancer and then her father to indifference and grief. The scandals were just the cherry on top of her messy life and ironically, also the reason she couldn't move forward with something respectable like running a charity.

Her new husband would change all of that. Had already started to.

The pièce de résistance of the event came with the first dance between husband and wife. Hendrix, whom she'd scarcely said two words to since that pantie-melting kiss, whisked her out onto the dance floor. He drew her close and when his arms came around her, the strangest sensation floated through her as they began to move to the classical piece that she'd have never picked out but fitted the occasion.

"Hey," he murmured into her ear. "How is Mrs. Harris doing?"

"I don't know. I haven't spoken to your mother." When he laughed, she realized he hadn't meant Helene. "Ha, ha. I'm out of sorts. It's been a long day."

"I know. That's why I asked. You seem distracted."

She pulled back a touch to look at him. "Ask me again."

The smile in his eyes warmed her, but then it slid away to be replaced by something else as their gazes held in a long moment that built on itself with heavy implications. "How are you, Mrs. Harris?"

A name shouldn't have so much color to it. If anything, it should have sounded foreign to her, but it wasn't strange. It felt...good. She took a deep breath and let that reality expand inside her. *Mrs. Harris.* That was her name. Rosalind Harris. Mrs. Roz Harris.

She liked it. Maybe she *should* have practiced writing it out a bajillion times on a piece of scratch paper. Then the concept wouldn't have been such a shock. There was a huge difference between academically knowing that you were changing your name and actually hearing someone address you that way. Especially when the man doing the addressing had the same name and you were married to him.

"I'm better now," she told him.

Understatement. Hendrix was solid and beautiful and he'd pulled off the wedding event of the season. Why hadn't she participated more in the planning?

Sour grapes. Nothing more complicated than that. She'd started getting a little too touchy-feely with the peanut butter and jelly analogy and he'd set her back on the right path with timely reminders of what they were doing here. For his trouble, she'd frozen him out and then used that as an excuse to pull back from a friendship with his mother.

Well, she was over it. They were married now and both of them knew the score. The no-sex rule wasn't in the way any longer. Thank God. They could spend all their time in bed and never have to talk about mothers, peanut butter or anything difficult.

"This was amazing," she said earnestly. "So much more than I was expecting. Thank you."

Surprise filtered through his expression. "I... You're welcome. I'm glad you liked it. The wedding planner did all the work. I just approved everything."

"I should have done it with you." The fact that she hadn't made her feel petty and childish. If nothing else, it was an effort that benefited her, so she could have done half the work. Then maybe she'd feel more like she'd earned the right to be called Mrs. Harris. "I'm sorry I didn't."

For the first time since their disastrous date, Hendrix smiled at her like he had that night in Vegas. As if he'd found the end of the rainbow and the pot of gold there was more valuable than he'd ever dreamed.

She liked it when he looked at her like that.

"It's okay. It wasn't any trouble." He spun her around as the last notes of the waltz ended and something a little darker and more sensual wafted from the string quartet on the dais in the corner. His arms tightened, drawing her deeper into his embrace. The crowd on the dance floor grew thicker as people filled in around them. "I'm enjoying the benefits of it, so it's all good."

His body pressed against hers deliciously. A slow simmer flared up in her core, bubbling outward until her nerve endings were stretched taut with anticipation. "The benefits?"

"Dancing with my bride, for one," he murmured. His hands drifted along her body with sensual intent, pressing her more firmly against him as he stroked her waist, the curve of her hip, lower still, and there was so much wedding dress in the way that she strained against his touch, yearning for the heat of his hand in places that hadn't been *touched* in so very long.

Dancing was a great excuse to let Hendrix put his hands on her in public. "I'm enjoying that part, too."

"It's been a long time," he said gruffly, "since I had free rein to hold you like this."

Yes, and judging by the oh-so-nice hard length buried in her stomach, he was as affected by their close proximity as she was. "You were a trouper about it."

"Wasn't easy. But it's over now. I can kiss you whenever I feel like it." To prove the point, he nuzzled her neck, setting off fireworks beneath her skin as he nibbled at the flesh.

"That's not kissing," she muttered, biting back a gasp as he cruised to her ear, molding it to his lips as he laved at her lobe.

"I'm getting there."

"Get there faster."

He pulled back and swept her with a glance that was equal parts evaluation and equal parts *I'm a second from throwing you down right here, right now.* "Is that your way of saying you're ready to leave?"

"We can't," she reminded him and tried to ignore how desperately disappointed she sounded.

This was a networking event as much as it was a wedding. Helene had a throng of people around her, and the movers and shakers of Raleigh stood at the bar. If the bride and groom dashed for the door fifteen minutes after the reception started, that wouldn't go over well.

"No," he agreed and bit out a vile curse that perfectly mirrored her thoughts. "We need tongues wagging with positive comments about us, preferably with lots of praise about how respectable we are."

Exactly. Especially if they spouted off at the mouth around her father. He needed a whole lot of reassurance that Roz had turned a corner, that her photo ops with naked men were a thing of the past. From here on out, the only scandal associated with her name should be more along the lines of serving the wrong wine at a party she and Hendrix threw for Harris Tobacco Lounge executive staff.

"So maybe we don't leave," she said as a plausible alternative began to form in her mind. Oh God, did she need that alternative. Fast. Her insides were already tight and slick with need.

His expression turned crafty as he considered her comment. "Maybe not. Maybe there's a…closet in the back?"

"With a door. That locks."

His thumb strayed to the place along her bodice where it met the skin of her back and heat flashed as he caressed the seam, dipping inside just enough to drive her insane and then skimming along until he hit the zipper.

"One tug, and this would be history," he said, the hazel in his eyes mesmerizing her with the promise as he toyed with the hook anchoring the zipper to the bodice. "It feels complicated. Challenging."

"Maybe you don't start there," she suggested and swayed a little to give the couples around them the impression the bride and groom were still dancing when in reality, her attention was on the perimeter of the room where two very promising hallways led to the back of the reception venue. "You might have better luck checking out how easily my skirt lifts up."

"Mrs. Harris, I do like the way you think." In a flash, he grabbed her hand and spun to lead her from the dance floor.

Well then. Looked like the honeymoon was starting early. She had no problem with that and she was nothing if not ready to ignore the fact that the bride and groom were still dashing for the door fifteen minutes after the reception started but with this plan, they'd be back in a few minutes. At least ten. Maybe once wouldn't be enough. Was married sex better than one night stand sex? Oh God, she couldn't wait to find out.

Breathlessly, she followed him, ignoring the multitudes of people who called out to them as they scouted for this hypothetical closet with a door that locked. In a true wedding day miracle, off the kitchen there was a linen closet full of spare tablecloths and empty centerpieces. No one saw them duck through the door, or at least no one who counted. They passed a member of the waitstaff who pretended he hadn't noticed their beeline through the back rooms where guests typically didn't tread. Whether it was a testament to his discretion or the fact that Hendrix and Roz were tied to powerful families, she didn't know. Didn't care.

All that mattered was the door had a lock. She shut it behind her with a click and flipped the dead bolt, plunging the room into semidarkness. Maybe there was a light but before she could reach for it, Hendrix pinned her against the door, his mouth on hers in an urgent, no-holds-barred kiss. No time to search for a light. No time to care.

Her knees gave out as the onslaught liquefied her entire body, but he'd wedged one leg so expertly between hers that she didn't melt to the ground in a big hot puddle. She moaned as his tongue invaded her mouth, heated and insistent against hers. He hefted her deeper into his body as he shifted closer.

Too many clothes. She got to work on his buttons, cursing at the intricacy of his tuxedo. Shame she couldn't just rip the little discs from the fabric but they had to reappear in public. Soon. Giving up, she pulled the fabric from his waistband so she could slide her hands under it.

Oh, yes, he was warm and his body was still drool-worthy with ridges and valleys of muscle along his abs that her fingers remembered well. He pressed closer still, trapping her hands between them, which was not going to work, so she shifted to the back as he gathered up her skirts, bunching the fabric at her waist. Instantly, she regretted not making him take the time to pull the dress off. She wanted his hands everywhere on her body, but then she forgot to care because his fingers slid beneath the white lacy thong she'd donned this morning in deference to her wedding day.

"I want to see this thong later," he rumbled in her ear as he fingered the panties instead of the place she needed him most. "It feels sexy and tiny and so good."

"It feels in the way," she corrected and gasped as he yanked the panties off, letting them fall to her ankles. She toed off the fabric and kicked it aside. She needed him back in place *now*. "Touch me. Hurry."

Fast. Hard. Frenzied. These were the things she wanted, not a speech about her undergarments. This was sex in its rawest form and she knew already that it would be good between them. She hoped it would put them on familiar ground. Eliminate confusion about what they were doing here.

"What's your rush, Mrs. Harris?" He teased her with short little caresses of his fingertips across her shoulder, down her cleavage, which ached for his attention, but had far too many seed pearls in the way for that nonsense.

"Besides the hundreds of people waiting for us?"

Her back arched involuntarily as his fingers found their way beneath the tight bodice of her dress to toy with her breasts. Heavenly heat corkscrewed through her core as he fingered her taut, sensitized nipples.

"Besides that."

"You're my rush," she ground out. "I'm about to come apart and I need your hands on me."

She needed oblivion like only he could give her, where all she could do was feel. Then it didn't matter that he was totally on board with a closet quickie for their first time together as husband and wife. Neither of them did intimacy. It was what made their marriage so perfect.

"Like this?" His hand snaked between them to palm her stomach and she wiggled, hoping to get it lower. He complied inch by maddening inch, creeping toward the finish line with a restraint more suited for a choirboy than the bad boy she knew lurked in his heart.

He'd licked her in places that had never been touched by a man. He'd talked so dirty while doing it that she could practically give herself an orgasm thinking about it. They were having sex in a closet with five hundred oblivious people on the other side of the wall and he had every bit of the skill set necessary to make it intoxicating. She needed *that* man.

"Hendrix, please," she begged. "I'm dying here."

"I've been dying for weeks and weeks," he said and she groaned as he wandered around to the back, wedging his hand between her buttocks and the door to play with flesh that certainly appreciated his attention but wasn't the part that needed him most.

Practically panting, she circled her hips, hoping he'd get the hint that the place he should be focusing on was between her thighs. "So this is my punishment for not letting you have your way with me until now?"

"Oh, no, sweetheart. This is my reward," he murmured. "I've dreamed of having you in my arms again so I could feel your amazing body in a hundred different ways. Like this."

Finally, he let his fingers walk through her center, parting the folds to make way, and one slid deep inside. Mewling because that was the only sound she could make, she widened herself for him, desperate for more instantly, and he obliged with another finger, plunging both into her slickness with his own groan.

"I could stay here for an eternity," he whispered. "But I need to—"

He cursed as she eased her way into his pants, too blind with need to bother with the zipper. Oh, yes, there he was. She palmed his hot, hard length through his underwear and it wasn't enough. "I need, too."

Urgently, she fumbled with his clothes and managed to get the buttons of his shirt partially undone, hissing as he withdrew his magic hands from her body to help. But that was a much better plan because his progress far eclipsed hers and he even had the wherewithal to find a condom from somewhere that she distinctly heard him tear open. That was some amazing foresight that she appreciated.

Then her brain ceased to function as he boosted her up against the door with one arm, notched his hard tip at her entrance and pushed. Stars wheeled across her vision as he filled her with his entire glorious length. Greedily, she took him, desperate for more, desperate for all of it, and he gave it to her, letting her slide down until they were nested so deep that she could feel him in her soul.

No.

No, she could not. That was far too fanciful for what was happening here. This was sex. Only. Her body craved friction, heat, a man's hard thrusts. Not poetry.

Wrapping her legs around him, she gripped his shoulders, letting her fingers sink into the fabric covering them because even if it left marks, who cared? They were married and no one else would see his bare shoulders but her.

He growled his approval and it rumbled through her rib cage. Or maybe that was the avalanche of satisfaction cascading through her chest because Hendrix was hers. No other woman got to see him naked. It shouldn't feel so good, so significant. But there was no escaping the fact that they were a unit now whether he liked it or not.

They shared a name. A house. Mutual goals. If he didn't like peanut butter and jelly, he should have come up with another plan to fix the scandal.

Shifting ever so slightly, he hit a spot inside her that felt so good it tore tears from her eyes. The position sensitized her to the point of madness and she urged him on with her hips as he drove them both into the stratosphere, the door biting into her back as she muffled her cries against his suit jacket, praying she wasn't smearing makeup all over his shoulder.

That would be a dead giveaway to anyone who bothered to notice. And she liked the idea of keeping this encounter secret. Their own little wedding party.

Explosion imminent, she rolled her hips until the angle increased the pressure the way she liked it. Hendrix grabbed one thigh, opening her even wider, and that was it. The orgasm ripped through her and she melted against him, going boneless in his arms until his own cry signaled his release.

He gave them both about five seconds of recovery time and then let her legs drift to the floor so they could hold each other up. Which she gladly did because he'd earned it.

"That was great for starters," she muttered against his shoulder because it felt expected that she should reiterate how hot—and not meaningful—this encounter was. "I can definitely report that took the edge off, but I'm nowhere near done."

There was so much more to explore. Best part? She could. Whenever she felt like it, since they'd be sleeping in the same bed. Married sex had a lot to recommend it.

Someone rattled the doorknob, nearly startling out of her skin.

"You have the key?" a muffled voice from the other side of the wall called.

Oh, God. They were about to be discovered.

Seven

Where was her underwear? It was so dark in here. Had she kicked them to the left? Panic drained Roz's mind and she couldn't think.

The doorknob rattled again. Whoever it was probably had no idea that the bride and groom were in the closet. But they were probably packing a cell phone with a camera. They always were.

Stuffing her fist against her mouth, Roz jumped away from the door and knelt to feel around for her panties, dress impeding her progress like a big white straitjacket for legs. Hendrix fumbled with his own clothes. His zipper shushed, sounding like an explosion in the small room. At least he'd gotten that much covered. Any photographs of this tryst would be of the dressed variety. But still not the commemorative moment they'd like captured digitally for eternity.

The door swung open, spilling light into the closet, and Roz had a very nasty flashback to a similar moment when she was twenty, with the obvious difference this time being that she was wearing a wedding dress and the man tucking in his shirt behind her had recently signed a marriage license.

Two white-coated waiters stared at her and Hendrix and she'd like to say her years of practice at being caught in less-than-stellar circumstances had prepared her for it, but it was never as easy as tossing her hair back and letting the chips fall where they may.

Besides, she refused to be embarrassed. Everything was covered. Married people were allowed to be in a locked closet without fear of judgment—or she wouldn't have bothered to go through with all of this. The wait staff was interrupting *her*, not the other way around.

She shot to her feet and it was a testament to her feigned righteous indignation at being disturbed that she didn't break an ankle as one of her stilettos hit the ground at an awkward angle.

"Um, sorry," the one on the left said, and he might as well have hashtagged it *#notsorry*.

His face beamed his prurient delight, like something naughty was showing, and she had half a moment of pure horror over not actually locating her underwear. She tugged on her skirt to make sure it wasn't caught on itself, but then Hendrix came up behind her, snaking an arm around her waist. Claiming her. They were a unit and he had her back.

She leaned into him, more grateful than she had a right to be.

"Can you give us a minute?" he said smoothly to

the interrupters and actually waited for the one waiter's nod before he shut the door in their face. Brilliant.
Why hadn't she thought of that?

Hendrix flipped on the overhead light, the white
lace scrap on the floor easily identifiable at that point.
But instead of letting her fetch her panties, he tipped
her chin up and laid a kiss on her lips that had nothing
to do with sex. Couldn't. There were people outside
who wanted inside this closet and they'd been busted.

"I wasn't finished, either," he murmured against her
mouth by way of explanation.

She nodded, letting his warmth bleed through her
via their joined lips, mystified why that sweet, unnecessary cap to their closet hookup meant so much. Eventually, he let her go and they got everything situated
well enough to mix in polite company again. Hendrix
reopened the door and they slipped past the waiters
hand in hand.

Her husband's palm burned against hers. She
couldn't recall the last time someone had held her hand,
like they were boyfriend-girlfriend. Or whatever. They
were married. Nothing wrong with holding hands. It
was just…unexpected.

"You okay?" Hendrix said softly, pulling her to the
side of the short hallway that led to the reception area.
His attention was firmly on her, but before she could
answer or figure out why his concern had just squished
at a place inside, more people interrupted them.

Why couldn't everyone leave them alone so she
could spend about a dozen hours exploring why everything with Hendrix felt so different now that she'd
signed a piece of paper?

Hendrix's arm went tense under her fingers and she

turned. Her father. And Helene. They stood at the end of the short hall, varying expressions of dismay and relief spreading across their faces.

Oh, God. The very people they were trying to help with this scandal-fixing marriage. Now it was obvious to everyone that she couldn't resist Hendrix, that she had something wrong with her that made it impossible to wait for more appropriate circumstances before getting naked with the man.

"We got a little concerned when we couldn't find you," Helene said with a smile. "But here you are."

Her father didn't smile. He crossed his arms and even though he could look her in the eye when she wore stilettos, she still felt small and admonished even before he opened his mouth. Marrying Hendrix had been a last-ditch effort to do *something* her father approved of. Looked like that had been a vain effort all the way around.

"Glad to see that you're dressed," her father said and it was clear that he was speaking directly to his daughter.

The *for once* was implied and sure enough, flooded her with the embarrassment she'd managed to fight off earlier, after being discovered by wait staff. Thank God their parents hadn't been the ones to fling open that door.

"That's not really your concern any longer," Hendrix said to her father.

She did a double take. Was he sticking up for her?

"It is my concern," her father corrected. "This marriage isn't guaranteed to remove all of the social shame from the photographs. Additional fodder could still be harmful and Roz is quite good at feeding that fire."

"Still not your concern," Hendrix corrected mildly and his hand tightened around hers.

As a warning to let him handle it? She couldn't speak anyway. The knot in her throat had grown big enough to choke a hippopotamus.

"Roz is my wife," Hendrix continued. "And any bad press that comes her way is my responsibility to mitigate. She has my name now. I'll take care of her."

Okay, there might be crying in her immediate future.

"Hendrix," she murmured because she felt like she had to say something, but that was as much as her brain could manufacture.

With that, her husband nodded to his mother and swept Roz past the inquisition that should have ruined her day. Instead, Hendrix had relegated that confrontation to an insignificant incident in the hall.

How had he done that? She snuck a glance at him. "Thank you. You didn't have to do that."

He shot her an enigmatic smile. "I did so have to do that. Your father should be proud of you, not throwing you to the wolves."

"Um, yeah. He's never really appreciated my ability to keep my balance while having sex against a door."

Hendrix laughed at that, which actually made her relax for what felt like the first time all day.

"I appreciate that skill." He waggled his brows and guided her back into the reception where they were swallowed by the crowd, none of whom seemed to notice they'd been gone.

If it was at all possible to receive an indicator that she'd made the right decision in marrying Hendrix Harris, that moment with her father had been it. Half of her reason for agreeing had to do with gaining approval from a man who had demonstrated time and time again that she could not earn his respect no matter what. That possibility had been completely eliminated…only to be replaced with a completely different reality.

Her husband wasn't going to take any crap from her father.

Maybe she didn't have to, either.

And that's when she actually started enjoying her wedding day.

Despite Paul Carpenter's comments to the contrary, the wedding had apparently gone a long way toward smoothing over the scandal. The snide looks Hendrix had witnessed people shooting at Roz when they'd gone to the florist, and even to some degree during their one date, had dwindled. There were lots of smiles, lots of congrats, lots of schmoozers.

And what kind of crap was that?

It was one thing to have an academic understanding that they were getting married so that Helene Harris for Governor didn't take unnecessary hits, but it was another entirely to see it in action. Especially when he was starting to suspect that some of the issue had to do with what society perceived as his "bad taste" to have mixed it up with the wild Carpenter daughter.

He was fixing it for her. Not the other way around. What was just as crazy? He liked being her go-to guy. The dressing-down he'd given her father had felt good. No one deserved to be judged for a healthy sexual appetite when her partner was a consenting adult.

He needed to get the hell out of here and make some

wedding day memories at home, where his wife could do whatever she so desired without anyone knowing about it.

"Let's go," he growled in Roz's ear. "We've been social for like a million hours already. Everyone here can suck it."

"Including me?" Her gaze grew a hungry edge that had all kinds of appealing implications inside it, especially when she dragged it down his body. "Because coincidentally, that's exactly what I had in mind."

"Really?" His groin tightened so fast it made him light-headed.

"True story," she murmured. "Or didn't you get the memo earlier that I wasn't done?"

Wheeling, he waved at his mother and snagged Roz's hand to lead her to the limo that waited patiently for them at the curb of the North Ridge Country Club. He'd paid the wedding coordinator a hefty sum to manage the logistics of the reception; she could handle whatever came after the departure of the bride and groom.

The limo ride took far too long—a whole ten minutes, during which he kept his hands off Roz like a good boy because this time, he didn't want quick.

Slow would be the theme of his wedding night.

Except his wife smelled divine and she cuddled up next to him on the roomy leather seat, letting her fingers do some serious wandering over his lap. Strands of Roz's dark hair had pulled out of the bun-like thing at her crown, dripping down in sexy little tendrils, and all he could think about was how it had gotten that way—his fingers.

He'd like to tug on a few more strands while deep inside her.

By the time the limo pulled up to the house, which his housekeeper had lit up for their arrival, his hard-on could cut glass and his patience had started to unravel.

"Inside," he growled. "Now."

To help her along, he swept her up in his arms to carry her over the threshold because it seemed like a legit thing that people did on their wedding day. She snuggled down into his embrace, looping her arms around his neck, and then got busy testing out his ability to walk while she nibbled on the flesh near his ear. Her tongue flicked out, sending a shower of sparks down his throat, and he stumbled, catching himself immediately. Wouldn't do to drop his new wife.

"Unless you'd like our wedding night to be memorialized with a trip to the ER, I'd suggest waiting five seconds for any more of that," he advised her, which she pretty much ignored. Now that he was on to her and better able to compensate, he walked faster.

They cleared the double front door, barely, as she'd started exploring his collarbone with her lips. There was no way he was doing stairs in his current fully aroused, highly sensitized state, so he let her slide to the ground and hustled her to the second floor.

Roz beat him to the gargantuan master suite that he'd yet to christen properly. He shut the doors to the bedroom behind him. In Vegas, they'd had a strict rule that no surface would go untouched. His bedroom's decor had been pulled together by a professional and contained solid pieces stained with a shade of espresso that was so dark, it looked black. Not one Carpenter piece in the bunch, not even the woman beckoning him with a hooded, enigmatic expression that portrayed her very naughty thoughts.

Good God she was gorgeous in her white dress. She had the fullest lips that needed nothing extra to be lush and inviting. He could write poetry to her mouth for a decade. And her eyes…they did a thing where they were both transparent and mysterious all at the same time.

Would he ever get tired of her face? What if they were the kind of couple who actually stayed married on purpose, affording him the opportunity to watch her age? One day he might wake up and wonder where her looks had gone. But he didn't think so. She'd still be Roz inside and that was the part he wanted with a burning need he scarcely recognized.

And need was supposed to be his wheelhouse. When he couldn't quantify something related to sex, that was a problem. It felt too much like the intimacy that he religiously avoided.

No, the real problem was that they weren't having sex yet. Sex eliminated all of the weirdness with pure mechanics of pleasure. And while he was busy composing sonnets to his wife's beauty, she was standing there staring at him like he'd lost his mind, likely because he hadn't made a move on her yet.

Clearly, he was slightly insane. What was he waiting for?

Striding forward, he did the one thing he hadn't been able to do thus far. He spun his bride to face away from him, undid the catch on her zipper and yanked it down. The strapless dress peeled from her body, baring her back and oh, yeah, that was nice. Her spine beckoned and he bent to fuse his mouth to the ridges, working his way down until he hit the hollow above her buttocks. Laving at it, he adding some lip action until he earned a sharp little gasp from her.

This was what he'd come for. Blinding, carnal pleasure. All of the other internal noise? Not happening. The faster he got to a place where he couldn't think, the faster all of the stuff inside that shouldn't be there would fade.

That spurred him on enough to want more. Easing the dress down her hips, he pushed her gently, encouraging her to step out of it. That sexy little thong that he'd thus far only felt was indeed amazing in the light. It formed a vee down between her cheeks like an arrow pointing the way to paradise and he groaned as he recalled how much time he'd spent pleasuring her in that exact spot while in Vegas. It was worth a repeat for sure.

Falling to his knees, he slid his tongue beneath the lacy bands, following the dip down and back up again. He accompanied that with a leisurely exploration of the backs of her legs, ending with a nice tour of the covered area between her cheeks. That's when her legs started trembling, whether from excitement or exhaustion he couldn't be sure. He'd have to come back later.

Right now, his bride needed to be more comfortable. He had a lot more where that had come from.

He picked her up in his arms again and without the binding dress, it was so much easier. And more rewarding as her bare breasts were *right there* for his viewing pleasure. That was a much better place to focus his attention.

Laying her on the bed, he looked his fill as he stripped out of his own clothes, impressed that he'd found the stamina to take the time. The last sock hit the floor and the appreciation in Roz's gaze as she watched his show thoroughly stirred him.

The closet gymnastics had done nothing to take the edge off. Roz was dead wrong about that. He wanted her all over again with a fierce urgency that demanded absolute surrender.

Crawling across the mattress and up her body, he took the liberty of kissing his way to the perfect globes of her breasts, licking one bright, hard tip into his mouth. Her flesh rolled across his tongue. Divine. He sucked harder and she arched up off the bed with a tiny gasp. Not enough. Teeth against the tip, he scraped at it while plucking at the other one with his fingertips.

She felt exquisite in his hand. Silky. Excited. She pushed against his mouth, shoving her breast deeper, and he took it all, sucking her nipple against the roof of his mouth. That had driven her wild once before.

It did again. That simple movement got her thrashing under him, driving her hips against his painfully hard erection. The contact lit him up and felt so good, he ground into her stomach with tight circles. *Inside. Now.* His body was screaming for release, shooting instructions to his muscles to tilt her hips and drive to completion.

Not on the agenda. Not yet. He had to slow it down.

Grabbing her hips, he peeled away from her luscious body and kissed down the length of her stomach until he hit her thighs. That lacy thong covered her and as much as he hated to see it go, it went.

He pushed her legs open and kept going. Gorgeous. The faster he sated her, the slower he could go because she was making him insane with hip rolls that pushed her closer to him, obviously seeking relief from the fire that was licking through her veins.

Or maybe that was just him.

Her secrets spread wide, he paused just a moment to enjoy the visual, but she was having none of that.

"Put your mouth on me," she instructed throatily. "I've dreamed about your wicked hard tongue for weeks and weeks."

Oh yeah? That was enough of a compliment to spur him into action. The first lick exploded across his taste buds, earthy and so thick with her desire. For him. This was his wife, who was wet and slick *for him*. It was nearly spiritual. Why didn't they tell you the mere act of signing a piece of paper had so much significance?

That was a discovery best explored further through hands-on experience. Her juices flowed over his tongue as he drove deeper, added a finger to the party, swirled along her crease until she started bucking against his face and still she seemed to crave more.

He gave it to her, sliding a wet finger between her cheeks to toy with her while simultaneously working the nub at her pleasure center with his teeth. Her thighs clenched, and she rocked against his fingers, pushing them deeper, and then she came with a cry that vibrated through his gut.

That was not something he could possibly hear enough.

She sat up far before he would have said she'd had time to recover, pushed him free of her body and rolled him until she was on top. Looked like they were moving on. Noted. But he couldn't find a thing to complain about as she straddled his hips. She'd never taken off her white strappy stilettos and she parked one on each side of his thighs, easing her center into a place just south of where he really wanted it, but that fit with his need to go slow, so he let her.

He'd teased up a flush along her cheeks and her beautiful peaked nipples rode high on her breasts. As she stared down at him from her perch, she was the most gorgeous thing he'd ever seen, with those pursed lips and a sated sheen in her eyes that he'd been personally responsible for putting there.

He wanted to do it again. And again.

And finally, he could. He reached for her, but she shook her head, clamping her thighs tight against him as she laced his fingers with hers to draw his hands away from her body. She weighed practically nothing and it would be an easy matter to break free, but he was kind of curious what she had in mind that required him to stay still.

He found out when she released his fingers to trail her own down his torso until she reached his groin. All the breath whooshed from his lungs as she palmed him to stroke downward with one hard thrust.

Fire tore through his body in a maelstrom of need.

His eyelids flew shut as he struggled to breathe, to hold it together, to keep from exploding right there in her hand. She wasn't in a merciful mood obviously because she crawled backward to kneel over him, captured his gaze in her hot one, and licked him.

The sight of her pink tongue laving across his flesh nearly undid him. Then she sucked him fully into her mouth and he pulsed against her tongue and it was almost too much to hold back. He clawed back the release with some kind of superpower he had no idea he possessed.

Anti-Orgasm Man. He should get a T-shirt for his effort.

Except his wife had some powers of her own and worked him back into a frenzy in under a minute flat. This was going to be a very short honeymoon indeed if she didn't stop *this instant*.

"Whoa, sweetheart," he bit out hoarsely and tried to ease out from her mouth without catching his sensitized flesh on her teeth. She pushed him deeper into her throat in response, melting his bones in the process so it was really difficult to get his arms to work.

"Please," he begged as she swirled her tongue counterclockwise so fast that he felt the answering lick of heat explode outward clear to his toes. His head fell backward against the bed as his legs tensed and he genuinely had no clue what he was begging her to do—stop or keep going.

She took the decision out of his hands by purring with him deep in her mouth and the vibration was the tipping point. The release rushed through his veins, gathered at the base of his spine and pushed from his body like a tsunami, eating everything in its path. She took it all and more, massaging him to a brilliant finish that wrung him out. Spent, he collapsed back on the mattress, too drained to move.

"That was for following the rules," she told him with a smug laugh. "You deserve about ten more."

If he'd known that was the prize for proving to himself and everyone else that he could go without sex, it might have made the whole moratorium a lot easier. Without opening his eyes, he nodded. "You have my permission to proceed."

"Ha, I didn't mean right this minute."

She fell silent and the pause was so heavy that he opened his eyes. Roz was lounging on the bed between his thighs, decked out like a naked offering with one leg draped over his calf and an elbow crooked on the far side of his hip. It was the most erotic pose he'd ever seen in his life. And that was saying something considering the sizzle factor of the photograph she'd starred in.

"Thank you," she said. "For what you said to my father."

Her expression was so enigmatic, he couldn't do anything but let his own gaze travel over it in search of clues for what he should say next. *You're welcome* seemed highly lacking in weight given the catch he'd noted in her voice. Neither was this a conversation he wanted to have while in bed with a naked woman.

Except she wasn't any garden-variety naked woman that he had no plans to see again.

It was Roz. And he most definitely would be waking up with her in the morning. So many mornings that he was at a loss how to avoid the significant overtones of this kind of sex, where they were apparently going to talk about stuff between rounds of pleasure.

Maybe that was the key. He just had to move them along until they were back in a place where there was nothing but heat between them. Clearly he hadn't gotten her hot enough yet if she could still think about things outside of this room.

"Let's talk about that later, shall we?" he murmured.

The tendrils of hair around her face had increased exponentially and he itched to pull the entire mass free of its confines. So he indulged himself. Leaning up, he plucked pins from her dark hair. Slowly, he let chunks of hair fall to her shoulders, and the enigmatic, slightly guarded expression melted away.

Better. She deserved about ten more orgasms, too. Enough that she could only focus on how good he could make her feel and not the crappy stuff about her life that he had an inexplicable drive to fix for her.

"Tonight is about making up for lost time," he told her as the last pin fell free. "I thought I'd never see you again after Vegas. I can't lie. I wanted to."

Why had he blurted that out? They were supposed to be reeling back the true confessions, not throwing down more.

She blinked and let the tiniest lift of her lips register. "I'd like to say I forgot about you. I tried. Never happened."

And here they were. Married. It was something he was having difficulty reconciling in his mind when Roz fit so easily into the "hot fling" box in his head. Surely there had been a woman at some point in the past whom he'd seen more than once, but he couldn't recall the face of anyone but this one. She'd filled his thoughts so much over the past month or so that he suddenly feared he'd have a hard time getting her out when they divorced.

More sex needed, stat. Obviously. They were doing far too much chitchatting.

Reaching for her, he snagged her shoulders and hauled her up the length of his body, which went a long way toward reviving him for round two. She met him in a fiery kiss that shot sensation down his throat. Roz spread her legs to straddle him, this time hitting the exact spot he wanted her to be in, apparently on board with no more talking.

The heat built on itself instantly, putting urgency into their kisses, and the thrust of her tongue against his had sweet fire laced through it that he welcomed. This time, there was no need to go slow and he didn't waste the opportunity. Taking a half second to pull out the box of condoms he'd stashed in his bedside table in anticipation of their wedding night, he dove back onto her, rolling to put her under him so he could focus.

She needed oblivion. He could give her that. Taking her mouth in a fierce kiss, he let his hands roam over her amazing body, caressing whatever he could reach until she was moaning deep in her chest. Her blistering fingers closed around his erection, priming it, and then she reached for the condoms before he could. In what might be the hottest thing she'd done thus far, she rolled it on him, squeezing and teasing as she went, then notching him at her entrance.

He caught her gaze as he paused, savoring this moment before he plunged because it was his favorite. The anticipation built and she flexed her hips, eager for him but not taking the initiative, apparently content to let him go at his own pace.

Roz was his match in every way. The reality seeped through him as they stared at each other, their chests heaving with the exertion of holding back. And then he pushed inside and not even the feel of her mouth could match the exquisiteness of the way her silk caressed every millimeter. He sucked in a breath as she took him deeper, wrapping her legs around him to hold him inside.

The pressure and tension climbed until he had to move, to feel. Gasping, she arched against him, grazing her breasts against his torso, and that felt unbelievable, too. Sensation swirled, driving him faster and faster and she closed around him again and again, squeezing until she was crying out her pleasure. His second release built and she was still watching him, her eyes dark and sensual and so open that he fell into them, hopefully never to surface.

They exploded together and it was only as they came down, wrapped in each other's arms, that he realized that they'd done it missionary style, like a real couple. A first. He'd have said he hated that position but it had felt so right with Roz. Something warm lingered in his chest as he pushed hair out of her face. She kissed his temple and snuggled deeper into his embrace.

This was maybe the most sated he'd ever been in his life. And they hadn't even had sex that many times. Quantity had always been his goal in the past, but apparently quality trumped that. Because they'd gotten married? Because he knew they had tomorrow night and the next and the next, so he didn't have to cram all his appetites into a few hours?

Whatever it was, it felt different. He liked it. Who knew?

This was uncharted territory and he didn't quite know what to do with it. Sex hadn't decreased the intimacy quotient after all. But he'd always shied away from that because rejection wasn't something he dealt with well, or rather, more to the point, he'd never felt like finding out how well he'd deal with it.

His father had done such a thorough job of rejecting him that he'd lived most of his life with total hatred of a man he'd never met. That was what had made the pact with Jonas and Warren so easy. He had no interest in learning how much more it would hurt to be rejected by someone he'd fallen in love with. Obviously it had driven Marcus to a permanent solution. What made Hendrix so much more capable of handling the same?

The rational part of his brain kicked in. Honestly, he'd have to give a woman a chance to reject him in order to fully test that.

Had he been given an opportunity to do exactly that? Roz had been great so far in their relationship. Maybe she was the exception to the rule. Maybe he could test out having a little more with her…

He settled her a little closer, letting her warm him thoroughly, and snagged the sheet to cover them. They hadn't slept at all that night in Vegas, so this would be a first, too. Waking up with a woman had also been something he studiously avoided, but waking up with Roz held enormous appeal.

If "more" didn't work out, then they could get a divorce like they'd always planned. It was practically a foolproof experiment in something that he'd never have said he'd want but couldn't seem to stop himself from exploring.

Eight

Hendrix and Roz had opted not to go away for their honeymoon, largely because that was something real couples did. But also because Helene had already scheduled a splashy fundraiser, the biggest one of the summer, for four days after the wedding. The event was supposed to generate the majority of the money needed to push her campaign through to the election. In other words, it was a big deal.

Helene had specifically asked them to make an appearance so it didn't seem like they were hiding. *Go big or go home,* she'd said with a smile and Roz hadn't really been able to find a good argument against attending. Though she'd racked her brain for one because a big social event with plenty of opportunity for her to feel like she still wasn't good enough to be associated with the Harris name didn't sound like fun.

The afternoon of, Hendrix came home from work

early carrying a bag emblazoned with the name of an exclusive store that Roz knew only carried women's clothing. Intrigued, she eyed the bag.

"You entering a drag queen revue that I don't know about?" she asked from her perch on the lounger near the window of their bedroom. It was an enormous room in an even more enormous house that felt genuinely empty when her husband wasn't in it. Probably because it was his, not hers.

Or at least that was the excuse she kept telling herself so she didn't have to think about what it meant that she sometimes missed him. That she thought about him all day long and only some of it was sexual.

"Maybe." He waggled his brows. "Let's see if it fits."

He pulled the dress from a layer of tissue paper and held it up to his chest as she giggled over his antics. But then the dress fully unfurled, revealing what he'd picked out. Oh, God, it was gorgeous. Red, with a gold clasp at the waist that gathered the material close.

"I think it would fit me better than you," she said wryly. "Is this your subtle way of getting me excited about the idea of hanging out with North Carolina's movers and shakers?"

"Depends." He shot her an adorable smile that made her pulse beat a little strangely as the dress became the second-most-beautiful thing in the room. "Did it work?"

Oh, it worked all right, but not even close to the way he meant.

"Only if it goes with the gold shoes I have in my closet." She held out a hand for the gown because the whole thing felt inevitable. "I'll try it on. But I'm only wearing it because you picked it out."

The silk slid through her hands like water as she laid it on the couch, then stood to wiggle out of her pants and shirt. The dress was strapless on one side and came up into an elegant over-the-shoulder style on the other. It settled against her curves like it had been made for her and fell to the ground in a waterfall of red. A high slit revealed enough leg to raise some eyebrows, which she sincerely hoped Hendrix would use as a convenient way to get his hands on her during dinner.

"You look amazing," he said quietly and when she glanced at him, pride glinted from his eyes.

"You have good taste," she shot back, mystified why the compliment pleased her so much. The gift as a whole pleased her in ways she'd never have expected. No man had ever bought her clothes before. She'd never had a need for one to, nor would she have accepted such a gift from anyone else.

Sure, there was an agenda buried in the middle of his gesture. He needed her by his side at his mother's thing and now she couldn't use *I have nothing to wear* as an excuse to weasel out of it. But she didn't care. The dress fit like a dream, clearly indicating her husband paid attention to details, and the way he was looking at her made her feel desired more sharply than anything he'd done in their entire history. That was saying something.

She half expected him to reach for her, but he started chattering about something that had happened at work earlier as he stripped out of his suit, then went to take a shower. Too bad. She'd be happy to show up late but he wasn't on board with that.

The limo ride was uneventful and she started to get antsy. The wedding hadn't been too bad in terms of dirty looks and noses in the air. But she'd been the bride and it was practically a requirement that people treat her nicely on her wedding day. This fundraiser was a whole different ball game and she didn't often do this kind of society thing. For a reason.

Only for Helene would she brave it. And because Hendrix had done something so unexpected as buy her a dress.

"Nervous?" Hendrix murmured as they exited the limo. "I'll hold your hand."

"You're supposed to," she reminded him blithely. "Because we're married and making sure people are fully aware of that fact."

When he clasped her fingers in his, though, it didn't feel utilitarian. Especially when he glanced down at her and smiled like they shared a secret. "I'm also doing it because I want to."

That warmed her enormously. For about two minutes. Because that's when she saw her father. Whom she had not realized would be in attendance. Of course he'd wrangled an invitation to the premiere Helene Harris for Governor event of the season. Maybe Helene had even invited him of her own free will.

Roz's chest turned to ice.

"I wonder if there's a closet in this place," she said into Hendrix's ear with a little nuzzle. If she could entice him into a back hall, they could spend an hour there before anyone even noticed they'd arrived. Then there wouldn't be a big to-do about them disappearing, and she could get good and relaxed before braving the hypercritical looks and comments.

Hendrix smiled at a few people and snaked an arm around Roz, pulling her close. But instead of copping a feel, like she'd have laid odds on, he held her waist in a perfectly respectable fashion. "Maybe we'll look later."

"Maybe we should look now." She slid her own arm around his waist in kind, but let her hand drift south with a caress designed to remind him they were at their best when they were burning up with need for each other. Though why she had to be the aggressor in this situation, she wasn't quite sure.

Instead of shooting her a salacious grin that communicated all the naughty thoughts in his mind, he pulled her into a shadowy alcove away from the crush. Oh, this had possibilities. The area wasn't enclosed, but could be considered private. Emboldened, she slipped the button free on his tux jacket, gauging exactly how much cover it might provide if he had a mind to get handsy.

That got her a smile, but without much carnal heat laced through it. No worries. She could get him hot and bothered pretty quickly and let her fingers do some walking. But he just laced his fingers with hers and pulled them free of his body.

"Roz, come on."

That didn't sound like the precursor to a hot round of mutual orgasmic delight. "I'm trying to, but you're not helping any."

"Why do we always have to have sex in public?"

Agape, she stared at him. "I must not be doing it right if you have to ask that question."

"I'm being serious." Their fingers were still entwined and he brought one to his mouth to kiss the back of her hand tenderly. "There's no one on earth who gets me more excited than you. We're not talking about whether or not you have the ability to get me off, but why you're trying to do it in the middle of my mother's fundraiser."

Guilt put her back up. "I guess the thrill is gone. And so early in our marriage, too. I thought that didn't wear off until at least after the first year."

He rolled his eyes. "I literally just told you this is not a conversation about how much I desire you. I'm trying to figure out why you have a seemingly self-destructive need to have sex in public. That's what got us into this marriage in the first place."

So now all this was her fault? "There were two people in that hot tub, Hendrix."

"Willingly," he threw in far too fast and that pissed her off, too. "I'm not pushing blame onto you. I wasn't saying no as you pulled me into that closet at the wedding. But I am right now. Wait."

He tightened his grip on her fingers as he correctly guessed she was about to storm off to…somewhere that she hadn't quite worked out yet.

"Sweetheart, listen to me."

And she was so out of sorts that she did, despite knowing in her marrow she wasn't going to like what he had to say.

"You want me so badly that you can't wait?" he asked. "That's great. I want you like that, too. The problem is that we both use that heat as a distraction. From life, from…I don't know. Crap going on inside. Whatever it is, I don't want to do that anymore."

The earnestness in his expression, his tone, in the very stroke of his fingers over hers bled through her, catching on something so deep inside that it hurt. "I don't do that."

He didn't even have the grace to go along with the

lie. "You do. We're cut from the same cloth. Why do you think we were both so willing to go through with this marriage? We understand each other."

Oh, God. That was so true it nearly wrenched her heart from its mooring. If he made her cry, she was never going to forgive him. She'd spent *thirty minutes* on her makeup. "What are you saying?"

His smile did nothing to fix the stuff raging through her chest. "I'm saying let's take our sex life behind closed doors. Permanently. Let's make it about us. About discovering what we can be to each other besides a distraction."

"So there's no more chance of public humiliation, you mean?"

He shook his head, dashing the out she'd handed him. "No. Well, I mean, yes, of course that is a very good side benefit. But I'm talking about removing the reasons why we're both so good at creating scandals. Stop avoiding intimacy and get real with me. At home."

That was the worst idea she'd ever heard in her life. "You first."

He nodded. "I'm at the head of the line, sweetheart. Get in the queue behind me and let's do this ride the way it was intended."

Her lungs hitched. "You're not just talking about laying down a new no-sex-in-public rule. Are you?"

"I don't know what I'm talking about." He laughed self-consciously, finally releasing her fingers to run a hand through his hair. "All I know is that my mom asked me to get married so her campaign wouldn't take a hit and all I could think about was getting you into bed again. Then we made a mutual decision that sex was off the table until after the ceremony. It really made me think about who I want to be when I grow up. An oversexed player who can't control himself? I don't want to be that guy. Not with you."

Stunned, she blinked up at him but his expression didn't waver. He was serious about making changes and somehow, she was wrapped in the middle of all of it. Like maybe he wanted to be a better person because of her. That was... She didn't know what that was, had no experience with this kind of truth.

"So where does that leave us?" she whispered.

He tilted his head until their foreheads touched. "A married couple who's expected at a fundraiser. Can we get through that and then we'll talk?"

She nodded and the motion brought his head up just at the right angle to join their lips. The kiss had nothing to do with sex, nothing to do with heat. It was a sweet encapsulation of the entire conversation. A little tender, a little confused and so much better than she'd have ever dreamed.

Somehow, she floated along behind him as he led her back into the fray and the fact that they hadn't gotten naked meant something significant. Hell if she knew what. Later tonight, maybe she'd get a chance to find out.

Turned out that Roz hadn't actually needed the orgasm to relax after all. Hendrix held her hand like he'd promised and generally stuck by her side through the whole of the fundraiser. The evening wound to a close without one snide comment being wafted in her direction. Whether that was because Hendrix had studiously kept her far away from her father—a fact she couldn't help but notice and appreciate—or because the marriage had really worked to soften society's opinion toward them, she couldn't say.

Ultimately, the only thing that mattered was that she ended the evening on a high she hadn't felt in a long time. Not even sex could compete with the burst of pure gratitude racing through her veins as the limo wheeled them toward Hendrix's house. Their house. It was technically theirs, for now, as he was sharing it with her. No harm in claiming it as such, right?

"I think that was a success, don't you, Mr. Harris?" she commented as he held the door open for her to precede him.

He shut it with a resounding click. "I'm sorry, I missed everything you just said outside of 'Mr. Harris,'" he murmured and propelled her up the stairs with insistent hands on her hips.

She let him because it suited her to get to a place where they could pick up their discussion from earlier. "You like it when I call you Mr. Harris? I can do that a whole bunch more."

"I insist that you do."

Once in the bedroom he sat her down on the bed, knelt at her feet and took enormous care with removing her shoes, unbuckling the straps with painstakingly slow pulls, watching her as he did it. His gaze flickered as he finally slipped off one shoe and then the other. He lifted her arch to his mouth, kissing it sensuously.

It was such an unexpected move that something akin to nerves popped up, brewing inside until she had to say something to break the weird tension.

"We got through the fundraiser," she said. "Is this the part where we're going to talk?"

"Uh-huh," he purred against her foot and dragged his lips up her leg.

It happened to the be the one revealed by the slit that opened almost all the way to her hipbone, so he had a lot of real estate to cover. Her flesh heated under his mouth, sending an arrow of desire through her core.

"First," he said. "I'm going to tell you how absolutely wild you drive me. Are you listening?"

He nibbled at the skin of her thigh and slid a hand up the inside of her dress, exactly as she'd imagined he would—at the table while they were eating dinner. She'd envisioned it being a huge turn-on to have his hands under her dress while they were sitting there with members of high society, especially given how sanctimonious they'd all been about the photograph. And Hendrix had taken that possibility off the table and opened up a whole different world at the same time.

This wasn't a turn-on because she was putting one over on the high and mighty. It was a turn-on because of the man doing the caressing. Exactly as he'd suggested, taking their sex life behind closed doors put a sheen on the encounter that she couldn't recall ever having felt before.

"I hear you," she whispered. "Tell me more."

His fingers slid higher, slowly working their way toward the edge of her panties and then dipping underneath the hem to knuckle across her sex. She gasped as the contact sang through her, automatically widening her legs to give him plenty of access.

"Wild." He gathered her dress in one hand as he slid up the other leg to bunch the red silk at her thighs. "Do you have any concept of how difficult it was to tell you no at the fundraiser?"

"Seemed pretty easy to me," she mumbled and immediately felt like a selfish shrew. "But I'm sure it wasn't."

"No," he agreed far too graciously instead of calling her on her cattiness like he should have. "I carried around a boner for at least half the time. This dress…" He heaved a lusty sigh as he trailed a finger from the fabric gathered over her shoulder down over her breasts, which tightened deliciously from no more than that light touch. "I'm going to have to do this the right way."

"Because you have such a habit of doing it wrong?" she suggested sarcastically.

"I mean, I can't take it off. Not yet." He speared her with a glance so laden with heat and implications that her core went slick and achy instantly, even before he put his hands under the skirt and hooked her underwear, drawing off the damp scrap to toss it over his shoulder.

Pulling her to the edge of the bed, he spread her thighs and treated her to the deepest, wettest French kiss imaginable. A moan escaped her throat as he lit her up from the inside out, heat exploding along her skin as Hendrix set fire to every inch of her body. He closed his eyes as he pleasured her and she could scarcely look away from the raw need plastered all over his face.

It should be the other way around. He had his mouth on her in the most intimate of kisses, and she felt herself coming apart as she watched his tongue swirl through her folds. His fingers twined through the silk of her dress, the one he'd given her as a sweet, unexpected gift, and that gave everything a significance she scarcely understood.

The release rolled through her, made so much more powerful by the fact that he was letting her see how much she affected him. He was still telling her how wild he was over her, and she was still listening. When she came, she cried out his name, hands to his jaw because she couldn't stand not touching him as her flesh separated from her bones, breaking her into a million unrecoverable pieces.

His eyes blinked open, allowing him to witness it as she slid into oblivion and it was a horrible shame that he wasn't right there with her. She wanted that, wanted to watch him come apart with abandon.

"Make love to me," she murmured and guided his lips to hers for a kiss that tasted like earth and fire. It was elemental in all its glory and she wanted more.

He got out of his clothes fast enough to communicate how much he liked that suggestion but when he reached for her, she pulled him onto the bed in the same position she'd just been in and straddled him, still wearing the dress.

"I might never take it off again," she informed him as she settled against his groin, teasing him with her still-damp core. Hard, thick flesh met hers and she wanted him with a fierceness she could hardly contain.

He groaned as she arched her back, thrusting her covered breasts against his chest. "It feels divine."

And that was enough of a recommendation for her to keep going, exactly like this. She pulled a condom from the gathered place at her waist, which she'd stashed there earlier in hopes of finding a closet at the fundraiser, but this was far better.

His gaze reflected his agreement, going hot with understanding as he spied the package in her fingers.

"I see you attended the fundraiser fully prepared to go the distance."

"Yeah. But it's okay. This is exactly the way our evening was supposed to go." How he'd converted her, she still didn't know. But it sure felt like how this ride should be experienced. If it wasn't, she didn't want to know about it.

Condom in place, she slid down until they were joined and he was so deep inside that there was no room for anything else. He captured her gaze and held it for an eternity, even as he slid his arms around her to hold her tight. It was the most intimate position she'd ever been in with another human being and it was so beautiful her heart ached.

And then it got even better as they moved in tandem in a sensuous rolling rhythm unlike anything she'd ever felt. Her head tipped back as she rode the wave of sensation and Hendrix fused his mouth to her throat, suckling at her skin. He murmured things against it, telling her how much he liked the way she felt, how sexy she was. The pretty words infused her blood, heightening the experience.

The release split through her body almost before she'd realized it was imminent. It was quieter, deeper than the first one. More encompassing. She let it expand, grabbing on to the sensation because it was something she wanted to savor. Hendrix's expression went tense with his own release and he drew it out with a long kiss, perfectly in sync with her in a way she knew in her bones would never have happened if they'd banged each other in a closet.

This was something else, taking their relationship to the next level.

He picked her up and set her on her feet so he could finally remove the dress and then gathered her into his arms to lay spoon style under the covers. She didn't resist, couldn't have. She wanted all of this to be as real as it felt, but as she lay there in the dark listening to her husband breathe, her eyes refused to stay closed.

None of this was going to last. She'd forgotten that in the midst of letting Hendrix prove they could have a closed-door relationship. She'd forgotten that their marriage had become intimate long before they'd signed any papers and she'd let herself get swept away in the beauty he'd shown her.

She did use sex as a distraction, as an avoidance tactic. Because she hadn't wanted to be in this position. Ever. But she'd let him change the dynamic between them.

They were still getting a divorce. She *couldn't* forget that part because it was the theme of her life.

She lost everything important to her eventually and Hendrix fell into that category just as much as anything else. This wasn't the start of a new trend. Just the continuation of an old one that was destined to break her heart.

Nine

Helene made a rare appearance at the office, bringing a huge catered lunch with her that the employees all appreciated. Hendrix let her have her fun as the company still had her name on it even though she'd transitioned the CEO job to him long ago. As the last of the potato salad disappeared from the break room and the employees drifted back to their desks, Hendrix crossed his arms and leaned back on the counter to contemplate his mom.

"What gives?" he asked with a chin jerk at the mostly decimated spread. "You get a large donation or something?"

Her lips curved into the smile that never failed to make him feel like they were a team. At last, it seemed like they were back on solid ground again.

Sure, she smiled at everyone, because she had the sunniest personality of anyone he'd ever known, but she was still his mom no matter what and he valued their bond more than he could explain.

"Paul Carpenter dumped five million in my lap. You didn't have anything to do with that, did you?"

He shrugged, wishing he could say it was an act of generosity and that she shouldn't read anything into it, but odds were good the donation came with strings. Carpenter had another think coming, if so. Having the billionaire as a father-in-law hadn't checked out like he'd expected. It chafed something fierce to have his hopes realized of being aligned with a powerful old money family, only to find out the patriarch was an ass.

"Not even close. I don't like how he treats Roz. If you recall, I might have given him that impression the last time we spoke at the wedding."

"Well, he's not the only one with a giving soul. The fundraiser was a huge success. I came by to thank you for hanging out with us old people."

Hendrix snorted. The day Helene could be described as old had yet to come. She had boundless energy, a magnanimous spirit and could still give women half her age a run for their money. "You're only seventeen years older than me, so you can stop with the old business. And you're welcome."

"You know what this means, right?" Helene eyed him curiously. "Your marriage to Roz worked to smooth over the scandal. My approval ratings are high. Seems like you did it. I don't know how to say thank you for this enormous sacrifice you made for me."

He grinned to cover the slight pulse bobble at what his mother was really saying—he and Roz had reached their goal much faster than originally antici-pated. Her speech had all the hallmarks of what you said as something was winding down. And he did not want to think of his marriage that way. "It was really my pleasure."

His mom stuck her fingers in her ears in mock ex-asperation. "I don't want to know. This time, keep your sex life to yourself."

"I'm trying." And it was working well. So well, he could scarcely believe how easily he'd slid deeper into his relationship with Roz. They fit together seamlessly and it was nearly too good to be true. Far too good to be talking about ending it already. "I really like her."

God, was he fourteen again? He was an adult who could surely find a better way to describe how his in-sides got a little brighter at the mere thought of his wife. But what was he supposed to say about the woman he woke up to every morning? Or about how he hadn't yet figured out why his marriage *wasn't* making him run screaming for the hills?

"I can tell," his mom said lightly. "I'm headed to see her next. You wanna come with me?"

His eyebrows shot up automatically. "You're going to see Roz?"

Helene and his wife weren't having lunch any longer even though he'd told Roz repeatedly that it was fine if she built a friendship with Helene. He still felt like he'd nipped that relationship in the bud prematurely. It didn't sit well and if they were mending the fences he'd knocked down, he definitely didn't want to get between them again.

"I am," she confirmed. "I can't put off my promise

to her any longer and still sleep at night. So I'm doing the clown thing. Full makeup and all."

"The press will eat it up," he promised and she nodded her agreement.

"Yes, I'm counting on it. It should be quite a circus, no pun intended."

He laughed, glad that despite the many other changes that had been forced on them over the years, they could still hang out and crack jokes with each other. He'd never censored one word to his mother and she was the one person he could be completely real with.

Well, not the only one. He could be real with Roz. He'd never censored anything he'd said to her either, a first. Usually he watched what he said to women because who wanted to give false expectations? But his relationship with Roz required absolute honesty from the get-go and it was a facet of their relationship he hadn't fully appreciated until now.

Tomorrow if he woke up and knew with certainty that he was done, he just had to announce it was time to file for divorce and she'd say okay. It was freeing to know he never had to pull punches with the woman he was sleeping with.

Not so freeing to be contemplating the fact that he'd practically been handed permission to bring up that divorce. He wasn't ready to think about that. They hadn't been married that long and surely Helene would want them to see this thing through a little while longer. Just to be absolutely certain that a divorce wouldn't undo all the good they'd done already.

"I have to admit, I'm intrigued by the whole clown idea," he told her. "But I have that presentation on restructuring the supply chain and I need to do a thorough sweep of the warehouse like I've been threatening to do for weeks."

Helene wrinkled her nose. "That sounds boring."

"Because it is. Being the CEO isn't all curly wigs and water-squirting flowers." Neither was being a political candidate, but she knew he was kidding.

"That's the benefit of being the boss," she reminded him and pushed him ahead of her out of the break room where his admin had started cleaning up the leftover boxes. "You can leave the boring stuff for another day and come watch me be a clown. It's for a good cause. And it's an opportunity to be seen with your lovely bride in a stellar photo op where everyone will not only be dressed but overdressed."

Seeing Roz in the middle of the day for no other reason than because he wanted to held enormous appeal that he chose not to examine too closely. And it was coupled with an opportunity to see what she did on a daily basis unobtrusively. He did have a certain curiosity about her charity. Because…*clowns*. It was such a strange thing to be passionate about.

"Sold." He buttoned his suit jacket. "Let me—"

"Not one foot in your office or you'll never emerge." Helene looped an arm through the crook of his elbow and tugged. "Ride with me in my car. We'll drop you off back here to get your car later."

And that was how he found himself at Carolina Presbyterian Hospital with his mother in clown makeup. The children's ward was a lively place, if not a little depressing. Easy to see why clowns might make the whole thing a tiny bit less awful. God willing, he'd never have to personally empathize with what these families were going through. He made a mental note to write Roz a check, which he should have done a long time ago.

He snuck a glance at Roz from the corner of his eye as he lounged in the spot he'd reserved for himself, which was well out of the way, yet afforded him a front-row seat for the show. His wife was gorgeous, focused and quite possibly the tensest he'd ever seen her, including the time they'd braved the florist, their wedding reception and, his least favorite, the encounter with her father in the hall after nearly being caught with their pants down.

Either she didn't like that he'd accompanied his mother or she was worried that something was going to go wrong with this once-in-a-lifetime opportunity to get buzz for her charity.

While Helene entertained the kids with stuffed animals she'd carried into the hospital in a big bag, Hendrix edged toward Roz, who had yet to acknowledge his existence. Not that he was nursing a teeny bit of hurt over that or anything.

"Hey," he murmured, mindful of the two separate news crews that were covering the gubernatorial candidate's foray into the world of therapy clowning, a thing he'd had no idea had a name, but apparently did.

"Hey." Her mouth pinched back into a straight line that he immediately wanted to kiss away.

Definitely tense and dang it if it wasn't on the tip of his tongue to suggest they find a closet somewhere because she was wound tight. But they weren't *that couple* any longer. For a reason. So he'd have to handle his wife's tension verbally. "You have a problem with me being here?"

"What?" She glanced at him and then immediately flicked her gaze back to Helene. "No. I don't care. It's a free country."

Which was the kind of thing you said when you *did* care but hadn't planned on letting anyone else in on the secret.

"Your shoes are too tight?" he guessed but she didn't smile at the joke.

"This is a big deal, Hendrix. I'm allowed to be nervous."

The sarcasm lacing the edge of her words was pure Roz, but he'd spent far too much time in her company to accept her comment as pure truth. She wasn't nervous. Tense, yes. But it wasn't nerves.

And like what had happened at their engagement party, he was nothing if not painfully aware that he could read her so easily because he was paying attention to *her*, not how best to get under that severe suit she'd donned like armor.

"She's doing fine," he told her with a nod toward his mom. "Come get some coffee with me."

Roz shot him another side-eyed glance, as if afraid to take her gaze off Helene for one second. "I can't leave. This is my charity on the line."

"On the line?" he repeated. "Like if Mom does the wrong thing, it's all going to collapse? You know no one is going to stop letting you do clowns just because she fails to make one of the kids smile, right?"

Her shoulders rolled back a couple of times as if she couldn't find a comfortable stance. "Maybe not. But maybe it's all going to collapse for other reasons."

That wasn't the fierce Rosalind Carpenter he knew. "If it does, that's not on you."

"It is," she hissed back under her breath. "Why do you think I needed your mother in the first place? Not because I thought kids would like to meet the woman who may be the governor by January."

"Will be," he corrected automatically because there was no way Helene was going to fail to reach her goal, not if he had anything to say about it. After all, he'd signed a marriage license to ensure that his mom got to move into the Governor's Mansion. The fact that his marriage had become so much more still wasn't something he had a handle on. "Why don't you clue me in on why Helene is really here if it's not to bring joy to some sick kids?"

Roz's eyes snapped shut and her chest heaved a couple of times through some deep breaths. "Actually, coffee would be good."

Despite being certain she'd found yet another avoidance tactic since she couldn't use sex, he nodded once and put a hand to her waist to guide her out of the room. After all, coffee had been his suggestion, but not because he'd intended to give her an out. It was a little uncomfortable to realize that while he might not be censoring his words with her, that didn't mean she was returning the favor.

And he wanted to know what was swirling beneath her skin. He wanted to know *her*. They might be on the downslide, but he couldn't contemplate letting her go, not right now. There was still too much to explore here.

Instead of taking her to the cafeteria where the coffee would be weak and tepid, he texted his driver to hit the Starbucks on the corner, then found the most private corner in the surprisingly busy children's ward.

He let Roz choose her seat and then took the opposite one.

She stared out the window, and he stared at her. The severe hairstyle she'd chosen pulled at her lush features, but nothing could change the radiance that gave her such a traffic-stopping face. When he'd left her this morning, she'd still been in bed, her long dark hair tumbling over her shoulders the way he liked it.

But he didn't think she'd appreciate it if he pulled the pins free right here in the middle of the hospital. "Coffee's on its way."

She nodded. "Thanks. I need it."

"This is the conversation you want to have?"

Her mouth tightened. "I didn't want to have a conversation at all."

"But you needed the air," he guessed and her wince said he'd called it in one. "Roz, I'm not going to bite. If you want to talk to me, I'm not going anywhere. But if you don't, then let's sit here while you collect yourself. Then we'll go back and do clowns with no one the wiser that you had an anxiety attack or whatever."

Her double take was so sharp, it should have knocked her off the chair. "Anxiety attack? Is that what it looked like? Could you tell I was mid-freak-out? Oh, God. Did any of the cameras pick it up? They did. Of course they did. They're all over the place and—"

"Sweetheart, you need to breathe now." He gathered up both her hands in his and held them in his lap, rubbing at her wrists as he racked his brain for information about what he'd accidentally triggered with his random comment. "Breathe. Again. Roz. Look at me."

She did and no, he hadn't imagined the wild flare of her irises a moment ago. Something had her spooked.

But she was breathing as instructed, though the death grip she had on his hands would leave a mark, particularly where her wedding rings bit into his index finger. Didn't matter. He didn't have any intention of letting her go.

His driver appeared with two lattes, set them on the table and vanished quickly. Hendrix ignored the white-and-green cups in favor of his alternately white-and-green wife, who, if he didn't miss his guess, might actually be about to lose her lunch.

"Um…" How did you go about delicately asking your wife if she had a positive test result to discuss? "Are you feeling faint? Do I need to call a doctor?"

What if she *was* pregnant? A thousand different things flashed through his head in an instant. But only some of them were of the panicked variety. Some weren't that unpleasant. Some were maybe even a little bit awed and hopeful.

"Oh, God, no!" she burst out. "Please don't bother anyone. I'm fine."

"Of course you are," he murmured and rubbed at her wrists again. "But maybe you could give me a little more to go on as to why we're sitting here in the corner not drinking the hot coffee that I got for us?"

She slipped a hand from his before he was ready to lose the contact and palmed her cup, sipped at the contents and shot him a fake smile. "See? Drinking."

"See?" He waved a hand in front of his face. "Still sitting here in the dark about what's going on with you. Roz, we're married. I've touched you in the most intimate places. I've done more illicit, dirty, sinful things with you than with anyone else in my life. You fell asleep in my arms last night. What is all of that but a demonstration of trust? There is nothing you can say to me that would change—"

"I'm afraid of clowns."

Oh, God. Now it was out there and Roz had nowhere to hide. She'd blurted out her deepest secret and even worse, she'd done it in the middle of Helene's shot in the arm for Clown-Around.

Hendrix wasn't laughing. He should be. There was nothing scary about clowns. Especially not when it was her mother-in-law underneath the makeup. Geez, she'd half thought seeing Helene all dressed up would be the magic bullet to fix all of the crazy going on inside that had only gotten worse the more Roz forced herself to be around the source of her fear.

"Okay." Hendrix's beautiful eyes flashed as he removed the coffee from her grip and recaptured her hand. As if he knew that holding her in place was something she desperately needed but didn't know how to ask for. "That's not what I thought you were going to say."

"No, probably not." Her mouth twisted into a wry smile designed to disguise the fact that she wished she could cry. "I wasn't expecting me to say it, either. It's dumb, I know."

He shook his head fiercely. "No. What's dumb is that you're holding all of it inside when I'm here. Tell me what I can do, sweetheart."

That's when her heart fluttered so hard that there was no way it could possibly stay behind her rib cage. *Now* she was feeling light-headed and like she might need a doctor to fix whatever he'd just broken inside her.

"Hold my hand," she mumbled because what else was she supposed to say when his impassioned statements might loosen her tear ducts after all?

"I am. I'm not going to stop."

He wouldn't, either. Because he was Hendrix Harris, the hero of her story, who stood up to her father and had such a good relationship with his mother that he'd willingly marry the wild Carpenter daughter with seemingly nothing to personally gain from it. In bed, he worshipped Roz. Out of it, he talked her down. He was everything she'd never have said she wanted—but did—and that was pushing buttons inside that weren't meshing well with clowns.

But at least she didn't feel like she was standing on the edge of a mile-high cliff any longer, legs about to give out as the darkness yawned at her feet. She could breathe. Thanks to Hendrix.

"I started Clown-Around because I needed to stop being afraid." He didn't blink as she blurted out her second-biggest secret, and he didn't interrupt with a bunch of advice on how to fix it. "I really thought it was going to work."

"Facing your fears is a good step," he agreed and shut his mouth expectantly, as if to indicate this was still a conversation and it was her turn again. He was good at that and she didn't mistake it as anything other than a skill.

That or he was just good at being with *her*, and she might appreciate that even more.

It was the thing she clung to as she spilled out the story of her eight-year-old self missing an entire semester of school because no one could figure out how to tell her she wasn't allowed to sit at the bedside of her dying mother.

At first, they'd tried. Her nanny would drive her to school, only to get a call from the headmistress that Roz had snuck out again. Fortunately, her father had found her at the hospital before the police had gotten involved, but his mandate that she not try that trick again had only fueled her need to both defy him and spend time with her mother. Sneaking out of school became great practice for later, when she did it to hang out with boys nearly twice her age.

As she recalled all of it for Hendrix, she didn't leave any of it out, especially not the ugly parts because he deserved to know what was going on with her, as he'd asked to.

"She was so sick," Roz recalled, not bothering to wipe the stream of tears that finally flowed. They'd just be followed by more. "The chemo was almost worse than the cancer and they'd come to get her for the treatments. I wouldn't let her go. There were these clowns."

She shuddered involuntarily, but Hendrix didn't say anything, just kept rubbing a thumb over the pulse point of her wrist, which was oddly comforting.

"Every day, I imagined that I was helping draw all the poison from her body when I sat by her bedside and held her hand. But they wouldn't let me go with her to the treatments and when she came back, it was like they'd sucked a little more of her life away."

Verbalizing all of this was not helping. If anything, the absolute terror of it became that much fresher as she relived how the two clowns wrenched her hand out of her mother's, with their big fake smiles and balloon animal distractions. They'd been employed by the hospital administration to keep her out of the way as the staff tried to care for her mother. She knew that as a rational adult. But the associations in her head with clowns and the way her mother slipped away more and more each day—that association wasn't fading like the psychologists had said it would.

"And now you know the worst about me," she informed him blithely.

Instead of responding, he dashed away the tears from her cheeks with one thumb, still clinging to her other hand as promised. His strength was amazing, and definitely not a quality she'd have put on her top twenty when it came to men. It was a bonus, particularly since he had twenty out of twenty on the list of what she'd have said would embody her perfect man.

What was she going to do with him?

Divorce him, most likely. Her heart lurched as she forced herself to accept the reality that all of his solid, quiet strength, the strength that was currently holding her together, wasn't permanent. She didn't get to keep things. The clowns were a great big reminder of that, one she needed to heed well.

"So what you're telling me is," he drawled, "that the worst thing about you is that you went through an incredibly traumatic series of events as a child and clowns were in the middle of it. And now they freak you out. Stop me when I get to the part where I'm supposed to cast the first stone."

She rolled her eyes. Miraculously, the fact that he was cracking jokes allowed her to reel back the emotion and take a deep breath. "Yeah, okay. It's not on the same level as adultery. But it's still real and scary and—"

"Something we need to deal with," he cut in, his

gaze heavy on her with sympathy and tenderness. "And we will. You know what most people do with fears? They run really fast in the other direction. You started an extremely worthwhile charity while trying to deal with *your* fear. I don't think I've ever been more impressed with a human being in my life than I am with you right now."

Okay, not so much with reeling back the emotions then. The tears started up again as she stared at him. "It's not working, though, in case you missed that part."

He shook his head. "Doesn't matter. We'll try something else. What matters is that you're amazing and you can't erase that by throwing down your failures."

She hadn't done anything special. But he had. She felt hollowed out and refilled all at the same time, and Hendrix was the reason. That scared her more than anything else that had happened today. "I don't think I can go back in there."

Which wasn't the biggest issue but the only one that she could reasonably be expected to address at this point. It was also the most critical.

Nodding, he squeezed her hand. "That makes sense. The problem is that you want to."

How did he see the things inside her so clearly? It was as frustrating as it was extraordinary. It meant that she needed to watch herself around him. If she wasn't careful, he'd pick up on the way her insides were going mushy as he sat with her in the corner of the children's ward holding her hand when he had a multimillion-dollar business to run.

"The problem is that I need to," she corrected. "This is my charity. Your mother is helping me enormously by bringing credibility to my organization."

And it was doubtful she needed to explain that her credibility was lacking. He understood how scandals affected everything—regardless of whether you deserved it—far better than anyone else in her life.

"Here's an idea," he said casually. "Why don't you be a clown?"

"Say what?" But she'd heard him and the concept filtered through all the angst and fear and found a small snippet of reason, latching onto it with teeth. "You mean with makeup and everything?"

"Sure." He shrugged. "Maybe you haven't been able to fix your fear because you're too far away. You can't just get near your fears. You need to be inside them, ripping the things to shreds, blasting them apart internally."

"Oh, sure, because that's what you do?"

The sarcasm didn't even faze him. He cocked his head and stared straight down into her soul. "Married you, didn't I?"

Before she could get the first of many questions out around the lump in her throat, one of Helene's staffers interrupted them, shattering the intensely intimate moment. Good. They'd gotten way too deep when what she should be doing is creating distance. The last thing she wanted to hear was how freaked he'd been to lose his independence and how great it was that he had an imminent divorce to keep his fears of commitment at bay. It wasn't hard to imagine a player like Hendrix Harris with a little calendar in his head where he ticked off the days until he could shed his marriage.

It was *very* hard, however, to imagine how she'd handle it when that day came. Because losing him was a given and the longer this dragged on, the harder it was going to be to keep pretending she wasn't falling for him—which meant she should do herself a favor and cauterize the wound now.

Ten

Hendrix didn't get a chance to finish his conversation with Roz. Helene's stint as a clown ended faster than anyone would have liked when one of the patients took a scary turn for the worse. Hospital personnel cleared the area and a calm but firm nurse assured Helene that someone would update her on the little boy's status as soon as they knew something.

A somber note to end the day. Hendrix couldn't stop thinking about how short life was, the revelations Roz had made about her childhood and how to pick up their conversation without seeming insensitive. But his own fears that he'd mentioned were as relevant now as they had been before he'd agreed to this marriage.

Even so, he wanted to take a chance. With Roz. And he wanted to talk about how rejection wasn't something he handled well, air his fears the same way she had.

But she insisted that he go back to the office with his mom so she could take her car to Clown-Around's tiny storefront and finish some paperwork. He wasn't dense. He'd given her a lot to think about and she wanted to be alone. What kind of potential start to a real marriage would it give them if he pushed her into a discussion before she was ready?

Distracted, he went back to work but he couldn't concentrate, so he drove home early. The expressway was a mess. Bumper-to-bumper traffic greeted him with nothing but red taillights. Of course. Probably because he wasn't supposed to go home.

It didn't matter anyway. By the time he got there, Roz wasn't home yet. He prowled around at loose ends, wondering when the hell his house had turned into such a mausoleum that he couldn't be there by himself. He'd lived here alone for years and years. In fact, it was extremely rare for him to bring a woman home in the first place. Roz had been unique in more ways than one.

By the time Roz finally graced him with her presence, he'd eaten a bowl of cereal standing up in the kitchen, chewed the head off of his housekeeper because she'd dared suggest that he should sit at the empty dining room table, and rearranged the furniture in the living room that he'd used one time in the past year—at his engagement party.

In other words, nothing constructive. He had it bad and he wasn't happy about it.

Her key rattled in the lock and he pounced, swinging the door wide before she could get it open herself. Cleary startled, she stood on the doorstep clutching the key, hand still extended.

"I was waiting for you," he explained. Likely she'd

figured that out given his obvious eagerness. "You didn't say you'd be late."

A wariness snapped over her expression that wasn't typically part of her demeanor. "Was I supposed to?"

"No. I mean, we don't have that kind of deal, where you have to check in." Frustrated all at once for no reason, he stepped back to let her into the house. "You weren't late because of me, were you?"

She shook her head. "You mean because of our earlier conversation? No. You gave me advice that I appreciated. I appreciate a lot of things about you."

Well, if that didn't sound like a good segue, he didn't know what would. "I appreciate a lot of things about you, too. On that note, my mother told me earlier today that things are looking really good for her campaign. She thinks the marriage did exactly what it was supposed to."

Roz swept past him to head for the stairs, scarcely even pausing as she called over her shoulder, "That's great."

A prickle of unease moved down his spine as he followed her, even though he probably shouldn't. She'd come home late and didn't seem to be in a chatty mood. He needed to back off, but he couldn't help himself. This conversation was too important to wait.

"It is. It means that everything we hoped this marriage would do is happening. Has happened. Her donations are pouring in. She helped your charity, and while I guess we don't know the results of that yet—"

"It was amazing," she said flatly and blew through the door of the bedroom to sink onto the bed, where she removed her shoes with a completely blank expression on her face. "I had calls from three different hospitals looking to form long-term partnerships. Helene's already agreed to do a couple more go-rounds for me."

"Wow, that sounds…good?" Her tone had all the inflection of a wet noodle, so he was flying blind.

"Yeah, it's good." She shut her eyes for a beat, pointedly not looking at him. "Things are going well for her. She told me that too when I called her. So we should probably talk about our exit strategy. It may be a little premature, but it's coming faster than I'd assumed and I'd really like to get started on it."

Exit strategy? "You mean the divorce?"

The word tasted nasty in his mouth as he spit it out. It reverberated through his chest, and he didn't like the feeling of emptiness that it caused. A divorce was not what he wanted. Not yet. Not before he'd figured out how to step through the minefield his marriage had become. He couldn't fathom giving up Roz but neither did he want to come right out and say that. For a lot of reasons.

The pact being first and foremost. It weighed so heavy on his mind that it was a wonder his brain wasn't sliding out through his nose.

She glanced up at him for the first time since walking through the door. "I was thinking it might be safe for me to move back to my loft. I miss it. This house is nice but it's not mine, you know?"

He nodded even though he didn't know. Hell, if she'd wanted to live at her loft while they were married, he would have accommodated that. They'd chosen his house for their marital experiment because it had historical significance and there was a possibility they'd do a lot of entertaining.

That possibility still existed. This conversation was

extremely premature, in fact. They couldn't get a divorce tonight.

But all at once, he wasn't sure that was his biggest problem. The divorce was merely symbolic of what was happening faster than he could wrap his hands around—the end of his marriage. "You're thinking of moving back to your loft soon?"

She shrugged. "Maybe tomorrow. No one is really paying attention to us anymore now that we're a respectable married couple. It would hardly raise eyebrows if anyone realized I didn't live here anymore."

"It might." The first tendrils of panic started winding through his chest. Roz was already halfway out the door and he hadn't had one second to sort through what he hoped to say in order to get her to stay. "I think it would be a mistake to split up too early. We might still be called on to attend one of my mother's functions. It would look weird if we weren't there as a couple."

"I don't know." Roz rubbed at her forehead again as if this whole conversation was giving her a headache. "I got the impression from your mother everything was fine. Maybe I don't need to be there."

Maybe I need you there.

But he couldn't force his tongue to form the words. What if she said too bad or laughed? If she really cared about him the way he cared about her, she wouldn't have even brought up the divorce. She'd have left that conspicuously out of the conversation. For the first time, she wasn't so easy to read and he was definitely paying attention to *her*, not her panties.

He'd had enough practice at it over the course of their engagement and marriage that it was second nature now to shove any physical needs to the back-

ground while he focused on what was happening between them. He didn't need the ache in his chest to
remind him that what was happening had all the hallmarks of the end.

Because he'd taken public sex off the menu of their
marriage? Surely not. The ache in his chest intensified
as he contemplated her. What a not-so-funny paradox
that would be if he'd ruined their relationship by at-
tempting to remove all possibility of scandal. Actually,
that was irony at its finest if so. They had a marriage
built on sex. Only. Just like he would have sworn up
and down was perfect for him. Who wouldn't want
that? He was married to a hot woman that he got to
sleep with at night. But apparently that wasn't enough
for her to stick around.

What would be? The continued irony was that he
wasn't even talking to her about that. Couldn't even
open his mouth and say *I'm falling for you.*

If he didn't use the word *love* in that sentence, he
wasn't breaking the pact, right?

He was skating a fine line between a mutual agreement to end an amicable fixer marriage and laying his
heart on the line for her to stomp all over it—and the
way this was going, the latter felt like more and more
of a possibility.

That couldn't happen if he didn't let on how this
conversation had the potential to rip him to shreds.

"We don't have to get divorced right away. What's
the hurry? Why not let it ride for a while longer," he
said casually as if his entire body wasn't frozen.

She blinked at him. "What would be the point?"

What indeed? All at once, the ache in his chest grew
way too strong to bear. Wasn't she the slightest bit sad

at the thought of losing what was great about them? The parts that were great were really great. The parts that were bad were…what? There *were* no bad parts. So what was her hurry?

"Because we enjoy each other's company and like the idea of being married?"

She recoiled. "You mean sex."

"Well, sure." Too late, he realized that was probably not the smartest thing to say as her expression closed in. "Not solely that."

But of course she knew as well as he did that sex was what they were both good at. What they'd started their relationship with. What else was there?

The black swirl in his gut answered that statement. There was a lot more here—on his side. But she didn't seem overly interested in hearing about that, nor did she jump up in a big hurry to reciprocate with declarations of her own about what elements of their marriage she might wish could continue.

"I can't, Hendrix," she said simply.

And without any elaboration on her part, his world fell apart.

It was every bit the rejection he'd been so careful to guard against. The only saving grace being that she didn't know how much those three words had sliced through all of his internal organs.

It wasn't Roz's fault that he'd hoped for something legit to come out of this marriage and ended up disillusioned. It was his. And he had to step into the role she'd cast for him whether he liked the idea of being Rosalind Carpenter's ex-husband or not.

It was fine. He still had a decade-long friendship with Jonas and Warren that wasn't in any danger. That was the place he truly belonged and it was enough. His ridiculous need for something real and legitimate with Roz was nothing but a pipe dream.

They didn't talk about it again, and neither did they settle back into the relationship they'd had for that brief period after the wedding. Hendrix hated the distance, he hated that he was such a chicken, hated that Roz didn't seem overly upset about any of it. He moped around until the weekend, when it all got very real.

While Roz packed up her clothes and personal items, Hendrix elected to be somewhere other than the house. He drove around Raleigh aimlessly and somehow ended up at his mother's curb on Cowper Drive, where she lived in a gorgeous house that he'd helped her select. It was Saturday, so odds were good that she was at some event cutting a ribbon or kissing some babies as she rallied the voters. But he texted her just in case and for the first time in what felt like a long while, fate smiled on him. She was home.

He rang the doorbell. Brookes, the head of his mother's security, answered the door. Hendrix nodded at the man whom he'd personally vetted before allowing him anywhere near Helene. Brookes had checked out in every way. On more than one occasion, Hendrix had wondered if there was something a little more than security going on between Brookes and his mom, but she'd denied it.

Given his reaction when Helene and Roz had lunch, he wouldn't have handled sharing his mother in that respect very well, either. He made a mental note to mention to his mother that he'd recently become aware that he was a selfish crybaby when it came to anyone intruding on his territory, and that maybe she should think about dating anyway despite her son's shortcomings.

"Hey, you," his mother called as she came out of her study wearing a crisp summer suit that had no wrinkles, a feat only someone as stylish as Helene could pull off. "I've got thirty minutes before I have to leave for brunch. Unless you want to be my plus one?"

He shrugged. What else did have to do besides watch the best thing that had ever happened to him walk out of his life? "I could do worse."

Her brows drew together as she contemplated him. "What's wrong, sweetie?"

"Why does something have to be wrong?"

She flicked a subtle hand at Brookes, who vanished into the other room. "Not that I don't enjoy seeing you, but when you come by on a Saturday and start talking about a date with your mother like it's a good thing, I'm concerned. Spill it. Did you have a fight with Roz?"

"No fight." There would have to be a difference of opinion for there to be a fight and he'd agreed with every word she'd said. There was no point to continuing this farce of a marriage. "You said yourself that things were fine with your campaign. You even went out of your way to tell us both that. So what else would be the natural conclusion to a fixer marriage but a fast, no-fault divorce once the problem is fixed?"

Besides, he was pretty sure the black swirl in his gut that wouldn't ease meant he'd been right all along to never have a woman in his bed twice. Better all the way around not to fight Roz on her insistence that it was over. What was he supposed to do, open himself

up for exactly the same kind of rejection that had dev-
astated Marcus?

His friends wouldn't have an ounce of sympathy
for him either, not after he'd violated the pact. Jonas at
least might have had some understanding if Hendrix
had managed to find someone who loved him back like
Jonas had. Warren wouldn't even let him get the first
sentence out and would get started on his own brand of
rejection. Hendrix would be dealing with Roz's evis-
ceration *and* lose his friends.

Thankfully, he hadn't even tried.

His mother cocked her head. "So, what? You're done
with Roz and thought you'd hang out with your mom
for the rest of your life?"

"Sure. What's wrong with that?"

He and his mother were a unit. The real kind. Maybe
not peanut butter and jelly, but better because they'd
been there for each other over the years when neither
of them had anyone else. His mom would never reject him.

Nor did she have a life of her own with someone
great who took care of her. Guilt swamped him as he
wondered if he had something to do with that.

"For a Harris, you're being a moron," she said coolly.
"I told you and Roz that my campaign was fine because
I wanted to take that out of the equation."

"Well, congrats. You did and now we have no reason to be married. What else would you have expected
to be the outcome of that?"

"A marriage, Hendrix. A real one. I didn't come up
with the idea of you marrying Roz *solely* to save my
campaign. It was a great benefit and I genuinely appre-

ciate it. But I want to see you happy. She's it for you, honey. I could see it in the photograph."

"What you saw was chemistry," he countered flatly before the hopeful part inside could latch onto the idea that he'd missed something crucial in this whole messy scenario. "We have it. In spades. But there's nothing else there."

"That's ridiculous. You might have figured out a way to lie to yourself, but I have thirty years of practice in reading you. I saw you two together. I listened to Roz talk about you. There's more."

On *his* side. Sure. Not hers.

"Doesn't matter," he growled. "She's out. She told me straight to my face that it was over. Unless you're suggesting that I should resort to chaining her up in the basement, I have to accept that it's indeed over. I wasn't given a choice."

Clearly exasperated, Helene fisted her hands on her hips and despite the fact that he'd been taller than her since he'd turned seventeen, she managed to tower over him. "So, let me get this straight. You told her that you were in love with her and that you might have married her to fix the scandal, but now you'd like to see what it looks like if you stay married because you want to. And she said 'forget it, I'm out'?"

He shifted uncomfortably. How had his mother conjured up the perfect speech to describe the things in his heart when he couldn't have spit out those words at gunpoint? "Yeah. Basically. Except not quite like that."

Or at all like that. He hadn't given her the opportunity to hear those things because it was better not to lay it all out. Saying that stuff out loud meant Roz could counter it easily. Who wanted that kind of out-right rejection?

"You didn't tell her, did you?" His mother's gentle tone still had plenty of censure in it.

"I don't deal well with rejection," he mumbled.

"Call Channel Five. There's a newsflash for you."

Her sarcasm wasn't lost on him. The fact that he hadn't told Roz meant he *never* had to deal with it. Instead, he was hiding at his mother's house.

He didn't deal well with relationships, either. He'd spent the whole of his life yearning to belong and holding on with a death grip where he did eke out a place. Neither had led to a healthy balance.

"You don't deal well with it because you have no experience with it. Plus it sucks," she told him. "No one wants to stand in line to let another person hand out pain and misery. But sweetie, Roz makes you happy, not miserable. Why don't you want to fight for that?"

"My father..." He swallowed. He hadn't mentioned the bastard in probably fifteen years and he didn't like doing it now, especially as his mother's mouth tight-ened. "He didn't even know me and he rejected me. How much worse would it be if I told Roz that I wanted to stay married and she said no anyway?"

"Let me ask you this. How bad does it hurt now?"

Horrifically bad. Worse than he'd allowed himself to admit. Talking about it wasn't helping. "Pretty much like a constant stomach ache."

She rubbed at his arm in that comforting way that only moms knew how to do. "That's also what it will feel like if she says no. So you'd be no worse off. But if you tell her and she says yes, how much better will that feel? Also, you should remember that your father didn't reject you. He rejected me. You didn't even exist yet, not as a real live person he could look in the face and then say he didn't want. You can't let someone else's mistakes cause you to make mistakes of your own."

"You think letting Roz go is a mistake?" His gut was screaming *yes* at a million and five decibels, drowning out the very excellent points his mother was making.

"The important question is whether you think that. But I wouldn't have encouraged you to marry her if I didn't think she could be much more than a mechanism to fix a problem. I'm shocked you didn't realize that already." His mother's voice broke unexpectedly and he glanced at her to see tears gathering in the corners of her eyes. "Just when you think your kid can't surprise you… You really were doing this whole thing for me, weren't you?"

He scowled. "Of course. Well, at first. You're the only mom I have and you're the greatest. Why wouldn't I do anything you needed from me?"

It hadn't hurt that marrying Roz on a temporary basis gave him the perfect excuse to avoid rejection. Too bad it hadn't worked out that way.

"Good answer." She grinned through her tears and then turned him toward the door with a little push. "Now I need you to go home and tell Roz to stop packing because you have important stuff to tell her. Do that for me and at some point in the future we'll laugh about how you almost really screwed this up."

His spirit lightened so fast that it made his head spin. She made something hard sound so easy. Hendrix took two steps toward the door and then stopped. "What if—"

"What-ifs are for losers who can't carry the name

Harris, sweetie. In other words, not you." She hustled him toward the door in an almost comical one-two shuffle. "I didn't raise a coward and I'm not going to be satisfied until I have grandbabies. So just keep that in mind."

Babies. The same emotions reappeared that had flooded him back at the hospital when he'd had a small suspicion Roz might be sick for reasons that had nothing to do with clowns. That might have been the clincher. He was too far gone to do anything other than take his mother's advice. "More favors? Marriage wasn't enough for you?"

"That's right. And more important, it's not enough for you, either. Chop, chop. I have a brunch to get to."

His mother closed the door behind him and he got all the way to his car before letting loose with the smile he'd been fighting. Helene Harris was one-of-a-kind. And so was his wife. He had to take a chance and tell her how he felt about her, or he'd never forgive himself. This was his best shot at being a part of something that made him happy and he'd given it a pass instead of fighting for it.

Hopefully, Roz was still at home so he could convince her to stay for reasons that had nothing to do with sex and everything to do with a promise of forever.

The moving company Roz had called made short work of transporting the boxes of clothes, shoes and other personal items she'd taken to Hendrix's house. Good thing. She wasn't in any mood to handle logistics right now.

Hendrix had left earlier, probably to go celebrate his forthcoming independence, and the fact that he was gone was good, too. She could leave without an extended goodbye that would likely yank more tears from her depths that she didn't want to lose. The first and second crying jags of the morning had already depleted what small amount of energy she still had after packing the boxes.

What was wrong with her? There had never been a scenario where she wasn't going to lose this marriage. Why was it hitting her so hard? Because she hadn't prepared properly for it to end? Maybe because it had ended so quickly, with almost no protest from the man she'd married, never mind that she'd stupidly begun to hope things might turn out differently.

That was the problem. She'd fallen into this bit of wonderful she'd found with Hendrix and forgotten it would soon vanish like so many other things in her life.

The moving truck pulled away from the front of Hendrix's Oakwood home and there was nothing left for Roz to do except follow it to her loft. Except she couldn't force herself to pull into the parking garage. She kept driving. The moving company had preauthorization with her building security and they were professionals who didn't need a neurotic, weepy woman supervising them.

Clown-Around could always use more attention. The boost Helene had given the organization surpassed Roz's wildest dreams. Becoming a Harris had launched her into a place that being a Carpenter had never touched. In more ways than one. The thought of how often she'd been *touched* as a Harris depressed her thoroughly.

The paperwork on her desk held zero appeal. She scouted around her tiny office for something else to do, finally landing in the supply closet. It could use organizing. All of the clown makeup and props had fallen into disarray after Helene had stopped by, and frankly, the last thing Roz had wanted to do was surround herself with the trappings that still held so many horrible memories.

But she was already so out of sorts that for once, the wigs lining overhead shelves and the multicolored outfits on hangers at her back didn't bother her. They were just costumes. Easily donned and easily taken off. She grabbed one of the wigs and stuck it on her head.

See? Easy. Not scary. Just some fake curly hair in an outrageous color.

All at once, she sank to the ground and put her face in her hands as the sheer weight of everything overwhelmed her.

Clowns hadn't taken her mother from her. Cancer had. For that matter, no one in a red nose had forced her father to stop caring about her—unless she was doing something he disapproved of, which he cared about plenty. Floppy shoes had done nothing to get her in trouble or bring down society's censure over a racy photograph. She'd done all of that on her own.

Clowns weren't the problem. She was. She'd assigned so much blame to the crappy hand fate had dealt her as a child that she'd practically let it ruin her life. It was only because luck had handed her Hendrix Harris on a silver platter that anything good had happened.

She didn't want that to be over. She didn't want to live each day scared to death to assign importance to the man she'd married. Most of all, she wanted to know what it felt like to know she could wake up each day next to someone who got her. Someone who loved her.

She'd been so busy looking for the hammer about to drop on her happiness that she hadn't considered the possibility that there was no hammer. Hendrix had even said they could put off the divorce, yet she'd let herself become convinced it was better to get it over with rather than see what might happen if she stopped assuming the worst. Maybe they could have tried being married for a few more weeks and let things develop. Go a little deeper.

If only Hendrix was here, she'd tell him that's what she wanted before she lost her nerve.

A chime sounded at the front door as someone pushed it open. Great. She'd forgotten to lock it again. She had to get better at remembering that or else move her offices to a more secure location. Anyone could wander in off the street.

But when she popped out of the closet, cell phone in hand in case she needed to dial 911, the nerves in her fingers went completely numb. The phone slipped from her grip and clattered to the parquet flooring.

As if she'd conjured him, Hendrix stood just inside the door, as gorgeous in a pair of jeans and a T-shirt as he was out of them. Because he had the same smile on his face regardless, the one that he was aiming at her now. The same one that had flushed through her on that dance floor at the Calypso Room a million years ago when she'd first caught sight of him.

"Hendrix Harris," she'd murmured then. And now apparently, as she realized she'd spoken out loud.

"Rosalind Harris," he returned easily, which was not even close to what he'd said to her that night in Vegas but almost made her swoon in a similar fashion. "I like what you've done with your hair."

Her fingers flew to her head and met the clown wig. Oh, God. She started to pull it off and then defiantly dropped her hand. "I'm practicing."

"To be a clown?"

She shook her head. "Facing down my shortcomings. How did you know I was here?"

Which was only the first of a whole slew of other questions, ones that she couldn't seem to get out around the lump in her throat. Hendrix was so close that she could reach out and touch him. She almost did. But she'd given up that right because she was an idiot, clearly.

"I didn't. I went to your loft first but the moving guys said they hadn't seen you. So it was worth a shot to come here. I saw your car outside."

"You were looking for me? That's funny. I…" *Need to tell you some things*. But she had no idea how to take the first step. When she'd wished he was here so she could say what was in her heart, she hadn't actually thought that would happen. He was so beautiful and smelled so delicious and familiar that her muscles had frozen. "You could have called."

"I wasn't sure what I was going to say. I, um, drove around a lot so I could practice." His smile reappeared. "I guess we're both doing that today."

Oddly, the fact that he seemed nervous and unable to figure out how to navigate either melted her heart. And gave her the slimmest glimmer of insight that maybe she'd been completely wrong about everything. "Were you practicing something like, 'watching my mom at the hospital made me realize I have a lifelong dream to be a clown'? Because that can be arranged."

Instead of laughing or throwing out a joke of his

own, he feathered a thumb across her cheek. "More like I messed up and let you pack all your stuff so you could leave me, when that's not what I want."

Her whole body froze. Except for her heart. That was beating a mile a minute as something bright fluttered through it. "It's not?"

He shook his head once, never letting go of her gaze. "You're my peanut butter *and* my jelly. Without you, I've got two useless pieces of bread that taste like sawdust. I want a chance to see what kind of marriage we can have without all the extra baggage. I mean, not to put too much pressure on you all at once." He hesitated, looking so miserable that she feared he would stop saying these beautiful things. "I'm trying to say that I want—"

"I love you," she blurted out. Oh, God. What was wrong with her that she couldn't stop behaving like a dimwit when it came to this man? "Not that *I'm* trying to put pressure on *you*—"

"I love you, too," he broke in and she was pretty sure the dazed look on his face was reflected on her own. "I'm changing my answer."

"Because you're a dimwit, too?" Maybe she should stop talking. "I mean, I'm a dimwit. Not you. I was scared that I was going to lose you—"

"No, you're right," he agreed readily. "I'm a complete and total dimwit. I have a problem with rejection so I try really hard to avoid it."

"I wasn't— I mean, I would never reject..." Except for when she'd told him she couldn't stay. She should have stayed. What if he'd never come looking for her? She would have missed out on the best thing that had ever happened to her. "I messed up, too. A lot. I should have told you I was falling for you and that I didn't want a divorce."

Something tender filtered through his gaze. "Funny, that's exactly what I practiced saying to you in the car as I drove around the whole of Raleigh. You stole my line."

"So that's it then? I don't want a divorce, you don't want a divorce. We love each other and we're staying married?" It sounded too good to be true, like a situation ripe for being ripped from her hands. Her pulse wobbled. This was the part where she had to calm down and face her fears like an adult who could handle her life. "I have a hard time trusting that all good things aren't about to come to an instant end."

She swallowed the rest, wishing he'd run true to form and interrupt her with his own revelations. But that didn't happen. He did hold out his hand and when she clasped it, the way he squeezed back was better than any time he'd ever touched her, bar none. Because it was encouraging, accepting. A show of solidarity. *I'm here and I'm not going anywhere*, he said without saying a word.

That loosened her tongue fast. A multitude of emotions poured out as she explained how clowns and cancer and rebellion and marriage had all tumbled together in her head. How she wasn't afraid any longer. She wrapped it up by pointing to the wig. "I'm inside my fears. Blasting them apart where they live. You gave me that. That, along with about a million other reasons, is why I can tell you I love you."

Sure, she still didn't want to lose him but she had absolute faith that if that ever did happen—regardless of the reason—she'd find a way to be okay.

"My turn." Hendrix reached up and plucked the wig off of her head, then plopped it onto his own. "This is the approved method to work through all this stuff, right?"

She nodded as the tears spilled over. "You look like a dork."

He just grinned and patted his red curly hair. "I look like a man who has finally figured out the key to dealing with the idiotic crap running through his head. I almost gave you up without a fight because I was convinced you were going to say thanks but no thanks if I brought up the things I was feeling. Color me shocked that you beat me to it."

"Not sorry."

"I'm just going to insist that you let me say 'I love you' first from now on."

"That's a much better marriage deal than the first one you offered me. I accept." Roz fished her wedding rings from her pocket and handed them to him solemnly. "As long as we both shall live?"

He better. She wasn't a serial wife. This was forever and she knew beyond a shadow of a doubt that she'd love him until the day she died.

He slid the cool bands onto her third finger and it was a thousand times more meaningful than the actual wedding ceremony. "I do."

Epilogue

Jonas and Warren were already seated in the corner booth when Hendrix arrived—late, because his wife had been very unwilling to let him out of the shower.

"This seems familiar," he joked as he slid into the seat next to Jonas and raised his brows at Warren. "Down to you being buried in your phone."

Warren glanced up from the lit screen and then immediately back down. "I like my job. I won't apologize for it."

"I like my job too but I like conversing with real people, as well," Hendrix shot back mildly, well aware that he was stalling. "Maybe you could try it?"

With a sigh, Warren laid his precious link to Flying Squirrel, his energy drink company, facedown on the table. "I'm dealing with a crap-ton of issues that have no solution, but okay. Let's talk about the Blue Devils why don't we? Or maybe the Hornets? What's the topic du jour, guys?"

Hendrix picked up his beer and set it back down again. There was no easy way to do this, so he just ripped the Band-Aid off. "I'm not divorcing Roz."

A thundercloud drifted over Warren's face as Jonas started laughing.

"I knew it." Warren put his head in his hands with a moan. "You fell in love with her, didn't you?"

"It's not that big of a deal." Hendrix scowled at his friend, knowing full well that it was a big deal to him. "Jonas did it, too."

Warren drained his beer, his mouth tight against the glass as his throat worked. He put the glass down with a *thunk*. "And both of you are really stretching my forgiveness gene."

"It was a shock to me too, if that helps."

"It doesn't."

Jonas put a comforting hand on Warren's arm. "It's okay, you'll find yourself in this same situation and see how hard it is to fight what you're feeling."

"I'll never go against the pact," Warren countered fiercely, his voice rising above the thumping music and happy hour crowd. "There were—are—reasons we made that pact. You guys are completely dishonoring Marcus's memory."

Marcus had been a coward. Hendrix had only recently begun to reframe his thoughts on the matter, but after seeing a coward's face in the mirror for the length of time it had taken for him to figure out that love wasn't the problem, he knew a little better what cowardice looked like. "Maybe we should talk about those reasons."

Instead of agreeing like a rational person might, Warren slid from the booth and dropped his phone into his pocket. "I can't do this now."

Hendrix and Jonas watched him stride from the bar like the hounds of hell were nipping at his heels. Dealing with rejection did suck, no two ways about it. But he was getting better at it because he wasn't a coward, not any longer. He was a Harris through and through, every bit his mother's child. Helene had raised him with her own special blend of Southern grit and he'd turned out okay despite never knowing his father. He was done letting that disappointment drive him to make mistakes.

"Welcome to the club." Solemnly, Jonas clinked his glass to Hendrix's and they drank to their respective marriages that had both turned out to be love matches in spite of their bone-headedness.

"Thanks. I hate to say it, but being a member of that club means I really don't want to sit around in a bar with you when I could be at home with my wife."

Jonas grinned. "As I agree with the sentiment, you can say it twice."

Hendrix made it to his house in Oakwood in record time. Their house. His and Roz's. She'd moved back in and put her loft up for sale even though he'd told her at least four times that he'd move in with her. His Oakwood place was a legitimate house but wherever Roz was made it home.

He found her in the bedroom, spread across the bed. Naked.

"Thought you'd never get here," she murmured throatily. "I was about to send you a selfie to hurry you along."

"So our next scandal can be a phone-hack leak of our personal photo album?" His clothes hit the floor in under thirty seconds.

"No more scandals. We're a respectable married couple, remember?" Roz squealed as he flipped her over on the bed and crawled up the length of her back.

"Only in public. Behind closed doors, all bets are off."

She shuddered under his tongue and arched in pleasure. "See what you've done to me? I'm a total sex addict, thanks to you. Before we got married, I was in the running for most pious fiancée alive."

"Not sorry." As much as he enjoyed Roz's back, he liked her front a lot better. That's where her eyes were and he'd discovered a wealth of intimacy in them when they made love, an act which he planned to repeat a million more times. He rolled her in his arms and sank into her.

She was his favorite part of being married.

* * * * *

She was a professional. On duty.

She didn't have time to picture running her fingers through that messy hair of his. Or…or… Her gaze rose from his mouth, quirking up at the corners as it was, to meet his eyes. They really were the soft blue of a star sapphire. She curled her fingers against her belt. Would the stubble on his face be rough or as soft as his hair looked?

"Darlin', you really shouldn't look at a man that way." His gruff voice was both a caress and a wake-up call.

Quin barely controlled a full-body shudder. She needed to think of ice baths and blizzards. Snow and ski slopes. High mountain air. Invigorating. Not warm. Not sexy. She took that step back, both physically and mentally. He laughed and the sound was dark and warm like fudge brownies just out of the oven. Her mouth watered.

Coffee. She needed coffee. And fresh air. Like right this minute.

THE COWBOY'S
CHRISTMAS
PROPOSITION

BY
SILVER JAMES

First Published in Great Britain 2017
By Mills & Boon, an imprint of HarperCollins*Publishers*
1 London Bridge Street, London, SE1 9GF

© 2017 Silver James

ISBN: 978-0-263-92840-2

51-1017

Our policy is to use papers that are natural, renewable and recyclable products and made from wood grown in sustainable forests. The logging and manufacturing processes conform to the legal environmental regulations of the country of origin.

Printed and bound in Spain
by CPI, Barcelona

Silver James likes walks on the wild side and coffee. Okay. She LOVES coffee. A cowgirl at heart, she's been an army officer's wife and mum, and worked in the legal field, fire service and law enforcement. Now retired from the real world, she lives in Oklahoma, spending her days writing with the assistance of two Newfoundlands, the cat who rules them all and the characters living in her imagination.

As always, thanks to my family for putting up with the craziness when I'm on deadline—and that includes my wonderful Harlequin Desire team, Charles, Stacy and Tahra, plus all the amazing Harlequin folks. And a special thanks to a special reader, Anita Bartlett, for our discussion of brothers from a sister's point of view.

One

Deacon Tate was a country boy at heart. He loved life on his Oklahoma ranch—driving the tractor, singing to the cows, riding his horse and stopping to watch the setting sun wash a blaze of colors across the red dirt of home. He would sit on his front porch as twilight softened the landscape, strumming his guitar while waiting for the fireflies to come out to play. He was also a free spirit. He loved life on the road, living on the tour bus, appearing in a different city every night. He fed off the energy of the crowd, absorbing their excitement through his skin by osmosis.

Performing live was in his blood, but he was ready for some downtime in his Red, White and Cool tour. The Sons of Nashville's manager had purposely scheduled this leg of the tour close to home. After tonight's performance at the Thunder River Casino just outside of Oklahoma City, the band would take off the week before Thanksgiving and Deke would be heading home to his ranch. Then the Friday after, they had a concert at the BOK Center in Tulsa.

They were done for a month after that. The break couldn't come soon enough.

He sang into the microphone, but his eyes were on the female fans lining the front of the stage trying to get his attention. He flirted with them with winks, and by appearing to sing directly to one or another. He loved women. All women. And he'd only been exclusive once.

The lights dimmed, a stool appeared on stage and he picked up his acoustic guitar and sat down. One blue spotlight picked him out. Head down, he strummed a few chords. The cheers and whistles slowly faded as he played. The chords gave way to the melody he plucked on the strings. The band remained silent, unsure of where he was going. Performing this song was totally unplanned. He'd written it for his cousin Cash's wedding but hadn't recorded it.

Deke's little brother, who was also the keyboardist for the Sons, was the first to recognize the song. After Dillon's piano riff, their guitarists, Bryce and Xander, picked up the tune and Kenji, the drummer, found the rhythm. Ozzie picked up the bass line without missing a beat.

"Are you ready to take a walk?" he crooned into the microphone. "Darlin', are you ready for me?" The crowd started to sway in time to the music and the groupies lining the stage pressed forward. Deke closed his eyes. "Are you counting the minutes? Can you feel my heart race?" He riffed on the guitar. "From this day forward, you'll never walk alone. I'll shelter your heart. I'll be your home. You are my love song, my forever song, the last song that I'll sing."

He poured out the rest of the words, his voice growing husky with emotion. Deke had watched each of his cousins find and fall in love with the women who completed them. Something inside him wanted the same thing, in a vague someday way. But none of his brothers had taken the plunge and there was something wrong with that picture. The Barrons were the wild bunch, the Tates the steady gatekeepers. Well, except for him. His mother said often and loudly that he was more Barron than Tate, but her eyes twinkled when she said it.

Deke sang of finding love, of losing it. He sang of getting it back and when he sang the chorus again, the women in the front row had faces slick with tears. His voice broke a little as he finished the last few lines and added, "You'll be my home, my love song, my forever song and the last song I ever sing."

The spotlight went out. Stunned silence filled the theater, where 2,500 fans were jammed in wall-to-wall. Then pandemonium erupted. Strobes flashed and spotlights probed the stage, but Deacon had disappeared. People screamed and whistled. They clapped their hands and stomped their feet. When the band launched into the opening strains of "Native Son," the noise volume doubled. Normally, this song was the finale but tonight, it was the encore.

When it was over, Deke and the band retreated backstage to the dressing rooms. The party had already started. Local radio personalities filtered in, some with contest winners tagging along. A few VIPs—politicians and business leaders—crowded around, congratulating him before moving along to the free bar and buffet. A low-level headache throbbed behind his eyes, and Deke only wanted to get on his bus and go home.

A loud squeal caught his attention and he looked up just in time to catch an armful of curves and red hair. Lips smacked his cheek. "You sang our song!" Roxanne Barron screamed.

Deke winced and was thankful when his cousin Cash peeled his wife away. He was surrounded now by family. His brothers, Cooper and Bridger, were harassing Dillon, the baby Tate. Cash was doing his best to contain Roxie, while his other cousins and their spouses, Chance and Cassidy, along with Cord and Jolie, laughed.

"You totally have to record that song, Deke," Cassidy said. "And have Jolie and I mentioned that we're totally PO'd you didn't write songs for our weddings?"

He ducked his head, slightly embarrassed. He'd been on the road and missed both Chance's and Cord's weddings though he'd played a cover song at their brother Clay's. Forcing his headache away, he listened to his cousins and their wives chatter and his brothers tease Dillon. This was family and he loved his.

There was life and love here. Sound and confusion. Friendship and flirting. Deke wasn't quite so ready to go home now, knowing his house was empty. There'd be no lights on, unless someone had gone by. He had a ranch foreman who lived on the property, keeping an eye on things when Deke was on the road or recording in Nashville, but he doubted the man would think of switching on lights.

The party finally wrapped up and those who lingered spilled into the parking lot. The band would ride the tour bus to Oklahoma City. Those who lived in Nashville had reservations at the Barron Hotel. They'd sleep during what was left of the night and fly home later in the day.

The roadies would break down the sets, instruments and sound systems, and leave the semitrucks and trailers in the secured storage yard where the local guys stored their vehicles during tours. That was where Deacon had left his pickup. He was ready to get home, even if the place would be dark and silent when he arrived.

"Mr. Tate!" The agitated yell disrupted his reverie; he and his three brothers all looked up. "Deacon!" The tour bus driver, Max, clarified. He was all but jumping up and down, alternating between waving and wringing his hands.

"Maxie? What's going on?"

"I didn't know what to do, Mr. T. I called the police and I was gettin' ready to come inside to get you but I couldn't leave it."

"Calm down, Max. Police? Why would you—" Deke's question was interrupted by a loud wail.

The driver pointed at a basket perched on the curving steps leading into the bus. "That's why, Mr. T. I found a baby."

Quincy Kincaid carefully sipped the hot coffee in her to-go cup. Five more hours until her shift change at 7:00 a.m. Her night had been quiet so far. A few speeders. Backing up a Cleveland County deputy on a domestic. She checked the dash clock on her Highway Patrol cruiser. Four hours, fifty-five minutes. And then she was off for three days before her next set of duty days, putting her that much closer to her vacation. Seventeen days, most of them spent far away from everyone. And one more item marked off her bucket list.

Aspen, Colorado, and Rocky Mountain high country, here she came. She'd saved up vacation time and money for this trip since she'd graduated from the Oklahoma Highway Patrol academy five years before. Five-star hotel. Beautiful scenery. Learning to ski. And Christmas far away from her family. She wasn't a Scrooge. Christmas was okay. It was her family that drove her batty.

Another sip of coffee, and she discovered it was cool enough to drink without caution but still hot enough to be satisfying. Thunder River Truck Stop always had fresh coffee, no matter the time of day or night. She gazed toward the bright splash of LED lights just over a mile down the road. The casino, like the truck stop, was a 24-7-365 operation. She'd set up here earlier and had caught some speeders leaving the concert. Deacon Tate and the Sons of Nashville. The concert had sold out and she'd been lucky not to get roped into extra security duty at the casino. That had gone to the off-duty guys who wanted to pick up extra money for Christmas.

The only present she was buying this Christmas was for herself—the trip to Aspen, to stay in that five-star hotel through the holidays. No family—not that hers really cared. No responsibilities and woo-hoo for that. Just snow and pine trees and mountains and, if she was lucky, a hot guy to share drinks with while sitting in front of a roaring fire. Quin rolled her head on her neck and eased the tightness in her shoulders. Only four hours and forty—

"Adam-109." The dispatcher's voice crackled from her radio.

"Adam-109."

"Respond to Thunder River Casino. In the parking lot. Report of a found infant."

She opened her mouth to respond when the import of the message filtered through her brain. "Say again, Dispatch."

"Report of a found infant, Adam-109. Look for the Sons of Nashville tour bus."

"Ten-four."

Seriously? A found baby? Who loses their baby? *Oh, wait*, she thought sarcastically. She was headed to a casino. People addicted to gambling did dumb things. Like losing their kids. Still, what did the band's bus have to do with the situation? Good thing she was less than five minutes away. She'd be able to satisfy her curiosity quickly. Unable to resist, she hit her overhead emergency lights but without sirens. Traffic stopped on the highway to let her exit the truck stop and she gunned her engine.

The tour bus wasn't hard to miss. It was one of those

custom motor coaches that cost more than most people's houses. Why people would call such a lavish vehicle a bus was beyond her comprehension. She'd worked event security a few times. Spoiled musicians and Hollywood people just irritated her.

She rolled up on the scene and notified Dispatch. Settling her Smokey Bear hat on her head, she stepped out of her cruiser, adjusted her weapons belt on her hips and strode toward the knot of people gathered around the open door of the motor coach.

A dark-haired woman was arguing with a tall man dressed like a cowboy holding a bundle in his arms. As Quin walked up, she overheard him say, "Forget it, Jolie. You can't have her."

Quin sighed. Was she walking into another domestic, only without backup this time?

"I just want to hold her," the woman pleaded. "You let Cassie hold her. Besides, I'm a nurse. I should check her, make sure she's okay." The woman peered down at the bundle and cooed.

Someone dramatically cleared his throat and the entire group turned to look at Quin. She inhaled, set a stern expression on her face and trudged toward them. "I'm Trooper Kincaid," she announced. "What's going on here?"

Everyone started talking at once. Quin's piercing whistle silenced them—all except the baby, who was now crying. The guy holding the infant shifted positions, patting its back as he sort of did this dip-and-sway thing with the kid on his shoulder. The wails turned to little sobs and after a hiccup, the baby cooed, settling its head against the cowboy's chest.

"I'm Deacon Tate," the cowboy explained.

Of course he was. Quin would have banged her head against the side of the bus if she'd been standing close enough. "Is that your baby, Mr. Tate?"

"Not exactly."

"Care to explain?"

"Someone left her on my bus."

"There was a note," a beautiful blonde added helpfully.

"And Max found her," a redhead explained.

An older man wearing a plaid flannel shirt covering a paunch that hung over his belt buckle offered a little wave. "I drive the bus," he explained.

Quin closed her eyes. She hadn't had enough caffeine to deal with groupies and good-ol'-boy bus drivers, much less stars too handsome for her taste. When she opened her eyes, no one had moved. She pointed at the driver as she pulled out a notebook and pen. "You. Tell me your full name and what happened?"

"Max, ma'am. Max Padilla. After the concerts, I hang around backstage until the after-party starts to break up. Then I come out and warm up the bus. It's a diesel so it runs rough on cold nights if I don't. Plus, I like to get the heat goin' in the back so the guys are warm, you know?"

Holding on to her patience, Quin prompted, "The baby?"

"Well, yeah. I was gettin' to that. So anyway, I came out to start the bus and there was the usual stuff stacked up around the door."

"The usual stuff?"

"Yeah. Flowers and…" The man stared at his boots. Was he blushing? "And stuff that girls—fans—leave for Deacon and the boys."

"Stuff. What kind of stuff?"

A guy who looked Asian leaned forward. "We get love notes and T-shirts and—"

"Bras and panties," a younger version of Deacon Tate explained.

Why her? She was so close to end of shift. Quin made a pointed notation in her book: *Stuff!* She looked up, pretending Deacon didn't steal her breath. "And?"

When Deacon's younger clone opened his mouth, Deacon himself cut him off. "Shut up, Dillon. There was a basket tucked in with all the stuff." He glanced through the bus doors, and Quin noticed a wicker basket for the first time. "Little Noelle here was inside all bundled up in blankets with her diaper bag."

"You know her name?"

Another man, just as handsome as Deacon but with darker hair and eyes—because she'd just realized Deacon's were blue—stepped closer, an envelope in his hand, and introduced himself. "I'm Chance Barron."

That was a name she was familiar with. The Barron family attorney. Just jolly. Her night kept getting better and better. "And you are here why, Mr. Barron?"

"Deacon is my cousin. My wife, Cassie, and I were here for the concert."

"I'm Jolie Barron," the brunette added. "I'm an RN and I can check her over if my big goof of a cousin-in-law will give me a chance to hold her."

So these were *not* groupies. Quin studied everyone in the group of people standing around. Tates and Barrons were easy to categorize. That left the motley crew likely making up Deacon's band the Sons of Nashville. *Yippee.* She wondered if she could call this in and let Cleveland County handle it. As she mulled over that idea, another police vehicle rolled to a stop next to her cruiser. Chickasaw Tribal Police. The casino and surrounding area were technically tribal land. Maybe she'd just let them have it.

"The note that came in the basket states the child's name is Noelle and that she belongs to Deacon," Chance continued as the tribal cops approached.

She took the proffered piece of paper and read it before handing it to the nearest tribal officer. Quin arched a brow at the country music superstar. "How often does your…" She didn't want to say "baby momma." Considering who she was dealing with, she had to proceed cautiously. "Has this happened before? Your child being dropped off like this?"

"No." Deacon's voice was one step above a growl. The baby fussed and he automatically soothed her. "I'm not irresponsible, Trooper Kincaid. I don't have any children." He paused, then added, "That I know of."

Quin glanced at the Chickasaw officers and one shrugged. "Unless she's Indian, we don't have jurisdiction. You're state. Up to you to place her with DHS."

The Department of Human Services—the foster care system. Quin knew what that was like. She'd been in the system as a kid. She was reluctant to sentence a baby to Child Protective Services but she didn't have much choice. She keyed the portable radio mic clipped to her shoulder. "Adam-109, Dispatch. Notify DHS of an emergency pickup notice for an infant, my location."

Dispatch's response was drowned out by loud objections from the Tates and Barrons. One voice rose above all the rest.

"DHS can't have her. According to the note, she's mine."

Two

What the heck was he thinking? Deke *knew* this baby wasn't his. Or was she? He took precautions, though there was always a chance something might go wrong. Without knowing who the baby's mother was, he wouldn't be able to say for sure one way or the other. If he had any sense at all, he would hand her off to the female trooper—and why had he never noticed how sexy a woman in uniform could be? This one nipped at him like one of those yappy little ankle-biter dogs. He glanced at her, assessing the expression on her face. Okay, make that a Doberman.

Noelle cooed and rubbed her cheek against his shoulder. He always had been a sucker for little kids and the idea of this one going to strangers… He halted that thought because, okay, *he* was a stranger. But he wasn't. Her mother had claimed he was the father and left the baby's basket outside his bus for a reason.

Fatherhood. The idea was like that charity ice-bucket

challenge—chilling but with warm fuzzies underneath for doing something good.

Hadn't he spent the last hour contemplating family then going home to an empty house? A baby would complicate things but if Noelle *was* his, he'd step up and take care of her. Katherine Tate hadn't raised her boys to shuck their responsibilities. He might be full-grown but his mom would take a strip out of his hide if he didn't do the right thing.

Noelle cooed and his heart did a funny little lurch in his chest. The idea of being her father didn't seem quite so alien now. He tested the word *dad* in his head. It didn't freak him out—and it probably should have.

He glanced toward Chance, who shifted position so the trooper couldn't see Deke. His cousin mouthed the words, *Are you sure you want the baby?* Deke stared into Chance's eyes and nodded. Chance moved away from the group, phone pressed to his ear. Man, but it was nice to have a hotshot attorney right there. Things settled in his chest and he liked the feeling. He'd always wanted to be a dad, but at some nebulous point in the future. Maybe this was fate's way of telling him the time was now. Taking on the care and feeding of baby Noelle was the right thing to do. Yeah, this was the right thing for him to do.

"Have you thought this through, Mr. Tate?" The cop was still glaring at him through narrowed eyes.

"I have, Trooper Kincaid." He offered her the smile where his dimple peeked out. "Do you have a first name?"

"Yes. How are you going to take care of her?"

"What is it?" He'd like to take care of the trooper, for sure. The more he studied her, from her brown felt Smokey Bear hat to her shiny black roper boots, the more he felt that way.

"Are you avoiding my question, Mr. Tate?"

"No. What's your name?"

"Persistent, aren't you?"

"I am when I'm after something I want."

She blinked a few times as she tucked her chin in and leaned away. He'd surprised her. Her light-colored eyes narrowed and her generous mouth thinned out as she pressed her lips together in a disapproving sneer.

"I told you my name. It's Trooper Kincaid."

"I'm Deacon, Troop, but my friends call me Deke."

"I'm not your friend, Mr. Tate."

"But you could be."

She glanced around as if suddenly realizing they had an audience. He liked that he'd put her off balance. She hit him with a steely-eyed, no-nonsense glare. Deke was enjoying teasing her far too much.

"Mr. Tate. Please hand over—" Noelle wailed and the trooper looked panicked.

Deke patted the baby's bottom. Yup. The kid was wet. "I do believe she needs a diaper change." He turned for the bus.

Jolie stepped forward wearing what he called her stern-mother face. "I'll take the baby inside to change her."

As a guy, Deke should have turned over the task automatically, but he suddenly found himself oddly protective and…possessive of the baby. "I'm perfectly capable of changing a wet diaper, Jolie. Not the first time I've done it." He glanced at Cash and Dillon. "You two certainly gave me enough practice when I got stuck with babysitting duty."

Before Jolie—or anyone else—could argue, Deke snagged the basket, which still held the diaper bag, and climbed the curving stairs into the main living space of the coach. There were two captain chairs—one for the driver, the other for a copilot—just beyond the door.

Inside, leather couches the color of pewter flanked an eating area with a table and two benches next to the kitchenette. The walls were tiger-eye maple. The counters and tables were topped in granite veined with a handful of colors ranging from black to rusty pink to white. Deke dropped the basket and bag on the couch next to the table.

He heard someone clomping up the steps behind him. Without turning around, he knew who had followed him. "Have a seat, Troop. I'll be right back." He paused before heading to the back of the bus, again giving her the once-over. Her tan slacks were tailored to fit and not even the bulletproof vest beneath the dark brown uniform shirt could contain her curves. She'd slicked back her hair under the Smokey Bear hat and he couldn't tell the color, but thought it was blond or light brown. He really wanted to see the color of her eyes but the hat brim kept them shaded.

Trooper Kincaid wasn't the type of woman who usually caught his attention. Groupies knew the rules, played the game. Maybe he was intrigued because she was something different. Her stern authority didn't fit in his world, but there was some undefined *something* that drew him. He'd have to think about why later. First things first.

"Dig around in the bag for wipes, a fresh diaper and something to change her into, will ya? This onesie is wet now."

"This onesie is wet now?" Quin muttered as she bent over the couch and opened the diaper bag. "How does the man even know what a onesie is?" By the time he got back with several towels to pad the table, she'd found the items he requested. She noticed the wet spot on his chest. That explained the need for a clothing change but she was still mystified as to how he knew what the garment was called. She watched as he got to work, fascinated despite her best intentions.

This guy had *bad boy* written all over him. Now that she could see him in decent lighting, his sheer male magnetism hit her like a tackle from a Dallas Cowboys linebacker. He was undeniably handsome, with thick brown hair that fell around his high cheekbones and sculpted jaw. Five-o'clock shadow added a rugged layer to his face. Wide-set blue eyes held a twinkle that reminded her of a star-sapphire ring she once had. His black Western shirt and leather jeans fit him far too thoroughly for the welfare of the general female population. Herself included.

His fingers were long and dexterous, as would befit a guitarist, and he deftly changed the baby's diaper and clothing. He wore a leather thong around his neck and Noelle snagged it in one chubby hand. Deacon laughed and cooed at her, like he did this all the time. For all Quin knew, he might.

She tried to sift a bio for him out of her crowded brain. Not that she was a big watcher of entertainment gossip shows. Still, Barrons and Tates were often covered in the local news, but she couldn't recall hearing that he was married—or ever had been.

"Did you find any bottles in the bag? Or a can of formula or something?"

Lost in her musings, she startled at the sound of his voice. Luckily, he was still concentrating on the baby so he hadn't noticed she'd been staring at his butt this whole time. "Oh, yes. There are a couple of full bottles. Not sure what's in them."

He glanced her way, and that killer smile with a side of dimple guaranteed to dampen groupies' panties appeared. Quin refused to let it work on her. Much. She curled her fingers against her palms because they itched to push his hair back off his face and then tangle in the thick waves. His gaze focused on her mouth and she couldn't stop her quick inhalation, nor could she keep her chest from swelling and pushing against the rigid bulk of her bulletproof vest. This man was lethal and she needed to remember that.

He held out his hand and she passed one of the bottles to him. Deacon twisted off the lid, sniffed and then dipped his finger in to taste, which was such a guy thing to do. "Formula. I think. Let's pop it in the microwave for about fifteen seconds. We don't want it too hot." He caught her gaze on him, and the stars in his sapphire eyes blazed. "The formula, that is."

Quin just managed to avoid rolling her eyes. She wasn't some teenage fangirl fawning over the magnificent Deacon Tate. She retrieved the bottle from him and dumped it in the sink. "I'll make fresh." She snagged a can with a baby on the label and read the instructions. She pretended the whole time that her fingers hadn't tingled when they touched his skin. That her nose hadn't gotten a whiff of clean sweat and a scent deeper and more primal when she handed the bottle back to him. He settled on the couch.

Opting for discretion over valor because her body was fomenting mutiny, she retreated across the bus and sat on the matching couch to watch. She still couldn't get over how proficiently this guy handled the baby.

"You said you don't have kids?" she finally asked, removing her hat.

His gaze was sharp as he looked up. "Kinda hard to have kids without a wife."

That didn't stop a lot of celebrities but she didn't point that out. "Then how are you so good with the baby?"

He paused to burp the infant then cuddled her back in one arm with the bottle in her mouth. Quin attempted to read the expression on Deacon's face. She found a sweetness there that was almost as surprising as his competence.

"Only child?"

"Excuse me?"

"Not a hard question, Troop."

"Stop calling me that."

"Then tell me your first name."

Quin refused to throw her hands up in a fit of frustration. "Fine. Not that it's any of your business, but it's Quincy."

"Did you hear that, Noelle? Her name is Quincy."

The baby cooed, and Quin discovered she was grinning rather stupidly. She wiped that expression off her face and leaned forward so she could breathe a little easier in her vest. "And to answer your question, I'm not an only child. I have four older brothers."

Deacon peeked up at her from under lashes far too long and lush for a man exuding as much testosterone as this one did. "Ah, the baby in the family. I'm the middle and got stuck with baby duty, especially with Dillon. He was a late surprise for Mom and Dad."

She glanced out the tinted window behind her. "Dillon is in your band?"

"Yup."

"Was he serious?"

"About what?"

"The...*stuff*?" She wanted to bite her tongue. She didn't care if overenthusiastic fans embarrassed themselves by leaving underwear in tribute to the band. Nor did she care if maybe some of the owners of said lingerie ended up in the bedroom or one of the curtained bunks she could see when she glanced toward the back of the bus.

He laughed and set the bottle on the table. Shifting the baby to his shoulder, he patted her back until she burped again. Deacon checked her diaper, settled her back in the crook of his arm and gazed at Quin. "Yeah, he was serious. We get stuff like that thrown on stage sometimes, too. Goes with the gig."

She couldn't decide if he was being this nonchalant because he was so egotistical that he figured the thongs and *stuff* were his due or because he didn't care. Time was passing and Quin needed to get things wrapped up. "Is she really yours?"

"Who?"

"The baby," she said pointedly.

He studied her face and she flushed for no reason she understood. He broke their staring match first by peering down at the sleeping infant. That soft expression washed over his features again, and she wondered where the feelings came from. Maybe Noelle really was his. Her chest burned at the thought, and she didn't quite know how to handle the feeling. To cover it up, she asked again, "Is the baby yours, Mr. Tate?"

Before he answered her question, the sound of booted feet stomping up the steps drew their attention to the front of the bus. Chance Barron's gaze bounced between her and Deacon before he announced, "She is until you find her mother, Trooper Kincaid, and we clear things up."

Three

Deke didn't know whether to high-five his cousin or panic. Was his ego overriding his common sense on the outside chance Noelle was his? Babies were hard. He knew that, but while he didn't quite understand his attraction to the gruff cop, he was adamant about keeping the baby close until he knew definitively who the father was. Noelle was a cute little thing and deserved something more than becoming a ward of the state.

So yeah, he'd score this one for the good guys. Not that Quincy Kincaid was a bad guy. She wasn't a *guy* in any way, shape or form. She'd pushed to her feet when Chance came in. With her back to Deke, he could tell the hair twisted into a tight knot at the base of her neck was blond.

His blood warmed. There was something about the nape of a woman's neck that really stirred him up. Some men liked breasts, some a sweetly rounded butt. Him? The arch of a woman's neck and the lines of her back. He loved kissing his way down from the spot where a woman's hair met skin on her nape, across soft shoulders and down the valley of her spine. Shifting uncomfortably, he jerked his thoughts away from Quincy the woman to focus on Quincy the cop.

"I don't think you understand the situation, Mr. Barron. A Child Protection worker from DHS will be here shortly. Under the law, Mr. Tate has to relinquish custody. He has no proof the child is his."

"You're the one who doesn't understand, Trooper Kincaid." Chance stepped toward her, his phone held out. "I'll have the paper version of this court order here very likely before your DHS representative arrives."

Deacon exchanged a relieved look with his cousin while Quincy scanned the document on Chance's phone.

"Who can call a judge at three thirty in the morning and get a custody order signed?" she muttered. Inhaling in an obvious—to him anyway—effort to control her frustration, she passed the phone back to Chance. She added, more loudly, "We'll all just sit right here until DHS and your paperwork arrive. In the meantime, Mr. Tate—"

"Deke," he insisted.

"Mr. Tate." She arched one brow and glowered. "In the meantime, you can explain to me how you, a single man, plan to care for a baby girl. I seriously doubt this bus contains a nursery."

"Considering I'm headed home as soon as we settle things, it doesn't matter if it does or not."

He watched her pull in her chin, crinkle her forehead and scowl at him. Deke was just contrary enough to enjoy the heck out of putting that expression on her face.

"So, you have a nursery set up at your home? Which is where, by the way? You can't take the baby back to Nashville."

"Home is a ranch about an hour's drive from here. And I admit I don't exactly have a nursery."

"Yet," Chance interjected. "Cassie, Jolie and Roxie have gone shopping. You will have everything you need by the time we get this worked out."

"Wait until Mom hears about this." Deke all but chortled. His mother was huge on family and none of her wayward sons had provided her with a grandchild. None of them was married. As a result, she doted on Cord and Jolie's little boy, CJ.

Quin favored Chance and him with her scowl. She'd been outfoxed and her expression indicated she knew it. She stepped back as Chance approached him but he could see the wheels turning. She hadn't surrendered. Yet. And wouldn't it be sweet when she did.

Chance murmured in his ear, "Won't be anything fancy. They went to the all-night supercenter." He glanced down at the baby and got a goofy look on his face. Deke choked back a laugh. If Noelle stayed in the family for very long, he predicted a Barron baby boom by next autumn.

Pulling back mentally, Deke considered what he'd just thought. He wasn't as freaked out by the notion of keeping Noelle in the family as he probably should be. That idea was all sorts of wrong. He toured. A lot. Only coming home when he could. He could hire a nanny, keep Noelle on the road with him. Or leave her at home with a nanny… Nope. He didn't like that idea at all. He did like the idea of having a loving wife and family—no matter where he was. Only that idea was all sorts of wrong, too.

Wow. He knew that the magic baby smell worked on testosterone as easily as it did on estrogen, but it was supposed to have the opposite effect. Women were supposed to go all weird and want babies. Not men. So why was he going all mushy where the kid was concerned? Deke was honest enough to admit his head space had been strange all night long. And then he was hit with the possibility that he had a kid. He'd been blindsided, but he'd also responded viscerally to the idea. It was growing on him.

He barely noticed Chance leave as he stared down at the baby in his arms. The little imp had obviously bewitched him. He'd never lacked for female companionship, and until his rather maudlin reflections of earlier, being tied down with a wife and family was a foreign concept. Maybe his cousins' happiness *was* rubbing off on him. Maybe he just needed something more than a one-night stand. Maybe he'd get lucky with the very luscious Trooper Quincy Kincaid. Maybe she'd even wear her Smokey Bear hat.

Noelle whimpered in her sleep, reminding him of what was at stake here. Deep down, he knew that as soon as the baby's mother was located—and his family had the resources to find her—the situation would be straightened out. When it was, he'd get back to life as normal—a life full of long-legged cowgirls in Daisy Dukes while touring, then going home and sitting on his front porch with a cold beer and his guitar for company.

Quin's voice interrupted his reverie. "I don't believe for a minute you are naive enough to believe that baby is yours."

With one hand, he grabbed the basket and moved it closer. With profound gentleness, he transferred the little girl into it. She stayed asleep. After tucking a crocheted blanket around her, he brushed the tip of his index finger through her wispy gold baby hair.

The sexy cop standing a few feet away kept pinging his radar. She'd been gruff and in-your-face about Noelle, and he wanted to know what made her tick. They had some time to kill. He'd watched out the window as his brothers and Cash Barron organized rides and shipped almost everyone off.

Deke wanted to satisfy his curiosity about Trooper Kincaid and whether she was as aloof—and as immune to him—as she pretended to be. He watched her from under half-lidded eyes, not missing a detail. Shoulders back, feet apart, knees slightly bent, hand on the butt of her pistol. She looked like she was getting ready for a fight.

"Do I make you nervous?" he drawled.

Quin refused to retreat a step, though her common sense insisted it was the smart thing to do. Instead, she stood her ground. She was the trained law-enforcement officer here. She was in charge. Keeping her stance aggressive but controlled, she jutted her chin toward him and leaned ever so slightly in his direction.

"Absolutely not." Then she realized her hand was on the butt of her sidearm. *Oops.* With conscious effort, she loosened her grip and hooked her thumb in her belt. She'd be cool, calm, efficient, with a detached sense of control. She could send out those vibes. Absolutely. Because this man did not make her think of kissing those full lips of his even if she was wondering whether they were soft or firm. No. She would not go there.

She was a professional. On duty. She didn't have time to picture running her fingers through that messy hair of his. Or—or... Her gaze rose from his mouth, quirking up at the corners as it was, to meet his eyes. They really were the soft blue of a star sapphire. She curled her fingers against her belt. Would the stubble on his face be rough, or as soft as his hair looked?

"Darlin', you really shouldn't look at a man that way." His gruff voice was both a caress and a wake-up call.

Quin barely controlled a full-body shudder. She needed to think of ice baths and blizzards. Snow and ski slopes. Invigorating high mountain air. Not warm. Not sexy. She took that step back, both physically and mentally. He laughed, and the sound was dark and warm like fudge brownies just out of the oven. Her mouth watered.

Coffee. She needed coffee. And fresh air. Like right this minute. She squared her shoulders and glanced at her watch: 4:18 a.m. Despite Quin's hoping otherwise, the DHS worker likely wouldn't arrive until after sunup.

"It appears we will be here a while, Mr.—"

"Deke."

"Tate. Is there any chance you have coffee hiding somewhere in this place?"

He chuckled, and she didn't like the way his eyes crinkled at the corners. No. She didn't like that at all.

"I'll see what I can scare up." He turned away from her and she realized she needed what cops laughingly called a 10-100.

"I also…" She did not want to ask, especially when he turned around, leaned up against the counter by bracing his hips against it and looked at her.

"You also…?" He did that smile-and-dimple thing again.

"May I use your facilities?"

"My…" His eyes twinkled and she could tell he was fighting laughter. The big jerk. "Bathroom is that way."

"Thank you," she acknowledged stiffly. Marching past him, she made note of the six curtained bunks lining the hall between the living space and the bedroom she could see at the rear.

Just past the bunk area, through a wooden door, she walked into a bathroom that made the one in her condo look like it belonged in a cheap motel. There was a huge glassed-in shower, a marble countertop with sink and full-sized commode. It was luxurious. She closed the door for privacy.

When she was done, she washed her hands and let her curiosity get the best of her. She poked her head into the bedroom. The queen-size bed appeared to be on a platform. It was higher off the floor than she'd first thought. A pewter-colored comforter looked warm and inviting.

Then she stopped to wonder how many women had been in that bed. Time to make a right turn into the sanity lane.

A chair sat in one corner. A guitar occupied a metal stand and there was a microphone in its own stand on the opposite side of the chair. Did he record back here? There was a computer setup on the nearby desk.

Quin heard a throat clearing behind her and she whirled. Her face flaming, she met Deacon's amused gaze without blinking.

"See anything you like, darlin'?"

"Uh...no. Not at all. I was curious to see how the other half lives. That's all."

"Sure." That twinkle in Deacon's eyes had turned to a hard glitter. He stalked toward her.

Self-preservation made her back up, taking one step for each of his. The backs of her legs smacked into the bed and she almost went down—would have hit the mattress if Deacon hadn't reached out and grabbed her arm.

All but panting, Quin forced herself to calm down. She was embarrassed at being caught. She truly hadn't meant to snoop. Much. And then there was the proximity of Deacon—with his dark good looks, the smoldering gleam in his eyes and that mouth. She couldn't help staring at it.

"You're starin' again."

She gulped. Jerking her eyes upward, she attempted to inhale around the catch in her chest. It just wasn't fair to women that one man could be this...everything a man was supposed to be. "Oh. Uh...the coffee?"

"It's ready."

"Oh, good. Great. Yes, thanks. Thank you. Very much." She eased past him and fled toward the living area. She almost stumbled when Deacon called after her, his voice gruff, which invited all sorts of sexy thoughts.

"We're not done, Trooper Kincaid. Not by a long shot."

Four

Deacon fell into bed just before 7:00 a.m. While he appreciated all the help from the Barron wives—or the Bee Dubyas as his brothers called them—they'd exhausted him and Noelle. The baby had been passed around so much she was wailing before he could convince them to go home. It helped that he'd sent out a group text to their husbands to come get them.

But they'd worked some serious magic on short notice. He'd come home to a functional nursery, courtesy of the chain store that was open 24/7. His home was now filled with bottles, diapers, formulas and more clothes than a kid needed in the short term. The crib and playpen thingy were up and ready—not that any of the women put Noelle down long enough for the baby to use them. They'd also set up a baby monitor. As tired as he was, that was a good thing.

Noelle took thirty minutes to calm down. He'd put her in the crib then sat next to it, stroking her gently and singing to her until she fell asleep. Deke had fond memories

of singing Dillon to sleep and he sometimes wondered if
that was why they both ended up in the music business.
In the end, Noelle had been clutching his finger as her
eyes drifted shut and her breathing turned into little puffs.
He was in desperate need of at least a couple of hours of
sleep. Then he'd deal with the curveball life had thrown
him—and the intriguing Highway Patrol trooper he'd left
in the Thunder River Casino parking lot as she attempted
to placate the DHS caseworker.

Bacon. Deacon inhaled deeply. That *was* bacon he was
smelling. And biscuits. What the…? He jumped out of bed
and stumbled toward the kitchen. He was halfway down
the hallway when his brain caught up with his body. The
baby-monitor receiver on his bedside table had been turned
off. He backtracked to the baby's room and looked in.
Noelle was sleeping soundly.

By the time he reached the kitchen, he'd corralled the
panic and was mostly coherent. Until he recognized the
woman standing at his stove. He should have known she'd
come as soon as word leaked out.

"Mom, why are you in my kitchen?"

She leveled him with a look insinuating he was both not
too bright and maybe not her son as a result of that fact.

"Beyond the obvious, Mom."

She poured him a cup of coffee and placed it on the
island. He hitched his butt onto one of the bar stools and
gratefully accepted her peace offering.

"Your brothers and cousins are in quite the tizzy, son."

Okay. *Son* was better than his full name, but not by
much. "It was a crazy night, Mom."

"Uh-huh." She flipped the strips of bacon in the cast-
iron frying pan.

"It was late, Mom. Or early, depending on which side
of dawn you went to bed."

"Uh-huh."

"Cut me some slack here."

"Don't get snippy, Deacon. Is she yours?"

He studied the steam rising from his mug. "You've seen her."

"Yes."

"What do you think?"

"I think she's a darlin' little girl that somebody—preferably her parents—should love beyond all things."

"We're doing the swabs for the test this afternoon. Chance says it'll take about three weeks. While it's possible, I'm not sure she's mine."

"I figured, sugar. She could be, but I don't think she is, either. As disappointing as that is."

"Mo-o-o-o-m," he warned by stretching out the word.

"None of you are married, Deke, so I am not advocating any of you rush out and find…what's the term you young people use? Baby momma? No baby mommas. Your daddy and I raised you boys to be honorable men, to do the right thing. You'll find the right girl, marry her and *then* have babies. Until we get the paternity-test results, the baby needs looking after. We'll hope her momma decides to come back. 'Course, if she's yours, she's ours. But that's a whole different situation. On the chance she *is* yours, we'll look after her."

Deke slid off the stool, walked around the island to his mom and kissed her on the cheek. "Yeah, we will. So…is that why you decided to come over and fix breakfast for me?" He noted the pile of bacon and sausage patties, the cartons of eggs and the huge pan of homemade biscuits baking in the oven.

"I suspect the locusts will descend soon enough. You know how crazy the family went over Cord's little CJ. Noelle is a baby. That just trips switches like you wouldn't believe."

Except he would, because seeing the baby, hearing her cry and holding her? Yup, every last one of his switches had been tripped. "She might not be mine, Mom."

"If she isn't, what happens if her momma doesn't come back?"

And that was the elephant in the room, wasn't it? "I truly don't know."

"What's your gut say?"

"I brought her home, Mom. No way was I letting her go into the system. But to make a commitment lasting the rest of my life?" He stared out the window over the sink. The note claimed he was Noelle's father. Why didn't the mother confront him? Ask for support? Why hadn't she contacted him before the baby was born? So many questions and no answers. At least not until the DNA test. If the baby wasn't his and they didn't locate her mother, he had no clue what he'd do. "I just don't know, Mom."

"You were always my homebody, Deke. At least until you picked up a guitar. If you weren't out there singin' for your supper every night, you'd be right here with a sweet woman making babies for me to spoil."

He splorted coffee through his nose. She clapped him on the back, pounding a little harder than necessary, and passed him a dish towel to wipe up the mess he'd made.

"Mom, you do remember that I'm the one who took three different girls to prom. The *same* prom."

She scowled at him. "I'm not likely to forget. You were a sophomore and they were seniors."

Deacon coughed behind the towel. He'd also escorted two seniors his junior year, and another three his senior year. Going steady was a foreign concept to him. Heck, the likelihood of his dating a woman more than a couple of times in a row ranked right up there with the Cubs winning the World Series. He'd had one relationship with another country singer that was sort of exclusive and it had ended amicably with both parties going their separate ways. One gossip columnist had labeled him a serial dater. He enjoyed all sorts of women and sex was just gravy.

His mom pointed her finger at him. If there was one deadly thing about Katherine Barron Tate, it was when she brought her "mother finger" to bear on her unruly sons.

Luckily, her lecture was interrupted by a perfunctory knock on the front door followed by the entrance of his older brother, Cooper.

"I smell food!" His brother paused at the door to kick off his muddy boots. "Sorry I missed the concert, little bro. We had a situation on one of the wells last night." Cooper worked with Cord Barron at BarEx, the oil-and-gas exploration-and-energy corporation controlled by the Barrons.

Coop padded into the kitchen and kissed their mother on the cheek. "Mornin', Momma. Sure could use a cup of coffee."

"Is your arm broken? You know where the mugs are kept and the pot is right there staring you in the face."

Laughing, Cooper made himself at home. This was the way of the Tates. There were times Deke wished for boundaries but his big, boisterous family refused to acknowledge them. Before his mother finished the bacon and started a batch of scrambled eggs with onions and peppers, along with home fries, his younger brothers, Bridger and Dillon, had tromped in. The rest of his brothers were likely out of town—Hunter and Boone working with Senator Clay Barron in Washington, DC, and Tucker out in Las Vegas with Chase Barron.

Dillon set the big farm-style table without being asked while Bridger stirred the gravy. Cooper had ducked out to grab a shower, seeing as he was covered in dirt and grease. When he returned, he was wearing a pair of Deacon's jeans and a Sons of Nashville concert sweatshirt.

Noelle's whimper echoed from the baby monitor on

the counter, and Deke led the charge. Halfway down the hallway, he turned to glower, noting how his mother and Dillon hadn't followed. He grinned evilly. "Coop, you and Bridge go grab her. I'll get her bottle ready." At their eager nods of agreement, he began to head back to the kitchen, then added, "Oh, she'll need a fresh diaper."

Then he ran, laughing. But between the two of them, they got Noelle sorted out and appeared with her several minutes later in the kitchen. His mother took over the care and feeding of the baby while her "boys" ate their breakfast.

Quin was supposed to be starting her days off. She'd hit Troop A's headquarters building an hour after her shift change. She'd spent another hour filling out her report and filing it so the information would go up the chain. Whatever was to be done about baby Noelle "Doe" and Deacon Tate was above her pay grade.

Sneaking out the back door after stuffing the report in her supervisor's in-box, she wanted only home, a hot shower, a protein shake and bed. In that order. And when she woke up, she'd have shopping to do. Housecleaning. Laundry. All the mundane things that normal people did on their days off.

Two hours after she'd arrived home, her supervisor called, jerking her from a sound sleep. She was to report for duty as soon as she could get to Troop A headquarters.

So…

Here she was, rapping her knuckles on the lieutenant's office door and peeking in through the glass window. He was on the phone but he crooked two fingers and gestured for her to enter. Quin slipped inside and sank onto a chair.

Lieutenant Charles had one of the best poker faces in the Department of Public Safety. As hard as she tried, Quin couldn't get a read on the conversation or who he was talking to, until he ended the call. "Of course, Governor. Whatever we can do to assist."

Her brain went down all sorts of rabbit holes. The governor had lots of reasons to be calling the Oklahoma Highway Patrol, but direct contact with her supervisor at Troop A? It wasn't like he was in the chain of command at the state level. Not that she was paranoid or anything, but after last night, the idea of a political target located between her shoulder blades didn't seem all that far-fetched.

The lieutenant's opening salvo just confirmed her suspicions. "So, you had quite the Friday night."

"You have my report, sir."

"Ease down, Kincaid. Yes. I have your report. And multiple calls from the governor on down." His dry chuckle did little to settle her nerves. "The decision has been made to take you off regular patrol—" He held up his hand, palm facing her to stay the retort she'd opened her mouth to make. "Priorities, Kincaid. And this case is now yours. You'll be the DPS liaison with all the other law-enforcement entities involved. Basically, you're heading up a task force to locate the baby's biological mother, to expedite the investigation and to act as the bridge between law enforcement and Deacon Tate."

"Bridge? What does that mean?"

"That means you are to stay on top of him—"

Quin all but sputtered as her mind went places it had no business going, and all her feminine parts perked right up at the thought.

"And this investigation. You'll work in conjunction with Child Protective Services from the Department of Human Services. The assigned CPS social worker will contact you. There is to be no direct contact with Mr. Tate unless you are present."

The cop side of her brain finally overrode the rest. "Wait. What does that mean, exactly?"

"What it means—exactly—is that you need to work closely with Mr. Tate. He is not to be disturbed by CPS or any law-enforcement agency involved in this investigation. You're point, Kincaid. You take any questions directly to him."

Quin stared, working hard to keep her mouth from gaping. She finally uttered, "Are you kidding me?"

"This is not something to kid about."

"But—"

"No *but*s."

"Yes, there is a *but*, sir. I'm scheduled for vacation time next month."

"Then you better get busy and find the mother, determine if Mr. Tate is the biological father and round up any other pertinent information."

She sat there, staring, her brain emitting nothing but white noise as it tried to wrap itself around the situation.

"Dismissed, Kincaid."

Quin rose, pivoted and headed for the door. The lieutenant's voice stopped her just as her hand touched the knob.

"FYI, Kincaid. No leaks. If any information beyond what DPS releases about this investigation gets out, it's all on your head."

Her mouth felt numb, just like her semicoherent brain, but she muttered, "Yes, sir," then exited. But the lieutenant still wasn't done.

"You need to get out to Mr. Tate's ranch and talk to him, Kincaid. Welfare check on the baby and all that. ASAP."

Oh, whoop-de-do. She had plans for today and none of them included driving to Timbuktu to deal with a spoiled star. Except there was a baby involved and seriously, what single guy was truly capable of 24/7 child care?

First, she had to locate directions. Then she'd just *drop in* on the man himself. And give him a piece of her mind.

Five

When Quin pulled up in front of Deacon Tate's gorgeous log home, she found a driveway full of vehicles. She parked at the end of the line and trudged past a dark-colored Dodge Challenger. She noted the manufacturer's badges. It was an SRT Hellcat HEMI muscle car—a model that cost almost as much as she made in a year.

The next vehicle was far less flashy—a black Ford Expedition, platinum edition. A white four-wheel-drive Ford F-250 pickup with the emblem for Barron Exploration plastered on the door was parked close to the walkway leading to the front door. Next to it was a Lexus LX 570, its metallic pearl-white paint almost blinding in the bright winter sun.

So much for confronting Tate alone. Quin marched up the fieldstone walkway and stopped at the double-wide wooden doors. She looked but couldn't find a doorbell, nor was there a door knocker—just a numeric keypad. Using the heel of her fist, she banged on the door.

A muffled voice called from inside. She pounded the door again. And waited. She had her hand on the handle when the door was jerked open. Off balance, she fell into a hard body. Muscular arms gripped Quin's waist, steadying her. Heat spread from strong fingers, radiating through her Kevlar vest to tease her skin.

She looked up into a pair of star-sapphire eyes and got a little lost in their mysterious depths.

"Don't just stand there, Deacon," a woman's voice ordered. "Let the poor girl in."

"Certainly." A boyish grin teased his mouth, and Quin's heart did a funny little flutter kick. "Please come in, Trooper Kincaid. We were just having breakfast. Are you hungry?"

She was so focused on his mouth that her brain went to the one place she didn't want it to go. She blinked to break the spell he'd cast. Quin once again considered the effect this man had on his female fans, and she frowned at the thought of the lingerie collection he and his bandmates probably laughed about.

"Quin?"

"I'm not hungry."

"Of course you are, hon. Come on in and sit. I'll get you a plate." The feminine voice came from inside the house and wasn't asking.

Quin watched Deacon walk through the large open living area toward a fabulous kitchen. Like the rest of the house, it looked as if it should be the centerfold in a decorating magazine.

"Don't dawdle, hon. Food's gettin' cold."

As Quin trailed in Deacon's wake, she studied the other people gathered around a granite island that looked big enough to land a small plane on. There were three men, two of whom she recognized from the previous night, and an older woman. The family resemblance was strong.

Deacon stopped at one of the bar stools and pulled it out for her. She settled on it and a plate heaped with bacon, sausages and eggs appeared in front of her. Deacon snagged flatware and a napkin—cloth—for her use.

"Share the biscuits and gravy, Cooper," the woman said. "I'm Katherine Tate. I take it you've met my sons Deacon and Dillon. These are two of my other sons, Cooper and Bridger. Coffee or something else t'drink?"

Her head was spinning a little. "Oh, coffee, please."

"Cream or sugar?"

She glanced at the oldest of the men present, though he wasn't *old*. Quin guessed him to be in his midthirties. "A little sugar, please, and vanilla creamer if you have it." She offered a tight smile to the men's mother. "Nice to meet you, Mrs. Tate. I'm Quincy Kincaid. I've been assigned by OHP as liaison on this case."

Katherine's eyes narrowed. "Case? This isn't a case, Miz Kincaid. This is a little girl. Who has a name." At that moment, a soft mewl issued from a soft-sided criblike thing Quin hadn't noticed upon her arrival. "I'll get the baby, Deacon. Finish your breakfast before it gets cold. And take your hat off, Miz Kincaid."

Quin removed her hat and set it on the stool next to her. Ignoring the stares from Deacon's brothers, she concentrated on the food in front of her. She forked eggs into her mouth and chewed carefully. The silence filling the room was so thick she could have been wearing earplugs. She couldn't even hear the four men breathing and that was saying something.

The stalemate broke when Katherine Tate returned, the baby slung easily on one hip. Quin supposed that after seven sons, Mrs. Tate would have had lots of practice with infants. Transfixed, she watched as Deacon's mother did a sort of slinking, rocking walk toward them.

The woman was suddenly right there standing between her and Deacon.

"Here." Mrs. Tate thrust the baby forward and Quin braced for it, figuring she was meant to be the recipient. But Deacon's mom passed Noelle to him. Feeling idiotic, Quin let her arms fall to her sides and swiveled to stare at her plate.

"She's clean. I'll fix her another bottle but you feed her this time. Eat fast."

"Yes, ma'am," Deke muttered around a mouthful of biscuit.

"Don't talk with your mouth full."

"Yes, ma'am." This time his voice was clear, his mouth empty.

Quin was fascinated. These men were all adults—well, all but Dillon maybe. He looked like a big man-child and she suspected that since he was the baby, he got away with everything. But it didn't matter that they were grown and held impressive jobs; this woman owned them. Then again, it was rather cute the way they got all goofy and treated her with respect. They weren't like Quin's brothers in any way, shape or form. Then again, she and her siblings hadn't grown up in the lap of luxury like the Tates.

Deacon scraped the last bite of eggs and potatoes off his plate, chewed vigorously and swallowed. She couldn't take her eyes off his mouth or his throat. And she was impressed by the way he had the baby propped up on his lap and was holding her so confidently in the crook of his left arm.

Mrs. Tate handed the bottle and a clean dish towel to Deacon. "I'll clear your plate. Go feed our little girl."

"You sure you don't wanna feed her, Mom?"

The woman looked aghast and wagged her index finger in his direction. "I only fed her this mornin' because you hadn't had your coffee, Deacon. I did my time with the seven of you. You're on your own now."

Quin stiffened when she realized Mrs. Tate was staring at her, the look in the older woman's eyes speculative. She slid off the stool and picked up her plate to carry it... somewhere. The sink?

"Just leave it, hon. Coop and Bridge are on dish duty."

The two brothers groaned but it was a good-natured sound, and Dillon gloated. His mother pointed at him. "You need to go get the trash in the nursery and take it out."

"Aw, Mom," Dillon protested.

She leveled a look at him that made Quin straighten her spine and bite her tongue to keep from offering to do it just so the woman would stop glaring.

"Quin?" Deacon called to her.

Whew. A reprieve. She hurried into the great room and stood near the large leather chair Deacon occupied. Noelle was draining her bottle with vigorous sucking noises. This was Quin's chance to tell him what was going to happen and then leave. "Do you have a moment to talk? We have to get some things straight."

He arched a brow and nodded toward the end of the couch nearest his chair. "So talk."

Quin settled herself on the couch, cognizant of being the focus of attention—*everyone's* attention. "As I mentioned when I arrived, I'm the law-enforcement liaison in this case. We've started the investigation into the baby's circumstances. Once we locate the mother—"

"Do you think you will?"

"Will what?"

Deacon glanced down to hide his grin. He enjoyed knocking the stodgy trooper off balance. She had a script and every time he threw her off, she got flustered. He liked the color in her cheeks and the snap of blue fire in her eyes when she got angry.

"Find Noelle's mother."

"Of course we will. It's just a matter of time. Then DHS will do an evaluation and a determination will be made taking into account the results of the paternity test."

"You think she's unfit because she left Noelle with me." Okay, maybe he shouldn't have sounded so accusatory but something in Quin's tone rankled.

"That's not up to me to decide."

"But you have."

"Look, Mr. Tate—"

"Deacon."

"Mr. Tate." She glowered. "The woman left her baby out in the cold next to your tour bus claiming you are the father." She studied him through narrow eyes. "Though there might be a possibility you're the father, pending the test results, we just don't know. What I don't understand is why a single man, and a—a…" She waved one hand and bit out the next words like they tasted bitter. "A rich superstar would insist on accepting custody of a baby that might not be his."

Noelle started sucking air. Deke pulled the empty bottle away, settled her on his shoulder and patted her back until she burped loudly. He pushed out of the chair and stared down at Quin. "It appears that Noelle's mother knows me better than you do."

Cuddling the infant against his shoulder, Deke walked to the kitchen and settled on the bar stool he'd vacated earlier. Noelle was cooing and nuzzling against his neck. He was ticked off at Quin and her preconceived notions. What she thought she knew about him was obviously gleaned from scandal rags and cheesy entertainment shows on TV. He should just ignore the irritation but something inside him really wanted this woman to like him.

Yeah, fat chance of that.

His mother brushed past him, pausing a moment to whisk hair out of his eyes, the gesture both oddly endearing and annoying. He watched her roost on the couch next to Quin, looking every inch a Southern matriarch. His mom wore jeans, Western boots and a turtleneck sweater, but from her demeanor, she might as well have been wearing a designer dress and pearls.

The two women began to converse in low voices and Deke couldn't make out what they were saying over the noise his brothers made cleaning up. His mother's gaze danced between him and Quin, which made him a little nervous. Okay, it made him a lot nervous. Katherine Tate was a plotter, especially where her boys were concerned.

Thinking to tell his brothers to keep it down, he glanced around just in time to see Bridger nudge Cooper's shoulder.

"If I ever catch Mom lookin' at me the way she's lookin' at Deke, especially with a pretty woman in the room, I'm headin' for the hills."

Cooper grinned. "Smart man. I'd be right behind you."

"So what are we gonna do?" Bridger glanced at Coop.

"Sit back and enjoy the show." Cooper tossed his dish towel over his shoulder and leaned against the counter, crossing his ankles and arms.

"Y'all know I can hear you, right?" Deke scowled at them.

His brothers burst out laughing. Dillon, approaching the back door and holding a plastic bag at arm's length, jerked his head around. "What's so funny? What'd I miss?"

"You're too young to understand," Cooper teased.

"Seriously? You're going to pull that crap on me now?"

Dillon waved the sack to emphasize his point then gave Deke a sideways glance. "They're right about one thing. She is pretty. Think she'd go out with me?"

Bridger smirked. "Naw. You're too young for her."

"Hey, I'm twenty-two. I'm right at the peak of my sex—"

"You boys do know that Trooper Kincaid and I can hear you, yes?" Katherine didn't need to raise her voice to be heard.

"Yes, ma'am," four voices replied in unison, with Dillon adding, "Well, do you? Because she's really hot."

Bridger rolled his eyes. "Dude, we can't take you anywhere. You do realize that you're bird-dogging the woman our big brother is interested in, right?"

"Not to mention you're a baby," Cooper added. "She wants a real man, not a pimply-faced—"

Dillon shoved Coop. "I don't have pimples!"

Deke wanted to bash all three of his brothers. This was normal behavior anytime two or more Tates shared the same space, but today he needed a huge helping of *regular* normal to deal with the trooper. He couldn't help but wonder what she was thinking. She looked stern in her dark brown uniform and black leather Sam Browne belt, but he caught a hint of humor around her eyes. At least he hoped it was humor. Did she have a boisterous family like his? That would be a good thing. She'd understand the ribbing and his frustration.

"I still think she should go out with me." Dillon was a persistent little bugger.

"Then you think wrong. *She* thinks you're too young," Quin called out. She didn't even look their way but her voice carried.

Was she teasing Dillon? That made Deke feel like a fool because he was suddenly jealous of his little brother.

He needed to get some space and think through this situation—and this woman. She was not his type, not in any way, shape or form. Except it was turning out that she was exactly his type in every way, shape and form. He was so screwed.

Six

"Pay no mind to the boys, Quincy." Katherine Tate gave her an inquisitive look. "I may call you Quincy, yes? Trooper Kincaid is so…harsh."

Quin nodded out of habit. Mrs. Tate was one of those women so used to getting her own way she'd likely steamroll over any protestations Quin might make.

"Do you have family, Quincy?"

Mrs. Tate was getting personal now. Quin would have to walk this minefield with care—at least until she figured out the woman's angle.

"Yes, ma'am."

"Brothers?"

"Yes, ma'am."

Mrs. Tate laughed, a rich laugh much like her son's that reminded Quin of hot fudge on ice cream. She wondered what it had been like having this woman as a mother, especially since her own was 180 degrees opposite in personality.

"I shall remind the boys not to play poker with you. Tell me about your brothers. Are you close?"

"No."

"Ah."

Quin squirmed. That one syllable spoke volumes and what it said made her bristle. All teasing aside, she had the distinct impression that she was interviewing for a job.

"My brothers and I weren't particularly close, either. Of course, I often thought Daddy should have drowned Cyrus at birth but then I wouldn't have my nephews so I suppose it all worked out. Families are odd microcosms, don't you think?"

Quin wasn't sure what to say. Cyrus Barron had been a powerful man, not just in Oklahoma, but pretty much in the entire world. His six sons—one only recently acknowledged—were following in his footsteps. The family had fingers in every important pie and then some. She wasn't as familiar with the Tate brothers but knew several of them worked side-by-side with their Barron cousins.

"Yes," Quin finally answered. "They can be." Which was true enough. Odd and dysfunctional described her family rather well.

"How closely do you plan to…*supervise* my son, Trooper Kincaid?"

The abrupt change of subject caught Quin off guard. "Technically, I'm only here as a liaison, ma'am. A…facilitator, so to speak."

"In other words, the governor called your big boss, who called your immediate boss, who stuck you with this because no one wants to upset the governor. I still want to know your intentions, Quincy. You aren't comfortable with this situation. And you especially don't like the idea of my son taking care of a baby."

Yeah. She'd sure enough poked the momma bear. With a sharp stick. "I admit to reservations, Mrs. Tate, especially given the fact that your son is uncertain whether he's the father."

The only reaction she got was the quirk of a well-shaped brow and silence.

"Look, I'm going to be blunt here. Why would your son take in a child he probably has no ties to? Aren't you worried this is a scam? Some sort of shakedown for money?"

Quin didn't understand why Deacon and his family were making such a big deal over this. Didn't it make more sense to just turn over the kid? She breathed through her irritation and continued. "While we are making every attempt to keep the situation low-key, your son is a celebrity. It's just a matter of time before the story leaks to the media. What happens then? I'm a trained investigator, Mrs. Tate. As such, I have to question your son's motive."

That earned Quin another pointed look. "That explains quite a bit, young lady."

Well, crud. She was losing ground fast and she really needed Mrs. Tate on her side. Quin figured Deacon's mother might be the only person who could make him see reason.

"Be honest with me, Mrs. Tate. Are you really okay with your son taking in this child on a whim?"

"A whim?" Deacon's voice was cold enough to raise goose bumps on her arms. Quin had totally forgotten that he and his brothers were just steps away.

"What would you call it, Mr. Tate?"

Deke glanced at his mother. She had that weird look on her face again, her gaze bouncing between him and Quin like she was watching them play Ping-Pong.

"Compassion, *Trooper* Kincaid, something you seem to be seriously lacking."

When Quin pushed to her feet and went toe-to-toe with him, Deke's anger melted into something hotter. He dropped his gaze to her mouth, watching her talk but not really listening. His brain had taken him right to the heart of what he wanted to do with Quin's mouth. The fantasy was so vivid his hands were reaching for her when he remembered where they were and what was happening. He tuned back just in time, and she said, "Why would a man like you—"

"A man like me?" He folded his arms across his chest. Yeah, there'd be no touching or kissing now. "Care to elaborate?"

Quin sputtered for a moment. Deke was suddenly aware that his brothers had formed a semicircle behind him in a show of solidarity. He'd handed off Noelle to Bridger when the tone of the women's conversation had changed. His mother hadn't moved, but her face was now a blank canvas.

Inhaling, Quin focused on him. "Yes, Mr. Tate. A man like you. A rich man. A...star. Aren't you in the middle of a tour? Why in the world would you want to take on the care and feeding of an infant? I can't help but consider this might be a publicity stunt—a way to boost your media presence."

Deke held on to his temper only because Cooper put his hand on his shoulder and squeezed. Hard. "So...let me get this straight. You think I'm a publicity whore who would use a baby as a way to get on the entertainment news. The bottom line—" he was all but shaking now "—is you believe that because I'm rich there is no way I could be doin' something like this simply because it's the right thing to do."

Quin opened and closed her mouth several times, apparently unable to speak. That worked just fine for Deke. She'd said more than enough, and no matter how sexy she was, he doubted he could get around her preconceived notions. He and his brothers had been raised to work for a living. His daddy would have tanned their hides if they showed even a hint of the attitude this maddening woman was accusing him of having.

"Have I got that right?" He glared at her as he pulled his cell phone out of his hip pocket and dialed Chance. The conversation was short. "I don't care what you have to do but I want Trooper Kincaid removed from the case." With the phone still pressed to his ear, he said to Quin, "Since you've already decided I'm guilty, I'm damned if I do, damned if I don't. Here's the deal—until Noelle's mother is found, she is mine and I will take care of her."

Chance questioned him on the situation so Deke added, "She accused me of staging a publicity stunt. I want her gone." He cut the call.

"Mr. Tate—"

"I will give you five minutes, Trooper Kincaid. I will show you the nursery that's been set up. I will show you that not only am I capable, but that I *am* taking care of Noelle. Follow me."

Deke stormed off as his brothers quickly cleared out of his way. He glanced back, not to see if Quin was following him, but to check his mother's expression. The woman was smiling. What was up with that? He didn't care, though he probably should. He had enough problems on his hands with the prickly state cop.

His brothers wisely stayed in the great room. When Deke and Quin reached the guest room next to the master bedroom, he stood back and ushered her inside. She'd detoured past the kitchen to snag her Smokey Bear hat and it was perched firmly on her head. Deke noticed the quick cut of her eyes toward the open doorway of his bedroom as she hesitated. He'd spent a portion of his dreams plotting ways to get her into his bed. That had been a complete waste of time.

He followed her into the guest room. The Bee Dubyas

had done an amazing job. The queen-size bed had been moved into a corner to make room for the crib. The top of the dresser had been cleared and padded for a changing table. They'd even installed a thing that warmed the baby wipes. The drawers were filled with diapers and baby clothes. Toys dotted the glider chair and the baby monitor—a whole house system—was front and center.

Deke leaned a shoulder against the doorjamb and watched Quin examine the space that had been created literally overnight to accommodate a baby. He had to reach deep to level out his temper. Why should he care if this cop liked him? He was doing the right thing and her opinion shouldn't matter. Yet for some reason it did.

Whoever Noelle's mother was, she was looking for something better for her child. At least he hoped that was her motivation. What did he actually know? Maybe the woman *was* trying to set him up for a paternity suit, which was easily defended with DNA. The baby had been well taken care of, according to Jolie. And she'd come with all the stuff babies came with—diapers, bottles, formula, clothes.

Quin whirled and faced him, her eyes snapping with irritation. "I find it somewhat amazing that you had this cozy little nest all prepared for this baby who isn't yours." She waved a hand around the room. "Especially since you claim ignorance about the existence of this child before last night. When the CPS caseworker comes out for the home study, I'm sure she'll make note of it."

Deacon stiffened and gave her a narrow look. "What caseworker and what home study?"

She closed her eyes, breathed, in an apparent attempt to ratchet down her temper. Deke was almost sorry. Sparring with her was entertaining.

"The state won't just turn over the baby to you. It doesn't work that way in the real world. I get that you're

Mr. Nashville Star and all, but here you have to follow the same rules as everyone else. Doesn't matter who you are. And it doesn't matter which judge signed those papers your cousin had drawn up." She muttered that last part.

Okay, so who would guess the confounding woman was still feeling the sting of Chance's middle-of-the-night call to the judge?

She inhaled and continued. "I just don't understand why a megastar like *Deacon Tate*—who has doubts he's the biological father—would take on the responsibility of a baby."

Deke didn't miss Quin's switch to discussing him in the third person. "Is there a reason you don't like me?"

"What?" Evidently, his question caught her off guard.

"You don't like me. I'd like to know why. If I've done something to offend you or—"

"I don't...*dislike* you."

"But you don't like me, either."

"Look, Mr. Tate, I'm just doing my job. Liking you or not has no bearing."

Deke pushed off the door frame. "We're done here."

Her eyes snapped with temper again. "No, we aren't."

Quin marched up to him and once again, they were toe-to-toe. Her mouth was right there, all plump and glistening because she'd just wet her lips. Was he quick enough to catch that tongue before it disappeared from sight? She leaned toward him and her eyes went a little unfocused. Close. So. Very. Very...

And then they were kissing. It wasn't sweet. It wasn't sensual. It was hard and angry and they each fought to dominate. He cinched his arm around her waist and hauled her up against him. Instead of soft breasts, he encountered stiffness. She was wearing a bulletproof vest? And oh, yeah, she was wearing her weapons belt, complete with pistol. Deke had totally blanked out that she was in uniform. Why was that so freaking sexy?

His free hand knocked her hat off and fisted in the tight bun at the back of her neck. He used his grip to angle her head so he could deepen the kiss. He bit at her bottom lip, tasted her with his tongue. When she sighed, he plunged his tongue into her mouth, tasting her fully now.

Her hands gripped the plackets of his flannel shirt, and it felt like she was both jerking him closer and pushing him away. He didn't care. The only thing that mattered was that they were kissing. Deke watched her, smiled into the kiss as her eyes drifted closed. She wasn't fighting for control now and her surrender was one of the sweetest things he'd ever experienced.

Without considering the consequences, he turned them around, backing Quin up against the wall. His whole being responded to her body pressed against him and he really wanted to strip her out of all that brown. Brown wasn't her color. Naked was. He wanted to touch *her*, not the vest binding her tight. He broke the kiss to nuzzle the soft pulse point under her chin. Her breathing changed rhythm. That was good. He ground his hips against hers, the friction feeling so good against his erection.

"I—"

He cut off whatever she was going to say by kissing her again. She tasted of coffee. She smelled faintly of peaches and cinnamon and his mouth watered. Peach cobbler with ice cream and a cup of steaming coffee. His favorite dessert. At least until he got his mouth on Quin. And he would. He would taste her in all sorts of ways.

"Ahem."

Deke cut his eyes to the door. Wonderful. Dillon stood there grinning like a demented elf. That was when he realized Quin was thumping on his chest with her fists and shaking her head from side to side in an effort to break their kiss. He backed away and was enjoying the heck out of the look he'd put on her face. Her cheeks were rosy, her hair tousled, the bun all but destroyed. Her eyes were half-lidded with desire even as they narrowed in anger. Her lips were swollen and red and she was breathing hard.

He caught the flash of movement from the corner of his eye and just managed to duck out of the way of Quin's fist, aimed for his chest, not his face.

"You are despicable," she hissed before her glower swept across him to include Dillon. She pushed Deke out of her way and shoved past his little brother. Moments later, he heard the door to the guest bathroom close and lock.

"I've heard that about you," Dillon teased. "Definitely despicable."

"Shut up." There was no heat in his voice because, truth be told, he was feeling pretty cocky. He'd upset Quin's equilibrium enough that she hadn't wanted to slap him— she'd wanted to slug him. Perverse, he realized, but it still made him just a little proud he'd gotten to her. And he had definitely gotten to her. She'd been kissing him back just as hard.

By the time he got around Dillon, Quin had cleared the bathroom and he caught sight of her not-quite-tight bun disappearing down the hall. Of course, the sway of her hips in those tan uniform pants made him have to adjust himself as he followed her back to the living room.

Quin didn't pause as she headed straight for the front door. Deke stopped, and that was when Dillon shoved her hat into his hands. He wanted to laugh and wondered how long it would take for the staid trooper to realize she was technically out of uniform. He'd about decided to keep the hat as a souvenir—and an excuse to see her again—when she pulled an about-face, stalked back to him and ripped the hat from his hands.

One of her eyes was twitching, her lips were pursed

and bright red spots stained her cheeks. "Not a word," she growled, pivoting and marching toward the door again.

"Trooper Kincaid?" His mother's use of Quin's title stopped her as she reached for the door handle. Her shoulders stiffened and her back went ramrod-straight but she didn't look around.

"Yes?"

"Do you have pearls, dear?"

Seven

Pearls? What did pearls have to do with anything that had just occurred? Seriously? No, Quin didn't have pearls. Did she look like the kind of woman who would wear them? She turned to gape at Mrs. Tate. The woman smiled, waiting expectantly for her answer.

"Um, no, ma'am. No pearls."

"That's a shame, Quincy. Every woman should have pearls handy when she needs something to clutch. Do drive safely back to the city."

And just like that, Quincy had been dismissed. What was up with this family? Oh, yeah. They were rich and they could pretty much do whatever they wanted. Except she wouldn't let them get away with this—whatever *this* was.

She stewed all the way back to Oklahoma City—over the situation and her reaction to Deacon. Quincy couldn't relate to the Tates. She needed to understand the motivations behind Deacon's alleged altruism. Cause and effect.

Incentives. Reasons. What were they? Granted, her family wasn't any sort of benchmark but there had to be a payoff in it for Deacon. But what could it be?

She'd asked similar questions as a child when she'd been plucked out of her group home to spend Christmas with a rich family. Their mansion had been full of Christmas decorations with a big tree and lots of presents. A TV station even did a story. Quin figured she'd hit the jackpot until the day after Christmas. The family sent her back to the group home. She didn't get to keep any of the presents the TV camera filmed her opening.

Yeah, in her jaded experience, people—especially the wealthy—didn't do something for nothing.

Quincy was no closer to answers for any of her questions when she parked in front of her apartment. She could write her report—and wouldn't it be a doozy—and email it to the LT. Then she could finally get around to the other things she'd scheduled for her day off.

She was in line at the grocery store when her phone dinged—a message from the lieutenant. Quincy was still on the hook—a welfare check tomorrow and every day thereafter. So much for Deacon or Chance Barron getting her kicked off the case. Darn it. She kept reading. Her recommendation to call in DHS was under advisement and the baby was to stay where she was. Quin also needed to locate the mother ASAP.

Great. Just…great.

Days off were rescinded to be made up in comp time. Still, the sooner she found the mother, the sooner she could get her life back. She had time to close this case before boarding her plane for those two glorious weeks far, far away. Time to put her investigative skills to work.

Deacon stared at five of his cousins. Thank goodness Clay and his wife, Georgie, were still in DC. The rest of the Barrons—and their wives—had descended first thing Sunday morning, including Chase and Savannah, who'd flown in from Vegas. At the moment, the women were passing Noelle around and cooing over the baby like she was a porcelain doll. The men were staring back at him, their expressions bleak.

"What?" He sounded defensive.

"A baby? Seriously?" Chase cut his eyes to his wife, who was currently rocking Noelle. "What are you tryin' to do to us, cuz?"

"I've heard nothing but 'baby, baby, baby' since Friday night." Cord scrubbed his forehead with the heel of his hand. "CJ is all 'I want a brother, Dad.' And Jolie? She's got that look in her eye." He shuddered dramatically. "I'm just now getting used to being the dad of a real kid."

Chance laughed. "As opposed to a fake kid?"

"You know what I mean," Cord grumbled. "Babies don't talk. Or play ball. Or *do* stuff." He eyed the women. "And I'm betting Cassie is giving you the same pitch as the rest of the wives."

Lifting his shoulders in a philosophical shrug, Chance said, "I figure they can all get their baby fix hanging out over here."

Forgotten in the banter, Deacon growled under his breath. He didn't want these daily invasions. Okay, granted, it was sort of nice to take a break from the constant vigilance of watching over Noelle, but he'd scheduled this time at home to get away from crowds and people. He'd hoped to write some songs, to ride—though that was on the back burner now—and just hang out at the one place that gave him peace. Thank goodness none of *his* brothers was married; otherwise he'd have no time alone.

Cash poured another cup of coffee for himself. "Roxie treats that damn dog of hers like a kid. I think I'm safe for a while."

Nudging his twin, Chase laughed. "You love that dog as much as she does, Cash."

"Shhh. She doesn't need to know that. And I figure as soon as Pippa pops, they'll all have a new baby to fuss over." Cash winked at Kade before turning his gaze toward Deke. "So, you want Barron Security to look into the situation?"

Deke nodded. Cash was the one cousin he really wanted to speak to. "Yeah. There's not much to go on and that trooper is supposed to be investigating. Knowing the governor, the Oklahoma Statue Bureau of Investigation is probably involved, too. I'll keep Noelle until you find the mom. Then we'll figure things out from there."

"What happens if Cash doesn't find her?" Chance asked. "Have you thought about the future?"

Deke pursed his lips, considering his answer. He hadn't shaken the thoughts of settling down and starting a family that had been floating in his brain just prior to finding the baby. Not that he believed in karma or the universe dropping a big ol' sign like a baby on him, but he still wondered at the timing. The munchkin had been in his life not even forty-eight hours, yet he couldn't imagine not hearing her sleepy sounds through the monitor, not filling his nose with the sweet scent inherent to babies. Well, as long as they were dry. He chuckled.

"I can't honestly say, Chance. Keeping her would mean a lot of changes. I'd need to hire a nanny because I'm not an idiot. With my schedule, there's no way I could be a full-time single dad. After New Year's, we go back to touring for a couple of months. Then we plan to take time off, work on the new album. I could be here."

"You aren't seriously considering keeping this child, are you?" Chance's eyes narrowed and he looked like he was ready to launch into a lecture consisting of all the reasons it was a bad idea.

"I don't know, Chance." Deke held up his hand to stall further comment. "I'm aware of all the negatives. Trust me. And remember, I am not an idiot, despite what y'all, my brothers and my mom seem to think. Best-case scenario, the mother turns up soon, and we can help her through whatever it is that made her leave Noelle on the bus. Christmas is coming. I'm betting she—"

"There are other considerations," Cash interrupted. He glanced at Chance and got a slight nod in reply. "What if this is a setup? We can't ignore any ulterior motives the mother might have."

"I'm aware of that, too. That's why I'd rather you track her down and we figure out what her deal is before the cops do."

Cash nodded, exchanging another look with Chance, but it was Chase who spoke up. "I'll have our PR people work on damage control—"

"Chase—"

"Just in case, Deke. Let Cash do his job and let me do mine while waiting on results of the test. As family, we only have your best interest at heart."

The doorbell rang. Roxie popped up off the floor to answer it. The men sitting around the kitchen island swiveled their heads to see who had arrived.

"Speaking of best interests…" Kade, heretofore silent, waggled his brows suggestively.

Quin was startled by the redhead who opened the door. There'd been a whole new fleet of vehicles in the drive as she arrived; she should have suspected that Deacon's harem would show up. She wasn't expecting so many women, though. Then her brain kicked into gear. These weren't fangirls. No, that would have been too simple. She was facing the very formidable Barron wives.

"May I help you?" the redhead asked, one brow arched. She obviously wasn't expecting Quin.

"That's just the nanny state checking up on me, Roxie." Deacon's voice wafted above the sudden silence.

Roxie Barron. Quin put name and face together. Roxanne Rowland had married Cash Barron of Barron Security earlier in the year. Quin had done her homework and was finally matching names, faces and spouses. Roxie had been at the casino Friday night. Stepping around her, Quin stopped at the edge of the living area. The women were spread over the couches and chairs while the men were gathered in the kitchen. Odd, until she realized the baby was in the living room. She had to stifle a laugh.

The women fawned over the baby while the men huddled together, like there was strength in numbers, as far away from the kid as they could get. Quin couldn't help but wonder if there would be a Barron baby boom a year from now. She fixed her gaze on Deacon. He didn't look any happier to see her than she was to see him. She lowered her eyes the moment she recognized the heat in his. Warmth climbed up her neck, flushing her cheeks. She'd counted on his anger, in light of his instructions to Chance Barron, but this flare of desire between them knocked her off balance.

The tingling in her lips and the quivers lower in her body didn't help matters. Of all the guys she'd come across in her life, why did it have to be this one that got her thinking about monkey business instead of her job? She had nothing against men or dating, it was just that most of the ones she came in contact with weren't suitable because they were candidates for arrest, or they were put off by her job. The last thing she wanted or needed was to get involved with a spoiled star with daddy dilemmas.

"As you can see, Trooper Kincaid, Noelle is fine and

being spoiled rotten. Last time I checked the state statutes, spoiling a baby wasn't a felony."

She caught a twinkle in his eye. Was he flirting with her?

"No, just a misdemeanor, and bad parenting," Quin wanted to bite her tongue. She was not flirting back.

"Ah, I see. Good thing my attorney is present." His mouth quirked. He *was* flirting with her.

"He seems to be everywhere you are. That makes you a suspicious subject." She couldn't stop her response, even as she dug the hole deeper.

"Does that mean I'm a person of…interest?"

Quin curled her lips between her teeth to keep from answering. Innuendo dripped off his words. They weren't flirting. Really they weren't. Flirting with Deacon Tate was a bad thing, especially after that kiss—the one she was desperate to forget. She blinked and discovered he was halfway across the room, headed her direction.

"Suddenly at a loss for words, Trooper?" He was right there, inches from her face. Everything feminine in her body perked right up. This man punched all the right tickets and she wanted to take the ride. Except she couldn't afford the complications.

"A smart person only speaks when there's something worthwhile to say."

Deacon leaned in and whispered, "Oh, I have plenty to say, Trooper Kincaid. And not just with words."

She shivered, a reflex from his warm breath in her ear. Thank goodness she was wearing Kevlar because her chest brushed his and without the vest, Deacon would know exactly what he was doing to her. Working to control her expression, she leaned back so she could see his face. In doing so, she caught a glimpse of everyone else. Ten people were staring at Deacon like he'd grown two heads.

* * *

Deacon struggled to control his breathing and his desire. He wanted to take her into his arms. Or back her against the wall. Again. He wanted to taste her mouth. Again. And he wanted to do a whole lot more. Except they had an audience. How had he forgotten that? His cousins needed to leave. Right now. And Noelle needed a long nap. Immediately. And he definitely needed to get Quincy out of her uniform and into his bed.

Which was not the brightest idea he'd ever had. The woman obviously didn't like him—or his family. She seemed convinced he couldn't handle Noelle, that the baby would be better off in foster care. That wasn't happening. Despite their differences, he couldn't deny his attraction to her. She was…tough. Forceful. Strong. Beautiful. And sexy beyond belief.

They stood there, staring at each other, both of them breathing hard. Was she remembering the feel of his mouth on hers? Of their bodies pressed together? He was so hard he worried his zipper might break. Walking across the room had been torture and he hoped no one noticed the obvious. Standing close and breathing in her peach-cobbler scent left him throbbing.

One of his cousins whistled a tune Deke recognized— Jason Aldean's "Burnin' It Down." As much as he wanted to be alone with Quincy, it was best they had chaperones—even smart-alecky ones. The last thing he should do was get involved with the cop investigating Noelle's abandonment. He stepped back, which was harder than he'd anticipated.

"Why exactly are you here again?" Deke asked, focusing on business, not pleasure.

"I've been ordered to make a daily welfare check." She sounded breathless, if officious.

"As you can see, Noelle is once again healthy, happy,

fed and clean. Is there anything else, Trooper Kincaid?" He smiled slightly, figuring his dimple was putting a punctuation mark on the smirk.

"Look, Deacon, I don't want to traipse out here every day any more than you want me here."

"You're wrong there, darlin'. You have no idea what I want." He liked the way her eyes widened at his declaration as her cheeks turned pink again.

"I am not your *darlin'*." She did a decent impersonation of his voice.

"Yet."

"Ever." Her eyes got all squinty and her mouth scrunched up. The expression was so exasperated and cute it was all Deke could do to keep from kissing her right then and there. "*Argh*. Don't even," she threatened, backing away from him, one hand reaching back for the door.

"Same time tomorrow, darlin'?" He stepped toward her, grabbing for the door as she ducked away.

The door slammed shut.

Eight

Deke hadn't meant to slam the door. Really. The wind caught it and pulled it shut. Well, that was his story and he'd stick to it as he turned around and faced ten pairs of eyes. Eleven if he counted Noelle's. Except hers were screwed up tight and her mouth was open for a mighty wail. He was all too familiar with that expression but he knew how to preempt the crying jag.

He waded through the wives, plucked the baby from Jolie's arms and kept walking. Noelle's impending tears were a good excuse to hide away from his nosy family. He settled in the big, wooden rocking chair he'd installed in the makeshift nursery. Crooning a song and rocking always worked on the baby girl.

Deke had about ten minutes of peace before the door eased open. He was surprised to see Kade standing there.

"You draw the short straw?" Deke kept his voice soft and slightly singsong.

His cousin, only recently acknowledged as one of the late Cyrus Barron's sons, ducked his head to hide a grin.

"Naw. They probably don't even know I'm gone. That said, once you get out there, the questions are gonna fly. That trooper hit the radar of every wife and your reaction didn't exactly go unnoticed. Is there something we should know?"

Deke made a face, and Kade held up both hands in front of him, backing up a step. "Not my business. Got it. And it's not really the reason I'm here. I know you aren't running much livestock these days, but now that you're caring for the baby, if you need help, all you have to do is call. It's not like you have a wife or babysitter to leave Noelle with while you work down at the barn."

"Good point, but my foreman lives on the ranch. He'll cover everything until Christmas and then he's taking his family to Texas for the holidays. As long as the weather stays good, I can put her in—" Deke looked around "—something. That carrier thing that fits in the car-seat base. Or the buggy."

Kade's gaze settled on a box on the floor. Snagging it, he slit the tape holding it closed and pulled out something that resembled a small backpack. "You can use this, too. We have one like it. You stick the baby in it and strap it on, carrying her across your chest. As long as it's not sub-freezing, you could at least go feed the horses." Kade and his new wife were expecting, and apparently he'd done his homework. He looked down at the toes of his boots. "You do know you can't put her in the car seat in the truck and just...leave her, right?"

Deke didn't laugh, but he wanted to. "Yeah. Got that. She needs to be right there within sight because...helpless baby." He didn't add the "duh" but it was implied.

Laughing softly, Kade nodded. "Yeah, figured. But

you know, the women…" They exchanged knowing looks. "Have you thought about hiring a nanny or something?"

"Cash will find the mom before long. I can cope until then. Or call the Bee Dubyas in a pinch."

Kade laughed again. "That's true. Anyway, if you need me, I can come feed, or I can send one of my hands."

"Dude, you're going to have your own hands full soon enough. Pippa looks like she's ready to pop any day now."

Kade blanched and sank onto the end of the bed. "Yeah." He looked up, his expression bleak. "I'm terrified."

Gazing down at the baby now sleeping so peacefully in his arms, Deke murmured, "Yeah, I know the feeling."

Quin would have banged her head against the steering wheel but she was driving at highway speeds on the interstate.

Her visit with Deacon couldn't have gone any worse. As soon as she saw all the vehicles in the drive, she should have turned around and…what? Run away like a scared dog with her tail tucked between legs? She *really* needed to find the mother, like yesterday!

Determined to do just that, she headed toward Troop A HQ, rather than home. She had a change of civilian clothes in her locker there. It was Sunday. The place would be quiet and she'd have access to databases from the department computer that she wouldn't have on her laptop at home.

Eight hours later, her stomach burned from too much caffeine and too little food. She had a list of people to contact on Monday, when state offices were open. Leaning back in her squeaky desk chair, she closed her eyes and swiveled a little from side to side. She tapped out a rhythm on her desk with a pen. What if Noelle's mother wasn't a native Oklahoman? If she was simply a fan of

Deacon's, the girl could have come from any of the surrounding states.

Sitting up with a sigh, she made more notes: Arkansas, Missouri, Kansas, Texas. Midwives. Hospitals. She doodled on her pad, realized the black lines vaguely resembled a bus. How had she gotten to Thunder River? She added cab companies to her list. And bus lines. If the girl came in from out of state, maybe she got here by bus. With luck, they'd still have security footage at the station downtown.

Quin dropped her chin to her chest and rubbed her stiff neck muscles. She had no idea when the girl had arrived. It would take days to go through the footage and all she had to go on was a woman carrying a baby in a basket. *Needle, meet haystack.* Pushing back from the desk, she walked to the window, to discover that night had fallen. Time for a hot shower and a good night's sleep, then she'd hit the investigation hard in the morning, which was Monday. Ugh.

A half hour later, after a stop for fast food, she stood under the steaming spray of water in her shower. Tension melted from her body, and her mind drifted to the one place she really needed to avoid—thoughts of Deacon Tate. And that kiss. The feel of his body—far more muscular than she would have guessed—pressed against hers. With the weight and stiffness of her Kevlar vest between them.

She'd spent a lot of time observing the man. The way his long hair fell across his forehead. His dreamy blue eyes that could go from star sapphire to ice at the whim of his mood. Broad shoulders. Muscular arms and chest. Lean hips. And his hands. Yes, she pretty much had a love affair going with his hands. He had long fingers and the strength in them was evident every time he touched her. She knew his fingertips were calloused and rough from when he'd touched her bare skin.

And she was right back to their kiss. His kiss. He'd kissed her. She hadn't kissed him back. Nope. Not. At.

All. Quin thunked her forehead against the tile. That kiss could never repeat itself. It had been a huge breach of ethics. Not to mention that Deacon Tate could be dangerous to her equilibrium. And her heart.

Sleep was out of the question now. Her body was hot and achy. She slid her hands over her torso and stomach and pretended he was touching her. She replayed the kiss in her memory, the way his teeth nipped her lips, the way his tongue teased against hers. Quin could almost taste the way his skin had smelled—tart lemon and almond-like cookies, sage and cedar like walking in the woods.

So much for a hot shower. If she was smart, she'd switch the knob to Cold. Since she wasn't much of a masochist, she left the water temperature alone and just gave in to the urges created by thoughts of the sexy singer. She wasn't sure how much longer she could resist his charms.

Her visits needed to be perfunctory—a quick peek at the kid and then she'd hit the road. No problem. The less time she spent with Mr. Too Sexy For His Jeans, the better. And she needed leads to find the baby momma, who was the basis of this whole fiasco. The water went lukewarm and she shut it off. Nothing like a good dose of thinking about work to get her back on track.

Quin always volunteered to work Thanksgiving Day. Other troopers had families to share the day with and the last place she wanted to be was with hers. She'd rather be out on the highways making sure other families got safely to their destinations. Except this Thanksgiving, she had one extra duty. *Ugh.*

Not knowing how Deacon planned to spend the day, she'd called ahead…only to learn he was at his mother's place. With the whole family. Tates *and* Barrons. *Double ugh.*

She had a plan. She would duck in, make sure the baby

was happy and whole, and run. Because the last thing she wanted, after last Saturday and Sunday, was to be trapped in a house with all those people.

A Mercedes blew past her. She automatically hit her lights and siren and charged after the speeder. Quin called in the vehicle description and license plate. The car came back clear, meaning it wasn't reported stolen and the tag was up-to-date. Five miles later, the driver realized she was chasing behind. He pulled to the shoulder and the brake lights went off. Good. The driver had put the sedan in Park.

Still, she approached cautiously. Like domestics, seemingly normal traffic stops could go south in a hurry. "Please turn off the ignition," she called, easing up to the side of the car, one hand on the roof, the other on her pistol. The driver immediately complied. Quin leaned down to look in the window.

A very sheepish man with gray hair and Clark Kent glasses offered an apologetic smile. "I am so sorry, officer. I fear I wasn't paying attention."

She didn't acknowledge the apology. "License, registration and proof of insurance, please."

The guy patted his jacket, doing his best to look bemused. Quin's instincts kicked in. "Please step out of the car, sir."

She backed up to give him room. A second later, she had a fight on her hands. The guy erupted from the driver's seat, fists swinging. She ducked the first punch but the follow-through caught her on the cheek and it *hurt*. Still the man was out of shape and she wasn't. Quin had him subdued within a few short minutes, but she'd taken a few more licks in the process.

"What is your problem, mister?" she asked as backup arrived and hoisted the man to his feet.

"Do you know who I am?"

Quin closed her eyes, counted to ten and took a deep breath. "No. Because you decided to turn stupid before you handed me your driver's license." The man opened his mouth to tell her and she held up a hand. "Too late now and I don't really care what your name is. You assaulted a state trooper. You are going to jail."

About to lose her cool again, she backed away and let the other officers deal with him. In short order, the driver was identified, Mirandized and stuffed in the back seat of another trooper's cruiser. "You really should hit the ER, Quin," one of the officers said.

"Yeah, yeah. It's just a bruise and a split lip. There's another deal I have to take care of first. I'll stop by University Hospital on my way home just for the paperwork. My LT is gonna be really unhappy. He was off today."

After a bit of commiseration from the other troopers who had responded, Quin was back in her cruiser driving to the last place in the world she wanted to be. After dealing with this ego-inflated, entitled jerk, she was headed into a nest of more just like him.

The celebration wasn't quite in full swing yet. Deke was hanging out close to the front door. Not *hovering* exactly, but he wanted to be the one to answer when Quin arrived.

The place was crawling with Tates and Barrons. As far as his mother was concerned, the more, the merrier. She and his late uncle Cyrus were as opposite as two siblings could get, except for one thing: when it came to family loyalty, they'd been peas in a pod.

The sun was shining, the air chilly but comfortable and there would be football after lunch, but not on TV. Any shared holiday—Thanksgiving, Christmas, Easter, Fourth of July, it didn't matter—always ended in a game of pickup football between the Tates and the Barrons. This year, the game would be a little less cutthroat given that little CJ would be playing.

When the doorbell rang, Deke just managed to beat Dillon to it. They scuffled and Deke had his little brother in a headlock when the door opened. Quin stood there, her uniform rumpled, a dark bruise on her cheek threatening to spread to her eye, her lip cut and swollen.

"What the hell—" He pushed Dillon away and reached for Quin's arm, drawing her into the room. "Who hit you?" Anger sat like a frozen lump of cornbread dressing in his gut.

Dillon, standing beside him, sucked in air. "Dang, Deke."

"I'm fine," Quin insisted, looking distinctly uncomfortable. "I just had a small run-in with a speeder. Not a big deal."

"The hell you say." Deke normally didn't cuss. Katherine Tate had certain rules in her house and four-letter words were prohibited. At the moment, he really didn't care. "If you could see your face, Quin, you'd say different."

His mother was suddenly at his other side, having pushed through the mass of people who'd rushed the door after hearing Deke's raised voice. "Let the child in," she insisted.

"I'm not a child," Quin said.

"In my house, if you're hurt, you're a child. And you're bleeding."

"But I'm not—"

Deke brushed his index finger over her chin and held it up for her to see the bloodstained tip. "Yeah, darlin', you are. Come in."

"Come with me," his mom ordered.

She and Quin, followed closely by Jolie, disappeared into the interior of the house. All the rest of the family stood around in stunned silence until CJ piped up. "She had a bad boo-boo, Cuncle Deke. You shoulda kissed it. That's what Mommy and Daddy do for me."

Cuncle was a word CJ had coined to differentiate between his Barron uncles and his corresponding Tate cousins. Normally, Deke would have smiled at the kid but he was way too angry. Cord, CJ's dad, shushed him and suggested that they go see what was on TV.

Deke had to find out exactly what had happened and if Quin really was okay. He arrived at the door to the bathroom, standing just out of sight.

"Yes, Mrs. Tate. I fully intend on going to the ER. It's required by DPS."

His mother immediately scolded Quin. "You shouldn't be driving, young lady."

"Mrs. Barron—" Quin began.

"Call me Jolie."

"Will you please explain to her that I'm fine?" Quin sounded exasperated and frustrated.

Deke settled on a plan. He'd have to make arrangements for Noelle but he would insist on driving Quin to the ER. She still had a chip on her shoulder where he and his family were concerned and he had a major hankering to knock off that chip. To take care of her. Not to mention kiss her. Again.

Deke slipped out before he got caught eavesdropping and was sitting on a bar stool jostling Noelle on his knee when the three women returned. As he'd anticipated, his mother insisted Quin join them for lunch though it took the threat of calling her supervisor to get her to sit down and eat.

The Barrons and their wives gathered on one side of the massive farm table. The Tates lined the other. Deke's mom sat at one end and his oldest brother, Hunter, who served as chief of security for Clay Barron, sat at the other.

Deke did his best to steer Quin away from Dillon, but his irritating little brother grabbed the chair next to her when Tucker distracted Deke.

Taking matters into his own hands, Deke pulled out the empty chair on Quin's other side, picked up her chair—with her sitting in it—and set it down in the empty spot. Then he hooked the empty chair with his booted foot, dragged it into place and sat. He smirked at Dillon before turning a sunny smile on Quin. She was working her lips to hide her smile.

"Don't you have brothers?" he asked, acting all innocent.

"I do. Four of them."

"Then you should be used to stupid antics."

She raised an eyebrow over her uninjured eye and didn't bother to hide her own smirk. "You could say that."

"So," Dillon said, leaning around Deke, "did you get the license of the truck that hit you?" He *oofed* as Deke nailed him in the ribs with an elbow.

Their mother cleared her throat and gave Dillon and him her "mother stare." Then she smiled at Quin. "I suppose your brothers taught you lots of things growing up."

"Yes, ma'am, they did."

Dillon leaned over Deke again, still grinning. "Oh? Care to share?"

She fixed Dillon with a regal expression that was almost as good as his mom's. "They taught me what not to date."

Nine

Deke, taking a sip of water at the time, spluttered and coughed. Dillon was all too happy to pound on his back. When he could breathe again, his mom fixed him with a stare. "I like this one."

Great. His mother had never been subtle and the few women he'd brought to family gatherings had never measured up to Katherine Tate's strict standards for her boys. Now she put her seal of approval on a maddening cop who made him think very inappropriate thoughts about her and handcuffs. He managed to avoid looks from both women by keeping his head down and stuffing the traditional Thanksgiving meal into his mouth.

By the time lunch was over, Quin's shiner was a doozy and her eye was swollen almost shut. He exchanged a look with his mother over pumpkin pie. He was formally excused from clean-up duty. His mother was as concerned about Quin's injuries as he was and would back him up when he insisted on driving her into Oklahoma City to University Hospital to get checked out.

The argument was brief when he told Quin the plan. He paused to grab an ice pack from the freezer before gathering her up and ushering her toward the door. His brothers were teaching CJ to do whipped-cream shots straight from the can as he closed the door behind them.

Deke guided her to his truck, and she balked until he said, "Do you want me to drive your cruiser? Because, babe, I've always wanted to go code three."

"What about the baby?"

Laughter rumbled in his throat and he didn't even attempt to stop it. "Darlin', my mother has seven sons. Not one of us is married, nor do we have any kids. She's in hog heaven babysittin' that little girl. Not to mention the Bee Dubyas."

"Bee what-yas?"

He spelled out the words as he settled her into the passenger seat of his truck and buckled the seat belt before she could. Then he explained, "Bee Dubya. For Barron Wives. That's what we call them when they're runnin' in a posse like they sometimes do."

He handed Quin the ice pack and she gingerly pressed it against her cheek. Deke didn't miss the wince and found himself doing the same in sympathy.

Neither of them spoke on the drive to the hospital. Walking in with an injured Highway Patrol trooper was a fast way to get in and out of the ER. Her X-rays were negative. The lip was already scabbing over. Thanks to the ice pack on the trip into town, the swelling around Quin's eye was down but she had a heck of a shiner. The ER doc wanted her to go home to bed. Deke perked up at that instruction and grinned when Quin scowled.

She was hurt. A tender part of him that didn't often see

the light of day just wanted to offer comfort. The tenderness he felt toward this feisty woman should have made him nervous. He wanted to ascribe the feeling to being around the baby, but he had been contemplating a home and family before any of this happened. Bottom line? He was all kinds of interested in Quincy.

They ended up compromising, not that he was happy about it. He drove her back to his mom's, then strapped Noelle, snugly asleep in her carrier, into the base of the car seat in his truck, and followed Quin, who was driving her cruiser, home. "Just in case," he'd insisted. Of course, he hadn't mentioned his ulterior motives—like finding out where she lived. The strain of the fight was settling in and her muscles were most likely stiff. She couldn't take any of the super-duper pain pills the doctor prescribed until she was safely home.

Deke was right on her bumper as she keyed in through the gate of her complex and he slipped through on her tail. His mom would have his head if he didn't see Quin safely to her door. That explanation was on the tip of his tongue as she confronted him when he pulled up behind her cruiser.

He rolled down the back window so he could hear the baby if she stirred and stepped out of the pickup, hands up in surrender. "Don't care what you say, darlin'."

"Stop calling me that."

"Okay, Trooper Darlin'. Whatever you say. But I'm tellin' ya, my momma would have my head if she heard I'd just left you here and driven away. I'll sit here until you're safely inside."

She angled her head, and he could almost see the thoughts tumbling behind her calculating gaze. "You aren't going to insist on coming in?"

Deke gestured to the open window of his truck. "Little

bit is sleepin'. I'm not gonna wake her, and I sure don't plan on leavin' her alone in the truck."

He reached out and gently traced the tip of a finger along the uninjured side of her jaw. "The man who did this deserves to spend a long time in jail," he said, his voice quiet but threatening. She tensed at his words but he leaned in anyway and planted a soft kiss on the corner of her mouth. "Go get some sleep, darlin'. I'll see ya soon."

He gripped her shoulders, turned her around and gave her a nudge toward her condo. Deke waited until she'd unlocked the door before he climbed back into the truck. He didn't stop the grin when he saw her raise her hand and touch the corner of her mouth where he'd kissed her. Yeah…he planned on seeing a lot more of Trooper Kincaid.

The day after Thanksgiving, Quin awoke stiff and achy, and the thought of getting out of bed filled her with dread. She poked at her bottom lip and winced.

"Not too bright, dummy," she chided herself. Her lip was still swollen, as was that whole side of her face.

Quin brushed the tip of her index finger over the spot where Deacon's lips had brushed her mouth last night. She hadn't expected the kiss—or maybe she had, but not the sweetness of it, or the tenderness of his touch.

How could she be so stupid? There was no way she was getting involved with Deacon. No. Just no. It was all kinds of wrong on more levels than she could comprehend this morning. First, he was part of a case she was working on. Second, he was bad news and she didn't trust him. She needed the DNA proof from the paternity test. The results were slowed down by the holiday but she held out hope they'd arrive within the next couple of weeks. Discovering whether he was the father would answer a lot of her questions.

Did they have chemistry? Well, she was human. And female. And he was Deacon Tate. His fame put her off more than it attracted her, but she had to admit, he was sexier than all get-out when he was up on stage singing. She made a mental note to never use her computer at Troop A to watch his YouTube videos again.

So she was attracted to him. No big deal since she had no intention of ever stepping over the professional line again. And so what if he flirted with her. He was a man who lived for the adoration of his female fans. Obviously. He was charming. Handsome. Talented. Sexy.

Quin groaned. This line of thought was taking her nowhere. She rolled out of bed with as few movements as possible. A long, hot shower would ease some of the pain and would definitely help with the stiffness. Then she'd check in at Troop A to see if any new information about Noelle's mother had arrived. She was tugging on every string she had looking for a lead. Then she'd face the drive to Deacon's ranch.

An hour later, she walked into the briefing at Troop A to the sound of whistles and catcalls. She kept her cop face in place, ignoring them as she took a seat. Staff meetings only happened once a week. The rest of the time, troopers checked in with Dispatch and hit the highway—or other assigned duties—running. Just her luck, the briefing had been scheduled for today.

The lieutenant walked to the podium, stared around the room making a head count, then launched into the game plan for the holiday weekend. It seemed everyone but Quin would be back out on the highways for the travel rush. It rankled that the lieutenant singled her out to come to his office as they broke up.

As soon as he closed his office door behind her, she opened her mouth to complain but he interrupted with a brusque "How's the face?"

"Sore."

"I want you to go home." He shook his head at her. "No arguments. You still need to check on the kid, then you can work from home, where you'll be comfortable. You can follow up leads from there."

If she had any. Still, the idea of a long, hot bath, flannel pajamas and fuzzy slippers appealed.

"Rest up because I need you back on patrol duty tomorrow. And trust me, I'd be saying this to any trooper whose face looked like yours. You can arrange your check on Deacon Tate around the patrol schedule. Okay?" He flashed her a droll smile. "I know you've been chewing your leash, Kincaid. Get over it. You're very much in the public eye. We need to find the mother then turn this whole mess over to those with more political clout than we have."

"No kidding, sir."

"Then get to work."

"Sir, yes, sir."

When her cruiser rolled to a stop in front of Deacon's house, there were no other vehicles around. Weird. Every other time she'd been here, the place had seemed like traffic central. Did he have a garage? She got out and looked around. No movement anywhere. She strode up the walk and climbed the steps to the front porch. Still nothing. She knocked, then walked around the house peeking in windows. No movement. No sound.

Her emotions seesawed between worry and anger. On her second circuit of the house, movement down at one of the outbuildings caught her eye. She went back to her cruiser and drove to what turned out to be the barn. A man she'd never seen before was in the process of releasing several horses into a corral.

"Can I help ya?" the man called.

"I'm looking for Mr. Tate."

The man pushed his ball cap up and scratched at the thatch of hair that spilled across his forehead. "Well now, I probably need t'know why you're lookin' for the boss."

Quin approached the fence. "And you are?"

He walked over and stuck out his hand. "Matt McConaughey." He patted his ample middle and laughed at her skeptical expression. "I know. I get that reaction a lot. I manage the place for Deke when he's outta town. Now, why would an Oklahoma Highway Patrol trooper be lookin' for my boss?"

"The same reason I've been out here every day for the past week. He has a baby—"

"Oh, yeah. I heard about that." He pointed toward a house off in the distance. "I live over there. Don't pay much attention to the comings and goings at the big house."

"Well, I've been assigned to make a daily welfare check on the baby. I need to know where Mr. Tate is and, more importantly, where the baby is."

"Don't gotta clue 'bout the baby. Deke headed to Tulsa early this mornin'. The boys gotta concert there t'night."

A concert? In Tulsa? Where was the baby? Angry, she took out her phone and called the number she had for Deke. It went straight to voice mail. Why hadn't he told her he was leaving town? He knew she made this ridiculous trip every day. And was he stupid enough to drag the baby to a freaking concert?

Realizing she'd hung up before leaving a message, she called back. This time she left an earful. She ignored the grinning cowboy watching her. After ending the call, she didn't even try to mask her irritation, though she remained civil to the man. "I appreciate your help."

"I'm sure I'll see ya again, Trooper Kincaid. Drive safe now."

When she got to the ranch gate, Quin stopped the cruiser but let it idle. She would have to drive to Tulsa now. Except she had no idea where the blasted concert was taking place. She grabbed her cell and did a search. The Sons of Nashville were scheduled to play at the BOK Center, starting at 7:00 p.m. So why the heck were they already up there?

So much for a hot bath, flannel and fuzzies. No way would she task a Troop B officer with tracking down the errant singer. Nope. Quin wanted to tell him what she thought of him in person.

Two and a half hours later, she pulled up in front of the tour bus and parked. She was about to use her baton on the door when it swooshed open and a smiling Max Padilla greeted her.

"Well, howdy, Miss, er, Trooper Kincaid. I wasn't expectin' t'see you."

Quin stifled the irritation that had simmered into anger on the drive. It wasn't this man's fault that his boss was a major pain in her butt. "I'm here to see Mr. Tate."

He offered a grin and a little wink, which just added to her irritation. "I'm guessin' that would be Mr. Deke and not Mr. Dillon."

"That would be a good guess."

"He's inside the BOK, ma'am."

She didn't trust her voice so she dipped her chin in a clipped nod to acknowledge the information. Her body cringed with each stomping step she took to the backstage entrance and she hoped she had some ibuprofen in the cruiser. She pressed the button on the keypad and identified herself when security answered. It still took her another ten minutes to get to the room set aside for the band.

Listening at the door before knocking, Quin caught feminine laughter fluttering above the more guttural sounds from the men. If someone asked, she would have been hard-pressed to explain the emotions roiling inside her and she would never utter out loud the names she was calling Deacon.

She banged on the door and waited. Someone called, "It's open. C'mon in."

As Quin pressed down on the lever, she heard someone else say, "I hope that's catering. I'm starved."

Opening the door wide, she stepped into the room. Silence descended with the force of a thunderclap. A couple of guys wearing tour T-shirts exchanged nervous glances. One of the girls tittered. Another retained her seat in the lap of one of the band members and watched with an amused expression on her face. Scanning faces, Quin located Deacon sitting in the rear of the room, removed from everyone else.

"Well, well, well," he drawled. "Fancy meeting you here, Trooper Kincaid."

"We need to talk."

"Okay."

She stared around the room to make the point that she wanted the conversation to be private. He just grinned at her, that darn brow quirked in a mischievous arch. Great. She could ignore his appeal and if he didn't mind an audience, who was she to argue?

"Why didn't you tell me you'd be out of town?"

"Didn't know I needed to. Besides, it isn't much of a secret, darlin'. Every country station in the state has been advertising this concert."

"You could have told me." Okay, now she just sounded whiny. She inhaled deeply and blew out the breath to calm down. "You are aware that part of my duty as the lead officer on the baby Noelle case includes a daily welfare check."

"Is that why you've been comin' by the ranch?" He winked at her. "I thought you were comin' to see me."

"As if." When Deacon laughed, she realized she'd muttered that loud enough for him to hear. "Where's Noelle?"

She put every bit of haughty authority she was still cling-ing to into her tone.

"She's in Oklahoma City."

"Well, at least you didn't drag a baby all the way up here and subject her to—to…" Words failed and Quin re-sorted to waving her hands around the room. That's when she realized every person there was watching, fascinated by her exchange with Deacon. "What did you do? Call up one of your groupies to babysit? You can't be doing things like this, Mr. Tate. You have a responsibility to that child. One, I'll remind you, that you agreed…no, you *insisted* on accepting. You can't just drop a baby off willy-nilly."

He mouthed *willy-nilly* and curled his lips between his teeth in what appeared to be an effort not to laugh.

"I'm serious, Mr. Tate. I would think you'd have more sense than to leave that child with just anyone."

Deacon's expression morphed from one of playfulness to one tinged with irritation. "Ah. So you're accusing me of being so callous that I'd dump the little girl I'd agreed to take care of on just *anyone*?"

There was a trap here but Quin was tired, annoyed and in pain. She couldn't see it so rather than saying a word, she nodded.

"You mean just *anyone*…like my mother."

Ten

His mother. Of course. What was she thinking? Oh, wait, she hadn't been thinking.

The scene kept playing over and over in her memory as she drove back to Oklahoma City. There'd been no humor in his expression when he'd told her where Noelle was. Feeling like an idiot—as she should—Quin had stood there with her mouth all but gaping as the implications hit her. No one in that room had said a word and she could relate to how a deflated balloon felt. Exiting with as much grace as she could muster, she'd all but run to her cruiser.

And here she was, headed southwest toward Oklahoma City. Quin glanced at the speedometer. A steady seventy-five—the speed limit. She had a lead foot but she was tempted to ease off. Her speed dropped five miles per hour. She was in no hurry to see Mrs. Tate because she had every reason to believe that as soon as she left the green room at the BOK, Deacon had called his mother.

What could she say to the woman? Worse, what would

the woman say to her? Quin knew from the moment she'd first laid eyes on Katherine Tate that the matriarch would fight like a momma bear for her boys. Watching their interaction at breakfast that first morning, she'd figured Deacon was very likely a favorite son.

The closer she got to Oklahoma City, the slower she drove. Quin stretched out the drive as long as she could. Once she hit the city limits, though, she had no more excuses. She'd already notified Dispatch of her destination and received directions instead of an address. Having met the woman, Quin was surprised not to be headed to Nichols Hills or one of the other wealthy enclaves. Nope. Just like her son, she lived out in the country on the family ranch. Why couldn't these people live in the city like normal folks?

Quin pulled through the ranch gate and slowly drove up the gravel drive. As she passed, cows happily munching the winter-brown grass lifted their heads to watch. Who had cows in their front yard? A man on horseback rode toward the cows and waved at her. Okay, maybe they were cattle instead of cows. There was a difference. The road took a gentle curve through an alley of trees, their bare branches entwining overhead.

When she saw the house, she stopped her cruiser. It was nothing like what she expected. It was huge and sprawling, and if she'd driven up here on a dark, stormy night, she probably would have turned around and high-tailed it out of there. She'd read too many Gothic novels as a kid. The home positively loomed from the top of a hill. It had three stories, a gabled roof, columns and was covered in what the locals called giraffe stone. Two one-story wings stretched from each end. The porch ran the length of the main portion of the house, its white columns supporting a balcony accessible from the second floor.

Quin sighed deeply and squared her shoulders. The

sooner she could see the baby and run, the better. But when she parked she didn't get out of the car because she still had no idea what to say to Mrs. Tate.

The front doors opened and a tall woman in jeans, boots and a chambray shirt stepped out onto the porch. She jammed her hands on her hips and hollered, "You gonna sit out there all day, Trooper Kincaid, or are you gonna come inside and be civilized?"

There was no hope now. Infused with dread, Quin got out and approached. Her booted feet clomped on the steps, their cadence giving away her reluctance.

"Don't dawdle, girl. I got things to do before the sun goes down."

She quickened her pace and Quin looked up to meet Mrs. Tate's sharp gaze. She'd thought the woman was wearing a work shirt. She'd been wrong. The blouse was a chambray blue but carried the sheen of polished cotton. It had a scene of snow-covered evergreens and cardinals delicately embroidered across the front. Quin caught the soft off-white gleam of pearls at the open collar. Her gaze flicked up just in time to catch a fleeting smile on Mrs. Tate's face.

What was it about this woman and pearls?

"Mom will deal with her."

Deacon glanced up at his youngest brother. He expected to see a mischievous expression to match Dillon's teasing tone. He found sympathy instead. He nodded in agreement but said nothing.

"I wouldn't wanna be that trooper by the time Mom's done with her."

He shrugged absently, plucking a tune from his guitar.

"Look, Deke, I know y'all think I'm young and stuff but I'm not as clueless as I act."

"I know that." He strummed through a chord progression. "What are you after, little bro?"

"Nothin'. I just figure you might want someone to talk to. I mean, dude! You're a single dad. Out of the blue. How crazy is that?" Dillon dropped onto the couch beside him. "Are you worried about the test results? What if she's yours?"

"She's not mine, Dill Pickle." Deke reverted to his brother's childhood nickname in hopes the other man would go away.

"Then why are you fighting to keep her?"

"I'm not. Not exactly."

Dillon pushed the sunglasses propped on the top of his head down to cover his eyes. Then he dramatically pulled them down his nose and leaned forward, peering intently over those glasses. "Seriously?"

His brother's antics made him laugh, which Deke suspected had been Dillon's intent all along. "Fine. Busted. I don't think she's mine, though we need the DNA part of the paternity test anyway. Chance says women are coming out of the woodwork to claim Noelle. The police kept the contents of the note out of the news, and it hasn't leaked so far. That's one way we can determine a legitimate claim. The other will be a confirmation of mitochondrial DNA from the mother."

"Woo, listen to you, Mr. Smart Guy. Maybe those college classes stuck after all."

"Or I watch too many reality-based crime shows when I can't sleep."

They both laughed. Deke welcomed the companionship. But after a moment, Dillon continued his interrogation. "You know I'm gonna ask. Everyone is wondering but Mom told us to stay out of it."

With a long-suffering sigh, Deke said, "Go ahead. Get it off your chest."

"Why?"

Deacon played a few more chords, paused to make notations in a musical composition notebook, strummed again. "Christmas is coming up. I have the feeling the mother will come back for Noelle. If the baby is in the system, she might never get her back."

"Uh-huh." The disbelief in Dillon's voice earned him a look.

"Uh-huh, Dill. If it turns out she's capable of taking care of the baby, I'll help her get Noelle back."

"Why would you help her?"

He lifted a shoulder and continued composing the tune. "How desperate do you have to be to drop your baby off at a band's tour bus? I'm bettin' the mom's not much more than a kid herself. She saw the bus, got this harebrained idea and boom. I have a baby. If the mom is honest with me, and she's not strung out or something, I'll do what I can for her."

Dillon snatched the notebook and made his own notations before pushing it back. "Play it that way."

Deke did and smiled. "Much better. Thanks."

"You're welcome." Dillon listened to him play some more, then asked, "Now tell me the real reason."

That was the question of the day, wasn't it? Deke had been mulling over reasons since he'd first laid eyes on the angelic child. "I wish I knew. I took one look and fell in love with her. It's hard—taking care of Noelle. Lord knows I'm exhausted all the time. I lay awake at night listening to her breathe and start freaking out about SIDS or croup. Colic. She'll be teething before too long."

"Uh-huh."

Deke hummed a vocal line over the chords he was strumming, both stalling and gathering his thoughts. "It's crazy, Dillon, but I want a family. I look at the Barron

boys. I watch Cord with CJ. I see the others with their
Bee Dubyas. They're happy. They want to go home at
night. With Noelle around, I don't want to *leave* home.
I want to adopt her if the mother doesn't turn up. I want
to find a woman I love so much that I want to make our
own babies because I want Noelle to have brothers and
sisters. I want to fill my house as full as our house was
growing up."

Reaching over to feel Deke's forehead and laughing
when his brother slapped his hand away, Dillon said,
"Nope. No fever. You do realize that finding a woman
who wants seven kids in this day and age is like finding
a…" He flapped his hands in the air like he was searching for inspiration. "That kind of woman is so rare there's
nothing to compare it to."

"I don't have eight bedrooms and dang if I'll make my
kids share a bedroom. You had it easy, kid. Hunter was
already out of the house, plus Mom and Dad had added
on their master suite so you got your own room. I had to
share a room with Tucker. And he snored like a diesel truck
when he was two. I just want Noelle to have some siblings.
When a kid's an only child, it makes me kinda sad."

"Uh-huh." Dillon leaned away but he wasn't quite fast
enough. Deacon's fist tagged him on the biceps with a
teasing punch. "All right, all right," he laughed. "So, do
you have someone in mind?" He waggled his brows suggestively.

"No."

"Yeah, right. You answered my question way too fast,
Deke. I'm thinkin' you've taken a fancy to the trooper."

"No!" Okay. Maybe he shouldn't have been quite so
forceful with that denial because Dillon was now having
trouble breathing around the laughter. "She's not interested in me or kids, Dill. You've seen her. She goes white

every time someone even looks like they might hand her the baby."

"Mom likes her," Dillon wheezed.

"Shut. Up."

Dillon laughed harder. When he could breathe, he huffed out, "You *are* interested in her. Gotta say she certainly—"

"Don't go there, Dillon. I'm warning you." Deke was all but growling. His little brother was saved by a knock on the door.

"Yo, dudes!" Kenji stuck his head in. "We're on in, like, five."

Quin perched on the edge of a leather couch. A silver serving tray with a complete silver coffee-and-tea service reigned over a slate coffee table. Who still entertained a guest like this? Oh, yeah, a woman who wore pearls with her jeans and cowboy boots. She placed Mrs. Tate in her early sixties but this setup was a throwback to the *Leave It to Beaver* days of the fifties.

Mrs. Tate had convinced her to stay for dinner. Okay, she wouldn't take no for an answer. Quin had even been forced to hold the baby for a bit—just so she could ascertain for herself that Noelle was fine and well cared for, as Mrs. Tate explained. The dig in that comment was apparent and Quincy had blushed. Now, what seemed like hours later, here they were having tea and coffee.

Mrs. Tate sat regally, spine straight, shoulders square, chin up—her posture perfect. Quin had no trouble picturing this woman looking right at home in *Downton Abbey*. "I do appreciate you staying for a visit, Quincy. We're still friends so I can call you Quincy, right?"

"Of c-course." Darn it. Why did she have to stammer? Quincy steadied the china cup and saucer holding her coffee on her knee.

"Please call me Katherine. I suspect we might become better friends before all is said and done."

Katherine smiled at her and while it looked benign enough, Quin saw the shark swimming behind the woman's expression. Quin was skating on thin ice and she knew it. She nodded and offered a partial smile but kept her mouth shut.

"Since you have such a large place in my son's life, Quincy, I thought it wise for us to get to know one another."

"No, ma'am." At the woman's raised brow, Quin scrambled to explain. "What I mean, ma'am, is that I have no place in Deacon's life. I'm here only to deal with the baby during the course of my investigation. Once the mother is located and a determination is made about the best interest of the child, then I'm…"

"You're what, Quincy?"

"No longer involved."

"Are you involved?" That shark smile again. "With my son?"

"Good heavens, no!" Quin wanted to bite her tongue. Time to backpedal. "What I mean is, your son…I… There's… No. Just…no. We aren't involved. Not like you're insinuating. And we won't be. I'm a state trooper doing my job. Your… Deacon… He's…"

"Handsome?" Now Katherine's smile was cat-and-cream smug. "Talented?"

"Ah, well, yes. Of course he is. But he and I… We aren't…"

"Did you know my mother was a good Southern woman?"

Quincy's head spun from the lightning-fast change in subject. "I… No. I know nothing about your family."

Now Katherine's smile was indulgent. "But you should, dear. Momma came from Georgia. She met Daddy at a cotillion in Atlanta. He was this brash westerner come east to get gentrified because he'd already made his first million. He was a rancher and an oilman. Tall and handsome, and Momma said it was love at first sight. They eloped, much to her parents' consternation. At least until they got a gander at Daddy's bank account. That made him their favorite son-in-law."

The older woman's right hand went to her throat, her fingers lovingly stroking the pearl necklace framed by the collar and open placket of her blouse. "Momma always wore pearls, you see." She sat up straighter—if that was even possible—and her voice took on a deep Southern drawl. "She used to say 'A Southern woman always has a string of pearls, Katherine. They give her grace and beauty even when she's feeling clumsy and ugly. They give her something to clutch when she wants to wring her hands.'" Katherine added, in her own voice, "One must never wring one's hands, no matter how dire the situation, you see." She tilted her head as if listening to something outside and smiled.

Quincy heard it then…the soft whump-whump-whump of a helicopter. Wait? The Tates had a helicopter pad? *And* a helicopter? Who in the world was arriv— Deacon. Of course. Moments later, she watched through the wide windows of the living room as the helicopter landed, its door opened and Deacon ducked out. Before she could catch her breath, Deacon was striding into the room. He stopped to kiss his mother's cheek, then asked, "Where's my girl?"

"Upstairs, son, but she's sleepin'. Don't go botherin' her now. Girls need their beauty sleep."

He laughed and leaped up the stairs two at a time. "Just gotta make sure she's sleepin' sweet."

As soon as Deacon was out of sight, Quincy gulped down her lukewarm coffee and wondered how to extricate herself. He wouldn't be gone more than a couple of minutes and she had no clue how to avoid seeing him when he returned. Her instincts told her to just get up and run.

Katherine leaned over and patted her knee. "You really should think about getting some pearls, Quincy."

Eleven

Deacon had been doing his best to sleep in. Noelle had suffered a touch of colic and after a slightly panicked middle-of-the-night call to Jolie—because there was no way he was getting his mother involved—he'd loaded the baby into his truck and they'd gone on a road trip around the countryside until Noelle fell asleep. He discovered she preferred love ballads like Dierks Bentley's "Black" and Jason Aldean's "Burnin' It Down." Too bad those songs sent his thoughts rocketing straight back to the kiss with Quin that should never have happened. Though now that it had, Deke was more than ready to seduce Trooper Kincaid into his bed, bad idea though it might be. She didn't like him, didn't trust him. Maybe it was the idea of forbidden fruit...

He shook the thought out of his head. Any pursuit of the lovely trooper was a bad idea. Not to mention his mother liked her. That fact should have him running away as fast as he could go. Remembering his discussion with Dillon, he reminded himself that he and Noelle were just a job to Quin, that she didn't have a motherly bone in her body. Sure she was sexy, but she wasn't forever.

Half-awake, he continued contemplating the events of the past several weeks. Ignoring the prickle in the back of his mind about the test results being due any time, Deke thought about the sexy trooper. He was a perverse son of a gun for enjoying his daily visits with Quin, not to mention that he was totally smitten with the baby girl asleep down the hall. Needling the trooper to get a reaction out of her was becoming a favorite pastime.

He drifted into a light doze, the sexy cop filling his mind.

Pounding on the door roused him from a vivid dream about the trooper and her handcuffs. Huh, who knew? That kink was becoming more interesting. Wearing only sleep pants slung low on his hips, he stumbled to the front door. To avoid waking up to a horde of relatives, he'd reprogrammed the electronic unlock code. Punching in the new sequence, he expected to find his mother or one of the Bee Dubyas when he opened the door.

Instead, he got the very woman of his dream. He caught her with her hand raised, ready to knock again. Her eyes widened as her gaze trailed from his face, down across his chest—and lower. Already aroused, his body reacted even more. Did Quin's pupils dilate? Her nostrils definitely flared and yeah, there was pink in her cheeks probably not brought on by the chilly temperature.

"You're early." Deke yawned and scrubbed his fingers through his messy hair.

"Obviously."

"Come in. I'll make some coffee." He stepped back so she could walk through the door.

Deke remembered to shut the door as Quin slipped past him. She unzipped her uniform jacket and shed it, dropping it on the back of his favorite chair as she headed toward the kitchen. With one ear cocked toward the bedrooms, he padded barefoot after her. He should have gotten cold, standing there shirtless in the door while winter air swirled in, which also should have taken care of his obvious reaction to her. But no.

He started the coffeemaker and clicked on the baby monitor perched on the kitchen counter. Listening to liquid drip into the stainless-steel carafe, Deke faced Quin and leaned back against the counter, legs crossed at the ankles. He absentmindedly scratched his chest. Quin's sharp intake of breath reminded him that he had company. And that he was standing here mostly naked.

What would it take to get her mostly naked? *No, scratch that.* He wanted her completely naked. Or at least out of that dang bulletproof vest she wore. Yes, she needed the armor for her job, but he really wanted to see the woman beneath the uniform. Neither of them spoke until the coffeemaker signaled that caffeine was now available in hot liquid form. He poured two mugs and slid one across the island to his guest before he rummaged in the fridge for the vanilla creamer she liked. He'd bought a big bottle just for her.

After several deep gulps, Deke figured he was coherent enough to carry on a normal conversation—something more refined than "Happy hump day. Me man. You woman. Get in my bed. Now."

"So what brings you out here so early?"

Quin stared pointedly at the neon diner clock on the wall above his fridge. "Late night?"

Deke liked a snarky woman as much as the next guy, but this morning, it flat out irritated him. "As a matter of fact, yeah. The baby was sick. She didn't get down until almost five." He made a production of looking at the watch on his wrist. "I've had all of three and a half hours sleep."

Did she look contrite there for a whole second? If Deke had any sense at all—and according to his mother, that was a debatable question—he'd do everything possible to get this annoying, if sexy, woman out of his life and get on with things. He'd considered doing so, but something always distracted him. Noelle cried. His phone rang. Food needed to be cooked, dishes washed, naps. Besides, he was curious. About Quin. About…them.

"Sick?" Her voice sounded accusatory.

"According to Jolie, it was a touch of colic and something all babies get on occasion. Her solution was to bundle up Noelle, put her in the car seat and drive around until she fell asleep. I don't even want to talk about how many miles I put on my truck between one and five."

"You drove her around in your truck? In the middle of the night?"

Deke yawned and scratched his chest again while taking another swig of coffee. "Yeah, those are the same questions I asked Jolie. Since she is both a nurse *and* a mother, I figured she was the expert."

Quin's gaze was glued to his hand. He scratched again and then rubbed down his stomach. She looked a little glassy-eyed now. He'd considered stepping into the laundry room to grab a T-shirt, but given Quin's reaction to him being shirtless, he was now considering tugging his sleep pants just a little bit lower.

"Like what you see, Trooper Kincaid?" The words were out of his mouth before he thought about them, and maybe the lazy drawl in his voice was a bit of overkill, but Quin's reaction was immediate and sharp.

"You need to put on clothes, Mr. Tate."

And she needed to take some off. Color was surging into her cheeks, and he just couldn't resist poking at her. "My house, my rules."

She sputtered, her mouth opening and closing several

times before she managed to speak. "That's it. We're done. There is no way this child should—"

Noelle's coughing and crying came through the monitor loud and clear. He automatically headed toward her room. Quin didn't follow him, but her voice did.

"Perhaps you aren't cut out to be the caretaker of an infant, Mr. Tate. Why don't you give up this farce and just let me put her into foster care?"

And there she went again. Yeah, this time he would call Chance. Maybe.

Quin didn't feel like traipsing down the hall after Deke, who was ignoring her. She could hear the baby crying through the monitor. Moments later, the microphone picked up Deke's soothing voice.

"Shh, baby girl. S'okay now. I'm here. No need for tears. Are you hungry? Bet you need a fresh diappy, too. Let me check."

Quin heard the rustle of material and then a disgusted "whew-eee," followed by a low chuckle that did all sorts of things to her insides. That was so not fair. The man was changing a dirty diaper and she was plotting ways to get him to kiss her again.

"You are a sweet little stinky-butt, baby girl. Let's get you all clean now before we have to go see that mean ol' state trooper."

Was it her imagination or did Deke's voice get louder when he said that last part? Jerk. He probably knew she was listening to every word. She took back everything she'd just been thinking. She would sit here, finish her coffee, check the baby and skedaddle. She'd had quite enough of the egotistical man, standing around all seductive in those flannel pants showing off his tight abs and scratching through the just-enough-to-be-interesting thatch of dark hair on his chest, making her want to run her fingers through it. Nope. She. Was. Done.

Then he walked in with a dopey grin on his face as he looked at the baby cradled in his arms. Men shouldn't get that look on their faces when dealing with small, squirmy humans. Heck, as far as she was concerned, *women* shouldn't go all googly-eyed, but they did. Deke ignored Quin as he settled the baby into a carrier on the counter. Noelle cooed at him as he prepped her bottle and clapped her hands when he took her out of the contraption and settled into his favorite chair in the great room.

Swiveling on her stool, Quin watched him. She had to admit the guy truly was competent. He changed diapers. He made bottles. Judging by the basket of neatly folded clothes in the laundry room behind the kitchen, he knew how to run a washer and dryer.

"Ha. He'll make some woman a great wife one of these days," she muttered. Not that she cared. She wasn't in the market for a wife. Or a husband. And especially not a boyfriend. Her biological clock could just keep tick-tick-ticking along. Home and hearth weren't high on her priority list. But… She glanced around.

Every time she came out here, she got the same feeling. This wasn't just another house to Deke. This was his home. He had a residence in Nashville—she'd checked, but this log cabin was home. She caught the chuckle bubbling up before it escaped. Calling this house a log *cabin* was like calling the Barron Hotel a motel. Even so, the place felt…lived in. Comfortable. A place where you could take your shoes off, plop your feet on the coffee table and watch TV.

She looked into the living area at the soaring ceilings, the huge windows that opened to breathtaking vistas, the massive native stone fireplace flanked by bookcases filled with books. Curious, she slipped off the stool and tiptoed over to check some of the titles. There seemed to be no rhyme or reason to his "filing" system, or the types of books on the shelves. She took down a biography of Harry Truman. It was obvious from the wear and tear on the pages that the book had been read. She reshelved it, checked the Harry Potter book next to the biography. It, too, looked well-read and disheveled. Like its owner.

Quin did not want to like Deacon. She didn't want this case to get personal in any way, shape or form. But it had, despite her best efforts. There was just something about the guy that sucked people in. Whether it was his good-ol'-boy demeanor, those amazing blue eyes or his handsome face. Not to mention that honed body... She jerked her thoughts back to business. Treading dangerous ground, she reminded herself.

"You're thinking awfully hard over there." The whiskey-rough sound of his voice startled Quin out of her ruminations. Was there anything *not* sexy about the man?

"Actually, I wasn't thinking anything except I've made my duty call and I should get on with my day."

"Suit yourself. I *was* going to offer breakfast..." Was he wheedling?

"Sorry. Already ate." Quin settled her belt and strode toward the chair. Where Deke was sitting. Leaning against her coat. "I'll just grab my coat." She indicated it with a tilt of her head.

"Ah. Sorry." Deke leaned forward but only far enough that she could grab the collar and tug. He was such a jerk.

Yes. A jerk. Not a nice man. Not an aw-shucks country boy with blue eyes and a dimple. She needed to remember that if she was to get through this whole situation with her sanity intact. "Sorry I woke you. I'll try to schedule my visits a little later in the day, seeing as you aren't a morning person." Quin headed for the door. "I'll let myself out."

"Y'all come back now, hear?"

Was he mocking her? While she normally had a good ear for sarcasm, Quin couldn't tell. Yes, his drawl sometimes became more pronounced, but he did that to flirt, or win over an unsuspecting adversary. She was onto that particular shtick.

Don't look back. Don't look back. She couldn't help herself. She looked back. Deke had the baby up on his shoulder, patting her back. That so was not an image she wanted in her head on the drive back to Oklahoma City. Then the insufferable man looked up at her and winked.

The door slammed behind Quin and if the noise hadn't startled Noelle so that she cried and spit up some formula, Deke would have been totally satisfied by their interplay. She wanted him. And it irritated the snot out of her. Yup. She would share his bed before it was all said and done.

He pushed out of the chair and headed to the bathroom. Noelle needed a bath. He needed a shower. And then he had some work to do around the ranch. He had a crazy dream about Noelle, about teaching her to ride a horse. To play the guitar. She wasn't his. But she could be. Even if the paternity test turned out negative, adoption was an option.

What the hell was he thinking? He stared down at the baby splashing in the plastic tub secured to the broad granite slab covering the bathroom's vanity. Single parenting was hard—as he'd discovered while looking after her for almost a month. Still, Noelle owned a huge chunk of his heart. While easier, life without her would be so much lonelier, and he wondered if he truly wanted to go back to his life as it was before.

Noelle cooed at him and dang if she wasn't batting her eyelashes. She was a born flirt. The blue of her eyes was almost the same shade as Quin's. And though her fuzzy cap of hair was a pale gold, it might turn to a richer blond like the woman who'd just marched out of his house.

Wouldn't that be something.

Twelve

December was half over and Quin was so tired of making this drive. Coming out here to the ranch just added one more frustration to her day. She'd spent the morning peering over the shoulder of an Oklahoma State Bureau of Investigation agent and getting nothing but attitude for it. No one had been able to locate a birth certificate or any record of baby Noelle's birth. Without that, they had very little to go on in order to identify her mother.

The Chickasaw Tribal Police had assisted in getting security-cam footage of the parking lot. It pictured a young woman creeping up to the bus and depositing the basket, but her face was obscured. Quin had watched the footage over and over, noting the almost perfect timing between the mother leaving her baby and the appearance of the bus driver. Little more than a minute separated the two events.

She had lots of theories about the situation. Had the bus driver been in on it from the beginning? Who else would know the timing so precisely? Quin made a note to interview the man again. Then she wondered if the mother had been nearby, hiding and watching to make sure the baby was found quickly. If so, that indicated a level of caring. If not, then Quin would recommend termination of parental rights in absentia, clearing the way for the baby to go into foster care with a chance at adoption. She wasn't into kids but Noelle was a cute one. Some family would snap the baby up in a heartbeat.

Quin was honest enough to hope for as little time in foster care as possible. The vast majority of foster parents were wonderful, loving people doing their best for the kids shuttled through the system. Her own experiences weren't the norm.

All this was well and good, but living with a single superstar was not in the best interests of a little girl, no matter how rich the guy was, or how much power his family wielded. The whole situation still irritated her. She hated people who gamed the system, and from her observations, the Tates, with the assistance of the powerful Barrons, were masters at it. She'd bet dollars to doughnuts that they could have fast-tracked the DNA test but every time she asked for the results, Chance Barron, as Deacon's attorney, stonewalled.

The media had caught wind of the story and there was speculation. She'd fielded a few calls, answering questions with the ubiquitous "No comment." She had to assume that Deacon's "people" were doing the same.

To distract herself, she pulled through the drive-through of a fast-food restaurant and ordered lunch on the run: cheeseburger, salty fries and a big soft drink, plus a coffee for later. After receiving her order, she found a parking space at the edge of the lot, pulled in and scarfed down her food.

Sitting at a stoplight a short time later, Quin drummed her fingers on the steering wheel. She couldn't stall any longer—time to make the drive to the land of sexy singers. She shook her head and pressed the accelerator as the light changed to green. Deacon Tate was not sexy. Not to her. And that kiss they'd exchanged had meant nothing at all. Nada. She was a professional. And he was a pain in her...profession.

With Noelle down for her afternoon nap, Deke grabbed a fast shower, then got another cup of coffee and settled in his office to catch up on some work. Trying to schedule studio time around the tour had been a hassle. And now, with Noelle in his life, the thought of flying to Nashville didn't sit well. Maybe he'd invite the band to come back early. The guys could lay down some tracks in his home studio before their gig on New Year's Eve.

He sent out emails, along with pictures he'd snapped of Noelle. The munchkin was far too cute and she had him totally wrapped around her tiny fingers. Deke was man enough to admit that fact to himself and his family. He glanced at the calendar. Was it possible a month had passed since she'd come into his life? Was it possible to love a child who probably wasn't his as much as he'd come to love this one?

His phone dinged with an incoming text. Deke opened it and stared. He didn't want to fumble with letters on a screen. He wanted to hear his cousin's voice, needed the immediacy of a direct answer. He scrolled through his contacts, almost smiling when the first name on his VIP list was Chance Barron. What did it say about him that he called the cousin who was his attorney far more often than Chase, the cousin who ran Barron Entertainment and was technically his boss? When Chase had opened Bent Star Records, Deke was first in line to sign with the label.

His coffee cup was empty so he headed to the kitchen for a refill, hitting the call button on his cell as he walked.

Chance picked up on the second ring and Deke put him on the speaker so he could pour his coffee.

"You answered quick. Are you in the middle of something?"

"No. In fact, you caught me between stuff, so excellent timing."

"Is it really done?" Deke asked bluntly. He'd been as nervous as a pimply-faced boy meeting his prom date's father waiting on Chance to work his legal magic.

"Yeah, cuz. It's done. You're officially good to keep her until after the New Year."

For the first time in several weeks, the pressure in Deke's chest eased and he inhaled deeply. "Thanks, Chance." A brisk knock sounded on the door. Expecting his ranch foreman, Deke called, "It's open."

After a pause, Chance said, "Not a problem, Deke. You do know, though, that you can't keep her forever, right?"

Deke heard the other man blow out a breath. "You got the results back."

A long moment of silence had Deke fisting his hands before his cousin spoke. "Yeah. She's not yours. The test was conclusive."

A block of ice settled in his chest, but he breathed through it, the cold dissipated by a flash of fierce love for the little girl. He didn't want to give her up. "You're wrong, Chance. She *is* mine. If not by blood, then by heart. You need to figure out a way I can adopt her, so—"

"You can't do that!" The indignant voice cut him off midsentence, and Deke pivoted. Quin stood just inside the door all but vibrating with outrage.

With far more calmness than he felt, he said, "Do what you have to, Chance. I need to take care of something here."

"Yeah, I heard. Good luck with that, bud."

"What game are you playing, Mr. Tate?"

Mr. Tate? So she was back to using formality to keep him at arm's length. "Listen, Quin—"

"No. I'm through listening. I have no clue what sort of crazy publicity stunt you're staging but it's done. Your attorney just told you you're not the father. I'm taking the baby into custody and transferring her to DHS for placement in foster care. *Real* foster care, with foster parents who have been licensed."

"The hell you are." Deke exhaled. Reached deep to find the calm he needed to deal with this maddening cop. It would really help if he wasn't so damn attracted to her.

She edged around him, and he saw the calculation in her eyes. She was trying to maneuver past him to get down the hallway to Noelle's room. That wasn't going to happen.

"Results of the paternity test don't matter at the moment, Quin. Custody papers have been signed by a judge and filed. I'm Noelle's temporary guardian until a formal hearing can be held in January."

"You aren't fit to take care of a baby."

He arched one brow and all but dared her to follow up on that allegation. When she didn't, he waited some more. One thing he'd learned while dealing with her—Quin Kincaid was long on righteous indignation but very short on patience. He planned to use that to his advantage. Until Noelle wailed.

Deacon was down the hallway leading to the bedrooms before Quin could do much more than take a step. As she arrived in the nursery, he already had the baby in his arms and was jostling her gently. He was not-so-subtly checking for a dirty diaper and then he had the little girl on the top of the dresser-cum-changing table.

Quin didn't know how to react to this...domesticity. Deacon Tate was a superstar. He had *people*, as in "I'll have my people call your people," but none of those people were here in this designer log house that felt homey and warm. And since none of them was there, he was the one changing the baby's diaper. And not for the first time. What guy did that? Plus, he constantly proved her wrong about his caretaking capabilities.

But why? What was in this deal for him? He wasn't necessarily a Nashville bad boy. Something of a flirt, with a different girl at every event, but not...*bad*. As far as her investigation revealed, there'd been no scandal associated with him. He didn't need to rehabilitate his image with an act of kindness like this. On paper, Deacon appeared to be a genuinely nice guy who did good things for people, even if he was a serial dater.

But Quin was a cynic, due to her own childhood in and out of the system. She'd been used as a pawn by a rich family and knew from first-hand experience. No one was this altruistic—not without a big payoff. There had to be some sort of perk for a star to take on an abandoned baby that wasn't his. Her head hurt from unraveling his motivation. All the possible reasons were more tangled up than a plate of angel-hair pasta.

And what was the deal with wanting to adopt Noelle? Yeah, since the kid wasn't his, was this just a big ruse to gain points with his adoring public? It wouldn't be the first time a big star adopted a kid and it got splashed all over the news.

She glanced up to discover Deacon standing in front of her. A moment later, he handed off the baby, whom she grabbed by sheer reflex.

"Hey!" she called after his retreating back.

"She's hungry. I'm going to fix her bottle." He paused and glanced over his shoulder at Quin. "Unless you want to fix the bottle?"

"No, that's okay. I'll—"

He walked away, effectively cutting off her protest.

As Quin followed him into the spacious kitchen, baby Noelle cooed and her tiny fingers tangled in Quin's ponytail. She smiled, despite herself, and jostled the kid the way she'd seen Deacon do. Settling one hip on the wrought-iron bar stool by the kitchen island, she watched the far-too-sexy man bustle about. He spooned formula into the bottle, added water, put on the lid and shook, whistling the whole time. It was a catchy tune, and Quin tried to place the song.

"You wanna feed her?"

She gulped and shook her head, resisting the urge to back away. "No. Sorry. Not the maternal type." She wasn't, but she wasn't petrified of holding the baby. When had that happened? When had she grown comfortable in this house with these two?

Deacon smiled. And darn if that smile shouldn't have been outlawed. Women around the world would do anything to be on the receiving end of that smile and here she was, sitting in the man's house, two feet away, trying hard to resist him.

"I'm not so sure about that, darlin'," he drawled. The light in his blue eyes was soft, like the sun kissing the sky a moment after dawn.

Nope. She wasn't falling for this. For him. Not at all. She was a cop. That was all she wanted to be. She didn't have room for superstar boyfriends and cute babies and Parade of Homes houses. And hadn't she just been upset with him? What was up with her seesawing emotions? Bad news all around.

"Quincy?" He whispered her name across her cheek in a warm breath. When she focused her eyes, he was close—too close. If-she-puckered-her-lips-they'd-be-kissing close.

"Yeah?" Oh, good grief. Was that her sounding all breathy and—and…girly?

"The baby's hungry, darlin'."

"Oh." She blinked several times before she leaned back and surrendered Noelle to Deacon.

He had a dish towel slung over his shoulder and his muscular biceps barely flexed as he settled Noelle in the cradle of one arm. Was it possible for the man's eyes to go even softer? The look on his face was…serene.

While she was contemplating his expression, he caught her off guard, and swooped in to kiss her. With a swirl of tongue between her lips. Sweet, gentle, but still hungry. She leaned away, mindful that he was holding the baby, not sure if she was upset or glad he'd kissed her. "Why did you do that?"

He grinned, totally unapologetic. "Because I needed to taste you again." He walked away and settled into his favorite chair, adjusted the baby and plopped the nipple of the bottle in her mouth. Noelle sucked noisily.

Argh. Quin wanted to wipe her mouth. Or rinse it with mouthwash to get rid of his taste. She leaned over, trying to listen surreptitiously. Was Deacon crooning to the baby? He was! He was singing to her. Quin couldn't help herself. She slid off the stool and crept closer to hear his voice.

"Rainbows and ponies, sweet baby mine. Ribbons and lace, to make you look fine. He'll dry your tears, kiss away your fears. He'll sing you lullabies. You are his sweetheart, his precious child. Sweet as can be, baby of mine. Daddy will love you to the end of time."

Daddy. What had Deacon told his cousin? *If not by blood, then by heart.* Quin couldn't help but feel a little jealous. He'd bonded with the baby. Quin had to admit that it would be tough to remove Noelle from Deacon's care.

Despite her reaction when she overheard the conversation with Chance Barron, something sweet settled inside her as she continued to watch man and baby. When the bottle was empty, Deacon shifted Noelle to his shoulder to rub and pat her back until the baby emitted a sleepy burp. What was the male equivalent of the Madonna and child? Because what Quin saw sitting in that chair on a frigid December day was every bit as powerful.

What was wrong with her? She couldn't have feelings for this man. She wasn't maternal so why should this image move her to sniffles and make her feel like someone had just punched her in the chest? She was a state trooper. Deacon and the baby were part of her investigation. That was all. They shouldn't be more. They *couldn't* be. And she'd make sure they wouldn't affect her. Oh, yeah. She'd get right on that.

Just as soon as she got her heart back under control.

Thirteen

Quin needed a vacation. Desperately. She was scheduled to leave in one day. The last thing she needed was to see Deacon. She went brain dead anytime he looked at her with those sleepy, sexy eyes of his. Or if his lips quirked up in that teasing smile. Or his mouth took hers like he was starving for the taste of her. No. She had to start thinking with her brain instead of her libido.

She was annoyed. At him. At his whole family. She needed to hang on to that feeling to do what she had to do.

Because there had been a break in the case.

Bridger Tate and Cash Barron had located Amanda Brooks, Noelle's mother. A caseworker from CPS and Quin were both there when the men questioned the girl. And she was *just* a girl—barely eighteen, the baby's father long gone. She'd made noises at first about Deacon being the father but Bridger shut that down when he asked about a birthmark. Amanda went into great detail describing it. Only problem? Deke didn't have one. Then Cash mentioned the DNA evidence—or lack thereof.

The teen had burst into tears and confessed she just wanted Noelle to have a wonderful life. Deacon was her favorite singer. The note and leaving Noelle at the bus had been a desperate, spur-of-the-moment action. CPS's unwritten mission was to keep families together. While a tour bus didn't strictly fit the guidelines of Oklahoma's Baby Safe Haven law where a parent could leave an infant in an approved facility like a fire station without legal repercussions, the teen's intention had been to keep her baby safe. No one was inclined to prosecute though the CPS worker wanted the baby in state foster care while Amanda took parenting classes.

Bridger and Cash weren't on board with that plan. Quin recalled the conversation she'd overheard between Deke and Chance about adoption. The teenager didn't stand a chance against the power and wealth wielded by Deacon and his extended family.

And that had seemed to be confirmed when Amanda called the CPS worker first thing that morning and said she was voluntarily giving up her parental rights so Deacon could adopt Noelle. Quin had seen the writing on the wall as soon as the social worker called. Private adoption or not, Deacon shouldn't just get his way, and Quin was glad the state was stepping in. CPS was requesting an emergency hearing to terminate Deacon's temporary custody. Though Quin had seen how much he cared for Noelle, when people threw their money and influence around like that, it just plain ticked her off.

Today would be the last time she had to lay eyes on the irritating man. She had plane tickets. She had hotel reservations. And she was leaving tomorrow morning no matter what. Five-star resort. Sexy ski…what did one call the guys who hung out on the slopes? They definitely weren't ski *bunnies*, and ski bums seemed as derogatory as bunnies. Ah, well. She didn't care. In just over twenty-four hours, she would be ensconced in front of that roaring fire, aperitif in hand, admiring the beautiful people.

Speaking of beautiful people, she segued back into cursing Deacon under her breath. She did not want to see him. Or give him the chance to kiss her again. She *didn't*, despite what her libido whispered in her ear. That was why she'd tried to call. She'd made arrangements for someone else to do the welfare checks until Noelle was removed from Deacon's custody, and wanted to tell him to expect the CPS caseworker. She'd left messages to call her when he didn't answer the landline or his cell. Then she'd gotten worried. What if he'd gotten word of what was coming? Had he packed up the baby and run?

That was stupid. Just like her nagging worry that something had happened to him. That he'd slipped and fallen in the shower and was bleeding to death. Or was unconscious and drowning. All of which was totally ridiculous and she knew it. If she'd thought about the situation with any clarity, she would have just called his cousin-slash-attorney. She could still do that. Except...

Okay, so she might have a soft spot for the kid. And Deacon, idiot that Quin was. Tomorrow, she'd be on a plane and wouldn't return to duty for seventeen days. By then, she would have gotten Deke out of her system, and the whole baby thing would be in the hands of CPS and the lawyers. By the time she was back in Oklahoma, Deke would have found some other woman to torment. And kiss. Awesome. Just as long as it wasn't her. Because kissing him was just...

The back wheels on her cruiser squiggled as she pressed the brake pedal while approaching a stop sign. She'd been driving through a light fall of sleet and now hard little balls of sneet—a combination of snow and sleet—were bouncing against her windshield. Great. The polar express wasn't supposed to arrive in full force until *after* her flight left in the morning.

Seeing there was no traffic in either direction, Quin squirted through the intersection without coming to a full stop on the black ice in her lane. Why take a chance? She had better places to be and far better things to do. Luckily, half a mile farther on, she lost the asphalt pavement and hit gravel. For once, she didn't grouse about the state of the road. Gravel gave her better traction in the frozen precipitation.

As she turned onto the long, winding lane leading up to Deacon's house, she had a white-knuckled grip on the steering wheel. The windshield wipers were working overtime to clear the thick, fluffy flakes now falling. Great. Just…great. She would have her conversation with Deacon, check on the baby and get her tail home. She might even call the airlines to see if she could grab a flight out today. Just in case.

The snow drifting from the leaden skies was sticking to the ground and the temperature was dropping. Quin shivered despite her bulletproof vest and quilted nylon duty jacket. She parked near the front door and bolted onto the porch before adjusting her duty belt lower on her hips.

"Don't go in. Tell him he needs to answer his freaking phone. Make sure he and the baby are okay. Leave. Easy peasy."

Quin glanced over her shoulder. The snow was coming down heavier and the wind picked up. She knocked. And waited. She pounded. And waited. She tried the door. Locked. She was shivering now and debating returning to her car to grab gloves and her knit cap. She banged on the window. Waited. She returned to the front door. Her fist connected with the wood, the door opened and she all but fell into the warmth of the house.

"Quin? What are you doing out here?" Deacon looked surprised to see her. The baby was curled against his right shoulder, peeking out shyly.

"I've been trying to contact you all morning. Don't you ever answer the phone?"

He looked a little sheepish. "Noelle and I were down in the barn getting the animals settled before the storm."

Okay, maybe, that was a good excuse but… "You didn't answer your cell, either."

"Ah…" He shrugged and turned on his very lethal good-ol'-boy smile, complete with dimple. "Left it up here at the house—"

"Yeah, yeah, whatever," she interrupted. "You should call Chance."

"Chance my attorney or Chance my cousin?"

"Aren't they one and the same?"

"Yes…and no." He chuckled. "If I'm in trouble, he's my attorney. If everything is copacetic, he's my cousin."

"You people think you have it all figured out, don't you?" Quin was frozen to the bone, frustrated and angry—as much with herself as with Deacon. "Your inability to remember to stick your phone in your pocket necessitated me driving out here. In a storm. To make sure you weren't dead or something." Why had she added that last bit? This was why she should have turned around and left as soon as she saw that he and the baby were fine.

Deacon looked her over and tilted his head toward the massive stone fireplace, where a fire was burning cheerily. "Go sit on the hearth and get warm. I'll put Noelle in her crib and get you some coffee. Then you can tell me why you were worried about us."

Quin opened her mouth to argue but he was already halfway to the kitchen. She was still shivering so she moved closer to the fire. A few minutes wouldn't hurt, right?

Deacon returned carrying a large, steaming mug. She accepted it and took an experimental taste. Just the right temperature, just sweet enough with a hint of vanilla cream. How did the guy remember that?

The heat radiating from the fireplace felt good on her back as she swallowed several long sips. She found herself oddly relaxed. The place smelled of cinnamon and pine, though there was no sign of a Christmas tree or other holiday accoutrements.

Quin was falling under his spell again. She had to stop this. "Christmas is less than a week away. Not doing the decorating thing?" She sounded snippy. That was good. No sexy, kissy thoughts about this man. Staying irritated. That was the key.

"Decorating?"

"Never mind. The sooner this is done, the sooner I can get back to regular duty. This is my last day before vacation."

"Big plans?"

"Yes. I'm flying to Aspen for a ski vacation."

"With your boyfriend?"

"I don't have one. Not that it's any of your business." The man had kissed her and he was just now getting around to asking if she was attached?

"So…you're spending Christmas in a hotel?"

"Again, not your business."

"Fine. Sorry for being curious. Have fun, but I think you'll be surprised how lonely it can be."

"Lonely? The resort is booked full. Hard to be lonely with a lot of people around."

"*Hmmm.* Of course. All those families and couples. Fun times."

"You don't have a clue. Maybe I booked a singles package," she snapped.

He nodded sagely and made that *hmmm* sound in his throat again.

"Look, I'm not here to discuss my private life."

Deacon raised his arms in symbolic surrender. "Sorry. I thought we were friends."

"We can't be friends. This is my job."

"Are you always so blunt?"

"I'm a cop. It's part of the job description."

"Good to know."

"You still didn't answer my question about Christmas." And she was prolonging this conversation why? Because she couldn't help the insane curiosity teasing her brain.

"I'll do a tree but we always gather at Mom's. The whole clan. Big ranch breakfast then stockings and presents. We eat a massive turkey dinner with all the trimmings, and promptly fall into food comas." He sipped his coffee, one hip leaning against the back of the huge leather chair. "I'm not always home, though. In the early years, we were usually on the road. I've spent more than a few Christmases in a hotel room. Trust me, being home is way better."

"Easy for you to say," she muttered. Her parents and their on-again-off-again marriage were a hot mess. Holidays spent with her four brothers in and out of the foster-care system didn't engender fond memories. Even now, as adults, they weren't very close. And just that quickly, her temper was back.

Quin needed to wrap this up and hit the road before she said or did something totally inappropriate. Like kiss that smug smile off Deacon's face. Wait. No. She had no desire to get that close to him, with his shaggy hair hanging in his eyes just begging her fingers to brush it away, and those lips curling on one side, teasing her. She shook her head and defaulted to gulping down the rest of her coffee. She'd been there, done that, and wasn't about to do it again. Because if she surrendered to the need building in her, she wouldn't leave. And even worse, she'd forget that this man was someone she didn't like.

Her phone pinged with a text, saving her from falling further down that rabbit hole. Quin retrieved it from her coat pocket and read the message. The pick-up order had been delayed until after Christmas.

"You must be charmed," she said, reading him the text. So what if her sarcasm came out to play. The stars always aligned for people like Deacon, and if she had his luck, she'd go to Thunder River Casino and make a fortune. She headed toward the kitchen to deposit her mug. Time to hit the road.

"It's really coming down out there. Why don't you stay until there's a break in the weather? I was just about to make breakfast. Stay. Eat with me."

He'd walked up behind her, catching her unaware. Which freaked her out a little. She was very proud of her situational awareness, and the fact that he could sneak up on her was unsettling. She glanced out the huge window over the sink and blanched. The ground—what she could see of it through the snow now blowing horizontally—was covered in white swirls.

"I can't. I have to get back to Oklahoma City."

Deacon crowded her up against the counter. Why did he have to smell so good? Like almond, sage and lemon. The mug clattered in the huge farmhouse sink behind her, and her phone landed on the granite counter.

"I'm a really good cook." He seduced her with the dimple again. "Mom made sure all us boys could look after ourselves."

Quin snorted in disbelief. "Yeah, right."

"I even know how to sew. Do laundry. Pick up after myself. Put the toilet seat down." He winked and her insides melted. He was a rich jerk but a charming one. Still, she had plans, and her duty to do. Standing here wondering if he would try to kiss her again was not on her agenda.

"Good for you. I've made sure you and the baby were breathing. I need to hit the road." Squaring her shoulders, she announced, "The CPS caseworker will do welfare checks from here on out." She ducked past him and hustled toward the door. Deacon still managed to beat her and open it for her, ever the gentleman. He gave her a piercing look but said nothing about her announcement.

A blast of frigid wind lashed her face, and she hesitated. Snow had built up on her windshield and she'd have to brush it away before driving. Squaring her shoulders, she dove into the teeth of the storm.

"Get in the car and get it started," Deacon yelled above the howling wind. "Get warm. I'll get the windows."

She was already shivering so didn't pause to argue. He donned a heavy sheepskin jacket and was pulling on gloves. The cruiser started—thankfully. As soon as the temperature gauge climbed above C, she hit the heater and defroster full-blast.

Deacon didn't just clear her windshield, he knocked the snow off all the windows and stomped down the snow in front of her tires. Then he stood back and saluted. She rolled her eyes but gave him a wave as she put the car in gear and slowly pulled out.

Once she turned onto the section line road, she was fighting snowdrifts. The road ran directly east and west while the wind came from due north. The windshield wipers barely kept up and she caught herself hunching over the steering wheel to peer through the windshield.

Quin wasn't sure when she realized there were ruts in the road. They were too wide for her cruiser but she could put one set of wheels into the tire track and follow it. She concentrated on staying in the rut.

Something dark and huge loomed up in front her. Out of

reflex, Quin hit the brakes and jerked the wheel to the left. Her actions sent the car into a dizzying spin. She fought the centrifugal gravity created by the out-of-control vehicle. The car came to an abrupt stop. She slammed her head against the window and tried to breathe around the air bag as the car engine sputtered and died.

The bag eventually deflated and Quin took stock of her situation. She could sum it up in one word: bad. She reached for the radio and got nothing but static. Same with the MDT, the mobile data terminal. Her phone was in her pocket. No worries. She'd call Dispatch and they could send a wrecker for her. Except her phone wasn't *in* her coat pocket. Or any of her pockets. She unhooked the shoulder harness and banged her shoulder on the driver's-side door. That's when she realized the car was tilted at a crazy angle.

Running her hand over the floor, she couldn't locate her phone. Then she remembered. She'd set it down on the kitchen counter at Deke's. And in her fit of self-preservation, she'd walked off without it. She was stuck in the middle of nowhere in the blizzard of the century with no way to call for help.

Quin breathed through her initial panic. Her head was pounding but she was a trained professional. She'd been following tracks made by a tractor or road grader or something. They'd come back. Find her. If her car wasn't buried in a snowdrift by then. How far had she driven? A mile? Two? She'd been driving slowly so she couldn't be too far from Deke's. She'd just have to walk back to his house. The idea grated on her but she had little choice. She had gloves. A warm hat. She was tough. She could do this.

Squirming so she could reach around the MDT mounted between the seats, she snagged the passenger door handle and shoved. Nothing happened. Moving into a better position, she pushed again, using both hands. Still nothing.

After ten minutes, Quin considered using her pocket-knife to hack away the air bag so she could wrap up in it. She could see her breath and her fingers were going numb.

"Quin!"

Was someone shouting?

"Quin! Are you in there?" Someone pounded on the passenger door. No, not just someone—Deke.

"Deke! I'm here. I'm here!"

Metal groaned and then the door opened a crack.

"Thank God. Hang on, darlin'. I'll have you out in a flash."

He had something in his hands, like a long crowbar, and he forced the passenger door to open wider. He leaned in and offered her his gloved hands.

"Grab hold, Quin. I'll pull you out."

A small, feminist part of her rebelled, but her teeth were chattering too hard to speak. She grabbed his hands. He lifted her like she weighed nothing. Then she was in his arms and he was carrying her to a beast of a four-wheel-drive pickup. Depositing her in the passenger seat, he slammed the door shut and hustled around to climb in the driver's side.

"Wh-wh-what are y-you d-doing here?"

"Rescuing you, obviously."

Damn his dimple, but he was bundling her into a blanket and the heater was blowing.

"You forgot your phone. Soon as I realized it, I grabbed up Noelle and headed out. I figured to catch up to you before you hit the highway. Appears I did."

"You dragged the baby out in this? What if you wrecked? That's just plain stupid!"

He stared at Quin, dimple and eye twinkles gone. "I'm more prepared for this weather than you, *Trooper.*"

She bristled at the emphasis on her title. She was prepared. Sort of. She had a kit in the trunk—which she couldn't reach after sliding off the road. In her defense, every meteorologist in the state had missed the sudden arrival and escalation in the power of the storm.

He continued, "For your information, she's in this flannel sack thing and wrapped in a Pendleton blanket with the heater running full-blast. Fast asleep, I might add. I also have extra blankets, water, food, a candle—you did know that a big candle will heat a cab this size, right? I wasn't about to leave her at home alone. That's what stupid people do and I'm not stupid, despite what you continue to believe."

Okay, he had a point there. Leaving the baby alone would have been worse than dragging her outside and this huge truck seemed more than capable of tackling even the highest snowdrifts.

"Where would you be if I hadn't come along? It's not like this road is well-traveled in *good* weather. An Oklahoma blue norther with a side of blizzard? Most sane folks are snug at home riding out the storm. Which is where we're headed. Home."

Fourteen

The tracks his truck had made on the way to find Quin were quickly filling in as Deke drove back to the house. Turning around had been an exercise in caution and he'd almost given up, deciding it might be easier to just back up the mile they had to go. But he persevered. By the time they reached his place, Quin had stopped shivering, but she had a nasty knot on her head and he was worried.

He nosed the big vehicle in as close to the back door as he could. This area provided more shelter from the storm, as it was on the south side of the house. He squeezed Quin's arm to get her attention. She gazed at him, her eyes a little glassy. Not good. He'd have to check her for signs of concussion once they got inside.

"I'm going to take Noelle in, then I'll come back to get you. I'll leave the truck running for the heat. Okay?"

Quin blinked several times as if trying to remember where she was. "Oh. Yeah. That makes sense. I'll just get out and come with you.

"No, darlin'. Just stay in the truck. The snow's deep even if we're out of the wind. If you slip or anything, I can't help you while I'm carrying the baby. Just sit tight. Okay?"

"Okay. Yes. That makes sense."

She was repeating herself and his worry ratcheted up a notch. He had another electronic key in the house in case Quin managed to lock the doors while he was moving Noelle inside. The baby yawned as he got her, still wrapped and strapped into the carrier, out of the car-seat base. He slammed the truck door and waded through the growing snowdrifts to the service door. He set the baby carrier down in the mudroom and trudged back to the truck. When he opened the passenger side door, Quin all but fell into his arms. He got her hitched up into a princess carry and bumped the door with his hip to close it.

He slipped and almost went down but found his balance before he dumped either of them in the snow. Inside the house, Deke set Quin on her feet, made sure she was steady and turned to click the remote start key fob to turn off the truck. He had to sweep out a small pile of snow to shut the door. With the door latched against the wind, Deacon stripped off his gloves and coat and hung them on the wall rack in the mudroom. Luckily, he'd already fed and watered the horses. They'd be able to weather the storm. Matt had rounded up the small herd of cattle and secured them in a secondary barn before holing up in his own house.

"C'mon, darlin'. Let's get you warm, 'kay? And I want to take a look at your head."

"My head?" Quin reached up with trembling fingers, but he snagged her hand before she touched the bump.

"Yeah, don't think you want to touch it, sweetheart. You've got a whale of a lump on your forehead. Do you remember what happened?"

She squinted her eyes as she thought. "Uh-huh. I was

following a track. The snow was so thick I was watching the road right at the end of my hood. I looked up and there was something big blocking the way. I…" Color crept up her cheeks. "I made a rookie mistake. I hit the brakes and jerked the wheel."

"I didn't see anything in the road." He shook his head as she started to argue. "Hon, you were in the bar ditch for a while before I got there. Whatever that vehicle was, the driver probably never even knew you were behind him. C'mon. Get out of your coat. I'll take a look at your head."

An hour later, Quin was soaking in the whirlpool tub in the master bedroom, Noelle was in her automatic swing cooing happily and Deke had fielded phone calls from every female member of his extended family. Diapers. Check. Food and formula. Check. Backup generator. Check. Weather report: blizzard conditions, lots of snow. Check. Sexy woman naked in his tub. Double check. Eventually, she'd have to call her supervisor to explain the situation. She wasn't going anywhere until the storm blew itself out.

He made a fresh pot of coffee, then headed to his closet. Quin couldn't wear her uniform the whole time she was here. And as much as he'd appreciate the view of her in the robe hanging on the back of the bathroom door—a robe he'd never worn—Quin would need real clothes. He found a selection of sweats, tees and jeans that might fit and laid them out on the bed. The idea of Quin wearing his clothes was a real turn-on, not that he needed any encouragement in that department.

The bathroom door opened a crack, and Deke caught a glimpse of Quin's face. "Feeling warmer now?"

"Yes. Thanks."

"You found the robe on the door?"

"Yes."

"I laid out some clothes for you to try on. Weather guys

say we're stuck for at least forty-eight hours. Considering where I live, it'll probably be longer before a plow can get through." He wasn't about to mention the bulldozer stored in his equipment barn.

"No. Just nooo." The bathroom door closed and a *thunk* followed.

Deke rushed to the door and tried the handle. It turned but wouldn't open. "Quin? Are you okay in there?"

"No. I'm supposed to get on a plane tomorrow. I have reservations. Colorado. Skiing. Luxury resort. Remember?"

Deke worked to keep the laughter out of his voice as he said, "Hon? There won't be any planes in or out of Will Rogers Airport and Colorado is getting hammered by this same weather system."

"Great. Just…great."

He thought it was. Quin under his roof for an indeterminate period of time? Check. A chance for her to get to know him? Check. A chance to get her into his bed? Double check.

Quin hid in the bathroom—and what a bathroom it was, with a huge whirlpool tub, a shower big enough for six and a heated floor. The fluffy robe hanging on the hook swamped her but it would do. After a few minutes of silence, she opened the door a crack and peeked out. Deke was nowhere to be seen and the bedroom door had been closed.

She was in the process of holding a pair of soft, faded jeans up to her waist when Deke tapped on the door. Quin clutched the robe closed and held her breath. The door didn't open as Deke's muffled voice filtered through the wood.

"Feel free to go through the dresser and my closet. Grab whatever you need."

"Thank you," she called back. She had one pair of panties and the sports bra she wore under her uniform. Unless the guy was a real pervert and he kept fan *souvenirs*, she doubted he'd have any lingerie stashed in his drawers. But if he was a boxer kind of guy, she could improvise. Because there was no way in the world she was going commando with Deacon around. He was lethal to the female libido. She wanted as many layers as she could pile on.

Not that she was afraid of him. Nope. Not at all. It was *her* reaction to the man that was terrifying. He made her stupid when his dimple appeared. And when he sang to the baby? She swore she could feel it in her womb and her biological clock jangled like an old-fashioned alarm clock.

Wearing a pair of his boxers—and she so wasn't going to think about the intimacy of that—Quin tried on the pair of jeans she was holding. They fit surprisingly well, if a little loose in the waist so that they rode lower on her hips than she was used to. She snagged a white T-shirt, shrugged into it and followed up with a baggy sweatshirt on top.

Armored in borrowed clothes, she ventured into the main part of the house. The baby was rocking in a swing contraption, eyes closed, one fist in her mouth. Deke had changed out of his wet jeans and now wore a dry pair slung low on his hips, topped by a T-shirt that molded to his chest and arms like a second skin. How was he not freezing?

Deke turned around, and a slow smile creased his cheeks. That was so not fair. Quin struggled to control her breathing and heart rate.

"I started some soup. Hope you like grilled cheese sandwiches."

Dark came early while they waited on the soup. The wind continued to howl and the snow drifted higher around the windows. This entire day had been a disaster.

She stared out the window at the swirling snow. Deke appeared beside her.

"Want to decorate the tree after we eat?"

"Seriously?"

"Yeah. It's in the mudroom and I'd already dragged the decorations out of the attic. I haven't put up a tree in years but I really want one now." His dimple flashed at her as he smiled.

She hadn't put up a tree in her condo in…never. Decorating with Deacon sounded like fun. "Okay, sure."

The soup was hot, the grilled cheese gooey; the simple meal was oddly filling. She offered to do dishes while Deacon brought in the tree and got it set up.

He opened a box of ornaments and she admired the collection nestled on cotton batting. "Wow."

"Mom got these for me to celebrate my first concert tour. There's an ornament for each city we played."

Deke opened a plastic crate and found the tree lights. "Ah, good. Let's hope they work." He plugged them in and sure enough, the entire string lit up. She continued unpacking ornaments while he wound the lights through the branches of the Scotch pine.

When he stood back to admire his work, Quin couldn't help but tease him. "Don't you think there's a hole there on the left?"

He narrowed his gaze, studying the tree. "Where?"

Quin got up and pointed to a spot. "There." Then she moved the string up one branch. She backed away and nodded. "Perfect."

Deacon laughed and shook his finger. "I see what you did there."

As they decorated, Deke stopped to reminisce about some of the ornaments. Quin suspected each one had a story because they were all unique, but some seemed extra special to him. When the last one, a blown-glass New Orleans street car, was placed on the tree, Deacon reached for a small wooden box he'd set aside.

"Here," he said, handing it to her. Inside was another original—a hand-painted porcelain angel.

Quin was almost afraid to touch the delicate tree-topper. "She's lovely."

"I found her in a little shop in San Antonio."

She glanced up at the warmth in his voice. Quin made to hand it back but Deke shook his head. "Nope. The honor is yours. Up you go."

Before she knew what he had in mind, she was sitting on his shoulders, angel in her hand. She could just reach the very top of the tree to get the angel firmly clamped and braced. When Deke lowered her to the floor, his arm slipped around her shoulders as they gazed at the tree. She noticed that he'd arranged lights at the crown of the tree to highlight the angel.

"Beautiful."

"Yes, she is."

That was when Quin realized he was looking at her, and his expression sent shivers through her.

Day three of my captivity, Quin thought, the unspoken words sounding wry in her head. Despite the sexual tension that was so thick they could swim through it, she and Deke were getting along. She'd discovered he was funny, with a dry sense of humor. He was patient, as evidenced by the way he dealt with Noelle. And he was a talented musician. He'd serenaded her several times while she was curled up on the couch with a book. She couldn't remember the last time she'd read for pleasure.

The storm still showed no signs of losing its bluster. The electricity had flickered a time or two, but held steady. Deke assured her that the emergency generator would keep lights on and the fridge running if they lost power. At the moment, she was flipping through channels on the TV that dominated one wall of the great room. Deke was puttering around in the kitchen.

One of the daytime talk shows caught her attention when a picture of Deacon flashed on the screen and she paused to watch. What the five women were saying was just…drivel. And patently untrue.

She called to him. "You don't deserve this. To be paid back for your kindness with headlines and innuendos like these?" Quin glowered at the talking heads chatting on TV.

Deacon handed her a cup of hot chocolate with whipped cream and a chocolate-dipped pretzel for a stir stick. Dropping to the couch beside her, he tasted his coffee before answering. His voice held the shrug his shoulders hadn't made.

"It's how they make their living, Quin. I'm fair game." He looked mischievous and added, "Besides, they're staking out the Nashville condo because Bent Star leaked that I'd be spending the holidays there."

"Smart. But what they're saying still isn't fair."

Laughing, he said, "Neither is the fact I have to get out in the snow, trudge to the barn and feed the horses."

"Can't your foreman do that?"

Deke's brow furrowed and he looked genuinely puzzled. "Why would I make him get out in the cold to drive over here, and do something I can do quicker and easier? They're my horses. My responsibility."

Quin leaned back, studied him with her cop senses turned on. He truly didn't understand why she'd think he'd do anything else. This man had depths she was only beginning to fathom. That should scare her just a bit. Okay, a lot. She didn't want a relationship. Didn't want the complications or the investment—of time *or* emotion. And she certainly didn't want him to kiss her again. No way.

When Noelle fussed from where she lay in a portable

playpen-and-crib contraption, Deacon was up and striding to her before Quin could even process there was a problem. She watched him pick up the infant and soothe her with the sweet lullaby he'd written just for the baby.

That darn biological clock kept right on ticking, sounding like the alarm clock the Peter Pan crocodile had swallowed. Tick. Tock.

After changing and resettling Noelle, Deke plopped back on the couch and realized Quin was still watching that dumb talk show.

Her head tilted as she focused on him. He resisted the urge to squirm under her scrutiny. Then she asked, "You really don't care?"

"What is it the kids say these days? Haters gonna hate?"

"Something like that."

"I'm in the public eye, Quin. There are always rumors and innuendos. This deal about the baby is just one more. I don't pay much attention. That's why record company PR people make the big bucks."

She laughed, and Deke wanted to hear her do that more often. The sound was bright and shiny, like the Christmas lights he'd strung on the tree. He'd enjoyed decorating the tree with Quin. With her and Noelle in the house, the place felt like Christmas, felt like a real home. Not wanting to fully acknowledge that, he tuned back into the conversation.

"So, you aren't a social-media addict like so many of the celebrities?"

It was his turn to laugh, though he exaggerated a grimace. "I'm told I have a Twitter account. But seriously? A hundred and forty characters? Does that include spaces and periods?"

"I guess this means I probably can't stalk you on Facebook, either."

"There's a fan page for the band, but no, I'm not on there." Deke scratched his head and pushed hair off his forehead. "I'm pretty much a country boy. I mean—" He swept a hand around the room. "Not exactly Beverly Hills standards."

"Oh, I don't know. Looks luxurious to me. And even though we're snowed in, the house still has electricity. Heat. And most important from a cabin-fever standpoint, cable TV. That makes you special."

Deke wanted to make Quin feel special, and he wanted to taste her again. He leaned forward and without thinking too deeply about his intentions, said, "I'm going to kiss you now."

"Are you asking or telling?"

"Yes."

Fifteen

Deke didn't need to hear Quin's sharp intake of breath to know her answer. Her hands were already reaching for him. He dipped his head, caught her bottom lip between his teeth and nipped. Then he kissed her slowly and gently, but very, very thoroughly. As long as the baby stayed asleep, he had all the time in the world to seduce this woman.

Her fingers clutched his shoulders as her body tensed, even though her lips softened against his. She was such a study of opposites and he couldn't wait to explore every last inch of her. He released her mouth, found the spot on her neck where her pulse beat rapidly. Deke wanted to strip her down, spread her and enjoy her in every way.

He didn't have to be told to go slow as he leashed his own urgency. This was not the time. He'd take it slow and easy, like teasing a tune out of his guitar. That was the key. He would learn to play this woman.

She'd slept under his roof for two nights, though upstairs in the long-unused guest suite. They'd spent the days like an old married couple. They watched TV. Read. He played and sang to her and Noelle. Quin napped on the couch, her head resting on his thigh. He smiled against her skin. It had taken everything in him to not laugh out loud the first time she'd awakened in that position.

Deke returned to her mouth and kissed her deeply again, his tongue probing and tasting. She broke the kiss and leaned back. Her expression was serious as she studied him. Snagging one of her hands, he lifted it to his mouth, kissed each one of her fingers.

"If you could see yourself, Quin, with tousled hair and lips wet and swollen from my kiss."

That startled a laugh out of her. "Seriously? Where do you come up with this stuff?"

"Is it working?"

"No!" She was adamant but her eyes crinkled around suppressed laughter.

Winking, he pulled her close again and murmured against her lips, "I think it is."

She melted against him as he kissed her again. Emotions surged through him, feelings he wasn't sure he wanted to take out and examine very closely. The woman could get under his skin all too easily—already had, he realized. These last few days had shown him what he'd been missing. It was like life had just slapped him upside the head with a clue-by-four.

Deke didn't want to seduce Quin for the sake of having sex. Oh, no. It was far more complex than that. He wanted to make love to her. He eased her down on the couch, one hand teasing up the hem of the sweatshirt she wore. Calloused fingertips encountered smooth skin and he hardened. He wanted her naked and in his bed. Quin pressed her hands against his chest and pushed. He froze.

"What are we doing?" she whispered.

"If my mother had her way, I'd be a gentleman and say we were just making out. But I'm not a gentleman. I want you, Quin. I want you in my bed. I want to be *in* you."

She laid back against the cushions. "I have a duty—"

"Yes. To yourself. Do you want this to happen, Quin? If you say you don't, I'll get up and go take the next of many cold showers. I won't be happy. Damn, woman. Being cooped up in here with you has been torture." Deke sat up, knowing they needed to talk this through.

"When I first saw your car in that ditch? I couldn't breathe. I almost couldn't think. I was so damn scared that I'd find you really hurt." He swallowed hard. "Or worse. If you'd died... But you didn't. And I brought you home, darlin'. Not to my house, but home. Because that's what it feels like with you here."

She started to speak, but he silenced her with another quick, hard kiss. "Let me finish. Please."

He waited, holding his breath. Once he'd opened the gate on his emotions, there was no way to stop the stampede. Maybe he should have held back, taken time to examine his feelings, but it was too late. Quin nodded, looking uncertain, but he could deal with uncertainty. Deke breathed, his lungs burning from the infusion of oxygen.

"I know what you think of me—or what you used to think. You've had a chance to get to know me. I've been gettin' to know you since that night we met, standin' in the cold in the parking lot at Thunder River. You drive me crazy. So uptight. Proper. Even back then, I wanted to take your hair down, see if it was as soft as it looked. I wanted to tangle my fingers in it and kiss you sense-less. Damn, darlin', I think I've been hard for you since I looked up and you announced, 'I'm Trooper Kincaid. What's going on here?'"

Quin bit her lip to keep from smiling and he gave in to

the temptation to kiss her again. Her mouth opened for his questing tongue. His hand cupped her cheek and stayed after he broke the kiss.

"I've seen you every day since then. You've pissed me off. You've driven me crazy with your scent and your smile and being too cute even when you didn't know you were being cute. You've made me laugh. And you've made me want things only you can give me."

Deke shifted, grasped her and lifted her into his lap. "Do you know how hard it's been for me to keep my hands off you? The past two nights, I've climbed the stairs and stood outside your door like a lovesick hound. I listen to you breathe through the door and I wonder if you're really sleepin' or if you're thinking about me, about us making love."

He paused and gazed into her eyes, didn't like what he saw there. "You're gonna run." She stiffened, pushed away, but he tightened his embrace. "Your feelings haven't changed? Tell me, Quin. Put me out of my misery. Is there any hope?"

A sob gathered in her chest, struggled to escape from her throat. If she let it, she'd never be able to stop the ones threatening to follow. She didn't want this tidal wave of emotion flooding her senses. *Home.* That word had arrowed into her heart. What did she know of healthy relationships? And how could this man, this superstar with all the talent and money and women in the world, want *her*? She was a cop, and far from beautiful. Nothing more. Nothing less.

His hands cupped her face, holding her so she had to look at him. Feeling the heat from his palms, the rough touch of his fingertips against her cheeks, she saw. This wasn't a game. This wasn't a seduction—well, okay, maybe it was, but he wanted *her*. Every instinct she'd had pointed to that conclusion. He wasn't lying. About any of this.

Could she let go? He definitely turned her on and from the first, her feelings had bounced around from frustration, anger, doubt, humor, lust—lots and lots of that—and plain old affection. She *liked* him. Too much. And she desired him.

Quin wanted to surrender to her feelings, wanted to give in to the demands of her own body. *Take me*, she silently begged. *Love me and don't ever let me go.* Because if they did this? If he ever let her go, she'd never recover.

As if he heard her silent pleas, he gathered her in his arms and stood. How strong was this guy? Her breath hitched and she pressed her lips to his throat. His arms tightened and his step quickened.

"In my bed, Quin. Okay?" he asked against her hair, raising goose bumps.

"Yes."

He settled them on the bed, both still clothed. She rested against a pile of pillows and in a crazy moment, given the circumstances, realized he'd made his bed that morning. She laughed, and loved the way his gaze softened as he watched her. Then he began to stroke her. His hands were gentle, at once teasing and soothing, as if he was seeking to both give and receive comfort.

"So beautiful, darlin'," he whispered over and over as his questing hands found her skin. A moment later, he whipped the sweatshirt over her head and she lay bare. She tensed until she saw his face. Heat surged in her blood and she flushed. He meant his words. She *was* beautiful in his eyes. She relaxed, ready to accept him.

His lips were firm when they found hers, after kissing their way along her shoulder, neck and cheek. He took the kiss deep, but so gently she fell into it, into him. There was a hard, hot rush in her middle, though her mind drifted on the crest of her emotions, like a feather floating on the stormy sea.

Quin loved the feel of his rough fingertips as they found her now. She surrendered to the sensation, growing liquid and pliant beneath his touch. A haze of desire clouded her mind but she didn't fight it. She wanted—no, needed— to let go.

His fingers coasted over one of her breasts, and his mouth followed. Deke's tongue teased her nipple, circling until it pebbled and she was arching up to meet him with a gasp. "Yes," she sighed as his hand cupped the other breast, kicking her heart rate up another notch. She brushed her hands across his back, tugging at the shirt he wore. "Off," she demanded.

Deke complied with a low chuckle and she traced the shape of him, the muscles and feathering of hair on his chest and abdomen. Even if she'd wanted to stop, she wouldn't have been able to. Why had she resisted him until this moment? Oh, yeah. Her job. Duty. But as she fell further under Deacon's spell, all her doubts had fled until she arrived at this moment. Duty, with all its demands, was only a faint echo in her mind.

His mouth demanded more from her, his hands showing her the way. She was ready, needy, breathless with desire. She wanted more, wanted him. Now. Quin tried to tell him that, but her words turned into a moan as his hand trailed across her belly, then delved deeper, slipping beneath the elastic band of her borrowed sweatpants. Quin worried, for a moment, about her unsexy clothing. Then she looked up, saw the shimmers of heat in Deacon's gaze and knew it was all for her. Because of her.

Why was he taking so long? This endless torment of sweet touches and kisses was driving her to the brink. He finally stripped the sweats off her, leaving her exposed and vulnerable until he kissed her in the most intimate way possible. His tongue sent shivers into her core and raised goose bumps on her skin.

"Please," she begged, not knowing if she'd managed to speak the word.

His mouth and fingers sent her on a soaring spiral up and up until she couldn't breathe, until she hung suspended on the edge of something wonderful. And then she fell, her body racked with a shuddering climax, a climax much more powerful than any she'd had.

And he was there, waiting for her when she came down. Naked. Hot. Hard. And ready. They were both ready at last. He positioned his erection at her entrance and pushed in. "Yess-s-s," she hissed as he entered her all the way.

Deke rested his forehead against hers, panting softly. "Gotta know, baby," he groaned, his entire body tense. "Birth control?"

How could she have forgotten? She stiffened, tried to push him off.

"Shhh. It's okay."

"No—" But he was gone. He'd withdrawn, leaving her feeling empty and unsated even though she'd just experienced the most amazing climax. He sat on the edge of the bed, reaching into the drawer of his nightstand. She heard foil tearing. She watched his hands moving in his lap, and then he was back.

"I won't ever put you at risk, Quin. Never."

Something eased in her chest but he didn't move to enter her again. "I want kids. Someday. In the right time. In the right way. With the right woman. Okay?"

She considered his words. Was he saying she was the right woman? At that moment, she wanted to be. "Okay," she whispered. And then he was inside her again.

Quin rode a hazy wave of desire, her insides still fluttering from her earlier climax. He slid in and out of her, hitting spots, changing rhythm, drawing her center tighter and tighter until she was on the brink once again. She fought letting go, clung to a shred of control until, at last, they were both there in the same moment.

Deke throbbed inside her and a throaty groan ground from between his teeth. She let go then, filled with helpless shudders. Her orgasm set her body on fire. Skyrockets burst behind her eyes and in her core. Heart. Mind. Body. All of her was joined in perfect synchronicity with the man who lay spent and panting on top of her.

How had she resisted him so long? And most important, why? He filled her with a tenderness she'd never thought herself capable of feeling. He was suddenly kissing her face, her cheeks, murmuring soft words of comfort to her. That was when she understood her skin was slick with tears.

"God, baby, did I hurt you?" He moved to roll away, and she stopped him by wrapping her legs around his waist.

"No. No. I'm fine. I'm perfect. I..." She offered a bemused laugh. "I don't know why I'm crying. I'm happy. So very happy."

And she was, inexplicably so. Quin wanted to grab this feeling, capture it somehow and place it in a treasure chest like the one where Deke kept his angel. She wanted to keep it forever. Then, whenever she was feeling sad or unhappy, she could open the chest, take out the memory and experience it all over again.

"I think I'm falling in love with you."

His words took her breath away because she wasn't sure she hadn't done the same. She didn't reply, though, her feelings too raw and unfocused.

Chuckling softly, he rolled to the side but took her with him so that she was snuggled next to him. "Progress," he said, laughter hiding behind the word.

"What do you mean?"

"You didn't hit me. And you didn't run."

Sixteen

Christmas Day dawned with skies of pink and orange as the sun peeked over the horizon. Deke was already up and puttering in the great room. He'd done some major scrounging but he'd come up with some gifts for Quin. Some were pretty cheesy but he wanted the pleasure of watching her unwrap presents. If things went right, he had one special gift for her.

The throaty growl of a diesel engine drew him to the front windows. As he watched, a yellow front-end loader crawled up the drive pushing snow out of its way. A train of vehicles followed in its wake. The cavalry had arrived. Deke didn't know whether to laugh or get upset, though it didn't matter. His idyllic interlude with Quin and Noelle had come to an end.

He headed to the bedroom to give Quin a heads-up. She was still asleep when he woke her with a kiss. "Merry Christmas, sleepyhead."

"Mmm, Merry Christmas," she said around a yawn. Her eyes narrowed. "What's that noise?"

"The cavalry. My family has arrived to celebrate."

She leaped out of bed like a scalded cat, hissing and yowling as she flew into the bathroom. "Why didn't you warn me!"

He followed her in as she jumped into the shower before the water heated. He muffled his laughter as she yowled again. "If I'd known, I would have. I did warn you that Christmas is a big deal to my family. They decided to bring it to us this year."

"How did they get here?"

"Front-end loader with a plow." She poked her head out and glowered at him, her expression suspicious. Definitely time to retreat.

As the day wore on, Deke found himself watching from the sidelines, which suited him just fine. His mother and brothers had brought presents and food. Noelle and Quin were the centers of attention, and while he considered rescuing Quin, he didn't. He was too fascinated watching the interactions.

Bridger sidled up to him at the kitchen island. "You like her." Deke hoped his expression didn't give him away. "Whoa. Seriously?" Bridger nudged him. "So it's more. She's cool, big bro." Bridge lowered his voice even further. "You know we've talked to Noelle's mom. Chance and Cash are working out the arrangements, financial and otherwise. Are you *sure* this is what you want? Taking on a baby is a huge responsibility, Deke."

"I know. I love that little girl."

"I think you love someone else, too, bro." Bridger cut his eyes to Quin.

He'd been drifting along enjoying this thing between him and Quin. He liked her. A lot. Even when she drove him crazy—and man, did she do that in all sorts of ways. Since he'd talked her into his bed, his thoughts had turned to something more. Something permanent.

Deke considered his response. He'd been headed toward this since the moment Quincy Kincaid walked into his life. "Yeah, you might be right."

Later, after the turkey and dressing, after the pumpkin pie, Deke knew the moment had arrived. He slipped into his room and pawed through a wooden box hidden on a shelf in his closet until he found the box holding the ring he'd inherited from his grandmother. Wasting no time, he walked back through the kitchen, snagged Quin's hand and urged her into the mudroom. He handed her a coat and a knit cap and pointed to the brand-new pair of snow boots she'd received for Christmas. He still didn't know how his mother had accomplished all the presents.

"If you're dragging me outside for a snowball fight..."

"Nope. Just some time alone. I love my family, but..."

He shrugged into his sheepskin rancher coat and settled his Stetson on his head. He slipped the box into his coat pocket. Deke snagged a muffler hanging on the coatrack and wrapped it around Quin's neck and checked to make sure his family had retired to the living room. He held his index finger to his mouth, took Quin's hand and sneaked through the door leading to the expansive deck.

During the course of the day, the promise of blue skies had faded behind a layer of clouds. As Deke cleared off a spot on the wide railing circling the deck, huge, fluffy flakes began to drift down. The world was quiet and peaceful and the snow-covered fields created a soft backdrop to the vibrant woman he boosted up to sit on the rail.

"I feel like I'm in a snow globe."

"You look like it, too," Deke teased. He leaned into her and kissed a snowflake off her eyelashes. "We need to talk," he blurted.

Quin's expression turned bemused. "About what?"

"The way I feel. About you. I like you, Quin. You know that. But it's more."

"More?" Did her breath hitch?

"Yeah. More. Seeing you with my family, with Noelle. Being with you these past few days? I love you, Quin. Shhh—" He hurried to interrupt her protests. "Just let me finish. I know we haven't known each other long. I know circumstances have been...weird. But I know what I feel in my heart. You're one of a kind, Quincy Kincaid, and I want you to be mine. For now and always."

Her eyes were wide as she watched him and her throat worked as she swallowed. "What are you saying, Deke?"

"I love you, Quin. And I want to marry you. Make a family with you." He pulled the box out of his pocket and opened it.

She swallowed again and raised her eyes from the ring to meet his gaze. "Deacon?"

"Please say yes, Quin."

"Are you...are you sure about this?"

"More sure than I've ever been of anything in my life."

A hesitant smile curved the corners of her mouth, then spread all the way to her eyes. "Yes," she whispered. "Yes!" she shouted, throwing her arms around his neck.

"Yo, Deacon! You know it's not official until you go down on one knee, right?" Cooper yelled from the doorway.

Ignoring his family, Deacon slipped the ring on her finger. The ring looked antique, with a large sapphire encircled by diamonds. She stared at it, almost afraid to meet his gaze. What was she doing? This was crazy! She was nobody—a cop who got snowed in with a star. But she'd caught him looking at her, when he thought she wasn't aware of his attention. He wore the same soft expression she saw when he took care of Noelle.

He loved her. And from his family's reaction, they weren't opposed to this. She tried to make sense of things, of her emotions. Did she love him? Had she only answered "yes" because he'd surprised her? She met his eyes now, gazed deeply into them, searching for the truth of his feelings, the truth of her own.

Deacon looked...dazed. And happy. There was a tenderness in his look that came close to undoing her. Their chemistry had been explosive from the first, and she could admit that it was mutual. And while she wavered between exasperation and affection, there'd been distrust. Was it gone now? Because any sort of long-term relationship, much less marriage, had to be based on mutual trust.

"I love you," he whispered as a smile spread across his face. "I love you!" he all but shouted, much to the amusement of his family.

Something eased in her heart and she smiled. The hopes and dreams she hadn't considered before meeting Deacon were becoming reality. This felt right, *Deacon* felt right, being here with him and Noelle, who was babbling at everyone from Katherine's arms, felt right. Six brothers and a mother-in-law. This is what Quin was getting by saying yes.

She felt a little insecure when she offered the words back, but accepted their truth. "I love you, too, Deacon."

When they came back inside, he wanted nothing more than to spend the rest of Christmas Day alone with his new fiancée. His family had other plans. As a way to torture them, he put a movie in the DVD player. The chorus of groans that accompanied the opening credits for *Love Actually* was his reward.

"Suck it up, buttercups. This movie is a Christmas present to Quin and we're watchin' it."

Halfway through the movie, every last one of them had decided they had someplace else to be. Deke paused the movie. Dillon and his mother were the last to leave. After hugs and kisses with his mom, he made turkey sandwiches and brought them on paper plates to Quin. He settled on the couch with her and sort of got into the movie.

The fire had burned down to glowing embers but it still put out enough heat for the room to be cozy. Quin snuggled deeper under the fleece blanket he'd tucked around her. They'd both dozed off during a second movie and darkness cocooned them.

He kissed her, his hands smoothing the cashmere sweater that had been a gift. Pressing another kiss to the soft skin under her jaw, he felt her pulse tripping beneath his lips.

Languidly, not fully awake, Quin rolled into him with a small sigh. She arched her hips, seeking contact with his. Deke had always worried about the roughness of his fingertips, calloused from years of playing the guitar. Conscious of that, he lightly stroked over the soft, warm flesh of her belly. He moved slowly, removing her clothes until she wore nothing but skin.

He stepped away just long enough to strip out of his own clothes and grab a condom, then climbed back onto the couch and positioned himself so she was beneath him. He brushed fingertips across her throat, slid his tongue along the seam of her lips and whispered his erotic intentions in her ear, all meant to arouse her from sleep and send her to a place where pleasure was sweet.

She said his name, then said it again after he took her mouth in a kiss meant to charm. He cupped her breast, plumped it to taste. Her breath quickened and she arched, squirming beneath him and swiveling her hips. He knew what she wanted, knew she'd be wet and ready as he slid his hand down to cup her.

Fingers stroking, teasing, he gently pinched her tender flesh, and she catapulted from that drowsy half sleep straight into urgent demand. He hardened more but Deke was determined to bring her to full desire before he sought his own release. He ran his hands over her, exploring the curves, the softness over her well-toned muscles.

Touching her made his pulse pound, sending hot blood streaking through his body. Quin reached for him with her left hand and he saw the flash of diamonds and platinum on her ring finger. He was shocked by the ferocious desire the sight built in him. His legs tangled with hers, and quiet need flared into flagrant want.

In this moment, there was only sensation. Her mouth searched for his, and their lips met. Her hands clutched at his shoulders. They were in sync—moods, needs and desires matching. They both wanted more. He would give all that she wanted and he would take all that he could. He was greedy.

Awake now, she watched him sheath himself through half-lidded eyes. She lifted her knees, spreading wider for him, then locked her ankles across the small of his back. Bracing on one hand, he teased her entrance but she took him by surprise, surging up to take him in. He sank to the hilt in her wet, welcoming heat. Dang, but he loved this woman.

Quin gasped when he withdrew and as he pushed back in, she shuddered, already coming. He choked, his breath clogging his lungs as his heart thundered. He rode out her orgasm with gritted teeth. He tried to tell her how he felt, how much she meant to him, but words refused to come. She tightened her legs, drew him deeper inside her.

He had to hold on, had to make this last, make it perfect for her. Deke pulled out, amid her protests. He spent endless time arousing her again. With his fingers, his mouth, he teased and tantalized. Her body fascinated him. Curvy yet sleek, it filled him with joy. Her skin quivered where he touched her and his own reacted in kind.

"Again, darlin'."

"No, I can't," she panted.

To prove she could, he slid his fingers into her. Her short nails sank into the skin of his back and he bet tomorrow he'd have half-moon marks as evidence of her loss of control. Her breath gasped out in short puffs and her hips pumped against his hand.

Her wet heat seduced him and he wanted to bury himself again. One more moment and he would indulge himself. "Just let go, Quin."

Saying her name was like a magic word. She shuddered, cried out and hung on to him. He loved watching her face when she climaxed, the way her mouth opened, her lips wet from quick licks of her tongue. The way her eyes flew open then went half-lidded, her gaze warm and sensual. He didn't let up, urging her with his fingers to ride the crest of sensation while he watched. She quivered, her breath seemingly locked in her lungs, and he sent her over the edge again, then let her melt against him as he eased her back to earth.

Caught up in her pleasure, he let passion and love guide him now. She pulled him on top and her hand fisted around him, guiding him to the silken heat of her body. He slid inside and then found her mouth. She kissed him, and he forgot everything. There was nothing but the two of them.

Goose bumps danced across her skin with every brush of his lips. After three orgasms, Deke was almost surprised at her responses. She met each stroke, swiveling her hips and driving him deep inside. He took her hands, laced their fingers and pumped his hips. Faster. And she rose to meet him, skin flushed, breath catching, eyelashes fluttering. He grinned, neck muscles tensing as white-hot sensation built at the base of his spine, spilling out into him. He was going to make her soar again.

Her fingers squeezed his. "Deacon."

Just as calling her name had set her off earlier, a switch tripped inside him and his control broke. He surged against her and she met him, held him, as he shuddered and throbbed deep inside her. *Hold on*, he thought. He had to hold on because he was spinning off and he wasn't going without Quin. She held him back, clinging as they slid down into the quiet. He rested his head between her breasts, eyes closed.

Right here. Right now. Just like this. This was what life was supposed to be.

Later, she lay with her head on his chest, their legs entwined. Drowsy, he listened to the easy sound of her breathing and the crackle of the fire. His ring glistened on her hand. He kissed her temple and whispered, "Merry Christmas, darlin'."

Seventeen

Self-conscious about the glittering ring on her left hand, Quin kept her hands shoved in her pockets while riding in the wrecker back to the OHP garage. Deke, his foreman and others had dug her patrol car out of the snow just in time for the wrecker to pull it back onto the roadway. It wasn't drivable and she dreaded the paperwork she faced.

Quin walked through the door to OHP headquarters with a grin stretching her cheeks. She'd stared at Deke's ring on her finger while opening the door and she was positively giddy. Deacon Tate had asked her to marry him. And she'd said yes! She did a series of little dance steps as she headed toward the requisitions office.

The secretary noticed, which wasn't surprising. Quin figured her happiness was flashing like a neon sign in Vegas. Unable to resist, Quin showed her the ring and explained she'd gotten engaged for Christmas.

"That's so romantic," the woman said, gushing. "Who's the lucky man? Anyone we know?"

And that cooled Quin's jets. The media, already dog-ging Deacon, would latch on to this latest event and worry it like a meaty bone. Besides, the whole idea of marrying him was still new enough, still nerve-racking enough, that she wanted to keep Deke's identity a secret for a lit-tle while longer.

"No, probably not. He's not in law enforcement."

"Smart." The secretary handed over a pile of papers and pointed to an empty desk. "Have fun."

Quin laughed and after silencing her phone, set to work filling in the blanks that would lead her to getting a new patrol car.

Once she was done and waiting for one to be assigned, Dispatch contacted her and instructed her to appear at the main offices of Child Protective Services as soon as possible.

Thirty minutes later, she walked into a room at the De-partment of Human Services and wondered if she was fac-ing a board of inquiry. Two women and a man sat on the far side of a conference table. There was one lone chair on her side. She slid into it and braced herself.

"It has come to our attention, Trooper Kincaid, that you've spent the last week living with Deacon Tate." The younger of the two women, who'd been assigned as Noelle's caseworker, opened the discussion.

Quin straightened in her chair, hoping she didn't blush. "That's correct. I was at his home making a welfare check when the blizzard hit. I've just now returned to duty, though I'm technically on vacation. Why?"

"What did you observe while you were there?" the man asked.

"Observe?" Quin already didn't like the tone of his meeting.

"How did Mr. Tate react to your presence?" the older woman snapped.

Quin considered her words carefully, then answered, "Mr. Tate was very hospitable."

"I'm sure he was," the woman replied archly before conferring in whispers with her colleagues, all three of them glancing at her surreptitiously.

"Certain information has come to us," the caseworker finally said.

Just over an hour later, Quin stumbled out of the office. She hadn't believed them at first. The man they described wasn't the Deacon she'd come to know. She wasn't a foolish woman. She was a cop. A trained investigator. And she hadn't gone into this situation with stars in her eyes like some silly groupie. They had evidence, though.

According to information CPS had discovered, Deacon Tate, Mr. All-American Nice Guy, was a publicist's fabrication. He was considered difficult to work with and in need of further "humanizing." Quin read the reports, incredulous at first, then disbelieving. The tipping point was a memo from a senior record executive.

What better story to put out than Deacon Tate, the country boy with the heart of gold, had taken in an abandoned baby...and romanced the cop assigned to the case. It could be a women's cable network movie. Rich singer falls in love with baby and poor cop, he asks the cop to marry him, they adopt the baby and all live happily ever after.

The older woman's eyes had held pity as she explained the situation.

Bottom line? Deacon had offered Noelle's mother 25,000 dollars to buy the baby. Despite all the evidence, Quin hadn't believed it. Not at first. Not until they brought in Noelle's mother. Amanda confirmed that she'd received the money to sign private adoption papers, and that someone with the Barron law firm had taken her to a bank to set up an account.

CPS wanted Quin to testify against Deke. All her previous reservations came flooding back. He was a performer, right? She'd watched his music videos, even commented on how real he seemed acting out the songs' stories. She thought back, reviewed all the things she and Deke had done together. Had he just been pretending with her?

Quin should have known her engagement was too good to be true. Should have known a man like Deacon would never love someone like her, that his family would never take in a stranger. It was all some publicity stunt. Using a baby as a pawn was despicable. She knew that from first-hand experience. Her parents, that rich couple—they'd all played that game using her and her brothers. She twisted the ring off her finger and shoved it in the pocket of her uniform pants.

Deke sat at the kitchen island, one hip hitched on a stool, his music composition book spread out on the granite counter. Noelle was asleep in her playpen so he strummed his acoustic guitar softly, pausing to jot notes and words, though he was mostly distracted by other thoughts.

After he'd helped dig out Quin's police car yesterday morning, he'd gone into Oklahoma City with the baby for an appointment of his own. Chance had set up a meeting with Noelle's mother.

"Why?" he'd asked her. "Why accuse me of being Noelle's father?"

Amanda—Mandy, she'd asked to be called—had cried and apologized. "Your music, it always makes me feel special, Mr. Deacon, like you're singing straight to my heart. When Noelle's daddy took off, I didn't know what t'do. I don't got no family t'speak of. And you have such a big one. I'd gotten a ride to the casino thinkin' I might be able to get a job. I saw your bus sittin' there and I just…" The girl hung her head and wiped her tears with the handkerchief Chance handed her. "I just got to thinkin' what it would be like if you were Noelle's daddy, about what a wonderful life she'd have. I knew you'd love her. I didn't mean t'cause trouble for you."

Deke's heart had gone out to the girl and he'd decided to help her. She'd been so relieved and excited when he offered her what amounted to a scholarship—tuition and living expenses while she attended cosmetology school. He'd tried to call Quin on the way home, to tell her what he planned to do. In the end, he couldn't be truly upset with Mandy. She only wanted a better life for her daughter. Besides, he would have never met Quin.

Even coming back to a house with no Quin, he'd had Noelle, so the place didn't feel empty, as it once had. His life was becoming everything he hoped for. He'd found a woman he loved, a baby they'd raise together. Family. He would have a ready-made family.

Before she'd left yesterday morning, Quin had decided to stay in town. He didn't like sleeping alone. He missed her sweet, sleepy-eyed kisses first thing in the morning. He'd tried calling her several times yesterday, last night and this morning, but his calls rolled to voice mail and his texts when unanswered. Quin was a state trooper—an important job. She'd been out of pocket for a week and probably had lots of work to catch up on—even though she was supposed to be on vacation. But they were engaged and he thought she'd return his call when she found a moment.

Something dark suddenly crawled through him, a worry he couldn't quite shake. What if she'd accepted his proposal because she didn't want to hurt his feelings? What if she was ducking his calls because she didn't know how to break it to him—that she didn't love him and wanted to break up? No, that couldn't be why.

He thought back to what they'd done, what he'd said after the proposal. He'd told her over and over that he loved her. She'd said the same, out there on the deck with his family watching. But later, had Quin said the words again? Doubts wormed their way in despite his efforts to squash them. As a result, here he sat, at 10:30 a.m., fidgeting and full of nervous energy. He couldn't wait to see her again and was surprised at how much he missed her. After being stuck together 24/7 for a week, he was used to having her here. She'd left on Tuesday, it was only Wednesday, yet every time he looked up, Deke expected to see her on the couch reading or watching TV. And every time, the room was empty.

Someone knocked on the door, and his heart leaped. He wasn't expecting any family so it had to be Quin. But why didn't she just walk in? She knew he didn't lock the door when he was home. They were engaged, and this would be her home, too. She didn't need to knock.

He set the guitar on the island and jogged to the door. He threw it open, a welcoming smile on his face. Two strangers stood there—a woman bundled up in a puffy coat, looking pinch-faced and angry. A burly, gruff-faced Oklahoma County deputy stood next to her, and he spoke before Deke could.

"Deacon Tate?"

"Yes?"

The deputy shoved a piece of paper at him as the woman barged past, striding into his home. "Where's the baby?" she demanded.

"The baby? What's going on?"

"Read the order," the deputy said.

He did and shoved a hand in his hip pocket. The deputy stiffened and ordered, "Hands where I can see them."

Deke held his hands out to his sides. "I was just reaching for my phone, deputy."

"Don't make any sudden moves, *sir*. I have no way of knowing what you're reaching for."

The man's emphasis on the honorific wasn't lost on

Deke so he didn't bother arguing or asking the obvious question because yes, the deputy knew who he was. From his position he watched the woman grab up the baby, but when Noelle started crying, he tensed.

"What are you doing to her?" he yelled.

"It's no longer your concern," the woman barked as she returned holding the upset baby.

"At least get her travel blanket from her room. You can't take her out in this cold dressed only in her onesie!"

After a minute of hesitation, the woman acquiesced. 'Fine. He can show us."

The deputy shadowed him across the great room, the woman following. Deke stopped at the nursery door and caught the look of surprise on the social worker's face when she stepped inside. What had she been expecting? That he stuffed Noelle into a cardboard box to sleep? He pointed with his chin to the tall dresser. "Second drawer. There's a Pendleton travel blanket thing that works with her carrier and car seat."

"I have a car seat."

"Yeah, I just bet." The one installed in his truck was top-of-the-line and had the highest safety rating. He could just imagine what she had in her state car. They allowed him to retrieve the blanket, then they returned to the front door.

Deacon battled to stay calm, especially when the woman swept out of his house without allowing him to kiss the baby goodbye. Adding insult, the deputy waited until the woman's car disappeared.

"Word of advice," the man called as he got into his patrol car. "Don't follow."

Seriously? Did they truly believe he'd go tearing after the woman and kidnap the baby or something? Why would he do something that stupid when he had something far more powerful in his corner—his family.

What he didn't understand was what had triggered this removal. It wasn't until he was reading the order to Chance over the phone that realization crashed into him. Quin. She'd known about the order. That was why she hadn't returned his calls. Her name was listed as a witness for the state. *Given the current guardian's unusual attachment to the child, it is this officer's opinion that he will not willingly release the child to her natural parent.*

What the hell? Yes, he loved Noelle but if her mother truly wanted her back and was able to take care of her, he'd do everything he could to help.

"Deacon?" Chance sounded cautious. "I thought you and Quin were engaged."

"Yeah, me, too. I... What's going on, Chance? Why would they take Noelle like this?" But what he really wanted to know was why Quin would do this to him... to Noelle.

"I don't know. They used a juvenile court judge. I put in a call to Judge Nelligan. We'll get to the bottom of things. In the meantime, hang tight and find out what Quin knows."

Yeah, he'd like to do that but she would have to answer her damn phone for that to happen. After a long pause, he admitted, "She's not taking my calls, Chance."

Silence stretched over the phone line. "Aw, hell, Deke," Chance finally said. "Is it possible she set you up?"

Was he that big of an idiot, his family all fools to believe her? He didn't know if she was capable of doing this, if she was that cold. But why else would she have given testimony to take Noelle away from him? Quin's apparent betrayal ripped his heart out of his chest. A knife twisting in his gut would have been more humane. The damn woman had shared his bed, accepted his marriage proposal. Even now she wore his grandmother's ring. Well not for long if she was playing him.

"I honestly don't know, Chance. I... Dammit, I love her. I thought she loved me. At least that's what she said."

"I'll find out what's going on, Deke. We'll get Noelle back. I promise."

Quin felt queasy. The low-level headache she'd been fighting since finding out about Deacon yesterday roared back to life as soon as she entered Troop A headquarters. A few of her colleagues were there—some finishing up reports before going off duty, others checking in prior to hitting the road for their shift. Now that her part in the baby Noelle investigation was over, she could get back to patrolling Oklahoma's highways. She blew off the remainder of her vacation. She was desperate to stay busy so she didn't have time to think.

She hadn't slept well last night. Oh, who was she kidding? She hadn't slept at all.

Quin had done the right thing so it couldn't be guilt keeping her awake. She'd been an idiot to trust a sexy man who knew how to push every last one of her buttons. She had a duty to protect the innocent and what Deke had done was inexcusable. Deacon Tate as a single father? Ridiculous. As evidenced by his insane declaration that he loved her and wanted to make a family with her and that baby. They didn't know each other well enough to be in love—the week spent snowed in notwithstanding. And she should have known he was playing her.

Removing Noelle from Deacon's custody was the right decision. Amanda wasn't exactly in a place to take care of her child. But she'd told them she wanted to go to school. Get her own place to live. Find a job. Based on that, the CPS caseworker had drawn up a plan—one that included parenting classes. It wouldn't be easy but little Noelle would be safe with a foster family until Mandy got her life together. Quin hoped the girl would. Then the little family would be reunited and everything would be fine.

And Quin wouldn't have to deal with Deacon Tate. Because she'd been out of her mind to fall for his seduction. Granted, he was the sexiest man she'd ever been around—much less kissed and made love with. The man was...*gifted* in that department. Her cheeks warmed with the thought of what they'd done, but he was still a jerk. She had to remember that. He'd taken advantage of a naive girl. Quin didn't want to admit that she'd allowed him to take advantage of her, as well.

"Yo, Kincaid!" Fingers snapped in front of her face and she blinked, realizing she'd totally blanked out.

"What?" She glared at the smirking trooper standing in front of her.

"Whoa, Quin. You're the one with the thousand-yard stare. I called your name five times. Lieutenant Charles wants you."

"Oh, thanks." She headed to her supervisor's office as the other cop called after her.

"You should think about maybe getting more sleep. You look like something my wife's cat dragged in." He laughed and walked away before she could think of a retort.

Sadly, he was right. She did need more sleep. And obviously, her attempt at applying makeup that morning hadn't concealed her restless nights. Quin braced herself, her stomach twisting in knots at the thought of what faced her. She was pretty sure the entire coalition of the Barrons' and Tates' powerful friends was about to dump on her.

The lieutenant was in the break room pouring a cup of coffee and he looked up as she paused in the doorway. He preempted her question. "You have a visitor. Interview room A. You need to fix this, Kincaid." He turned back to his coffee, dismissing her.

Great. She'd done the right thing, and now it was all

coming back on her. Well, fine. Just fine. She'd go deal
with whatever minion Deacon had sent. She'd set that
person straight. Then she'd get back to doing her job. Full
of righteous indignation, she stalked down the hallway.

When she reached the interview room, Quin didn't
knock. She barged through the door. The person sitting
there jerked liked she'd been punched, one hand pressed
to her chest as she jumped to her feet. Quin halted two
steps inside the room as she recognized her visitor. Mandy
Brooks was the last person she expected to see. The girl's
eyes looked bruised from exhaustion and her posture indicated she was ready to bolt.

Quin studied her. In a nervous gesture, Mandy tucked a
lank strand of hair behind her ear with trembling fingers.
The kid looked beaten down by life and Quin didn't like
the resigned expression etched on the girl's face.

She gentled her voice. "Hey, Mandy. I wasn't expecting you. Here, sit down."

"I'm sorry, ma'am. I didn't… You…" The girl inhaled,
working to control the shaking in her hands. "I'm sorry.
You scared me bustin' in like that and all."

Approaching carefully, Quin hitched one hip on the
metal table, keeping a little distance between them. "My
fault, Mandy. I was expecting someone else."

"I…don't mean t'take up your time or nothin'. I know
you're really busy but… I just had t'talk to you."

Quin resisted the urge to rub her temples. She needed
to tread lightly here and the headache was making it hard
to concentrate. "It's okay, hon. What do you need to talk
'bout?"

Amanda twisted her fingers into knots, then spread
them to smooth down the worn denim covering her thighs.
"I gotta say this, ma'am."

"You can call me Quincy, Mandy."

"Yes, ma'am. I mean, Quin…cy. It's like this, you see.

I know you think you're helpin' and all but you're ruinin
everything." The girl's words ran together at the end, he
tone no longer hesitant.

Quin did her best to decipher what the girl was imply
ing. She gave up because she had no idea where Mandy
was headed. "I don't understand…"

"Of course you don't. You're strong, Miz Quincy
Strong and brave. Not like me. I'm not those things. Neve
will be. And see, that's what I gotta make you under
stand. What those people at CPS are doin'? Trying to keep
Noelle from Mr. Deke? That's just wrong."

Warmth suffused her cheeks as Quin attempted to curb
her temper. "Did he send you here?" It would be just like
the sorry son of a gun to send this poor girl in an attempt
to sway her.

"No! How could you even think that?"

The shocked indignation on Mandy's face, followed
quickly by fear, made Quin realize she sounded far harshe
than she'd intended. She breathed through her anger
worked to school her expression into something softer
something more sympathetic. How could she be upset with
Mandy? The girl had a huge crush on Deacon. Of cours
she would be protective of him. After all, Mandy had en
trusted the man with her baby.

"It's not like that at all, Miz Quincy. I—" Mandy
snapped her mouth shut and swallowed before continu
ing. "I haven't seen Mr. Deke since y'all took my littl
Noelle away from him. An' see? That's why I'm here
What y'all did, it's just wrong."

So much for soft and sympathetic. Before Quin could
respond, the shy, reticent girl she was familiar with dis
solved right in front of her, and in the girl's place stood
momma bear.

"How could you, Miz Quincy? You say you're my
friend but you go behind my back and you… Lordy. Yo

hurt him so bad. You hurt my baby girl. And you just keep on hurtin' folks for no reason."

Quin needed to regain control of this situation. "That's not true, Mandy. We're doing what is best for you and Noelle."

"No, you ain't!" Agitated, Mandy surged to her feet and paced the confines of the interview room. "I thought you understood. But you don't. You're just like all those people at Child Services."

"Mandy, please…" Quin kept her voice calm.

"No. You don't get it. Not at all. I'm broken and I always will be. The system broke me. And now you want to throw my baby in there to get chewed up."

"You aren't broken—"

"The devil I ain't! I'll always be broken. I'm not like you. You're strong. I'm not. And I won't ever be. No child deserves a momma who can't face the world and protect 'em. And I can't. That's why I gave her to Mr. Deacon. I knew he'd take care of her. Knew he'd love her. And he does. He brought her to see me so I could decide what t'do. He loves her with his whole heart. I see it every time he looks at her, every time he says her name."

Mandy brushed at her cheeks and cleared her throat. Quin was too stunned to speak.

"And you know what, Miz Quincy? He told me all about you. How he loved you, and how y'all were gonna make a family with Noelle. When he said your name, when he talked about the future an' you? He looked that same way. I'd give anything to have a man look like that when he thinks about me. Maybe you don't feel the same about him. That's on you, but don't take my baby away from that man—from the family that loves her and will take care of her for the rest of her life."

Tears flowed unheeded down Mandy's cheeks, her body racked with silent sobs. Quin was at a complete loss as to what to do. She wanted to comfort the girl but Mandy stood there encased in misery, arms around herself as if to contain the storm raging within her.

The door banged open, slamming against the wall. Both women whirled. Deacon stood there with Chance Barron, and two troopers. Part of Quin's brain recorded the difference between Mandy's reaction and her own. Mandy slumped in relief—like Deacon had just ridden in on his white horse to rescue her. Quin, on the other hand, felt detached from the scene, as Mandy's words trickled through her brain.

He loves her with his whole heart. I see it every time he looks at her, every time he says her name.

When he said your name, when he talked about the future an' you? He looked that same way.

Only he wasn't looking at her with love. Not at the moment. She'd always thought Deacon was easygoing. Boy, had she been wrong. The man standing there breathing hard looked like he *could* slay dragons.

One of the troopers cleared his throat and jerked his thumb in Chance's direction. "This guy says he's the girl's lawyer. And this one…" He gave Deke an assessing look. "He claims to be your fiancé. You need us to stay, Quin?"

"No. I'll handle this, Rizzo. Thanks." The troopers exited, shutting the door behind them.

"What did you do to her?" Deacon's voice fairly vibrated with anger.

That got her back up. "Me? Not a darn thing. What nonsense have you been telling her?"

"Nonsense? Oh, you mean like I love her little girl and want to adopt Noelle? Like I want to make sure Mandy gets her education and gets a chance to live a real life? Like I care about what happens to her and to Noelle? Like I loved you?"

"Don't fight," Mandy pleaded. "Don't fight because of me."

Deacon strode to the girl. He touched Mandy's shoulder, his hand and expression gentle. Jealousy stabbed through Quin, hot and fast like a bullet. She glowered at the pair through narrowed eyes until her cop training took over. She slowly regained control. Focused. And really looked at them.

That was when she realized there was nothing sexual in the way Deacon touched Mandy. His hold was careful, comforting, like a father's, or a big brother's.

"Go outside with Chance, Mandy," Deacon directed. "It'll be okay. We'll get this mess untangled. I'll fix it. You just have to trust me." He turned the girl over to Chance, nodded at some question in his cousin's eyes and waited until the door was closed behind them before he faced Quin.

Trust. That was what it boiled down to. Quin understood now. Mandy *did* know Deacon better than she did. He wasn't doing any of this for publicity, for recognition, despite evidence to the contrary—evidence she now suspected had been fabricated. He was doing it because he really was a good guy. A man so good he'd taken in an abandoned baby because it was the right thing to do. And then he fell in love with that baby and wanted to give her a home. He'd fallen in love with the cop who fought him every step, and wanted to make a home with her, too. Quin had hurt him deeply because, she realized too late, he had truly loved her. And she hadn't trusted him—or herself—enough to believe.

She turned away and pulled her cell phone from her hip pocket. Quin didn't understand why the numbers were blurry as she attempted to dial the social worker who'd removed Noelle. She felt Deke's glare knifing into her back.

"You callin' for backup now, Trooper Kincaid? Don't

bother. I'm leaving. You don't have to worry about seein' me ever again. Since you're not wearing it, you can deliver my grandmother's ring to Chance when you see him in court. We're done."

Quin's call to Child Services went to voice mail. She hung up. Her denial was on her lips as she turned to face Deke. Only the room was empty. He'd gone. She was left standing alone. Frustrated, she considered chasing him down so she could explain. That was when the truth hit.

She'd blown it as far as Deacon was concerned. He'd loved her. Loved her enough he'd wanted to spend the rest of his life with her. She'd been waiting for the other shoe to drop, quick to assign motives where there'd been none. Wrapping her arms around her waist, she bent over, sick to her stomach. She'd ruined the best thing to ever happen to her. Quin had destroyed any chance they might have had by her actions. Because she hadn't trusted Deacon, had believed the worst of him before hearing his side.

Tears streamed unheeded down her cheeks as she sank onto the metal chair. She felt numb, which was a blessing. When the pain finally came, she knew it would eviscerate her.

Eighteen

The last thing Deke wanted to do was sing in front of a crowd of strangers, but Chase had set up this appearance months ago when he was wrangling something out of the city fathers. Under normal circumstances, this appearance would be a piece of cake. But a hard-nosed cop had ripped his heart out and then stomped on it.

And God help him but he still loved her.

The boys continued to walk on eggshells around him. They'd come out to the ranch to work on some of the new songs for the next album. Yeah, the new stuff was maudlin as hell, and Dillon had been quick to ask what Deke had done to screw things up with Quin. Only he hadn't done a thing. Not a blasted thing.

He'd taken in an abandoned baby. He'd fallen in love with her. And he'd fallen in love with the stubborn woman assigned to the investigation. He'd given his heart to both, wanting to adopt Noelle and help her mother, and wanting to marry Quin. Who then betrayed him and took that baby away.

The rest of the band was in the front of the bus kicking back. Deke hid in the bedroom. He didn't want to do this gig. He wanted to go home. Alone. Yeah, he might pour a tumbler full of good Kentucky whiskey and write stupid songs about broken hearts that no one but him would ever hear, but he was entitled. He'd face the rest of his life to-morrow. Tonight, he just wanted to wallow in his misery.

Deke could hear the other guys out in the living area and he had to roll his eyes. They were playing rock-paper-scissors. The loser had to come get him. He consid-ered saving them the angst, then decided *naw*. Make them work for it. He put away the acoustic guitar. He wouldn't be strumming it tonight. Those broken-heart ballads had no place on a New Year's Eve playlist, though a few love songs were necessary. As much as he hated the thought of singing one given the sorry state of his own life, he knew their fans would be in a romantic mood.

Quin knew what she had to do. The problem was, she had no plan. And not much time to come up with one, much less execute it. She was in uniform and on crowd control, along with half of Troop A. The other half was out on the streets on drunk patrol. The night was cold but not frigid. The indoor venues were doing bang-up busi-ness. Deke and the Sons of Nashville were scheduled to take the outdoor stage in Bicentennial Park at 10:00 p.m. for a concert that ended just before midnight, when they'd lead the crowd in counting down to the New Year as the lighted ball climbed its anchor pole.

Her timing would have to be impeccable. If she dis-tracted him during the concert—made him even angrier than he already was—he or Chance would file a com-plaint against her. And if she approached him before the concert…yeah, he'd just ignore her like he'd been doing since he'd walked out of the interview room.

For two hours, she patrolled the downtown area, which was roped off for Opening Night, Oklahoma City's big New Year's Eve celebration. Even with the cold temperatures, the crowd was bigger than normal—thanks to Deacon Tate and the Sons of Nashville. Free concert? Oh, heck yeah! Their fans were all over that.

From nine to ten, she fretted and answered minor calls. A public drunk. A child who fell and cut her chin. A couple fighting over flirting with the opposite sex. She was also aware of the crowd gathering around the finale stage in the park. People came out of the Norick Downtown Library, out of the Oklahoma City Museum of Art and streamed from the art deco doors of the Civic Center.

The food trucks lined up at the edge of the outdoor venue had been doing a brisk business but now they were all but deserted. The stage was set up in front of city hall. The streets surrounding the venue had been closed to vehicular traffic and already the park area between the Civic Center and city hall was wall-to-wall people. She had to figure out something before Deke's concert began.

A soft rap on the door indicated the time to mope had come to an end. "Go away," Deke yelled.

"Having trouble hearing, bro," Kenji said as he entered. "You said 'C'mon in,' right?"

Deke had to work to hide his grin. Not only were the members of his band incredible musicians, but they were also the best kind of friends. "Yeah, something like that."

"You know the girl's not worth it, right, dude?" Kenji asked in his signature Tennessee accent. "And you know there's been a million songs written about this situation, right?"

To prove his point, Kenji burst into a slightly off-key rendition of Cole Swindell's "Ain't Worth the Whiskey." The rest of the band joined in from the front of the bus.

"We are so adding that to the list tonight," Dillon yelled.

Deke considered Kenji's words. Maybe he'd rushed things with Quin. Maybe he'd suffered a bruised ego at her hands, not a broken heart. Yeah, right. Asking her to marry him had not been a spur-of-the-moment decision. The idea had been fermenting in his mind almost from the moment he first laid eyes on her. Not that he believed in love at first sight but...yeah, he believed in love at first sight when it came to Quincy Kincaid. But loving her and forgiving her were two different animals.

Twenty minutes later, they were on stage, waiting to be introduced by the mayor of Oklahoma City. The crowd was estimated at close to 100,000. The night felt electric, energy pouring from the people spread out between city hall and the Civic Center.

Deke closed his eyes, focused. He would feed off the intensity of the audience, absorb their excitement. He lived for this. Loved it down to his very soul. Tonight, he would sing for them. And with luck, their energy would fill up the empty places in his heart.

As the mayor wrapped up the intro, Kenji started a pounding beat on his drums. Ozzie matched it with his bass guitar line. When the crowd erupted, spotlights lit the stage. The beat continued until things quieted down. A few measures later, Xander added a riff on the banjo, which Bryce followed, dueling banjos–style, with the same riff on his guitar. Dillon added the song line on his keyboard. And then Deke stepped front and center, launching into "Red Dirt Cowgirl," which he'd written for Chance and Cassidy when they got married.

The clock ticked toward midnight but as often happened when he was on stage, Deke lost himself in the music, in the crowd, in the sheer electricity shooting through the air. Until he looked down. And saw her.

* * *

Working along the outside edges of the crowd, Quin was drawn inexorably toward the stage. Like a moth to a flame. A bee to honey. Ants to a picnic. She was a walking cliché. Reaching the corner of the stage, she was no closer to forming a plan.

Time was running out. She needed to do something. And fast. The girls lined up in front of the stage caught Quin's eye. They all had big signs with printed messages on cardboard. And just like that, a plan popped into her head.

"Can I borrow your sign?" she asked the girl nearest her, all but yelling over the music blaring from nearby speakers.

The girl's eyes widened. "I recognize you! You're Deacon's Christmas cop. The one he fell in love with."

Wait. What? How could people know about her, about Deacon? Then it occurred to her—the press releases from the record-company PR department, and the statement from some executive the CPS people had shown her. She wondered if Deke knew they were still linked, and if he'd care.

"Yes," Quin said. "I need your sign, okay?"

The girl held out the piece of cardboard. "What'cha gonna do with it?"

"Try to hold on to the best thing that ever happened to me!" Quin grabbed the black Sharpie pen she habitually shoved in her hip pocket to mark evidence and scribbled on the cardboard. She waited until Deke looked her direction and then she hoisted the sign high over her head.

I'm Sorry!!!!

He stared right through her, his face blank. She needed another sign. Quin looked around but her new friend was

already on the case. The girl passed over another piece o
cardboard and Quin scribbled.

When Deke glanced her way, she was ready.

I Was Wrong. All Along.

He turned his back to the audience to do a riff with Dil
lon on the keyboard, which gave her time to gather more
signs and scribble furiously. When he faced the crowe
again, she moved to stand directly in front of him, he
new girl posse hard on her heels.

I Didn't Give You A Chance To Explain. Did I Mention I'm Sorry?

He still ignored her.

I Fixed It.

That got a narrowing of his eyes.

Noelle Will Be Home With You Tomorrow!

Did he just miss a chord? He was still singing but he'
stopped playing and his eyes bored into hers. She broke
eye contact when she dipped her chin to write the nex
set of signs.

Before I Get Out Of Your Life For Good...
I Just Want You To Know...
I Love You

Deke continued crooning the words of the love song
into the microphone, seemingly unmoved. She supposed

hat was her answer. This whole crazy, spur-of-the-mo-
nent deal had been a last-ditch effort. She offered him a
mile that felt small, tentative and very, *very* sad—which
/as exactly how she felt.

Quin handed the signs back to the girl and yelled above
he noise, "Thanks anyway. It was worth a shot."

Turning her back, she merged into the crowd and
/orked her way toward the street. The song ended to ap-
lause, whistles and shouts of approval. The microphone
queaked from feedback and Deke's voice surrounded her.

"Somebody stop that state trooper."

A solid wall of bodies formed between her and escape.
he stopped. Quin could have bulled her way through but
here was something in Deke's voice that made her swivel
round to face him instead.

"Come here," he ordered. Her heart skipped a beat as
he moved purposely toward the stage. He gestured for
er to come around to the side, then announced that Dil-
on was singing the next song—much to his little broth-
r's surprise.

Deke pointed out some steps and waved for her to come
p on stage. When she reached him, he pulled her out of
ight of the crowd and asked, "Did you mean it?" She nod-
led. "I'll have Noelle back tomorrow? For New Year's
)ay?"

"Yes. I talked to the juvenile judge. She's rescinding her
rder, reinstating your custody order." She scrubbed her
ace with the heels of her hands. "I was so wrong, Deke.
about you, about everything. CPS had all this evidence.
believed it because… I don't know why. I should have
alled you, let you tell me your side. Something inside
ne just…couldn't believe that you truly loved me. I'm so
orry. About everything."

Deke didn't say a word, simply stared at her as the

music curtained them from the world. After too many stuttering heartbeats to count, he asked, "Do you love me?"

Quin had to blink rapidly as her eyes filled with tears. "With all my heart. Noelle, too."

Once again, he remained silent and when he spoke it wasn't the words she wanted to hear. "I have to finish the show."

She nodded, mute, as she turned to the stairs and descended. She'd given it her best shot. Maybe someday he'd forgive her.

Deke slipped his phone from his hip pocket and with frantic fingers, texted Chance. He asked about Noelle's status, filling in his cousin on what Quin had said. His phone rang and he ducked behind the speakers, hoping he could hear Chance.

"Stand by, Deke. I'm checking my messages. Tell me exactly what Quin said."

He repeated her words, his chest so tight with compressed emotion he could barely get them out.

"I'm not that familiar with the juvie judges. I know Nelligan was about to get into a jurisdiction fight with her. I had one of my investigators looking into the situation so we'd have ammunition at the emergency hearing Nelligan set. All the evidence was generated through CPS. Quin was just a witness. Aha! Found it. The clerk emailed me. We can pick Noelle up at the foster home anytime after ten tomorrow. Congrats, Deke! You're gonna be a dad after all."

Air whooshed out of his lungs and he realized the crowd was cheering. Dillon's song was over. Without stopping to think things through, Deke walked over, removed his mic from its stand and walked to the front of the stage. He searched the crowd for Quin's face, found her standing in shadows off to one side. He launched into the next song on the playlist but kept his eyes glued to Quin.

She stood frozen, her eyes on him. Almost as if she was in a trance, she began to walk back toward the stage. People noticed he was staring, turned to look. A gaggle of female fans squealed and rushed to Quin, escorting her back toward the stage. People stepped aside so there was a clear path to where he was standing.

Quin told her feet to stop walking but they paid her no mind. She was six feet away from the stage when Deke finished his song to thunderous applause. As it died down, he spoke.

"You know it's not official until I get down on one knee, right?" And he did. He dropped down, right there on the stage in front of the whole crowd. "I love you, Quincy Kincaid. Will you marry me?"

"Yes," she said. Or thought she did. No sound came out of her mouth. But Deke must have read her lips because he was off the stage and she was flying toward him. He caught her midleap and swung her around, his lips finding hers with unerring accuracy. She'd missed his kisses, missed the hot, hungry taking of her mouth. Missed the way her heart skipped beats until it was perfectly synchronized with his.

He broke the kiss and murmured against her ear, "I love you, Quincy." He continued saying the words as he peppered her face, neck and shoulders with kisses.

Quin laughed. She couldn't help herself. Here she was in full uniform in the middle of a New Year's Eve concert, her arms and legs around the sexiest country music star in the whole world. "I love you, too," she answered each time he said it.

Then they were moving toward the stage. Deke loosened his hold on her long enough for Bryce and Xander to lift her up by her hands. Deke hopped up beside her. He swept her into his arms and kissed her again. While she was still lost in the kiss, the band started playing and the next thing she knew, Deke had her tucked up against his side. The mic was back in his hand and he was singing.

"I've been on the road for all my life. Knocking around with the boys. Never thought I'd settle down, much less with a wife."

Kenji played a sting on the drums—the sound often accompanying a lame joke—and Quin laughed as Deke didn't miss a beat.

"I'm headin' home. I'm comin' back to you. Back where I belong. Been on the road way beyond too long, an' I've been dreamin' 'bout you."

Deke cupped her cheek in the palm of his hand and gazed into her eyes as he continued singing. "My heart knew things would never be the same, the moment you walked through the door. My roamin' days are over, since you're gonna take my name.

"I'm headin' home." He launched into the chorus and the crowd sang along. Then they all got quiet—even the music went soft as Deke sang, "I need to get back to you, to the place I belong. 'Cause you hold my heart right there in your hand. I'm gonna love you for all my life, 'cause you make me a better man. Hang on girl, I'll be there soon. 'Cause I'm headin' home, I'm comin' back to you."

In that moment, standing there in Deke's arms in front of a huge crowd, she realized what she'd been missing her whole life. That sense of belonging, of *home*, and with this man, this wild, wonderful, sexy man with a voice that charmed the panties off his fans, she'd found what she'd been missing.

The crowd started counting down as the giant lighted ball rose beside the stage. "Ten. Nine. Eight..." they chanted, quickly getting to "Three. Two. One!"

The Sons of Nashville launched into a country-twang version of "Auld Lang Syne." She had the vague notion that Deke was supposed to be leading the singing but he was too busy kissing her and that was all right by her.

"Happy New Year," he murmured against her lips.

Yes. It truly was. "I love you."

And that's when fireworks lit up the sky—and her heart.

Epilogue

Quin faced the mirror, shocked at the reflection of the woman staring back at her. In the background, the Bee Dubyas buzzed like their namesake insect. The Barron Wives and her soon-to-be mother-in-law were…they were a force of nature. There was no other description. In just a few minutes, she would enter the ballroom at the Barron Hotel and say her vows, then she and Deke would formally adopt Noelle.

Katherine stepped up behind her. Before Quin could turn, the older woman draped a familiar pearl necklace around her neck and fastened the clasp. Pressing her cheek against Quin's, she whispered, "Welcome to the family, sweetie. Thank you for making my son so happy."

Quin had to blink hard to keep tears at bay as she reached up to touch the pearls. "They're beautiful."

"So are you, Quincy. So are you. When the time comes, I hope you'll share them with other Tate brides when my boys finally find their forevers."

"Of course I will!"

Smiling, Katherine turned her. "And then the necklace will come back to you and Deacon will place it around the throat of y'all's little girl when she goes to meet her own true love at the altar."

Ten minutes later, Quin joined the love of her life and the baby soon to be theirs, legally in addition to emotionally, in front of a bent willow arbor. Laced with peonies and lilies and Oklahoma blue ribbon, the arch was the perfect backdrop for their nuptials. Hunter, Deacon's oldest brother, stood as his best man. When the Bee Dubyas discovered she had no close female friends, they drew straws to see who would be her matron of honor. Quin thought it fitting when Cassidy, the first Barron bride, won.

Judge Nelligan read the rites, and Quin said, "I do" to the rest of her life.

"Are you trying to take advantage of me?" Quin's words were slightly slurred. Deke had finally managed their escape from the party downstairs and retreated to their suite. He'd gotten them both naked and in bed and now his tough trooper was being too cute for words.

His lips curved against her cheek. "Of course I am."

"Oh. Okay. Just checking." She giggled and hiccupped. "I knew that last glass of champagne was a mistake. I should have had cake instead."

He settled beside her, propped on one elbow. "The cake was awesome. Want me to go get you some?"

Quin laughed and his insides did that funny tightening, like a balloon expanding in his chest.

"You traipsing around naked might just break some poor woman's brain."

That made him laugh as he lowered his head to kiss her. After the kiss, he smoothed out her hair and just looked at her. He'd never thought he could love another so much. Yet here he was on his wedding night, in love with this woman. And their daughter. Their *daughter*. Noelle Katherine Tate.

She ran her fingers over his lips. "Why the big smile?"

Deke hadn't realized he'd been smiling, but the answer was easy. "Just happy, darlin'. And thinkin' about how much I love my wife and child." He waggled his brows. "Want to try makin' a brother or sister for Noelle?"

She waggled hers in reply. "Think you're up to the task?"

"Oh, heck, yeah."

"You know what they say, right?"

"About what?"

"Pride. Because…" Quin brushed her fingertips down his bare chest and they dipped below the sheet. She curled her hand around him. "Just as I suspected. You are definitely full of pride."

He covered a groan with a deep chuckle. Quin knew *exactly* how to get his attention and he loved her touch. Deke leaned over and savored her skin as he nipped and licked his way down her neck. She tasted delicious and looked so sexy lying beneath him. He kissed her, deeply, not so much taking as sharing this time. As much as he wanted her, he wanted things slow and sweet tonight even as their bare flesh rubbed together, creating its own heat.

Breaking the kiss, he eased back. "Hello, wife."

Her smile wreathed her face. "Hello, husband."

"I do like the sound of that."

"Me, too."

The need for her zinged through Deke, like a new song, the words and melody teasing him until he was compelled to write them down. In this case, he was going to record them with his body on hers. In hers.

Quin shifted, her arms urging him back over her. She stretched, arched and pressed her lips against his heart. "This is mine," she murmured.

"Always," Deke promised. "Just like you'll always be mine."

He stroked his hand over her, arousing and teasing even as she continued to stroke him in the most intimate way. His eyes closed of their own accord as he absorbed the pleasure of what she did. He'd found where he belonged, found what he wanted in life.

"Are you ready, darlin'?"

Her eyes sparkled with desire as she opened her thighs for him. He shifted between them and gazed down at the woman who completed his life. "I never thought I'd ever say this, but damn if you aren't sexy in those pearls."

Her peal of laughter was cut short as he slid deep inside her. Here was comfort. Here was love. This country boy had finally come home.

Wrapped around each other, they made slow, sweet love that quickly turned hard and fast, their need and desire swamping them both. When Quin fell over the edge, Deke was there to catch her. The same way she held him through his own climax a few moments later. Panting, she rested her temple against his scruffy jaw.

"Wow," she sighed. "That was so much better than cake."

Deke laughed and Quin laughed with him. Life with his tough Christmas cop would never be a piece of cake. And he'd have it no other way.

* * * * *

*Don't miss any of these cowgirl romances from
Silver James.*

**COWGIRLS DON'T CRY
THE COWGIRL'S LITTLE SECRET
THE BOSS AND HIS COWGIRL
CONVENIENT COWGIRL BRIDE
REDEEMED BY THE COWGIRL**

Available now from Mills & Boon Desire!

MILLS & BOON®

Desire™

PASSIONATE AND DRAMATIC LOVE STORIES

MILLS & BOON®

Why shop at millsandboon.co.uk?

Each year, thousands of romance readers
find their perfect read at millsandboon.co.uk.
That's because we're passionate about
bringing you the very best romantic fiction.
Here are some of the advantages of
shopping at www.millsandboon.co.uk:

* **Get new books first**—you'll be able to buy
  your favourite books one month before they
  hit the shops

* **Get exclusive discounts**—you'll also be
  able to buy our specially created monthly
  collections, with up to 50% off the RRP

* **Find your favourite authors**—latest news,
  interviews and new releases for all your
  favourite authors and series on our website,
  plus ideas for what to try next

* **Join in**—once you've bought your favourite
  books, don't forget to register with us to rate,
  review and join in the discussions

Visit **www.millsandboon.co.uk**
for all this and more today!